A PROMISE OF RUIN

This Large Print Book carries the
Seal of Approval of N.A.V.H.

A DR. GENEVIEVE SUMMERFORD
MYSTERY

A PROMISE OF RUIN

CUYLER OVERHOLT

THORNDIKE PRESS

A part of Gale, a Cengage Company

GALE
A Cengage Company

Farmington Hills, Mich • San Francisco • New York • Waterville, Maine
Meriden, Conn • Mason, Ohio • Chicago

LIBRARY OF CONGRESS CIP DATA ON FILE.
CATALOGUING IN PUBLICATION FOR THIS BOOK
IS AVAILABLE FROM THE LIBRARY OF CONGRESS

ISBN-13: 978-1-4328-4661-9 (hardcover)
ISBN-10: 1-4328-4661-2 (hardcover)

Published in 2018 by arrangement with Sourcebooks, Inc.

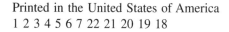

Printed in the United States of America
1 2 3 4 5 6 7 22 21 20 19 18

To Chance and Tucker,
two of the good ones.

"The test of civilization
is the estimate of woman."

— George William Curtis

PROLOGUE

On the last day of life as she knew it, Teresa Casoria stood at the rail of the steamship *Madonna* and watched the sun rise over America.

They had dropped anchor in the middle of the night, too late to see anything but twinkling lights to the east and west. Unable to sleep, she'd packed her one valise and brought it up to the deck at the crack of dawn. Now, she watched the pink light of morning move like a magician's hand over the entrance to New York Harbor, revealing tidy houses and colorful gardens and an old stone fortress along the shoreline.

Other passenger ships were anchored nearby in the quarantine grounds, also awaiting inspection. Although their upper decks were nearly empty, Teresa could see clusters of steerage passengers pressing against the lower rails, as eager as she was to see their new home. She felt a twinge of regret, wishing, not for the first time, that she had traveled in steerage herself. Her second-class shipmates seemed to have known that she wasn't really one of them — never treating her rudely, exactly, but simply looking right through her, as if she weren't even there. In steerage, she needn't have worried about having only two shirtwaists to wear, or which fork to use, or whether to give the steward money for bringing her a deck rug. She might have made some friends to share her hopes and fears with, and perhaps even practiced her English.

But these were ungrateful thoughts, and she quickly banished them from her mind. It had been extremely generous of Antonio to send her a second-class ticket. True, she'd thought him extravagant when she first received it, believing they should use the money for other, more important things after they were married, but when she saw the steerage passengers leaving the disinfection station in Naples with their heads shorn and their bags soggy from fumigation, she was thankful for his consideration. Now, with the dreaded Ellis Island immigration station looming up ahead, she was doubly thankful, for according to the Italian waitress in the single ladies' lounge, anyone rich enough to afford a first- or second-class ticket was presumed to be of sound mind, body, and character and therefore subjected to only the most cursory examination on board.

Even knowing this, she felt a stab of anxiety when she saw the cutter with the yellow flag bouncing toward the *Madonna* over the choppy water. If they sent her back now, away from Antonio, what would she have to live for? She groped for the cross that hung from her neck, forcing herself to stand up straight. She wouldn't give into fear now. If she'd listened to fear, she would have married doting but simpleminded Ciro. She would have accepted that her poor quarter of Naples was the only world she'd ever know and that dreams were for other, more important people. Instead, she had found real love and followed it to America, where everything she'd dared to dream was about to come true.

To her relief, the onboard inspection was as cursory as the waitress had predicted, and within thirty minutes, the passengers had been released and were preparing to disembark. Teresa returned to the rail as the ship steamed into the upper bay, watching with her heart in her mouth as the fabled lady of liberty rose up on the horizon, lifting her torch toward Teresa in welcome as if

11

she'd been waiting only for her. Just as Teresa was thinking she'd never seen anything more beautiful, the ship turned on its course, and New York City came into view, shimmering like a mirage in the distance. She gripped the rail and drank in the sight, determined to fix it in her mind forever.

As they steamed closer, the solid city facade broke into separate, pastel-colored skyscrapers standing shoulder to shoulder along the shore. Light glinted off the buildings' windows and flashed on their copper turrets, giving the scene an otherworldly glow. She was suddenly overcome with gratitude for the events that had led her to this moment. She didn't know what she had done to deserve such good fortune, but she promised God then and there that she'd do everything in her power to be worthy of it.

The blast of a whistle made her jump, breaking into her thoughts. Looking down, she saw a tiny tugboat darting straight across the bow of the enormous *Madonna*. A laugh of delight escaped her. *Truly, I am in America,* she thought, *where the small and the humble bow to no one.*

A few minutes later, they were moving up a river along the west side of the island, and she was looking into the beating heart of the city. *My city now,* she thought, her own heart beating faster in response. From every pier came the whir of hoists and the roar of donkey engines and the shouts of brawny longshoremen at work. Peering between the giant steamers and sailing ships that filled the slips, she saw a stone-paved street teeming with tangled carriages and clanging streetcars and overloaded wagons. On and on they steamed, past one battered pile dock after another, until she was beginning to think the city would go on forever.

At last, the ship slowed and started turning toward an empty slip. A boisterous crowd was waiting at the end of the pier, waving hands and handkerchiefs and shouting up to the passengers. Teresa searched their faces but didn't see Antonio among them. He must be waiting inside the shed, she decided. She grabbed her valise and hurried down to the lower deck — only to wait, quivering with nervous excitement, while the *Madonna* slowly warped in.

Finally, with tugs pushing, windlasses pulling, and deckhands shouting back and forth, the ship was secured, and the gangplank was dropped into place. Teresa rode a wave of passengers into the crowded pier shed, pushing through hordes of railroad and livery and boardinghouse agents as she searched right and left for Antonio. An official waved her toward the customs desk, where she handed over her landing card and the letter Antonio had sent her for this purpose, stating his occupation and address and confirming that Teresa was to be his wife.

"Is your fiancé here?" the man behind the desk asked her in Italian.

She looked once more around the crowded shed. "I don't see him, but he is coming," she answered in her best English, proud of how much she'd learned during her months working in Mrs. Hancock's kitchen, where only her employer's native language was allowed to be spoken.

Instructing her not to leave the shed until Antonio arrived to collect her, the man gave Teresa back the letter and sent her on to the inspection table, where her bag was opened and sorted through. And then finally, after all the months of waiting, it was over. She had made it, to America and Antonio.

But . . . where was her beloved? She continued to the door of the shed to look for him on the street outside, longing for the sight of his face and eager to see the look in his eyes when they fell on her. But he wasn't out there either. She stepped aside to let other passengers exit the shed, listening wistfully to their shouts of greeting and trying not to feel abandoned as they disappeared into the waiting conveyances. The *Madonna* was supposed to have arrived the day before, she reminded herself, but had been delayed and forced to remain in quarantine overnight. Antonio might have had important business to attend to this morning that had kept him from returning on time. No doubt he would come as soon as he was able.

The sun was now high in the sky, making the shed uncomfortably warm. She loosened her shawl and plucked at her damp shirtwaist, trying not to let her shoulders slump so that Antonio's first glimpse of her would be a good one. Gradually, the stream of departing cabin-class passengers slowed to a trickle and then stopped altogether. The steerage passengers came next, herded through the shed onto barges bound for Ellis Island. She watched them shuffle across the floor, their arms overflowing with baskets and bundles and swaddled infants, their faces reflecting equal parts hope and fear. And then, even they were gone.

As the last barge pulled away, her courage faltered, and her face grew hot with shame. She lowered her valise to the ground. Could he have forgotten? Or — God forbid —

changed his mind? But no, that wasn't possible; Antonio loved her more than the stars and the moon. He had told her so, and she believed him. She could feel the customs official's gaze upon her, making perspiration bead along her forehead. How long would they let her wait here? If he didn't come soon, would they force her to go to the detention room on Ellis Island — the room where people could disappear for months, or even years — while they decided what to do with her? What if they took her there and Antonio couldn't find her? What if they sent her back home?

She pulled Antonio's letter from her pocket and peered at the return address. Maybe she could find her way to him. But where was this 109th Street? She wished she had brought a map of the city with her. How could she have been so stupid, to come without a map? Hot tears sprang to her eyes. The fear was back, stronger and more insistent than ever. She fumbled for her handkerchief as the tears brimmed over.

And then, someone called her name. She lifted her head. Through the blur of her tears, she saw a man stepping out of a carriage at the end of the pier. He called to her again, opening his arms in greeting. Teresa's breath left her in a rush of relief. Shoving the handkerchief into her pocket, she scooped up her valise and, with a happy wave to the customs official, ran down the dock toward the carriage.

CHAPTER ONE

I raised the gun, training my gaze on the two boats that were moving shoulder to shoulder up the East River. Unlike the sleek college shells that regularly plied this northern end of the river, these were weathered four-oared barges, with wide beams and fixed seats and oarlocks attached directly to the gunwales. Their occupants were similarly unrefined — husky, broad-shouldered boys in mismatched sleeveless jerseys, who chopped unevenly at the water with their oars as they struggled to keep the boats abreast. I held my breath and readied my finger on the trigger.

"Now!" Finn shouted beside me.

I squeezed. A wave of wild cheering nearly knocked me off my feet as the boats crossed the invisible starting line at the foot of the pier and surged up the course, leaving churning pools in their wake. Handing Finn the starting gun, I grabbed the field glasses that hung from my neck and lifted them to my eyes. My sights landed first on the flotilla of bobbing watercraft that had come out to watch the Independence Day race, some decked out in green in support of Simon Shaw's Wieran Club, others waving the yellow flag of Dan Oakley's club from the adjoining assembly district. I aimed a little lower, sweeping across a peeling tugboat and a stretch of open, roiling water, until a magnified Simon suddenly popped into view. I jumped — and then, with a twinge of voyeuristic guilt, adjusted the knob to bring his features into clearer focus.

Simon was sitting in the stroke seat, setting the pace for the lads behind him. I could clearly see the determination on his sun-bronzed face, and the contraction of his muscles with each pull of his oar. The team had been practicing for several weeks, and Simon's already well-tempered physique had only improved with use. I dipped the glasses slightly to follow the sculpted lines of his shoulders and biceps, and immediately wished I hadn't. The sight sent a familiar flutter through my belly that I, in what seemed to have become a regular practice, tried vainly to ignore.

I dropped the glasses to my chest. Barely a day went by that I didn't think of the kiss

I'd shared with Simon the previous winter, after he helped absolve my patient of murder. To tell the truth, I'd been more or less waiting since then for him to take things up where we'd left off. But over the past six months, he hadn't so much as pecked me on the cheek. At first, I'd assumed he was just being discreet. After that memorable kiss, we'd agreed to continue exploring our feelings for each other despite the difference in our stations, trusting that, with time, we could overcome the prejudices against us. But we'd never articulated a strategy for accomplishing this feat, or discussed what our individual expectations might be. I knew that Simon, who'd once been my family's stable boy, was acutely conscious of the differences in our upbringings, and had concluded that he was avoiding public displays of affection out of respect for what he believed was my own sense of decorum.

When he proved equally chaste during our few private moments together, I'd decided instead that he was being chivalrous, remembering how I'd thrown myself at him in the stable all those years ago and not trusting me now to know my own mind or body. Embarrassing as this possibility was, I preferred it to believing he wasn't attracted to me. But as months continued to roll past without the smallest amorous advance, this explanation too was growing thin.

A drunken shout brought me back to the present. I raised the field glasses and scanned the florid faces of the spectators along the riverbank, trying to gauge the general level of inebriation and the corresponding likelihood that my services would be required. Although my interest and advanced training were in neurology and mental therapy, this wasn't the first time Simon had recruited me to tend to the bodily injuries of his constituents. As a Tammany captain responsible for delivering votes to his party's candidates, Simon was a sort of perpetual Santa Claus to the residents of his election district, providing them with whatever assistance they needed. I'd resisted his requests for medical help at first, thinking a general practitioner would be more qualified for the job. But as doctors had turned out to be scarcer than fur coats in the local immigrant neighborhoods, I'd become unexpectedly adept at stitching bashed skulls and bandaging bleeding knuckles. Today, my medical bag was stuffed with arnica and alum powder and catgut, just in case.

"Come on, Doc," urged Finn, grabbing my elbow. The spectators were streaming up the bank away from the pier, cutting through the adjacent stone yard and the produce stands of the Harlem Market to follow the boats upriver. Finn, who as the eldest of the Wieran Club boys had been saddled with my care by Simon, was clearly eager to be among them.

I picked up my bag and we joined the moving throng, staying as close to the bank as possible to keep the race in view. I watched with a shudder as a trio of half-naked boys jumped off the sewer pipe at 102nd Street and swam toward the boats with gurgling whoops of excitement, undeterred by either the clumps of sewage or the giant water rats that bobbed along beside them. The Oakley boat reached them first, rowing at a higher cadence than the Wieran boat, which was almost two seats behind. I heard unhappy muttering from a group of men sporting green Wieran flags and hoped there wouldn't be trouble. The rivalry between the two clubs had a long and contentious history. The day before, one of Simon's rowers had injured his hand at the bottling factory where he worked, causing some Wieran supporters to question why his machine had just happened to break after he took over another worker's shift. Luckily, the boy's injury hadn't prevented him from taking part in the race, which kept the grumbling from erupting into something ugly. Knowing how many bets had been laid, however, and how much beer was flowing along the twenty-block stretch of the course, I didn't trust the peace to last.

Fortunately for me and the Greens, by the time we arrived at 105th Street, Simon's boat had drawn even with the competition, whose faster pace had apparently proved unsustainable. Finn joined the Wieran supporters pressed three deep against the marble yard fence, cheering and pounding his neighbors on the back as the boats glided past. I drew up panting behind him, squeezing the stitch in my side and ducking reflexively as a firecracker exploded nearby. Fenced-in stone and coal yards lined the next several hundred feet of waterfront, blocking further progress by the spectators. A few of the more faithful had accordingly climbed down from the manure pier and were wading unsteadily into the water, shouting out drunken advice to the receding oarsmen. I was wondering if Finn expected me to do the same, when he turned and said, "Come on, Doc! This way!"

I followed him toward a black delivery van that was idling at the street corner. He opened the van's passenger door and half lifted, half threw me onto the seat before hopping onto the running board beside me. "Go!" he shouted, banging his palm on the roof.

Turning toward the driver, I was astonished to see that it was eleven-year-old Frankie the Pipes, one of the youngest Wieran Club members, whose moniker stemmed from an unusually high-pitched voice. At Finn's command, Frankie slid forward on his seat to stand on the clutch pedal and moved the gear stick into position. As he raised his foot from the pedal, the van lurched forward, straight toward a woman and child stepping off the curb.

"Frankie!" I cried.

"Sorry," he squeaked, swerving to avoid them before accelerating across 105th Street.

I turned and peered through the opening behind me, at three older boys who were standing in the back of the van. "Why is Frankie driving?"

"It's his pop's van," Donny O'Meara answered glumly.

"And I'm the only one who gets to drive it!" Frankie crowed, his narrow chest puffing with pride.

Simon had told me that Frankie's father, who eked out a meager living as a linen supplier, spent a large portion of his day in the local saloons and often enlisted Frankie to drive for him when he was "indisposed." I doubted, however, that this little junket would meet with Mr. Dolan's approval. "Did you ask your father if you could take it?"

He shrugged. "Couldn't," he said without meeting my gaze. "He ain't been home since last night."

I bit back a reprimand. Simon had introduced me to the current Wieran Club members shortly after we renewed our acquaintance, saying he'd welcome my advice on handling adolescent boys. I'd soon realized, however, that he had a far better grasp of the young male psyche than I ever would. Watching him manage budding rivalries, wounded pride, and the constant threat of fistfights, I'd come to understand that with these lads, a light hand was essential; you had to patiently draw out their better selves, not try to beat them out with a stick. Instead of scolding Frankie for taking the van, therefore, I merely grabbed hold of the door as he hurtled around the corner onto First Avenue and prayed that his father would remain oblivious for a few more hours.

We were now entering the heart of Harlem's Italian colony, where the Independence Day celebration was already well under way. Groups of dark-haired women in red and yellow shawls congregated on nearly every stoop, chatting among themselves or calling out to the barefooted children who gamboled around them, while vendors in jaunty caps strolled past them down the sidewalk, hawking colored ices and ropes of nuts and small tin pails carried on poles across their shoulders. On the roadway itself, a parade was in progress, with rows of red-shirted men moving in loose formation up the paving stones, weaving around clumps of matted refuse left over from the recent street cleaners' strike. We inched past them up the avenue, unavoidably becoming part of the boisterous procession. Somewhere behind us, a brass band struggled through a rendition of "The Star Spangled Banner," while what sounded like a campaign chant drifted back to us from marchers up ahead. Everywhere I looked, red banners with a bearded man's face and the words LA LIBERAZIONE E L'UNIFICAZIONE! flapped alongside the American flag, reminding me that today was not only America's birthday, but the birthday of Giuseppe Garibaldi as well. A memorial was being dedicated to the beloved

27

military hero on Staten Island this afternoon, and it seemed Italians all over the city were taking note.

An impatient oath rang out from the back of the van. "Could you shake it, Frankie?" urged Donny O'Meara, who I'd heard had bet a full week's wages on the race.

"Not without running someone over," I answered. Although the parading men were staying to one side of the road, much of the other side was taken up by women carrying giant wicker baskets and herding flocks of dark-haired children before them. Frankie tried to squeeze past a boy pulling two toddlers in a rickety cart but had to slam on the brakes as a hokey-pokey man darted across the street in front of us, ringing his big brass bell.

"So run 'em over," Donny growled. "We're going to miss the finish at this rate."

"Aw, keep your pants on," Frankie piped back.

Donny reached over the seat and squeezed the back of his neck.

"Get your meat hook off me!" said Frankie, twisting away from his hand and driving one wheel up over the curb in the process, nearly costing Finn his footing on the running board.

"Look, boys!" I interjected. "There's our

chance!"

The phalanx of marchers closest to us had paused to buy some ices, creating a widening gap between our van and the nearest intersection. Donny released Frankie, who somehow managed to get the van off the curb, through the gap, and to the corner without maiming anyone. Turning hard right onto 107th Street, he adjusted the throttle, worked the clutch and gear stick, and resumed his race toward the river, weaving deftly through a bevy of sanitation carts that were pumping chloride of lime into the alleyways. I had to admit, I was impressed. Although my family had owned a motorcar for more than a year, I myself hadn't learned the first thing about operating it. I decided to ask our chauffeur to teach me at the first opportunity.

We arrived at the foot of Pleasant Avenue in time to see the boats half a block upstream, with Wieran now well in the lead. Donny whooped his approval as we turned up the avenue and followed them north. Although the fans were sparser here, they still formed a nearly unbroken line along the riverfront, allowing us only occasional glimpses of the race. Finn fed us updates from the running board until Frankie, fed up with secondhand reports, sped ahead two blocks, jerked to a stop in the middle of the street, and jumped out of the van. I followed with the rest of the boys, running out onto the 110th Street pier just in time to see the Wierans row past, a full length ahead of the Oakley boat. Simon's skin glistened with sweat and river spray as he drove his oar cleanly, powerfully through the water, his timing steady as a metronome. The boys behind him were more ragged, their shoulders slumped and their mouths agape, but looked no less determined. The Wieran fans sent up an unholy roar, not stopping until the rowers were indistinguishable on the horizon.

While the boys lingered to watch the receding rowers, I started back toward the idling van. The Consolidated Gas Company facilities occupied the entire next block, and Jefferson Park the three blocks after that, which meant we were going to have to make another detour and rejoin the race farther north. I was consulting my pendant watch, trying to calculate where we should attempt to rejoin them, when a collective moan rose from the spectators behind me.

I turned and looked back toward the boys, who were staring upriver with matching expressions of dismay. Following their gaze, I saw the Wieran boat floating listlessly near the 112th Street recreation pier, its rowers at rest and their oar blades lying flat on the water.

"What the Sam Hill?" muttered a mustachioed man on the bulkhead, spitting out a wad of tobacco as the Oakley crew overtook the lifeless boat and continued up the course.

I ran back out over the pier to the boys. "What happened?"

No one answered me. I lifted my field glasses and found the boat in my sights. There was nothing obviously wrong with either the hull or the oarlocks. I focused on some swimmers splashing in the water near the end of the pier, wondering if they had interfered with the race somehow, but that wouldn't account for the rowers remaining at a standstill. Swinging the glasses back to the boat, I saw Simon shout to someone on the lower pier deck before turning to speak to his crew. The starboard oarsmen took two strokes, nosing the bow toward the pier, followed by a few more strokes by the rowers in the stern, and then the boat glided out of sight along the northern side of the pier.

"What's going on?" Finn asked.

I shook my head. "I can't see anything wrong with the boat."

"Maybe Henry's hand gave out on him."

31

"Maybe," I said, although I'd examined the boy's bruised hand myself and had been sure he was up to the race. "Or one of the other boys might have strained something." I scanned the waterfront up ahead. The quickest way to get to the pier would be on foot. "I'm going to walk from here," I told the boys. "Finn, see that Frankie gets the van back safely, will you?"

I hurried back to the van ahead of them to grab my medical bag and then started up the avenue. I was halfway to the gas company fence before I realized they were all still behind me. I swung around to face them. "What are you doing?"

"Going with you," Frankie squeaked. "We don't want to miss nothin'."

"You can't leave your father's van in the middle of the street!"

His elfin features took on a familiar, stubborn expression.

"Finn?" I entreated, looking to the older boy.

"Come on," said Finn, taking Frankie by the scruff of his neck and turning him back toward the van.

I continued alone up the waterfront, skirting the fence and cutting across the empty loading docks toward the recreation pier. The sun was hot in the clear July sky, and I was damp and flushed by the time I arrived in Jefferson Park a few minutes later. Apparently, the park had been the Italian paraders' destination, for red banners were everywhere in evidence, and a motley collection of brass bands near the pavilion was churning out a festive tune. I hurried on across the lawns, past children performing flag drills on the playgrounds and picnickers sprawled over blankets on the grass. Everywhere, the air rang with the shrieks of children and the happy chatter of adults.

As I drew closer to the recreation pier, however, I was struck by the unnatural quiet that enveloped it. There should have been a holiday band playing on the upper deck and couples dancing and children launching early rockets across the river. Instead, I heard only the flapping of the flags on the pier roof, along with a low murmur from clumps of people huddled along the north railings of the pier and on the adjacent esplanade, all with their backs to me. I reached the jam on the esplanade and rose up on my toes to look beyond it. To my surprise, there was a policeman on the other side, holding the bystanders back. Clutching my medical bag to my chest, I led with my shoulder and pushed my way through the crowd.

CHAPTER TWO

I broke through to the front and stopped short. A few yards up ahead, a wet body lay inert on the walkway, surrounded by Simon, a second police officer, and a fireman with a dripping rope coiled over one shoulder. For a few heart-stopping seconds, I thought it might be one of Simon's boys — until a quick count of the oarsmen huddled a dozen yards up the esplanade reassured me. Taking another, longer look, I realized from its clothing that the body was female.

I called to Simon, who came over and spoke a few words to the policeman standing guard. The policeman stepped aside to let me pass.

"What happened?" I asked Simon as he led me a few steps from the crowd.

"A couple of boys swimming under the pier found her caught up in some rotten pilings," he said, his face showing the strain of his discovery. "She'd been under for a while. We had to pull her out with a rope."

"Do you want me to take a look?"

"Better let the coroner's physician handle it. The ambulance is on its way." He glanced toward the rowers on the bank. "You could come check on the lads with me, though. I haven't had a chance to talk to them since we pulled her out."

We started toward the rowers, which required passing the lifeless body on the esplanade. We were nearly to it when a dusty police wagon drove up on the grass on the other side of the esplanade railing and sputtered to a stop, followed by a horse-drawn ambulance. We stopped to watch a non-uniformed man jump out of the wagon and climb over the rail to join the others by the body.

"That's Detective Norton, from the 104th Street Station," Simon said. "He's going to want to talk to me."

"Should I leave?" I asked.

"No, it's all right; he's a friend. I play poker with him and the boys from the station. I'll explain things to him."

The detective conferred briefly with the patrolman, then circled around the body toward Simon.

Simon nodded in greeting. "Jimmy."

The detective nodded back. "I understand

you found her?"

"I just pulled her out. We were in the middle of a race when some swimmers spotted her and called us over."

The detective turned to me, cocking an eyebrow. "And this is?"

"Our team physician, Dr. Genevieve Summerford," Simon said. "She was just about to check on the boys with me. They've had a pretty nasty shock."

I noted the telltale flicker of surprise in the detective's eyes upon hearing that I was a doctor and waited for the usual snort of disbelief, but he only nodded again before turning back to Simon. "You want to show me exactly where the body was, first?"

They started toward the river's edge, followed by the uniformed patrolman and the fireman, leaving me temporarily alone on the esplanade.

I took a tentative step closer to the drowned woman. Although I'd been trained to face all kinds of death with detachment, my personal memories sometimes made this difficult. The accidental death of my younger brother when I was twelve — a death I had long blamed myself for — continued to exert a hold on me, occasionally triggering emotions that caught me by surprise. Now, as I gazed at the crumpled form on the pathway with the stillness of death upon it, my breath began to thicken in my chest as an old pain echoed inside me. Giving myself a mental push, I crossed the remaining distance between us.

She was really more of a girl than a woman, I realized now, perhaps sixteen or seventeen years of age, lying on her side in a semifetal position with strands of damp, dark hair across her face. Her light-brown eyes were open and glistening, her olive complexion mottled by livor mortis. A finger-long gash, only partially healed, ran across her cheek, while a chain of purplish-red bruises marred the skin on her neck. Oddly enough, considering the season, she was wearing a long winter coat, trimmed with red and yellow braid on the cuffs and lapels. A small gold cross had fallen out from behind the unfastened top button and was hanging by a chain over one lapel. Glancing lower, I noted that the shoes were missing from her stockinged feet. "What happened to you?" I whispered.

Simon and the others were starting back from the water. I took a step back, wanting to hear their thoughts and hoping not to be expelled from the scene.

"The park keeper told Officer Dennis that he didn't see or hear anything unusual during the night or early this morning," the detective was saying as they drew up beside the body.

"Well, she couldn't have gone in within the last couple of hours," Simon replied. "She was stiff as a board when we found her. Not to mention that with so many people around the pier, someone would have been sure to notice."

It was true that if rigor mortis was already established when they found her, the girl must have died long before the morning's festivities got underway. I wondered if she might have fallen in somewhere upriver during the evening and been carried down by the tide.

"She could have been dead before she hit the water," the detective mused, crouching beside the body. "That would explain the bruises on her neck."

"You're thinking she was strangled?" Simon asked, squatting beside him.

The detective shrugged. "These dagoes have hot tempers. Could've been a jealous boyfriend, or a Black Hand kidnapping gone wrong."

I looked back at the lifeless body in alarm. Over the past two years, the Italian criminal element known as the Black Hand had established a disturbing presence in a number of American cities, nowhere more boldly than in New York. Engaging primarily in extortion, the group preyed mercilessly on its fellow countrymen, killing them or bombing their businesses if they didn't capitulate to its demands. Usually, these demands were made in a letter signed with a crudely drawn black hand, skull, or other sinister symbol.

In recent months, the group's activity had spread from the downtown Italian district of Manhattan into the newer colonies in Harlem and Brooklyn. As if tormenting their hardworking countrymen with knives and bombs wasn't enough, the extortionists had also taken to kidnapping their children, ensuring that even the most courageous succumbed to their demands. But until now, the kidnappings had always been of little boys. If the young woman lying before me had died at their hands, it could signal a whole new kind of terror for the city.

"That cut on her face looks too old to be from a recent attack," Simon observed. "It's already partially scabbed over."

"The bruises are fresh enough," Norton replied.

Though the bruises may have been fresh, I thought it unlikely that the girl had been dead when she entered the river. The inward curve of her body was typical of drowning victims, whose head and limbs tended to hang from their more buoyant chest cavities in the water, becoming locked in that position as rigor mortis set in. If someone had thrown her into the river, most likely they'd either mistakenly believed she was dead or had trusted the river to finish her off.

"We'll know more after the autopsy," Detective Norton said, straightening from his crouch.

The crowd had grown more unruly and was beginning to press in on the gathering on the esplanade. The police accordingly began a more aggressive clearing of unnecessary personnel, which unfortunately included me. Since Simon still had to make his statement, I continued alone up the esplanade to check on the boys. I spied Frankie's van parked on the grass a few yards ahead, and then Frankie and his comrades mingling with the oarsmen by the rail. A few seconds later, they spotted me as well and bounded over, pelting me with questions about the dead girl.

After telling them the little I knew, I gently probed the rowers' reactions to what they had witnessed. For now, at least, excitement over their macabre discovery and disappointment over the race's interruption seemed to be their primary emotions.

"D'you think they did it on purpose?" Frankie asked me.

"Who?" I replied.

"The Oakley Club."

I frowned at him. "Are you asking me if I think your competition threw that girl in the water, then had someone call the Wieran team over, just so they could win the race?"

"Yeah, that's it," he confirmed.

"No," I said. "I most certainly do not."

"I wouldn't put it past 'em," Finn opined.

"Well, you'd better not go around saying so," I cautioned, remembering the alcohol-fueled crowds of Oakley supporters.

Per Simon's instructions, I told the boys to row the boat back downriver to the launch float, assuring them he'd meet them at the clubhouse that evening for the scheduled bonfire and fireworks. A few minutes later, the boat shoved off, minus its stern pair, while the remaining boys carried the extra oars back to the van. I waited until they were safely away and then started back down the esplanade.

Word of the girl's death must have spread, for by the time I returned to the pier, the small group of spectators at its foot had grown into a pulsing mass several hundred people strong that spilled onto the adjoining lawn. With families scattered all over the park, I supposed there must be many daughters and sisters unaccounted for, causing the fear I saw in many of the faces. I edged my way through the throng as frantic shouts and murmured prayers rippled all around me.

"Mio Dio! La mia Vittoria!" shrieked one woman, pushing past me and around the overwhelmed policeman. She ran to the body and stared down at it for a frozen moment before dropping to her knees with a moan of relief.

I stepped into the void she'd created at the front of the crowd and called to Simon, who was helping a photographer unload equipment from the nearby police wagon.

"How are they taking it?" he asked as he joined me.

"Almost too well," I told him. "I let them know I'd be at the clubhouse tonight, in case any of them want to speak to me in private."

"I appreciate it," he said, the warmth in his eyes underscoring his words.

We watched in silence as the photographer set up a tall tripod so that its legs were straddling the drowned girl and then climbed a stool to attach his camera to the

42

top of it, with the lens facing straight down. Draping a dark cloth over his head, he removed the lens cap, inserted a glass plate holder, and pulled out the dark slide to make his first exposure.

"What will happen now?" I asked Simon.

"I expect they'll let all these people file past, once they're done, to see if anyone can identify her. If that doesn't work, they'll likely print up a circular with her photograph and show it around the local lodging houses and women's shelters to see if anyone recognizes her there. They can use the circular to check for a match in the missing persons files too."

I hoped it would be enough. But I knew that hundreds of unclaimed bodies were buried every year on Hart's Island, an unhappy consequence of the record-breaking numbers of foreigners pouring into the city. I hated to think that this sweet-faced young girl might join their ranks, her death dismissed as one more unfortunate but inevitable occurrence of immigrant life.

Detective Norton called to Simon from the police wagon.

"Looks like I'm needed," Simon said. "You might as well go; there's nothing more you can do here. I'll see you tonight, at the clubhouse." He started toward the detective.

I lingered for a moment longer, watching him confer over the detective's memorandum book with his hands on his hips and his legs planted solidly on the pavement, admiring the sturdy look of him. How steady he was, I thought with a sigh; how easily he seemed to handle whatever life threw his way . . .

A piercing voice broke into my thoughts. "Miss! Miss, please!"

Glancing over my shoulder, I saw a dark-haired girl, perhaps thirteen years of age, standing a few feet behind me at the front of the crowd, struggling to escape the grip of a stout old woman in a black dress and shawl. "Please, miss!" she cried again.

With a start, I realized she was calling to me.

She broke free of the old woman and lunged toward me. "Will you help me, miss?" she entreated, anxiety contorting her oval face. Her English, though accented, was easy enough to understand.

"Help you? How?" I asked in astonishment.

"Rosa, *torna qui!*" the old woman hissed.

The girl ignored her. "My friend is missing," she said quickly, reaching for a locket

44

that hung from her neck. "If I give you her picture, will you ask the police to make a *circolare* for her too?"

I stared at her, uncomprehending, until it dawned on me that she must have overheard my conversation with Simon. I was still trying to come up with a response when she unclasped the brass locket and thrust it in front of my face. It contained two small photographs: one of a younger version of the girl standing before me, the other of an older girl, about fifteen years of age at the time it was taken. The older girl was very pretty, with a shy smile that lit up her big, dark eyes.

"This is my friend, Teresa Casoria," she said, pointing to the older girl. "She came here on a ship to marry Antonio eight days ago. She promised she would come see me on my birthday — but that was four days ago, and she hasn't come. I fear something bad must have happened to her."

"Oh, I am sorry," I sputtered, "but I'm really not in a position to help . . ."

"You know the police," she said, gesturing toward Simon and the detective. "You can give them her picture and ask them to look for her too." She pried the picture out of its frame with her fingernail and pushed it into my hand.

I looked down at the picture and back at her, nonplussed but also moved by her distress. "You know, it's possible that your friend was simply turned back at Ellis Island. If she contracted infectious eye disease or favus from another steerage passenger —"

"Teresa didn't come in steerage," she broke in. "Antonio bought her a cabin ticket. She told me so."

"Well then," I said slowly, deciding to try another tack, "perhaps she simply forgot about your birthday. If she's just arrived in New York, she must have a great deal on her mind. Especially if she's planning to marry."

"No," she said with an emphatic shake of her head. "Teresa wouldn't forget."

"Rosa! *Dobbiamo andare!*" called the old woman, beckoning with a crabbed arm.

The girl glanced over her shoulder and turned back to me, her dark eyes pleading. "In Naples, when my mother died, Teresa was very kind to me. She used to stay after school to help me with my lessons, and tell me happy stories. She was like the sun to me, shining through a cloudy sky. When I learned we were moving to America, I cried for days because I didn't want to leave her. But she promised to write to me every month so that I wouldn't feel too lonely. And then last winter, she wrote to say she was coming to New York to marry, and I was so happy!" She paused, her eyes welling with tears. "But now something has gone wrong. I can feel it! Please, miss, you must help her. You must!"

I hardly knew what to say. "But you don't know for sure that she's in trouble," I insisted. "She could have just had a change in plans and taken a later boat."

She was shaking her head again. "She posted a letter to me the morning she left, telling me she was on her way and that she was bringing a present for my birthday. Besides, Antonio had already sent her the ticket."

"Well, have you spoken to this . . . Antonio? Surely, he would know if she's gone missing."

She looked surprised by my question. "I'm an unmarried girl, miss. I'm not allowed to walk out alone. And my grandmother won't go with me to talk to Antonio or to the police. She says I'm being foolish."

I was inclined to agree with her grandmother, although I felt it would be unkind to say so.

"His name is Antonio Fabroni," she added quickly, her expression brightening, as if it had occurred to her that I might ask him for her. "He has a house painting business on 109th Street. Teresa told me he lives with his mother over the shop."

"I'm sorry," I said firmly, "but if you're convinced she's gone missing, the best advice I can give you is to file a report with the missing persons —" I broke off as her grandmother stepped forward and seized her by the arm. Muttering darkly, the old woman started pulling her back through the crowd.

"Wait!" I called after the girl, holding out the picture. "Your photograph!"

"You can give it back to me after they find her," she called over her shoulder. "My name is Rosa Velloca, and I live near the church, on 115th Street. Thank you, miss! Thank you with all of my heart!"

CHAPTER THREE

"Are you sure you know what you're doing?" Simon asked from the other side of the kitchen, where he was mashing a bowlful of potatoes with a carpenter's mallet.

"Of course I do." Edging to my right to block his view, I raised my spatula again and searched for the proper angle of attack. I'd been hounding Simon for months to introduce me to his friends; now that he'd finally invited one for supper, I wasn't about to admit that I was in over my head.

The six spotted trout stared doubtfully up at me, as if all too aware of my domestic inadequacies. After the unsettling events of the morning, I'd thought it would be a comfort to retreat to the Wieran clubrooms and prepare a homey meal for Simon and his friend. It hadn't occurred to me to worry that I'd never actually learned to cook. I made up for that omission now as I glanced at the sputtering skillet, which my housekeeper, Katie, had advised should be "hot enough to crisp 'em up, but not so hot as to burn 'em." A moment ago, the butter had been a golden, aromatic puddle, but while I'd been struggling to get the slippery corpses into the pan, it had turned an alarming shade of brown.

Once again, I lowered the spatula and scooped one of the fish off the plate. Once again, it slipped off the spatula's face — and this time would have landed on the floor, if I hadn't just managed to catch it in my apron. I shot a glance at Simon, but he appeared to be absorbed in mashing the potatoes. In desperation, I grasped the trout's tail with my free hand and swung it into the cast iron skillet, where it landed with a satisfying hiss. I grabbed two more and tossed them in after it, gazing down at the trout in relief as they sizzled in the browning fat.

I did so want the evening to go well and for Patrick and me to get along. Unfortunately, this was not a foregone conclusion. Just as many of my acquaintances would never accept as an equal a man who'd once been my family's stable boy, many of Simon's milieu, I had learned, felt nothing but scorn for those born into wealth and privilege. Two months ago, I'd taken what I considered the first step in breaching this divide by introducing Simon to my old school friend, Emily Clark, at a picnic in Central Park. To my relief, Emily had delighted in his company. Despite my repeated requests, however, Simon had failed to reciprocate. When I'd finally asked him outright if he was embarrassed to be seen with me, he'd claimed it wasn't me but his friends he was worried about, fearing they might be "a bit rough" for my taste.

As I believed I'd already demonstrated my ability to get on with people from all walks of life, I didn't wholeheartedly accept his explanation. In fact, I told him that if he didn't invite a friend, any friend, to join us for dinner on Independence Day, he needn't expect me to act as medical officer at the morning's race, as the participants of said function would surely be too rough for my delicate sensibilities. Though I'd only been teasing, he must have detected my underlying hurt, or perhaps he'd simply been unable to find another medical volunteer. In any event, a few days ago, he'd informed me that his policeman friend, Patrick Branagan, would be joining us on the Fourth for dinner.

"You might want to take that pan off the heat for a minute," he suggested now, glancing toward the stove, "to let the butter cool down."

"I was just about to do that," I said, reaching for the iron handle. I lifted the skillet only a few inches before dropping it back onto the stove. "Ow!"

I heard Simon expel his breath. The next moment, he was at my side, dish towel in hand, pushing the skillet off the burner.

"Our pans at home don't heat up like that," I muttered, although I couldn't actually recall ever handling one.

He gestured toward my hand. "Let's see it."

"It's fine," I said, curling my fingers into a ball at my side.

He reached for my wrist and turned my hand over, revealing a nasty red stripe across the palm. "Bloody hell, Genna," he said with a sigh. "Why couldn't you just let me cook the fish?"

"I'm perfectly capable of cooking six little trout," I insisted, trying to tug my hand away.

"And what if you're not?" he asked, refusing to let go. "Is that such a terrible thing?"

As usual, I found it impossible to dissemble under his all-too-penetrating gaze. Abandoning further bravado, I admitted, "I just don't want your friends to think I'm a . . . a 'helpless toff,' " repeating the phrase I'd heard a sailor utter disparagingly in the saloon a week before. "I *ought* to know how to cook. I don't know why I never learned."

"Maybe because you were busy learning other things," he said with a crooked smile. "Like how to be a doctor."

"Well, there was that," I conceded, smiling back a little despite myself.

He traced a line beside the welt with his thumb. "Does it hurt much?"

I didn't answer immediately, too riveted by the sensations he was generating in the hollow of my hand. "Not much," I managed finally. "I doubt it will even blister."

He carefully unfurled my fingers, checking for burns across the upper joints. I had a sudden memory of watching him at work in my family's stable as his hands moved gently but surely over a sore foreleg or a steaming flank. *That one has magic hands,* our chauffeur, Maurice, used to say. It was true, I thought now, my eyelids flickering involuntarily as his thumb grazed each paralyzed fingertip.

The sensations stopped. I looked up to find him watching me, his smile gone, his expression very still and intense. I held his gaze, hardly breathing, seeing what I was sure was desire in his eyes. *Finally,* I thought, my pulse leaping in response. I leaned toward him, lifting my face, my entire body alight.

He abruptly released my hand. "You'd better go run that under some cold water. I can finish the trout." Turning back to the stove, he wrapped the towel around the handle and gave the pan a shake.

I hurried to the sink, not wanting him to see the blush of confusion that was racing up my cheeks. Was I the only one who wanted more of what we'd tasted, all those years ago? Even now, my body pulsed with the memory of it: my dizzying expectation as I carried the apples down to the stable, propelled by a yearning I couldn't even identify; young Simon's eyes, gleaming like jet in the lamplight, when he came down from the loft and found me standing there. And then, dear God, the brush of his lips across my face, and the pressure of his fingers unbuttoning my chemise, and the bone-deep ache his touch provoked . . . I closed my eyes with a shiver. Although he'd stopped before we'd done anything "irreversible," it had been the most thrilling event of my life to date — and neither my mind nor my body seemed to want to forget it.

Unfortunately, I'd never stopped to consider the possible consequences of my actions. Thanks to my foolishly forward behavior, Simon and his mother, who'd been our parlor maid, were removed from our employ — and my life — while I was sent for an extended stay abroad so that I might mingle with more suitable young men. In the years that followed, still filled with shame over the incident, I'd managed to convince myself that my youthful attraction to Simon had been merely a random phenomenon, that he, who as my daily riding escort was the male with whom I'd come in most frequent contact, had simply been the readiest target of my ascending, pubescent chemistry. But when he reappeared out of the blue last winter in magistrate's court, I felt the same molten charge that I'd experienced in my adolescence, like hot current surging through undergauged wire. I knew then that my attraction to him was rooted in something more than circumstance. I knew I wanted more of him, and the way he made me feel. But it was beginning to seem as though my wanting might be in vain.

There was no time to dwell on this most recent disappointment, however, for Patrick was due to arrive at any moment. Composing my features into a mask of cheerful expectancy, I dried my hands and carried a vase of yellow roses into the dining room. Though no one could call this hard-used room elegant, I thought it looked inviting enough, with the flowers in my mother's crystal vase on the table and light from flickering candles warming the buff-colored walls. As I rearranged the blossoms, I tried not to think of what my parents would say if they knew I was entertaining male guests in the rooms of the Wieran Club, which was located above Simon's saloon. I'd taken advantage of their European sojourn to test the limits of social propriety, spending far more unsupervised time in Simon's company than was strictly proper considering the lack of any formal understanding between us, often in settings I was sure my parents would consider unseemly. I appeased my conscience with the thought that, although the club members weren't scheduled to arrive until later that evening, the club rooms were at least officially open, which ought to be adequate defense against any allegations of scandalous behavior.

I heard the sound of a boot on wood, and then the hallway door flew open. A flush-faced man in rolled-up shirtsleeves stood on the threshold, holding a foaming growler in each hand. "The reserves have arrived!" he announced in a brogue as muscular as his forearms.

"Patrick! Good man," said Simon, emerging from the kitchen. "I was afraid you'd forget."

"You're payin' for it," Patrick said with a grin. "The least I can do is carry it upstairs." Though he was shorter and stockier than Simon, he had the same dark, wavy hair and square-cut features. He also had the same twinkle in his eye, I noticed, which I was beginning to think was an Irish birthright.

Simon was striding toward him, reaching for the pails of beer, when Patrick moved aside to allow a young woman to enter. Simon stopped short on sight of her.

"Hello, Simon," she said, stepping into the room. She was black-haired and fair-skinned, with brilliant blue eyes that flashed when they lit on him.

Patrick shot Simon an apologetic glance. "When she found out I was having supper with you, she insisted I bring her along."

"I had to see for myself that you were still alive," the woman said to Simon, with an Irish lilt nearly as pronounced as Patrick's. "You've been so scarce these past few months, I could hardly believe it." She slid off her wrap and held it out to him, holding on for a moment longer than was necessary when he reached for it. Fluttering her dark lashes, she added, "I hope you don't mind."

"Always glad to see an old friend," Simon said, removing the wrap from her grasp. He gestured toward me. "Kitty, Patrick, this is Genevieve."

I extended a hand to Kitty. "How do you do?"

She shook my hand limply, looking me coolly up and down. Her dress was very flattering, if more revealing than current fashion dictated, with a shirred, off-the-shoulder bodice in sapphire-blue taffeta that matched the brilliant color of her eyes. I suddenly wished I hadn't chosen the dull, gray costume I was wearing. I had thought it would put me on equal footing with our company, but with Kitty's arrival, I'd only ended up looking dowdy in comparison.

"The boys'll be arriving soon for the festivities, so if we want any peace, we'd better get to it," Simon said, ushering our guests toward the table. He took charge of the beer, while I set out another plate for Kitty and went to fetch our dinner. A few moments later, we were all seated at the table, Patrick and Kitty across from Simon and me. When our plates were full and the beer had been poured, Patrick raised his glass in my direction. "To new friends," he said.

I lifted my glass with a smile.

"And to old ones," Kitty added, leaning forward to raise her glass toward Simon, revealing an impressive expanse of bosom in the process.

Simon glanced at me over his glass, looking uncharacteristically sheepish. I cocked an eyebrow and sipped my beer.

"I heard it was you who pulled that girl out of the river today," Patrick said, wagging his fork at Simon.

Simon put down his glass. "I'm sorry to say you heard right." He shook his head. "It's a shame. She couldn't have been more than sixteen. Does Norton have any idea who she is yet?"

"Not that I've heard."

"Now why do you boys want to talk about a dead girl when you've got two live ones right here?" Kitty protested.

I too would prefer to speak about something else. It wasn't just the drowned girl I wanted to forget; young Rosa's face kept popping up in my mind, wide-eyed and imploring, waiting for me to shed light on her friend's disappearance. As I'd expected, my request that Detective Norton do something with the missing girl's picture had fallen on deaf ears. A missing person's report would have to be filed, the busy detective had told me, before any action could be taken. As I'd already told Rosa the same thing, I believed I'd discharged any duty I might owe her. And yet, those pleading eyes wouldn't leave me alone . . .

"All right, what should we talk about instead?" Simon asked, settling back in his chair.

"Why don't you tell us how you two met?" Kitty suggested.

Simon and I glanced at each other. After two beats of silence, I answered, "I sought Simon out last winter when a patient of mine got into legal trouble. I knew he was the captain of the election district where my patient lived, and I thought he might be able to help." It was the stock answer I'd come to rely on whenever I was asked this question.

"A patient?" Kitty asked with a frown. "You're a nurse, then?"

"Genevieve's a doctor," Simon said, smiling in my direction.

"Get off," Kitty scoffed.

"No, it's true, I am," I told her. "A medical psychologist, to be exact. Which means I treat functional disorders of the mind."

She sat back, her eyes narrowing as she digested this information. "You must have had a lot of schooling," she said finally.

"Well, yes, I suppose I have. I was lucky to be able to attend Johns Hopkins Medical School."

She sniffed. "I've never cared much for book learnin', myself. S'pose I've been too busy learnin' about life firsthand."

I nodded, sensing she believed we were in some sort of competition but refusing to take the bait. "You would have liked my old anatomy professor, I think. He always said that learning from books was no substitute for real life experience."

She smiled thinly and sipped her beer.

Patrick draped a beefy hand over the back of her neck. "Kitty works in a white goods factory. But she's aiming to set up a shop of her own one day."

"That's right," Katie confirmed, lifting her chin. "It's going to be the best lingerie shop in all of New York, sellin' only the finest silks and trimmings." She turned to stroke Patrick's cheek with her forefinger. "And Patrick's going to help me, aren't you, Pat?"

Apparently, whatever Kitty's past with Simon had entailed, she had since moved on to Patrick, who appeared unperturbed by this chain of events. He grinned in response, pulling her toward him to give her a lusty kiss. She broke away and chucked him playfully under the chin. "Mind your

61

manners, lovey," she murmured. "Dinner before dessert."

I didn't know where to look, unaccustomed to such open displays of affection. I glanced down at my plate, and then over their heads, and finally to my right, toward Simon. My heart sank as I saw that he was watching Kitty with a mix of amusement and . . . not admiration, exactly, but . . . appreciation. Yes, he was enjoying the way she purred and pouted and kept Patrick effortlessly enthralled. Is that what Simon found attractive? A woman who wore her sexuality like a luxurious fur coat? If so, he must find me very prim and constrained indeed.

But if that was true, I wondered, trying not to choke on the lump of mashed potato in my mouth, why was he bothering to spend time with me? We could have gone our separate ways, once my patient's case was resolved and I no longer required his help. Why had Simon decided to pursue our unconventional acquaintance if he wasn't even attracted to me? God knew he didn't owe me anything; I was the one in his debt, several times over. Perhaps, I thought, he'd felt an initial attraction, but it had faded as we'd spent more time together, and now he regretted his decision. With women like Kitty at his beck and call, I couldn't really say that I blamed him.

"Is that right, Pat?" Simon was asking. "You're goin' into the ladies' undergarment business?"

Patrick grinned. "Why not? I've never been one to turn down a sure investment."

"Investment, is it?" Simon chortled. "Police work must be paying more than I realized these days."

"Pat's been promoted to roundsman," Kitty informed him, wrapping a possessive hand around Patrick's bicep. "And he's been puttin' in lots of extra hours."

"Promoted!" Simon said, laying down his fork. "Why didn't you tell me?"

Patrick shrugged.

"He doesn't like to talk himself up," Kitty answered for him. "But they know a good man when they see one."

"Well, this calls for a toast," Simon declared. He raised his glass toward Patrick. "May your pockets be heavy, and your heart be light —"

"And good luck pursue you each morning and night!" Kitty finished for him. They all laughed and quaffed their beer, while I smiled along and tried not to feel like an outsider.

"How's your ma doin', Simon?" Kitty asked when the gaiety had subsided. "I haven't seen her in a month of Sundays."

I held my breath, shooting a glance at Simon. He hardly ever mentioned his mother in my presence, a fact I suspected reflected a continuing animosity toward me on her part. I couldn't fault her for blaming me for her dismissal all those years ago, but I did think it important to attempt a reconciliation if Simon and I were to have any hope of a future together. Last month, I'd suggested he bring me along to Sunday dinner at his mother's sometime — a suggestion he had studiously ignored, making me fear things were even worse than I'd imagined.

"She's well enough," he answered Kitty. "Thanks for asking."

"Still reading the cards?"

"Only for friends and family. She gets tired if she overdoes."

Kitty turned to me. "Has she done a reading for you yet?"

"A reading?"

"Has she told your fortune?" she spelled out impatiently, as if I were being deliberately obtuse.

"Oh . . . no, not yet," I said, both embarrassed by my ignorance of Mrs. Shaw's abilities and irrationally jealous of Kitty's familiarity with them.

"You're in for a treat then," she said with a knowing nod. "She's got the gift, she does."

I was glad when Simon changed the subject a moment later, although I found myself once again relegated to the sidelines as the conversation moved from a recent boxing match, to a cinder-blinded fire horse, to a popular local bartendress known as Buttermouth Bel. Only when the discussion turned to Police Commissioner Theodore Bingham, a colorful and contentious figure about whom I was relatively well informed, did I finally see an opportunity to join in.

"I hear Mayor McClellan is being pressured to fire him," I said, passing Simon more potatoes. "Because of the transfers." General Bingham's first promise when he took office eighteen months earlier had been to root out police graft. Graft, of course, depended on long-standing relationships between the city's political machine, the gangs who helped keep it in power by perpetrating fraud at the polls, and the police who allowed those gangs to operate. It also depended on each police captain's intimate knowledge of the illegal drinking, gambling, and disorderly resorts within his precinct, from which he could, if he was so inclined, extract a monthly protection fee. The previous fall, to sever these lucrative connections, our bold commissioner had taken the unprecedented step of transferring all but one of his eighty-six police captains to new precincts. The reaction had been predictable, with much gnashing of teeth by all parties concerned.

"McClellan's not going to fire him," Patrick said. "It'd only make him look as crooked as the rest. Besides, Bingham's too popular. People like the way he's going after the Black Hand."

The commissioner's second promise had been to crush the mushrooming Italian criminal organization, whose ruthless activities were creating hysteria among even the city's non-Italian residents, who feared they would eventually become targets.

"Speaking of which," Simon said, "has anyone been arrested for the bombings on 107th Street?"

"Not yet," Patrick replied.

Simon shook his head. "Does Hurley even have a plan?"

"There's not much the captain, or anyone, can do," Patrick said. "Not without witnesses willing to come forward. The damned dagoes would rather stick knives in their own throats than squeal on one of their own. It makes it impossible for us to do our job."

As newspaper commenters liked to tell us, the Italian immigrants had brought a deep distrust of police and the legal process to America, born of centuries of abuse in their homeland at the hands of those in power. They lived, accordingly, by a code that required victims of crime to seek their own justice, and even to shield their assailants from the law.

"Couldn't they talk to you in private, like?" Kitty asked.

"They're too scared," Patrick said. "They think these crooks have magical powers. They cross themselves if you even mention the Black Hand."

"I thought the Italian squad was making inroads," I ventured. Our previous police commissioner had taken the first step toward addressing the "Italian problem," creating a squad of six Italian-speaking men tasked with infiltrating the immigrant colonies, forming alliances, and gathering intelligence on suspected criminals. But it was Commissioner Bingham who had given the squad real teeth, enlarging it to thirty-five men, renaming it "the Italian Legion," and promoting its head, the quick-fisted but incorruptible Joseph Petrosino, to the rank of lieutenant.

"They've made some big arrests, to be sure," Patrick said, "but for every thug they put in jail or deport, another three spring up. We've had more kidnappings in the last six months than we did all last year."

"Detective Norton thinks the girl they found in the river might have been a Black Hand kidnapping victim," I told him.

He cocked an eyebrow. "That would be a first. Far as I know, they've only ever taken young children before. And only boys at that."

"Well, I think it's disgraceful, stealing little children right off the streets," Kitty joined in. "Isn't there anything you can do to stop it, Pat?"

"Not if the victims won't even show us the letters or let us in on the ransom exchange."

"What about the 'secret service' Bingham keeps asking for?" Simon asked.

I waited with interest for Patrick's answer. I knew that, in what some considered an overreach of authority, Commissioner Bingham was agitating for the creation of a special unit modeled on the federal Secret Service, which would have unlimited discretion in dealing with Italian crime and report only to him.

"I wouldn't hold your breath," Patrick said, refilling his glass. "He's been asking the Board of Aldermen for funding ever since he took office, but they just keep turning a deaf ear."

"Well, someone better do something," Simon said, "or things could get ugly around here. There's no love lost between the Irish and Italian gangs. With public opinion at their back, I wouldn't be surprised if the Duffy Hills and Red Peppers start lynching every Italian they can catch south of 102nd Street."

"We don't want a repeat of New Orleans," I agreed.

"Why? What happened in New Orleans?" Kitty asked.

"The lynching of those Italian prisoners?" I prompted.

When her face remained blank, I elaborated. "An angry mob attacked and killed eleven Italian prisoners charged with murdering an Irish police chief. The king of Italy demanded immediate punishment of the attackers and reparations for the victims' families, but our government refused, saying the American legal system had to establish the guilt or innocence of the parties first. The Italians recalled their foreign minister in response, and introduced resolutions in their parliament calling for a punitive naval strike on our shore."

"Wait a minute," Patrick said. "Are you telling me the dagoes were threatening to attack the United States?"

"Well, yes," I said, warming to my subject. "It was a matter of national pride for them, you see. Of course, there was no attack, but that's why we started building up our navy, to protect against future threats. Before it happened, we didn't have a single modern battleship, but when the Spanish-American War broke out a few years later, we had a whole fleet." I took a sip of my beer, proud to have had something of interest to contribute at last, and waited for their response. My little riff, however, seemed to have brought the conversation to a halt.

Finally, Patrick, who'd been watching me with a bemused expression, turned to Simon and said, "She's a smart one, ain't she?"

"That she is," he agreed with a wry smile.

I smiled back uncertainly. I hadn't meant to sound like a stuffy schoolmarm.

I was relieved when the clock on the mantel struck the half hour a few moments later. "I'd better get dessert," I said, rising to my feet.

"I'll help," Kitty said.

Before I could protest, she was out of her chair and lifting the two nearest plates. "It'll give us a chance for some girl talk," she added.

As I could think of only one subject that we had in common, it was with some reluctance that I cleared the remaining plates and followed her into the kitchen.

CHAPTER FOUR

Kitty deposited the dishes in the sink, then leaned back against the table and watched me with a speculative air while I fetched bowls of strawberries and whipped cream from the icebox.

"So, are you serious about him, or just slummin'?" she asked as I started doling the strawberries onto dessert plates.

I paused in midscoop. "I beg your pardon?"

She shrugged a shapely shoulder. "I wouldn't have figured you for his type, but I can see from the way he looks at you, he's smitten. I just want to know if it goes both ways."

I was too glad to hear she thought Simon was smitten with me to be offended by the directness of her question. Indeed, I would have liked to ask her just how, exactly, he looked at me, but my pride wouldn't allow it. "I care for Simon a great deal."

She studied my face for a long moment. "Fair enough," she said, pushing off from the table. "I ain't one to be a sore loser. Besides, I've got a pretty good thing going with Patrick."

"Yes, he appears to be very much in love with you," I said, relieved that we seemed to have reached some sort of understanding.

"Ha!" she crowed. "Love's got nothin' to do with it. I give him what he wants, and he takes good care of me. He bought me this dress," she added, pirouetting on the linoleum floor. "Ain't it a whizz?"

"It's beautiful."

Her face grew thoughtful as her attention returned to me. "You know, you could be a real looker if you tried. I could give you a few tips, if you like."

"I didn't think I was doing so badly," I said with an awkward laugh, spooning out the rest of the strawberries.

"Oh, you've got the goods, all right. But what's the point of having 'em if you're going to keep 'em under lock and key? It's not every woman who catches Simon's fancy. If you want him to stay interested, you need to make him feel like a man." She winked at me. "And that means showin' him your womanly assets."

After seeing the way both Patrick and

Simon reacted to Kitty, I had to believe there was something in what she said. But I found the idea of manipulating a man with my "womanly assets" repellent. "I'd like to believe that a woman's physical attractiveness isn't everything. I should think a meeting of minds would be just as important in a long-term relationship."

She tipped back her head and cackled. "Think whatever you like, dearie, but it's a man's little head, not his big one, that decides how long he's going to stick around, and Lord help you if you don't know that by now."

I found it difficult to look at Simon when we returned to the dining room. He must have sensed that something was amiss, for I could feel his eyes following me as I busied myself handing out the dessert plates and replenishing the cutlery.

"That looks delicious," he said as I sat down beside him, giving me an encouraging smile.

On the other side of the table, Kitty lifted a cream-topped berry in her fingers and, with a sidelong glance at Patrick, delicately licked it clean. Patrick watched in dumbstruck fascination, his own fork hanging forgotten in the air.

Could men really be that simple? I wondered crossly, mashing a berry between my own teeth. As a doctor, I had a fair understanding of the baser human instincts and their importance to the survival of our race. I would have liked to think, however, that thousands of years of civilization had put the "little head," as Kitty had called it, in its place.

"Mmm," Kitty murmured, licking a fleck of cream from her finger and winking at me across the table. I decided I'd had entirely enough winking for one day.

A few minutes later, the clock struck the quarter hour. "We'd better put a hole in it," Patrick said, having apparently regained his senses. "I'm on the eight o'clock shift." He lifted his nearly full glass and drained it in one long gulp. Simon had told me that under Commissioner Bingham's new five-platoon schedule, officers now spent six hours in reserve before going out on patrol, which they could use to sleep and/or sober up, barring emergencies. Watching Patrick down his umpteenth glass of beer, it struck me that this might have been one of the commissioner's most valuable contributions to the city to date.

The first of the Wieran Club boys were already thundering up the hallway stairs when we opened the door to show out our guests. The rest of the members straggled in while Simon and I were washing up, all loud and "full of taspy," as Simon would say, clearly eager for the celebrations to begin. If any of the oarsmen were suffering psychic distress from seeing the body at the pier, they were doing an excellent job of concealing it. Finn, as the eldest member of the club, started things off by climbing on a chair to deliver the customary reading from the Declaration of Independence, gesturing theatrically as the rest of the boys hooted their approval. "And for the support of this Declaration, with a firm reliance on the protection of divine Providence, we mutually pledge to each other our Lives, our Fortunes, and our sacred Honor!" he finished in a grand crescendo, sweeping his arm through the air.

From there, the evening proceeded in a whirlwind of frenzied male energy. After distributing rockets and Roman candles, Simon led the boys down to the street, where kegs of beer and tables heaped with sandwiches had been set up on the sidewalk. With the help of other block residents, the boys built an enormous pile of boxes, barrels, and fence boards in the center of the pavement and set the mound ablaze. The street was soon swarming with people, young and old alike, all apparently bent on creating the maximum amount of noise and smoke. Strings of Chinese crackers popped and snaked from the fire escapes, while Catherine wheels spat out sparks from every other door. Toddlers wandered down the sidewalk blowing on tin trumpets, watching their older brethren light giant crackers or launch bottle rockets from the curb. Those too poor to afford firecrackers simply packed gunpowder into cracks in the sidewalk and set it alight, or grabbed burning boards from the fire and ran with them down the street, loosing long trails of sparks.

I stood near the door under the saloon canopy and watched it all with my heart in my mouth, waiting for someone to get hurt. I had insisted that all club members receive the tetanus antitoxin offered by Board of Health supply stations prior to the holiday, so at least they were safe from death by lockjaw, but there was always the danger of losing one's finger or one's eyesight to exploding powder or of being shot by a stray bullet. Although Simon forbade the use of even blank cartridges, not everyone on the street and bordering avenues was so disciplined, as the constant pop of pistol fire attested.

My fears were temporarily forgotten,

however, as I watched Simon interact with the boys. The lads clearly held him in great affection. I supposed he was one of the few people who'd ever given them something without expecting anything in return — for survival in the tenement districts, I'd come to learn, was a struggle from which children were not immune. It wasn't unusual for the oldest siblings in a family to be sent into the streets to fend for themselves before they could even tie their shoes. More often than not, these outcasts were forced to become petty thieves, snatching fruit from the peddlers' stands or bread from the cooling racks to survive. As they got older, they might progress to siphoning sugar from sacks on the docks or stealing coal from delivery chutes or lifting merchandise from cars in the train yards. A few would make a stab at honest labor, shining shoes or peddling pencils or newspapers, but the competition for turf in such industries was fierce, and their older street brethren would soon be demanding an extortionate cut of their meager proceeds. Eventually, the gangs, in constant need of reinforcements, would recruit them as lookouts and decoys, providing a twisted sense of "family" and cementing them in a life of crime.

Simon's Wieran Club offered something

different. Although the neighborhood boys were often attracted initially by the club's free meals and athletics, they stayed for the camaraderie and sense of pride they gained while advancing through its ranks. In between sporting events and excursions, they learned carpentry, machine repair, and accounting. Once Simon felt they were ready, he found them jobs in local businesses or put them to work for the Tammany machine. I knew that in the more heavily populated, politically important districts of the Lower East Side, Tammany club recruits were often used to cast illegal ballots and intimidate opposition voters at the polls. But Simon didn't condone such practices, believing he could win votes honestly by serving his constituents' needs. Apparently he was right, for in the last two elections, he'd delivered over ninety percent of his district's votes to the Tammany-backed candidate, without the use of dirty tactics at the polls. Meanwhile, his club recruits were all leading relatively productive, mostly law-abiding lives. It was a record, I thought, that even my Tammany-loathing father could admire.

Simon came to stand beside me, his watchful eyes taking in all the activity on the street. "Having fun?"

"If being in constant terror of injury and mayhem constitutes fun, then yes, I most certainly am."

"Don't worry. We haven't had a serious injury yet."

Even as he was saying this, one of the older boys starting swatting at his smoldering pant cuff with an unexploded rocket.

"Use the hose, Tommy," Simon called to him.

I groaned and closed my eyes.

"Sorry about the unexpected company at dinner," Simon said a moment later.

"There's no need to apologize," I assured him. "After all, I've been pestering you to introduce me to your friends, and now I've met two of them."

"Kitty's not the first friend I would have chosen to introduce you to. She's a darb, for sure, but I can't imagine any two women more different than you and her."

I wasn't quite sure how to take this. "Have you known her long?"

"Since I was seventeen. She was living down the block on Leroy Street when my mother and I moved in. Mum's sight was failing, and she needed someone to help her keep house, so I hired Kitty to come by for a few hours each week. I, ah, got to know her pretty well."

"So I gathered."

He turned to me with a frown. "She's not usually so . . . prickly. I'm guessing she must have found you pretty intimidating."

"*She* found *me* intimidating? I thought she was going to cut my heart out with a spoon. I do hope you weren't the great love of her life."

"Me? God no," he said, looking back out over the street as a toddler was almost trampled by three running boys. "Hey, Tim, mind your little brother!" he called. "We had some fun together," he continued, "but it was never serious. Kitty just doesn't like giving things up."

I shot him a sidelong glance. For all Simon's experience with women, he didn't seem to recognize when one was carrying a torch for him. "She has an awfully utilitarian view of the male-female relationship," I mused. "Was she always so practical?"

He chuckled. "That's Kitty, to a T."

"I rather pity Patrick if his money ever runs out."

He shrugged. "She hasn't had it easy. She's had to make the most of what she's got to survive." He gave me a quizzical look. "I suppose that shocks you?"

I considered the question. "No, not really," I said after a moment. "It isn't so different from marrying for money, after all, or exchanging one's wealth for a title, or any of the other trade-offs you hear about women making every day. It's just that I, personally, could never do it."

"Don't say never until you've walked in another person's shoes."

"There are always other choices."

"Like starving?" he retorted. "Or watching the people you love suffer?"

I stiffened, stung by the sharpness of his tone. "I'm sorry; I suppose you're right. I can't know how I would act until I'd actually lived Kitty's life."

"No, I'm sorry," he said with a shake of his head. "I'm being an arse. It's just that I was hoping you'd like my friends."

"Oh, Simon, I don't *not* like them. After all, I hardly even know them yet. But I do trust your opinion, and if you care for them, I'm sure I'll come to appreciate them in time."

He smiled ruefully. "What I ought to be saying is, thanks for going to so much work and putting on such a nice supper."

"Yes, you should," I replied in a tone of mock indignation. "And you're welcome."

We remained in the doorway for another quarter hour, with Simon pointing out some of the more colorful neighborhood residents and shouting to the boys from time to time. But although harmony had been restored, I couldn't stop thinking about his outburst. I understood now why he'd been reluctant to introduce me to other people in his life: he had appreciated, more than I, how difficult it might be. The fact was that while I truly believed I could find some common ground with Patrick — and even Kitty — if I tried, I was far less confident that we could ever become truly close. And what would life as a couple be like for Simon and me without the richness and support of mutual friends?

Once the rockets and crackers were gone and the bonfire was reduced to embers, we all traipsed over to East River Park for the public fireworks display. I sat between Simon and Frankie on the grass, oohing and aahing with the others at each dazzling explosion and singing along with the band when it played between displays. Watching the boys' upturned faces soften in amazement under the magic in the sky, it occurred to me that I'd never before enjoyed fireworks so much.

When all that remained were wisps of smoke and a ringing in our ears, the boys wandered off in search of further entertainment and Simon offered to walk me home. I happily consented, eager to spend some time with him alone. He helped me up from the grass, tucking my hand under his elbow as we started across the lawn. It was a small gesture, but every part of me thrummed in response.

The blocks just beyond the park were still full of merrymakers, echoing with the sounds of firecrackers and police gongs. As we continued further west and north, however, the celebrations became more subdued. Many of the houses along Madison Avenue were dark, their owners gone to the country or to their yacht clubs for the holiday. There were still occasional clusters of people on the sidewalk, however, returning from the theater or from private parties, and as we walked arm in arm toward Ninety-Second Street — Simon in his workday outfit of boots and suspenders and rolled-up shirtsleeves, me in my conservative but expensive gray suit — we attracted more than one curious stare. I pulled Simon closer, wanting him to know I was proud to have him at my side.

When we were two blocks from my home, a stout older woman in an enormous feathered hat stopped short on the sidewalk beside us. "Doctor Summerford?"

It took me a moment to recognize her. "Mrs. Richards!" A few months ago, Mrs.

Richards, an acquaintance of my aunt's, had discovered that her daughter, Serena, was secretly volunteering at a settlement house, an undertaking Mrs. Richards considered both dangerous and unseemly. When Serena not only refused to stop working at the settlement, but also threatened to stop eating if her mother forced her hand, Mrs. Richards sent her to me for "fixing." After a single session, I'd concluded that the girl was displaying a healthy rebellion toward her overly domineering mother and tailored the rest of her "treatment" to helping her learn to manage her mother in less confrontational ways.

"I see you've decided to stay in the city after all," I said, extending my hand. Serena had told me her mother was threatening to haul the family off for an extended stay in the White Mountains to ensure that her daughter had no more contact with the "germ-infested" clients of the settlement house.

She took my hand, looking Simon up and down with a frown. "Serena and I have come to an agreement," she told me. "I've given her permission to work at the settlement so long as the doctor there guarantees it's safe for her to do so. I must confess, I didn't realize how much good these settlements do until I received a personal visit from Alva Belmont, seeking my help."

"I'm glad to hear it," I said, delighted to know our strategy had succeeded. Aware of her mother's social aspirations, Serena had engineered the visit from Mrs. Belmont — who was a member of the settlement board, in addition to being a pillar of high society — by intimating that her mother was itching to make a large donation.

Mrs. Richards turned a jaundiced eye on Simon. "I don't believe I've had the pleasure."

"This is my very good friend, Simon Shaw," I told her. "Simon, Mrs. Richards."

He held out a hand. "Pleased to meet you."

She stared at his hand with unconcealed distaste before taking it briefly between her fingertips. "Do I recall correctly that your parents are abroad, dear?" she asked, turning back to me.

"Yes, in Italy. Having a wonderful time, according to their postcards."

She sniffed. With another glance at Simon, she said ominously, "I'll be sure to tell them I bumped into you, when I see them next." Turning on her heel, she continued down the street.

"She's awfully high up the tree," Simon

said, frowning after her. "I've met gang members with better manners."

"I'm so sorry."

"Someone ought to tell her she doesn't own the sidewalk."

"The reason she's so snooty is because she's only one generation removed from the tenements herself, and desperate to dissociate herself from her humble beginnings," I told him, mortified by her rudeness. "She probably wouldn't acknowledge her own father if he passed her on the street."

"So why do you put up with her?"

I sighed. "Because I need more paying clients, and she could be a valuable source of referrals." In the six months since I'd opened my psychotherapy practice, I had acquired exactly five paying patients, two of whom were abroad for the summer. My therapy class at the settlement had gratifyingly expanded to eight women, but it claimed only a single hour of my time each Sunday and provided no financial remuneration. Though I'd been working hard to broaden my referral base, the combination of my gender and my youth was making this difficult. My dream of renting a flat over my tiny Madison Avenue office and moving out of my parents' house had accordingly been postponed for the indefinite future, a fact that had me chafing at the bit — for although Father was trying hard to respect my desire for independence, so long as I remained under his roof, I feared the old patterns would be difficult to break.

It was clear to me from Simon's expression that he considered my reasons for tolerating Mrs. Richards insufficient, but he kept his thoughts to himself as we continued the last block up Madison and turned left onto Ninety-Second Street. Although most of my neighbors' houses were dark, the lights were glowing softly at number 7. I slowed my pace as we approached, reluctant to bring the evening to a close, already wondering when I'd see him again. I knew that, come August, he'd be spending every spare minute at his fledgling stable in Saratoga, and I was hoping to spend as much time together as possible before then.

At the bottom of the steps, we stopped and turned to each other. I gazed up at his face — the face that had figured so largely in my daydreams when I was hardly more than a child, and that had grown only dearer with time — and waited, acutely aware of the moment's potential.

He returned my gaze, his dark eyes inscrutable.

What would Kitty do now, I wondered, to

make him take her into his arms? Feign a swoon? Murmur something suggestive in his ear? I remembered how she'd fluttered her eyelashes to such charming effect, tucking her chin toward one shoulder in a way that managed to look both seductive and vulnerable at the same time. Perhaps that was something I could try. Rotating my shoulder upward and inward, I ducked my head and batted my lashes, gazing at him sideways.

He frowned at me. "Somethin' wrong with your shoulder?"

I stifled a grimace. "My shoulder's fine," I said, batting my lashes more vigorously, in case he hadn't noticed.

He leaned closer, his frown deepening. "Something in your eye, then?"

I dropped my shoulder in defeat. "Yes, but it's gone now." I could never be like Kitty, I realized. I could only be me.

And yet . . . he wasn't backing away. Was it possible, I wondered, that just being me was enough? I turned my face up to him and searched his eyes, not caring if he saw the longing and confusion that were warring within me, needing to know if he felt the same for me as I did for him.

I thought I saw his shoulders soften, as some strong emotion I couldn't quite read flashed across his face. He raked a hand through his hair, his gaze moving from my eyes to my mouth and back again. *Yes,* I inwardly coaxed, recalling the exquisite sensation of his lips against mine, trying to mentally bend him to my will . . .

He straightened and pulled away.

I bit my lip to suppress a groan. Was it some absurdly rigid notion of gentlemanly conduct that was restraining him? Did he think that that was what I wanted or expected? I grasped his hand and pressed it between my palms. "Simon, I do hope you know it would be all right if you wanted to . . . that is, I wouldn't mind at all if you . . . well, if you felt like —"

"I'd better get a leg on," he broke in, easing his hand from my grasp. "I was supposed to be at an assembly district meeting thirty minutes ago."

I shut my mouth and stepped back, feeling as though I'd been slapped. "Yes, of course. Good night then." I started clumsily up the steps, my humiliation complete.

He waited like a proper gentleman until I was over the threshold and then, shoving his hands into his pockets, turned and walked quickly back the way we'd come.

90

CHAPTER FIVE

I spent Friday morning visiting the pastors of three nearby churches, hoping to drum up some referrals for my practice. While the first two merely heard me out with polite disinterest, the last was familiar with the benefits of mental therapy and promised to recommend me to his parishioners should the need arise. Not even this bit of good news, however, could lift the despondency that had settled over me since Simon's unambiguous rejection the evening before.

There was no reason — or more accurately, no reason I wished to embrace — for Simon's refusal to engage in even the smallest of physical intimacies. He was neither a prude nor a slave to social convention, which meant the only possible explanation was that his feelings for me had cooled. I'd tried hard to reject this conclusion as I'd lain sleepless during the wee hours, holding on to the many recent instances when I was sure I'd sensed his keen regard. Ultimately, however, I'd had to conclude that I'd only been seeing what I wanted to see. Apparently, Simon's interest in me was no more than the interest one had in an old and valued friend. If I wanted to preserve a shred of dignity, I was going to have to adjust my own feelings accordingly and stop chasing after him like a lovesick schoolgirl.

Immediately upon my arrival home, I went into the telephone closet and put a call through to the Barge Office. The only thing that had distracted me from thoughts about Simon, as I'd tossed and turned in bed the evening before, was the equally distressing memory of young Rosa's entreaties. Plagued by the persistent feeling that I was betraying the girl's trust — however much I'd tried to refuse it — I'd decided that I would at least try to ascertain whether her missing friend had taken the steamship to New York as originally planned.

The official who answered my call told me that a Teresa Casoria had indeed arrived in New York on the steamship *Madonna* nine days earlier, traveling second-cabin class. According to the ship's manifest, she was in good health upon her arrival and allowed to disembark at the Thirty-Fourth Street pier. I slowly hung up the receiver, unsettled by the news. So the girl had not changed her mind or been detained as I'd proposed. I could only hope that she had forgotten about her promise to visit Rosa in the excitement of reuniting with her fiancé.

After a quick lunch of cold ham and toast, I sat down to finish writing my lecture on the influence of the mind in the causation and cure of disease, which I was planning to present at the next meeting of the East Side Ladies' Guild in hopes of winning some patients from its fold. I found myself struggling to focus, however, and after two unproductive hours, I finally decided to clear my head by walking down to the Wieran clubhouse to collect the vase I'd left there the previous evening. The vase was one of my mother's favorites, and I was eager to retrieve it before someone used it for a game of ninepins.

The club rooms were dark when I arrived, as I'd expected for this time of day. Groping for a match and taper, I crossed to the dining table and lit the mantle on the overhead lamp. The light fell over the yellow roses on the center of the table, still fresh and dewy in my mother's vase. I eyed them dispiritedly, seeing in the flowers a reminder of my dashed hopes of the evening before. I lifted the vase and carried it into the kitchen, tempted to toss the roses into the bucket for the rag and bone man, but transferred them into a jar instead before emptying and drying the vase. I started back through the dining room, and was halfway to the hallway door, when I heard a noise from the adjoining meeting room. I stopped to listen. There it was again: the distinct sound of somebody crying. Lowering the vase back onto the table, I crossed to the meeting room door and cautiously turned the knob.

The crying stopped.

I cracked the door open and looked inside. Frankie "the Pipes" Dolan lay on a cot against the wall with a rumpled sheet pulled up over his chin, his tearstained cheeks shining in the gray light from the window. "Frankie?" I started toward him.

He watched my approach without speaking, his eyes far too sad and hopeless for an eleven-year-old boy.

"What's happened?"

He didn't answer.

"Are you hurt?"

"Arrghh," came his muffled reply.

I tugged down the sheet that was covering his face. "What?"

"Arrghh," he said again.

His mouth was hanging in a fixed, open position. Peering closer, I noted that the pillow beneath it was wet with drool. "Can't you close your mouth?"

He shook his head.

Crouching beside him for a better look, I saw that there was an abrasion along one side of his jaw and that his bottom lip was bruised and swollen. "Did somebody hit you?"

He nodded.

The blow, I deduced, must have either fractured or dislocated his jaw. I cradled his face between my hands and peered inside his mouth. There was a cut on the inside of one cheek, probably made by his teeth, but no bruising or bleeding around the jawbone. Nor could I feel any deformity of the mandible when I pressed on it. I palpated the area in front of both ears and felt telltale depressions where the condyles had moved out of their sockets. "I think it's just dislocated," I told him in some relief.

He closed his eyes, squeezing out a fresh trickle of tears.

"Don't worry, Frankie, you're going to be fine. I'm going to bring you to the hospital, and they'll fix you up in no time."

His eyes flew open and he shrank back on the cot, pulling the sheet up over his nose.

"What's the matter? Don't you want to go to the hospital?"

"Ahh ahr," he said, shaking his head.

"It won't hurt, I promise. I'll make sure they give you a few whiffs of ether first."

"Ahr ahr," he said more vehemently, his eyes pleading now.

I sat back on my haunches, wondering if there was something else he was afraid of besides the procedure. Why had he come here to the empty clubhouse, after all, instead of going to someone for help? My mind drifted back to the last few times I'd seen him, and the answer hit me like a blow to my own jaw. "Oh, Frankie . . . It was your father, wasn't it? He hit you when he found out you'd taken the van."

He turned his face away.

That would explain his reluctance to go to the hospital; he was afraid they'd set the "Gerry man" on him. Elbridge Gerry's Society for the Prevention of Cruelty to Children was the bogeyman of the tenements, the stuff of nightmares for children who'd rather suffer a parent's beating than be separated from everything they knew.

"But we have to fix it," I said, stroking back his hair. "And the sooner the better. I could do it myself, but I don't have any ether on hand, not to mention a proper inhaling apparatus."

His face swiveled back toward me, eyes

96

alight. "Yah!" he exclaimed. "Yuh juah!"

"What?"

He bolted upright on the cot. "Yuh juah!" he said again, pointing at me.

"You want me to do it?"

He nodded so vigorously that I was concerned for his jaw. "I can't, Frankie, not without sedation. Now come on, let's get you down there . . ."

He grabbed onto the edge of the cot with both hands, his freckled brow buckling in determination.

I considered my options. I couldn't very well drag him to the hospital if he didn't want to go. And it was true that I was familiar with the latest reduction technique. I'd only actually performed the procedure once, however, for an asylum inmate who'd dislocated her jaw while biting another resident — and only after she'd been given so much ether that I could have driven a screwdriver through her head with no reaction. I wasn't sure I could manage it without relaxing the musculature first. The last thing I wanted to do was put Frankie through more distress.

I rose from my crouch to ease my stiff thighs, reviewing possible sedatives. He couldn't swallow properly, so a tablet of Veronal or a shot of whiskey was out of the question. I supposed I could administer a few drops of chloroform — I had a vial in my kit at home — using a handkerchief for a mask. But chloroform had been known to stop the heart of pediatric patients, and I wasn't sure I had sufficient experience to safely dose him . . .

I looked down in surprise as Frankie grasped hold of my hands.

"Yuh juah," he said again quietly, waggling my hands to and fro and nodding in encouragement.

I slowly released my breath. His bravery put my own self-doubts to shame. "All right, Frankie. Let's give it a try." Fortunately, with a saloon directly beneath us, the implements I required were right at hand. I told him to lie down and rest until I got back, then made my way downstairs.

I was hoping that Simon wouldn't be in the saloon, for I'd like some time to adjust to our new footing before seeing him again. Normally, he made a point of being there between the hours of four and six p.m. so that the residents of his district could stop in to see him on their way home from work, but today was not a normal day. According to the morning paper, last night's celebration had resulted in at least 196 fires and seven deaths, in addition to scores of injuries from stray bullets, exploding cartridges, and wayward firecrackers. I expected that Simon would be working later than usual as a result, paying court fines, fixing damaged property, and doing whatever else he could to help ease the holiday hangover.

When I entered the saloon, however, I saw him already seated at the bar, listening to two men with their caps in their hands who appeared to be asking for his assistance. I paused inside the door and watched from a distance, struggling with a groundswell of emotions as I tried to view him in a new, platonic light. He was wearing his court clothes, which meant he'd added a waistcoat and collar to his usual, informal attire. Unfortunately for my purposes, he had already rolled up his shirtsleeves and removed his tie to loosen the collar, which lent him an appealingly piratical air.

Although he must have been tired after his busy day, he appeared to be taking a genuine, unhurried interest in the men's problem, listening attentively to their impassioned recital and inserting the occasional concise question. They, in turn, regarded him with the sort of hopeful respect usually reserved for presidents or popes. When they were done, he slapped each one on the shoulder and shook their hands. They walked past me out of the saloon, standing decidedly taller than they had before.

I started toward the bar. Some of the regulars saw me coming and fell silent, tipping their caps. I smiled at them, hoping to put them at ease, wondering if they'd ever get used to me. "Billie," I called to the bartender as I drew up beside Simon, "could you spare a couple of corks?"

"Genna!" Simon exclaimed, swiveling toward me. "Where did you come from?"

From the look on his face, I could have sworn there was no one else he'd rather see. But then, everyone tended to feel that way, I reminded myself, when they were the subject of Simon's undivided attention. Adopting a breezy tone, as if I hadn't just been begging him to kiss me the night before, I answered, "I dropped by to pick up my mother's vase and found a surprise waiting for me in the meeting room."

"What kind of surprise?"

He listened in silence as I told him about Frankie's injury, deepening lines around the corners of his mouth his only visible reaction.

"I think I may be able to fix his jaw," I finished, "but I'm afraid it will only happen again if we don't do something about his home situation." Although I'd become somewhat inured to the open and casual display of violence since traveling in Simon's world, certain kinds of violence — like that inflicted by a parent on a defenseless child — still stuck sharply in my craw. Understanding the psychological underpinnings of such behavior did not make it any easier to stomach. Nor did it point to an easy solution, in Frankie's case at least. If his father was reported and prosecuted for assault and battery, the judge might very well refuse to convict, believing that Frankie's misconduct deserved a good beating, in which case Frankie would likely incur another beating for his father's trouble. If the father was convicted and sent to Blackwell's Island, on the other hand, his wife and children would likely starve without his earnings. And if Frankie was removed from his parents' care and sent to live at an institution or with another family, there was no saying he wouldn't endure even worse treatment, without the small comforts afforded by being with his natural kin.

"I'll have a talk with his da," Simon told me.

"I'm not sure a talk will be enough."

"I can be persuasive when I need to be."

The edge in his voice made me look at him more closely. He had the drawn, preoccupied air I'd noticed on a few prior occasions, when the daily crises of life in the district became almost too much even for him. "Long day?" I asked, suppressing an urge to smooth back the lock of hair that had fallen over his eye. Changing my feelings for him, I realized with a pang, was going to be even harder than I'd imagined.

He nodded. "And it's not over yet. I've still got to find housing for a boy whose father was sent to the workhouse, and there's a bar mitzvah I promised to go to. I just stopped by to see if there was anything urgent waiting for me here."

I nodded in sympathy. Apparently, Simon's job as electoral district captain was to have a finger — and sometimes an entire arm — in everything that went on in the lives of his constituents. Just this week, in addition to providing bail for the usual lot of drunk and disorderly miscreants, he had found living quarters for a family displaced by fire, solved a pushcart peddlers' dispute, paid for a pauper's burial, and persuaded an Irish livery operator to hire a delinquent Italian boy. This last had been especially tricky, he'd explained, because of the animosity between the Italians and the Irish in his district. He had accomplished it by promising to recommend the livery service to a florist he knew, for use in all of its deliveries. As far as I could tell, the whole Tammany enterprise was a web of such mutually beneficial relationships. Despite the misgivings of people like my father, who hated the political machine that had held the city in its grip for so much of its history, I liked to think that its activities helped more people than they hurt, and usually people of the neediest sort.

Billie slid a beer and a cheese sandwich in front of Simon, who tucked into them as if he hadn't eaten all day.

"And these are for you," the bartender said, handing me the corks. "Although if it's Colombian spirits you're brewing, you didn't get them from me," he added with a wink, referring to the wood alcohol that passed for a beverage in some of the more desperate parts of town.

"Thanks, Billie, but I'll be using them for purely medicinal purposes."

He grinned. "That's what they all say."

I turned to go.

"Genna, wait." Simon emptied his beer glass and put it down. "I'm coming with you." Pushing the rest of the sandwich into his mouth, he rose from the stool and followed me back upstairs.

Frankie was sitting up on the cot when we entered the meeting room.

"Look who I found," I said.

"Hey there, Frankie." Simon crossed to the cot and sat down beside him. "How are you feeling?"

Frankie attempted but failed to say something intelligible.

I saw Simon's jaw clench, but his tone was teasing as he ruffled the boy's hair and remarked, "Say now, I know I've asked you to pipe down on occasion, but don't you think this is going a little too far?"

A mirthful noise emerged from Frankie's mouth.

"All right, let's get you fixed up," I said, with a matter-of-factness I was far from feeling. Although I appreciated Simon's concern for the boy, I would have preferred to attempt the procedure without his watchful eyes upon me. "Come sit here," I instructed Frankie, pulling a chair into the center of the room.

He walked over and settled himself on the chair.

I held the two corks in front of him. "Do you know what a fulcrum is?"

He shook his head.

"When you put a board over a barrel to make a seesaw, the barrel is the fulcrum. It helps you lift the person sitting on the other end of the board. These corks are going to act like fulcrums, helping me to lever your jaw back into place. Understand?"

He nodded gamely, his trusting eyes locked on mine.

I inserted one cork between the upper and lower back teeth on each side of his mouth and then walked around to stand behind him. Simon leaned toward us with his elbows on his knees, watching intently.

I laced my fingers under Frankie's chin. "When I say 'now', I want you to take a deep breath, and then slowly let it out," I told him. "Ready?"

" 'eady," he replied.

Dear Lord, I thought, *don't let me make things any worse for this boy than they already are.* "All right, Frankie. Now." As soon as I heard him exhale, I started pulling up on his chin, concentrating on applying pressure evenly to both sides. I could feel his neck tightening and his shoulders rising higher and higher in resistance. I forced myself to pull harder, and then harder still, picturing the condyles moving downward and backward over the articular eminences.

A grunt of pain or protest escaped him. I winced in sympathy and was just about to let go when I heard the condyles slip back into their sockets with an audible *pop.*

Frankie raised a tentative hand to his jaw. "You did it!" he marveled.

"Don't talk just yet," I said, slumping behind him in relief. "You could dislocate it again. I'll go get something to wrap it with." I went into the kitchen for a clean dish towel and carried it back to the meeting room. "This will keep you from opening your mouth too far and dislocating the jaw again," I told him, wrapping it under his chin and over his head.

"Hey, I ain't gonna wear that," he protested, pulling back.

"Don't talk," I reminded him, struggling to pull the ends into a knot.

"I ain't wearing it," he repeated through gritted teeth, pushing it off.

"Frankie . . ." Simon growled.

"Why not?" I asked, dropping the towel into my lap.

Frankie glared at me. "Because the boys'll say I look like one of them mummies, that's why."

Since mummies had been an abiding topic of conversation among the club members ever since our recent excursion to the

106

Metropolitan Museum, I couldn't honestly gainsay this concern. I thought for a moment. "How about like this then," I said, wrapping the thick towel around his neck and tying it in front, so that it supported his jaw from below. I leaned back to check the final effect. "Goodness, you look just like a Tenth Avenue Cowboy," I exclaimed, knowing full well that every warm-blooded boy in the city dreamed of being one of the horsemen who rode down the Tenth Avenue tracks, warning pedestrians of oncoming freight trains.

He sat up straighter, fingering the towel. "Yeah!" he repeated, his eyes shining. "Just like a Tenth Avenue Cowboy!"

I smiled, although it just about broke my heart to witness the wonder that had somehow managed to survive in this hard-used little boy.

"I want to see," he said and ran out to the hallway water closet to look in the mirror.

Simon smiled and shook his head. "That was very impressive, Doctor."

"I'm just glad it worked. It's been a while since I tried it." I started dragging the chair back to the wall.

"I'll get that." He jumped up and crossed to the chair, pausing with his hand on the back of it. His eyes swept over my face, full of such warm regard that, despite all my sensible intentions, I found myself holding my breath again.

"The boys are lucky to have you," he said. "They may not always show it, but you've come to mean a lot to them."

"They've come to mean a lot to me too." I hesitated, then added, "You all have." I held his gaze, waiting for him to respond to my implicit invitation and let me know that my doubts had all been for naught.

He started to say something but stopped, looking away. "Well," he mumbled finally, "I just want you to know how much I appreciate your helping them. I know there are other things you could be doing with your time." He hoisted the chair and carried it back to the wall.

Although the words were kind, they rang hollowly in my ears. It was gratitude he was feeling, on behalf of his boys. Nothing more, nothing less. It was time I finally believed it and moved on.

We walked Frankie down to the sidewalk, where Simon was hailed by a man in overalls just leaving the saloon. While the two conversed, I crouched in front of Frankie and checked that his wrap was secure as he squirmed under my ministrations.

"Try not to chew on anything hard for a few days," I told him, "or to yawn without supporting your jaw." *And stay out of your father's way,* I wanted to add but knew it would only embarrass him. I pushed the hair out of his eyes, wishing there was something I could do to put a smile on his somber young face. "Say, Frankie, do you like ice-cream sandwiches?"

He shoved his hands into his pockets. "I dunno."

"You don't know? You mean you don't care for them?"

"I mean I ain't never had one," he said with a scowl.

I found this hard to comprehend. The ice-cream sandwich vendors had become a summertime fixture on practically every East Side block, selling their portable treats for only a penny a piece. It was a very frugal family indeed — or a rather hard-hearted one — that could never spare a penny for a child's treat. "Then today's your lucky day." I took a penny from my purse and held it out. "You're going to buy yourself an ice-cream sandwich on your way home, to celebrate our successful procedure."

"I don't need no ice-cream sandwich," he said, his proud refusal belied by the wistful gleam in his eye.

"Of course you don't *need* it. But you most certainly deserve it, for being such a brave patient." I moved the penny closer.

He hesitated a moment longer, then took it from my fingers — not realizing, I guessed, that he was licking his lips as he did so. I stood and watched him walk off down the street, a little piece of my heart going with him.

I glanced toward Simon, who was still occupied with the man at the door. Normally, I would have waited to chat with him some more, and perhaps even strolled with him to his next appointment. But I was going to have to stop looking for opportunities to spend time together. It would only cause me pain to remain in frequent contact, when what I wanted was out of reach. And so I forced myself to go, giving him a wave as I started down the sidewalk.

"Genna, wait!" He patted the man on the shoulder and crossed over to me. "You asked me to tell you if I learned anything more about the drowned girl. I didn't want to talk about it in front of Frankie, but I ran into Detective Norton today after court, and he brought me up to date."

Images of the dead Italian girl came rushing back to me, temporarily pushing aside my personal woes. "Do they know who she is?"

"They've got a name, yes."

"And do they know what happened to her?"

He rubbed the back of his neck uneasily. "Why don't we go into my office, where we'll have some privacy." He pulled the saloon door open and ushered me inside.

CHAPTER SIX

I followed him into the half-full dining room, past the silent piano, and through a door in the back wall of the saloon. I hadn't been inside his office since the day I'd come to seek his help in absolving my patient from murder the previous winter. It was as sparsely furnished as before, containing nothing but a ceiling lamp, a large round table, and half a dozen chairs. He followed me in and closed the door.

"Norton had the autopsy results," he told me.

I nodded, waiting for more.

He studied my face. "You sure you want to hear this?"

"Of course I do."

"You'd better sit down, then."

I lowered myself into one of the chairs. He certainly had my full attention.

Dropping onto the seat beside me, he began, "There was a letter in the dead girl's coat pocket, postmarked in March. The ink was blurry, but they could still make out most of it." He extracted a piece of paper from his pocket and began to read from penciled notes. "The letter was addressed to a Lucia Siavo in Durazzano, Italy, which, according to the interpreter, is a small hill town on the outskirts of Naples. Detective Norton confirmed with the Board of Immigration that a Lucia Siavo from the village of Durazzano was listed on the manifest of the steamship *Citta Di Napoli,* which arrived in New York three weeks ago. According to the manifest, Lucia traveled alone, in steerage. She was seventeen years of age, five feet two inches tall, and had black hair and brown eyes. The coroner has confirmed that the height and other features match the girl in the river." He looked up. "While Norton can't be positive yet, he's assuming the dead girl is this Lucia Siavo."

"Lucia," I repeated softly.

Turning back to his notes, he continued, "The letter is signed by someone named Marco, who calls her 'my sweet Lucia' and talks about sharing his love and prosperity with her and raising a family in America. He also refers to an enclosed steamship ticket."

"So she came here to marry."

"So it seems," he said, returning the paper to his pocket.

"What did the autopsy reveal?"

He hesitated, shifting on his seat. I braced myself for whatever he was finding so difficult to tell me.

"They're calling it a drowning," he said.

"So . . . not strangulation," I said, my own conclusion confirmed.

"No. But there were . . . signs that she'd had sexual relations recently."

I frowned at him. "Well, you did say she came here to marry." Even as I said it, however, I remembered that she'd worn no wedding band.

He shifted again on his seat. "The coroner told Norton that she was only wearing undergarments under her coat. And she . . . well, she appeared to have been manhandled pretty badly."

"Oh, I see," I said slowly. "You mean that she was violated."

"There were also several burns on her body."

"Burns?" I repeated.

"Cigarette burns."

I stared at him. "Someone raped her and then burned her with a cigarette?"

"Actually, they think there must have been repeated assaults, since some of the injuries were older than others."

I swallowed. "You're telling me that she was raped and burned repeatedly, over a period of time. And the bruises on her neck?"

"Probably also incurred during the sexual act."

I sat back in my chair.

Reluctantly, he added, "They also found a syphilis lesion."

I closed my eyes, not sure I wanted to hear more.

"The detective thinks she may have been shanghaied directly from the boat and forced into prostitution."

"Dear God." I pictured the sweet-faced girl I'd seen on the esplanade, arriving in New York full of hopes and dreams for her future, and walking instead into some unholy nightmare. For a moment, I put myself in her shoes and felt the weight of her terror. But only for a moment. Some things were too horrible even to imagine. I opened my eyes. "I thought they were taking precautions at Ellis Island to make sure that sort of thing couldn't happen."

"According to the detective, it still happens more than you might think."

I remembered the scandal a few years back when it was discovered that representatives of the so-called Swedish Immigrant Home, purportedly there to welcome and help new arrivals, had actually been abducting single women from Ellis Island and selling them into prostitution. And that had only been the tip of the iceberg. Numerous investigations by vigilance committees across the country had since determined that New York was at the heart of a booming international "white slave" trade, supplying thousands of girls each year to brothels as far away as South Africa, Australia, and the Panama Canal. I had read about it, shaken my head over it, and thanked God it could never happen to me. But until now, it had never seemed entirely real.

"His theory makes sense, timewise," I said after a moment. "A syphilis chancre typically appears about three weeks after exposure and disappears a few weeks later. If she wasn't already infected when she arrived in New York, then it must have happened shortly after she got here. Have the police been able to locate her fiancé, to confirm he didn't meet her at the boat?"

"Not yet. Unfortunately, he didn't sign his last name, and there was no return address on the envelope. Norton's checking to see if he filed a missing persons report with any of the precincts."

Three long weeks, the girl had gone unaccounted for. I stared at the scarred tabletop as imagined scenes of her captivity raced unbidden through my mind. "Assuming the detective's theory is correct," I asked, "how did she end up in the river?"

"He thinks she must have managed to escape from wherever they were holding her, which would explain her attire. She wouldn't have been allowed to keep any respectable street clothes, except for the coat, which would have been too expensive for her handlers to replace."

"And they caught her, and threw her into the river so she couldn't tell anyone what they'd done," I finished sickly.

But Simon was shaking his head. "She would have been too valuable a commodity to kill. Besides, if they wanted to silence her, they would have made sure she was dead before they threw her in."

"Then . . ." I cocked my head in question. I thought again of the victim's simple peasant coat, and the crucifix she'd worn until the very end. "Oh my God, of course," I said, breathless with understanding. "She did escape, didn't she? She just wanted it all to end."

We were both silent for a time.

I bolted suddenly upright, remembering

Rosa's missing friend. "Oh, Simon, you don't think the same thing could have happened to Teresa, do you? The missing girl I told you about?"

"I'd say that's highly unlikely," he reassured me. "Thousands of immigrant women arrive here each week, and most of them get to where they're going without any problem."

"But Rosa said she's been missing for days . . ."

"She *thinks* she's missing. You told me she hadn't actually checked with the fiancé. She may be already married and settled in, for all you know."

"Yes, I suppose you're right," I said, sinking back in my chair, wanting to believe that what he was saying was true.

"Besides, this is all just theory so far. Lucia Siavo could just as well have become a prostitute of her own volition."

"Why on earth would she do that, when she had a husband waiting for her?"

"I knew a man who sent for his sweetheart in Ireland to come over, after he'd made a success of himself," he said by way of answer. "She was four months pregnant when she arrived. He turned his back on her, refusing even to pay her ship fare back home. A year later, he found out she was walking the streets to support herself and her child."

"But there was nothing in the coroner's report about a pregnancy, was there?"

"All I'm saying is that it's too early to jump to any conclusions."

Early or not, it was hard for me to believe that any woman would voluntarily choose a life of such degradation. "Does the detective have any idea who might have taken Lucia, assuming she was, in fact, abducted?"

"He's guessing it was someone working for one of the downtown Italian disorderly houses."

I shook my head in confusion. "He thinks she escaped from a downtown brothel, then came all the way up to Harlem to drown herself? Why wouldn't she just jump off the nearest pier?"

"The theory is that they were bringing her up to a customer, and she escaped in transit. Apparently, Italian prostitutes are hard to find in Italian Harlem. Of course, there are plenty of disorderly resorts further up, around 125th Street, but the girls there are mostly Polish and Slavic, with maybe a few Irish mixed in. Apparently, Italian men would rather spend their money on a girl who speaks their own language."

"Does the detective have any particular

operator in mind?"

"He's not familiar with the downtown resorts, but he said he was going to check with some precinct detectives down there to see if they had any ideas."

This struck me as a rather roundabout way to investigate. "It seems to me this would be a perfect case for the Italian Legion. Surely, they'd stand the best chance of getting to the bottom of it."

"You're probably right, but from what I hear, Petrosino's squad is spread pretty thin dealing with the Black Hand. And now that this girl's death has been ruled a suicide, there isn't even a murder involved."

I gaped at him. "I would think that kidnapping a girl and forcing her into prostitution warrants their attention nonetheless!"

He threw up his hands. "I'm not saying it doesn't. But Petrosino's men have to sleep and eat, just like everyone else."

I drew a calming breath. "I'm sorry, I just find this all very . . . disturbing."

"Of course you do. I understand."

I wondered if he really did understand — if a man was even capable of the awful, empathic sense of violation that this girl's vile treatment had evoked in me. Although he didn't say so, I suspected he thought I was taking the thing too much to heart.

Maybe if I had seen as much senseless cruelty as he had, I could view her destruction more objectively, understanding it as part of the tapestry of tragedy and triumph that was urban life. Maybe if I hadn't experienced tragedy in my own past, I could convince myself that I lived in some separate, protected reality and needn't concern myself with the misfortunes of others. Instead, something seemed to be taking root inside me, turning my horror to anger, pushing me to take a stand against whatever dark forces had run roughshod over an innocent girl.

"Mr. Shaw?" Billie called through the door. "Ralph Cameron's here to see you."

"Thanks, Billie," he called back. "That'll be about his son," he explained. "He was picked up for vagrancy this morning."

"I should be getting along anyway," I said.

He walked me back to the entrance. I turned to face him, realizing it might be some time before I saw him again, feeling a stab of loss that cut all the way to the bone.

"You all right?" he asked, peering at my face.

"I'm fine. Will you telephone me if you learn anything more about Lucia?"

He frowned at me. "You ought to try to forget about her, Genna," he advised.

"There's nothing anyone can do now about what happened."

I heard him in dismay, feeling more alone than ever. After my ordeal last winter, when I'd nearly been killed myself while trying to save my client, all I'd wanted was to hunker down in my protected corner of the universe and lead a life of work and simple pleasures. I certainly had no desire to become involved in another police investigation. But I couldn't turn a blind eye to what poor Lucia had evidently been forced to endure — and I didn't see how Simon could either. I wanted to challenge him, to make him see that forgetting wasn't the answer. But it had become clear that it was no longer my place to question Simon's actions or beliefs. So instead, I forced a noncommittal smile and hurried out the door, leaving him frowning in my wake.

I walked blindly down the sidewalk, reeling from the day's discoveries. Was there no end to the cruelty in the world? Little Frankie's battering had been bad enough; what Lucia appeared to have endured was almost beyond comprehension. Confinement, rape, torture — this was a very different sort of violence than that carried out by an alcoholic father who'd been raised by the fist and was carrying on the tradition. Nor was it a simple crime of impulse, triggered by random opportunity. It took planning to do what Lucia's captors had done. Planning, and a terrifying insensibility to her suffering. I couldn't forget about it even if I wanted to.

An elevated train rumbled out of the station at the end of the block, bound for Harlem and points north. I stopped short on the sidewalk and stared up at it. It was true that I couldn't undo what had happened to Lucia, but perhaps there was a chance I could keep it from happening to someone else — someone whose fate, for whatever reason, seemed to have been delivered directly to my door. According to Detective Norton, women were still being abducted in New York City on a not infrequent basis, despite attempts to make the ports and terminals safer. Simon's assurances notwithstanding, it didn't strike me as farfetched to think that Teresa Casoria might be one of them. Teresa was from the same part of Italy as Lucia. Like Lucia, she had come alone to America to marry. According to Rosa, she had disappeared without a trace. What if she was in trouble and I was the only person in a position to help? What if, this very second, someone was torturing her the way they'd apparently tortured Lucia? Could I just sit by and hope it wasn't so?

I swiveled on my heel and strode back into the saloon. Simon had already returned to his office, but Billie fetched me the business directory from under the counter. Rosa had told me that the name of her friend's fiancé was Fabroni, and that he lived with his mother above his shop. Leafing through the pages, I found Fabroni Painting listed at 317 East 109th Street, smack in the middle of Italian Harlem. That had to be him. I was going to speak with Mr. Fabroni and find out once and for all if Teresa was missing. If she wasn't, I would have wasted a few hours of my time. If she was . . . well, I didn't know exactly what more I could do if my fears were confirmed, but at least I would have done something.

A few moments later, I bounded up the steps to the El station, where I paid my nickel, dropped my ticket into the chopper, and joined the dense crowd waiting on the platform. It was the end of a hot summer workday in Yorkville, and the odors of sweat, pickling brine, and cigar smoke hung heavily in the humid air. The press of bodies only added to the heat, and by the time the train arrived, I was perspiring through all my under layers. Luckily, I was able to grab a spot in the forward end of the first car behind the motorman's box, where a pleasant breeze blew back from the open doorway. I declined a young man's offer to give me his seat, grabbing onto the overhead strap instead as the car rumbled into motion and peering with interest out the windows.

Except for my recent jaunt the day of the rowing race, I hadn't been north of Yorkville in years, and as the train rattled uptown, I gazed with astonishment at the vista unfolding before me. Thirty years before, the Harlem Flats had been nothing but empty fields, crisscrossed by rivers and streams. While I was growing up, the stagnant pools that festered in the lower-lying areas had been gradually filled in with ashes and covered with a layer of clay, in the dim hope that someone might want to build there in the future. Now, it seemed, that future had arrived. I'd expected to see a mix of vacant lots and row houses and old frame dwellings dotting the landscape; instead, the dense development that had once been confined to the river's edge seemed to have spread across the entire East Side.

It was not, alas, an appealing sight. The tenements lining the avenue and side streets were of the cheapest sort, doubtless thrown up in a hurry to capitalize on migration to the area when the elevated train lines were built. There were no parks or fine buildings to break their flat-faced monotony, nothing to lead the eye skyward except spindly legged cisterns on the tenement roofs and the occasional belching chimney of an electric plant. As block after block of the cheerless landscape rolled past, it was hard to feel anything but pity for its inhabitants.

And yet, when I disembarked at 106th Street and descended from the platform, I seemed to enter a different world altogether: a noisy, crowded, colorful place that, though littered with trash and pierced by the screech of the elevated trains, pulsed with an intriguing energy. I joined the flow of pedestrians up the avenue, watching sharp-tongued women haggle with vendors hawking fruit and hats and oilcloths from pushcarts under the tracks. A weary-looking group of laborers in hobnailed boots and jaunty red scarves ambled past me, their blue shirts dusted with powdered schist, calling out to old men playing cards on the sidewalk. My ears caught on passing fragments of foreign conversation, while my nostrils twitched at tantalizing aromas that drifted from the open windows.

I was so busy taking everything in that, at first, I took no notice of the man walking a few yards ahead of me. When he reached the next corner and turned right, however, I realized he was Simon's friend Patrick Branagan. Although he wasn't wearing his police uniform, his profile was unmistakable. By the time I arrived at the corner, he was already a dozen yards down the side street. I watched as he stopped to speak to a group of young boys spinning tops on the sidewalk, dropping a coin into one of the boys' hands and then pointing to the saloon next door. The boy jumped to his feet and started back in my direction, while Patrick continued into the saloon.

As I wasn't inclined to follow him into a drinking establishment just to exchange what would likely be some awkward hellos, I continued on through the intersection. A moment later, the boy passed me and trotted ahead to the next corner, turning right onto 108th Street. I reached the corner and idly watched his progress while I waited for the intersection to clear.

Some tables and chairs were set up in front of a café halfway down the block. The boy slowed as he approached them, scanning the customers enjoying coffee and pastries, before turning toward an elderly, bearded man in an old-fashioned felt hat who was sitting at one of the outer tables. The two exchanged a few words. Slowly, as if his bones were creaking in protest, the old gentleman drew a black leather satchel from under his seat and held it up to the boy. The boy grabbed the handle and ran back toward the corner where I was standing. The old man watched him go, then pushed himself up from the table with the help of a cane and limped down the street in the opposite direction.

I stared after the boy as he dashed past me and back the way he'd come, disappearing around the corner onto 107th Street. *What was that all about?* I wondered. The officer in the intersection blew his whistle, signaling it was safe to walk. I joined the pedestrians surging across, my thoughts returning to Teresa Casoria and the task at hand.

At the next block, I turned right and started toward the river. Although the light was beginning to fade between the buildings, drifts of barefoot boys were still out on the street, batting balls with broom handles or pitching bottle caps on the sidewalk, their shouts echoing off the walls and hanging in the still evening air. Here and there, a woman nursed a baby on a stoop or leaned out a tenement window to watch the boys at play. I supposed I ought to feel anxious, walking in such unfamiliar environs, but no one bothered me as I made my way across town. Indeed, the whole neighborhood exuded an air of weary relief, punctuated by the distant hoot of factory whistles signaling the end of the day shift.

I was halfway between Second and First Avenues, swerving to avoid a boy pushing a cartload of shavings from the ice house floor, when, from the corner of my eye, I saw the gilt lettering on the side of a truck parked at the curb. *Fabroni Painting, 317 E. 109th St., N.Y.,* the letters read. Looking to my left, I saw *Fabroni Painting* applied in the same gold lettering across the bottom-floor window of the four-story brick building directly opposite. I approached the window and looked in.

Though it was dark inside, I could make out a small desk with a telephone on one side and a stack of paint-splattered ladders and folded tarpaulins on the other. I stepped back a pace and looked up, feeling a quiver of apprehension. What would Mr. Fabroni think of a total stranger bursting into his home and asking questions about his bride? Belatedly, it occurred to me that my unsolicited visit might not be well received, despite my good intentions. I hesitated, and even considered turning around. Rosa's face swam up in my mind again, however, urging me onward.

I entered the building foyer and read the names on the letter box. The Fabronis lived in number 2A. Straightening my hat, I started up the steps to meet them.

CHAPTER SEVEN

From the landing, I could see that the door to apartment number 2A was ajar. I crossed the hallway and looked in. The door opened onto a small kitchen with a stove and sink along the back wall. A modest parlor adjoined it on the left, where two men and a young woman were eating supper. The parlor windows were open, allowing a current of air to flow through the apartment to the open entry door. I cleared my throat and knocked tentatively on the doorjamb.

A middle-aged woman all in black, whom I hadn't even noticed at first, detached herself from the stove and stepped toward me. *"Sí?"* she asked with a frown, looking me up and down.

Although I knew some Italian from my travels abroad, it had been a while since I'd used it, so I decided to try English first. "Good evening. I'm looking for Antonio Fabroni. I understand he lives in this building?"

The three people in the adjacent room all turned at the sound of my voice. The younger of the two men rose from the table and started toward me. He was quite a handsome fellow, with a confident gaze and a slight swagger to his step.

"I'm Antonio Fabroni," he said, dabbing his mouth with a napkin.

"How do you do," I said, extending my hand. "I'm Dr. Genevieve Summerford. I saw your truck outside and was hoping I'd find you at home."

He took my hand, his face brightening at the mention of his truck. "So you are in need of a house painter?" he asked with a smile.

"Oh, no. Actually, I'm here to inquire about your fiancée, Teresa Casoria."

The woman in black froze behind him, while a fork clattered onto a plate in the parlor.

Antonio's grip tightened on my hand. "What do you know about Teresa?" he asked, his smile evaporating.

I licked my suddenly dry lips. "Only that a friend of hers was expecting to see her a week ago and was concerned when she didn't arrive. She's been terribly worried

132

that something may have happened to her."

"Who is this friend?" he demanded.

"Is it true then? Has she gone missing?"

"Please, who is this friend," he asked again, "and what does she know about Teresa?"

"Her name is Rosa Velloca. I met her by chance in Jefferson Park, during the holiday celebration. She told me Teresa had befriended her in Italy and asked me to help find her."

He spoke briefly in Italian to the woman, who shook her head in response. "I don't understand," he said, turning back to me. "Why would this Rosa think you could help?"

"It's rather a long story," I said, trying to extract my fingers from his grip. "Perhaps if I could come in and explain?"

He looked down, seeming surprised to find that he was still grasping my hand. "Forgive me," he said, releasing it. "I have forgotten my manners. Of course, you must come in." He turned to the woman. "Mama, set a plate for our visitor."

"Oh, that's not necessary," I protested.

Ignoring me, he called out something in Italian to the man and woman already seated at the parlor table, which I roughly translated as *You go. We'll talk later.*

133

The man rose, taking the arm of the young woman and lifting her from her chair. He was a big man, about twenty years older than Antonio, with a bushy mustache and a deformed or mutilated ear. The woman was a few years younger than me, with hollow cheeks and downcast eyes. The two walked past me out the door without a word and continued toward the rear apartments.

"Come, miss," Antonio urged, gesturing me toward the table, where his mother was already spooning a stew of some sort onto a fresh plate. Seeing that he wasn't going to take no for an answer, I crossed into the parlor and sat down.

He sat beside me, palms on his thighs and eyes flashing with barely contained impatience as he waited for me to begin.

I dutifully spooned a morsel of stew into my mouth while his mother hovered in the background. A medley of flavors and textures, spicy and salty, chewy and tender at the same time, exploded over my tongue. "Oh my, this is delicious," I said with a gasp.

"My mother is an excellent cook," Antonio agreed. He lifted a half-full wineglass and drained its contents while I savored another, larger spoonful. "And now," he said, putting down the glass, "you will please tell me what you know of Teresa."

Laying down my fork reluctantly, I told him about the discovery of the drowned girl, the events that had inspired Rosa Velloca to confide in me, and the immigration bureau's confirmation of Teresa's arrival.

He listened closely, his brow furrowed. "I should have been there to meet her, at the boat," he said when I was done. "But I was late. For this I will never forgive myself, if she has been harmed."

"You haven't seen or heard from her then, since she arrived?"

"No, I haven't."

Hesitantly, I asked, "Do you have any reason to believe that she might have changed her mind about the marriage? Gone to stay with someone else, perhaps?"

He frowned at me. "I almost wish that that were true. At least then, I would know that she is safe. But she sent me a letter the morning she left, telling me that she loved me and was on her way."

I nodded, remembering that Rosa had also received a letter sent on the morning of Teresa's departure. "I understand you paid for her ticket," I said after a moment.

"Of course."

"I don't suppose she might have been deceiving you as to her intentions, to gain passage to America?"

His eyes flashed with indignation. "Teresa would never do such a thing!"

"I meant no offense. I'm only trying to consider every possibility."

He crossed his arms over his chest. "That is not a possibility."

I glanced from him to his mother, who was watching us intently, her face puckered with worry or disapproval. She stood next to a sort of altar set back against the wall, which contained several half-burned candles, a statue of the Madonna, pictures of assorted saints, and a framed photograph of a young girl in a white dress and veil, flanked by Antonio, his mother, and a handful of others. "What about her family in Italy?" I asked, turning back to Antonio. "Have you been in contact with them?"

"I sent them a telegraph a week ago, asking if they had heard from her. They replied that they had not."

"Perhaps she met with an accident, then, after she disembarked."

"I went to all the hospitals. They have no record of her."

I sat back in my chair. It seemed we were all out of acceptable explanations. Which meant we were going to have to consider the less palatable ones. "Do you think it's possible, Mr. Fabroni, that someone who knew of your impending marriage might have kidnapped Teresa in order to extort money from you? A member of the Black Hand, perhaps?"

He blinked. "The Black Hand?"

"I understand you run a successful business. That would make you a potential target."

"If *La Mano Nera* were involved, I would have received a demand letter, and I assure you that I have not."

I studied his face, wondering if he was telling the truth. Patrick had said that more times than not, the victims of extortion letters were unwilling to even admit they'd been targeted. But if Antonio already knew who took his fiancée, I didn't think he'd be sitting here speaking with me. "What do you think happened to her, then?" I asked finally.

"I don't know. But I will find out."

His mother muttered something behind me.

"Basta, Mama," he said with a sigh. To me, he explained, "My mother believes I have brought this trouble on our home by choosing to marry an Italian girl. She wished me to marry someone born in this country so that we would be 'real' Americans. But we cannot choose who we love, can we, signorina?"

I glanced over my shoulder at his mother in surprise; I'd have thought she'd prefer a daughter-in-law from the old country. Perhaps she'd believed an American wife would help ensure her son's success here. "How did you and Teresa meet?" I asked Antonio.

"We met when I returned to *Napoli* last autumn, for my uncle's funeral. She and her mother delivered the flowers to the church." He shook his head, his eyes shining at the memory. "She was the most beautiful girl I had ever seen. I stayed for three months instead of two weeks. I couldn't leave until she had promised to be mine."

"From what Rosa told me, she has a very kind heart, as well."

He frowned. "I'm sorry I haven't met this Rosa. You say that she and Teresa were friends in Italy?"

"Yes, they went to school together apparently, although Teresa must have been a few years ahead of her. Teresa befriended Rosa after her mother died, and when Rosa's family left Naples to come here a few years ago, she and Teresa continued to correspond."

Mrs. Fabroni said something I couldn't understand.

"And Teresa told this girl that she was to be my wife?" Antonio asked me.

"Oh yes, Rosa knew all about you. She wanted to speak with you herself, when Teresa didn't come to visit, but her grandmother wouldn't allow it. That's why I'm here. I had hoped I'd be able to put her fears to rest."

He nodded slowly, pursing his lips. "Perhaps I should go speak to this girl, to see if she has any idea where Teresa could be."

"I'm afraid she has no more idea than you do. She fully expected Teresa to come visit her on her birthday."

"Still, if she was a friend of my *fidanzata,* I would very much like to make her acquaintance. Where does she live, do you know?"

I tried to remember what Rosa had told me. "I only know that she lives near a church, on 115th Street."

"The Church of Our Lady of Mount Carmel," he said with a nod, glancing at his mother.

"She'll be terribly distressed to hear that Teresa never reached you. I wonder if . . . well, I wonder if you might consider waiting to speak with her, just until the police have had time to conduct a proper search. I assume you've reported Teresa missing?"

His face suddenly went blank. "There is

no need for the police."

"But if Teresa's in trouble . . ."

"There is no need for the police," he said again, more firmly. "I will fix this myself."

Was this the Italian code of honor I had heard about? Or was Antonio refusing to admit to himself how precarious Teresa's situation might be? Either way, I didn't think trying to handle things himself was going to improve his fiancée's chances of being found. "There is another possible reason for her disappearance," I said slowly.

He cocked his head.

"The drowned girl I told you about also traveled here alone from Italy to marry. The police believe she may have been abducted, shortly after she arrived."

"But I told you, there has been no ransom letter for Teresa, which makes kidnapping unlikely."

"I don't mean abducted for ransom." I drew in a breath. "I mean abducted into prostitution."

He stiffened. "What are you suggesting?"

"Only that you ought to do everything you can to find Teresa as soon as possible. And that includes involving the police."

"If anyone has harmed Teresa in such a way," he hissed, "they will pay for it dearly. And I will be the one to make them!"

"Mr. Fabroni," I said in alarm, "you may not be aware, but the laws here deal rather harshly with people who try to take things into their own hands. You could jeopardize your future with Teresa if you attempt it."

"La necessità non ha legge," he shot back.

I silently worked out the translation: *Necessity knows no law.*

Crossing his arms over his chest, he added, "I will do what must be done."

Mrs. Fabroni came to stand behind her son, glowering at me over his shoulder.

It seemed we had said everything there was to say. "Well, I've kept you long enough." I pushed back my chair and stood up. "I hope with all my heart that you find Teresa, Mr. Fabroni. Perhaps if you do, you'll be so kind as to let me know." I extracted a card from the case in my bag and laid it on the table.

He rose and followed me to the door.

"Signorina," he said as I was stepping over the threshold.

I turned.

"If Teresa has fallen into evil hands, as you suggest, you could put both her and yourself in danger by asking too many questions. I urge you to speak no more of this to anyone."

I tipped my head to acknowledge his

concern. I did not, however, make any promises.

To my surprise, Simon was sitting on the stoop when I arrived back home, eating a bag of peanuts. I felt the usual flare of excitement at the sight of him and immediately initiated the mental gymnastics required to snuff it out. "What are you doing here?"

"Katie told me you weren't home yet, so I thought I'd wait outside," he said, offering me a peanut.

I shook my head. "I mean, why are you here at all?" The surprise of seeing him must have flushed out some suppressed anger I'd been harboring since the night before, for the words came out more harshly than I'd intended.

He raised an eyebrow, but said only, "I thought you'd be interested to hear that I stopped by Frankie's place and had a chat with his father."

"Oh yes, I am interested." I sank onto the seat beside him, my wounded feelings once more taking a backseat to my concern for Frankie. "How did it go?"

"I have a feeling things are going to be easier for the boy from now on."

"How did you manage it?" As a rule,

142

Simon preferred the carrot to the stick. But I couldn't think of any incentive that could keep a man in check once he was in a drunken rage. "Did you threaten to report him to the police?"

He shook his head. "Too indirect."

"How then?"

"I told him that if he ever hit any of his children again, I'd break both of his arms."

"Ah." I nodded appreciatively. "And would you, really?"

"Of course not."

I had to admit, I was disappointed to hear it.

"I'd only break one of his arms," he continued, "so he could still drive his truck. I wouldn't want to make paupers out of his wife and children." He grinned at me, and I couldn't help laughing, despite everything.

"Where've you been, anyway?" he asked. "Katie was starting to worry. She expected you home hours ago."

"In Harlem, talking to Teresa Casoria's fiancé." I might as well have said I'd been visiting John Johnson, the notorious wife slayer on Murderer's Row.

"By yourself?"

I shrugged. "I needed to find out if Teresa was with him or if she'd really disappeared."

"Crimus, Genna." He shook his head.

"Why are you so determined to get involved in something that's none of your affair?"

It stung to hear him say it. "Why did you talk to Frankie's father?" I shot back.

"That's different."

"Is it?"

Something between a sigh and a groan rumbled through his throat. "You couldn't at least have waited for me to go with you?"

"You didn't seem terribly interested in what had become of her."

"Well, I'm interested in what happens to *you.*"

Another shard of anger broke free, lodging in my craw. Why did he say things like that, when he must know how I would interpret them? "Are you really?"

"What does that mean?"

"Nothing," I said, looking away. I picked up a pebble and scraped it along the edge of the step.

"Of course I care what happens to you. Why would you doubt it?"

I snorted. *Where to begin?* I thought, but I didn't reply.

"This is about last night, isn't it?" he asked after a moment.

I kept scraping away at the limestone.

"Genna."

"What?"

"Would you look at me?"

I looked at him and, to my horror, felt my eyes flood with tears.

He blew out his breath. "You can't think I didn't want to kiss you."

I swiped the tears from my eyes. "Then why didn't you?"

He looked out over the street, the muscles clenching along his jawline. When he turned back, his eyes were nearly black with intensity. "Because I'm not playing to win one hand. I want the whole shebang."

I stared back at him, trying but failing to make sense of this response. "I don't understand."

"Why do you think you were interested in me, all those years ago?"

"I don't know. For all sorts of reasons."

"I was the poor, uneducated son of your parlor maid. Not the usual stuff that girlish dreams are made of."

"I didn't care about any of that."

He tipped his head. "I believe you. But that's not to say it didn't figure in your attraction."

"If you mean I liked that you didn't take guff from anyone and that you had the strength and intelligence to make your own way in the world, then yes, that was part of it."

He smiled ruefully. "But only part. You picked me, Genna, because your body was wakening, and you were achin' with it, and you, being you, needed to figure out what it was all about. But you couldn't very well roll in the hay with one of your fancy gentleman friends, now could you? That would have ruined your reputation. With me, you figured you were safe. And you would have been, if it wasn't for that worm-hearted scullery maid who turned us in."

"That's ridiculous!" I protested. "I wasn't thinking about my reputation."

"I'm not saying it was a calculated decision. But somewhere in the back of your mind, the way you'd been raised, you had to be aware of the risks and want to protect yourself from what people might say."

"I see. So you're not only accusing me of slumming to satisfy my frustrated carnal desires, but of being too cowardly to defy the disapproval of my family and friends as well!"

"I'm not 'accusing' you of anything. I don't fault you, for any of it. You're as red-blooded a woman as any, with a red-blooded woman's natural desires. You can't help that the rules are different for women than for men."

I shook my head, aghast at this unflattering explanation for my adolescent behavior. "Even if what you're suggesting were true," I sputtered, "what could it possibly have to do with things between us now?"

"You think you want me, but what you're feeling is lust, not love. You want to finish what we started in the stable. Well, fine. Believe me, I want the same thing. Jaysus, do I want it. But I'm not going to be just an experiment, like that poor sap you bedded in medical school. I want you to want *all* of me. The whole package."

My mind raced back to what I'd told him about Roger Milton, the fellow medical student I'd chosen to relieve me of my virginity when my ignorance of the sexual act had finally become too much to bear. It was true that I'd chosen him in part because he was graduating a few days later, making it unlikely I'd ever have to see him again. But that had been an entirely different situation. "I do want all of you!"

"You sure about that?"

"Yes!"

He chucked a peanut shell into the gutter. "Then marry me."

I gaped at him.

He turned back to me. "You heard me right. Give the word, and I'll have a magistrate here in thirty minutes."

It was a good thing I was already sitting down, or I would have dropped in a heap onto the steps. Simon *did* want me, as much as I wanted him. I felt a smile as wide as New York harbor splay across my face. Marry Simon. Live with him as man and wife, joined in body and mind. It was what I had fantasized about, practically since the day I'd met him. I pressed a hand against my stomach to suppress the violent fluttering there.

And yet . . . and yet. My smile faded as the implications sank in. Yes, I'd dreamed this might happen — had hoped we could figure out how to make it work, despite the odds against us. But we *hadn't* figured it out yet, not by a long shot. I tried to imagine moving into a flat over the saloon, or perhaps into a house with Simon and his resentful mother, living among people who regarded me as a pampered and not quite trustworthy intruder, while my parents invited us for chilly, formal dinners twice a year and my childhood friends scratched me from their address books. I could see my referrals of paying clients drying up and my practice shriveling, my dream of economic self-sufficiency falling by the wayside.

"You know I want to be with you," I said finally. "But we can't just rush into things.

We need more time . . ." I petered to a halt.

"Don't worry," he said, tossing another shell across the sidewalk. "I didn't expect you to say yes. I just want you to call a spade a spade." He turned and looked at me, his eyes steely. "The fact is, Genna, that you don't know what you want yet. And I can't be all in while you're still standing on the sidelines."

I swallowed, feeling a mix of shame and resentment at being put in this position. "My reservations have nothing to do with my feelings for you. You must know that. It's just that . . ." I hesitated, not quite sure where the heart of my resistance lay. "I need to establish my practice first, for one thing," I said, grabbing onto the simplest explanation.

"And you're afraid rich folks won't want a doctor who's married to the likes of me. I twig the problem." Tossing the empty peanut bag after the shell, he added, "Although I'm sure there are plenty of poor folks who could use your help."

"Yes, but they can't pay enough for me to live on. I need at least *some* patients with resources."

He shrugged. "I make enough money for us both."

"I could never give up my work!"

"Who asked you to? All I'm saying is that I could provide for us, while you take care of the people who need help."

Well, yes, I supposed that might work, although I wondered how many people from the tenements would have both the time and the inclination to seek out psychotherapy. I'd only been able to recruit the women for my Sunday class because of Reverend Palmers's not very subtle threats to cut off their access to the clinic dispensary if they didn't attend.

"And then, of course, there are my friends," he went on. "Although, just so you know, I do have a few who've read a book or two."

I bit my lip, unable to say that this hadn't been a concern.

He frowned at me. "But of course, that's not the biggest reason, is it? We both know what that is: you're worried how your father would take it."

Although I liked to believe that I was no longer controlled by my father's opinions, the stab of anxiety I felt as he said this made me realize that it was true. "He's coming around, Simon," I said, pleading now. "He just needs more time to get to know you. I'm sure once he does, he'll understand what I see in you."

He eyed me skeptically. "Your father has no interest in getting to know me."

I had to admit that my father had shown no propensity as yet to become better acquainted. "Well, what about your mother?" I returned. "You won't even let me see her, so I can only imagine how much she resents me."

"The difference is, I'd marry you anyway."

"And come to hate me for driving you apart."

He shook his head. "It won't work, Genna," he said calmly. "You can't put this on me. I know what I want, and if someone else doesn't like it that's their problem."

There was no defense I could make to that. I fell silent, aching with shame. Simon had given me a chance to be as brave as he was, and I had failed.

He sighed. "Oh, for God's sake, stop looking so guilty. I know you've got more to lose than I have. The last thing I want to do is push you into something you'll regret." He stood to go, brushing off his trousers. "Like I said, I just think we should be clear on where things stand." His eyes bored into mine, clear and determined. "You're not ready to marry me, Genna. And I'm not going to make love to you until you are."

CHAPTER EIGHT

I pulled out the clumsy stitches I'd just embroidered on the napkin, part of a set to be sold off by the East Side Ladies' Guild in support of its many charitable interests, and started over again. I'd never been much good at needlework, but tonight my fingers were particularly uncooperative, straying like unsupervised children over the cloth as my mind endlessly rehashed my conversation with Simon. In the hours since he'd made his rather glib proposal, my guilt over turning him down had changed into roiling resentment. It was all well and good for him to declare he didn't care what other people thought, but I knew how close he was to his mother and what her estrangement would mean to him. It was naive to think we could live a satisfying life in our own little bubble, cut off from the people who meant the most to us.

And it wasn't just our parents' reactions

we had to think about. Except for the Wieran Club boys, most of the residents of Simon's district with whom I'd come in contact had regarded me with, at best, a sort of puzzled curiosity and, at worst, hostility and suspicion. It was my sincere hope that, like the boys, they would all come to know and accept me over time — but until then, I'd be no asset to a man whose job depended on the trust and fellowship of his constituents. Likewise, although I expected my handful of close friends to come around, Mrs. Richards's reaction to Simon had reminded me that I couldn't count on my larger circle of acquaintances to overlook the difference in our stations. Although I was prepared to jettison any incorrigible snobs who refused to be won over by Simon's charm, the winnowing process would need to be a gradual and tactful one if I wanted to preserve my oldest and dearest connections — something I'd like to do not only for personal reasons, but as a source of potential referrals as well.

It wasn't only Simon's dismissal of my concerns that irked me, however; I couldn't help suspecting that he was using the sexual card to manipulate me. What was the point of refusing me even the slightest intimacy? He couldn't really believe that I only wanted to use him to indulge my sexual curiosity. Nor did I see how exchanging a few kisses and caresses with me, without a formal commitment first, would cause him any grievous pain. His willful declaration of abstinence could just as easily be interpreted as an attempt, whether conscious or not, to force me to agree to marry him before I was ready.

It might also, it occurred to me as I stabbed absently at the napkin with my needle, have something to do with his long-simmering animosity toward my father. I was sure it galled Simon that the man who'd treated him so badly in the past still had the power to come between us. It didn't seem outlandish to think that, in the face of this, he might use the one thing he had over me — my desire for him — as a lever to make me declare my allegiance once and for all. Whatever his reasons, he had managed to paint me as a sexual aggressor or, even worse, a sexual supplicant in our relationship — an odd and exceedingly embarrassing position to be in.

"Are you going to finish that, or just keep torturing it?" Katie asked from her chair across the sitting room, nodding at the napkin as her own gnarled hands made short work of a glove repair. We'd taken to sitting together occasionally in the evenings, something Katie never would have done while my parents were at home but which we both took tacit pleasure in. Although she'd been originally retained as a cook, and still insisted on wearing a uniform, Katie had taken over many of the general house-keeping duties after my little brother died, when my mother was paralyzed with grief. She'd also become a sort of surrogate parent, tending to my small sorrows and injuries when Mama was unavailable and making sure I completed my school work. Though she was now plump and gray with age, her eyes were as sharp as ever, and she usually knew — practically before I did — when something was troubling me.

"I'm afraid I'm all thumbs tonight," I said, dropping the embroidery hoop into my lap.

"I saw you talking with Simon earlier on the stoop," she said, her voice carrying the merest hint of a question. Katie would never pry; this was simply her way of inviting my confidence, should I have anything I wished to discuss.

I hesitated. Katie had grown quite fond of Simon when he was a youngster, living with his mother over the stable, and despite her frequent fretting over what my involvement with an Irish saloon-keeping politician might mean for my future, I knew she trusted the adult Simon to have my best interests at heart. If she thought he was causing me trouble, however, she'd be the first to rake him over the coals.

"I treated one of his boys for a dislocated jaw this afternoon," I said finally. "Simon just stopped by to tell me how the boy was faring." I said nothing more, reluctant to tell her, or anyone, about the embarrassing conversation that had taken place between us.

I heard the hall clock chime the half hour, and returned my embroidery to its basket. It was time to make my call. Proceeding to the hallway telephone closet, I asked the operator to put me through to Second Deputy Police Commissioner Bugher at his home. Despite what Antonio Fabroni had said, I still believed that the Italian Legion should be alerted to his fiancée's disappearance, and since no one else seemed disposed to bring it to their attention, I had decided to do so myself. Commissioner Bugher, a former navy man, lived two blocks away and was friendly with my father, who had visited him at his shooting preserve in Maryland just the previous spring. As the official responsible for supervising the detective bureau, I thought it might be prudent to ask him for an introduction to Detective Petrosino, to ensure that the busy detective would find time to see me. I'd calculated that calling him after the dinner hour, when he was known to enjoy a glass of whiskey or two, might yield the best results.

To my delight, when Commissioner Bugher answered my call and heard the reason for my request, he promised to telephone the detective personally in the morning. I hung up the phone and trotted upstairs to bed, planning what I would say to Petrosino and hoping that the prospect of our meeting would keep thoughts of Simon's unsettling remarks at bay.

Alas, this hope went unrealized, and I arrived bleary and lead-headed at the breakfast table the next morning after another nearly sleepless night. Katie, on the other hand, was uncharacteristically fidgety, flitting around me like a fly around a bulb with her cap askew.

"That's plenty," I said, holding up a restraining hand when she attempted to spoon a third helping of creamed eggs onto my plate. You'd never know, from the heaping contents of the pan, that I was the only Summerford currently in residence. "I hope you're planning to eat some of this yourself.

I'd hate to see it go to waste."

"I already had my breakfast," she informed me, dumping another dollop onto my plate. "I want to get an early start to the station."

With my parents away and our maid on loan to the Fiskes during their absence, I had urged Katie to take the weekend off to visit her sister in New Jersey. She had protested, of course, but I'd gradually whittled away her resistance, assuring her that I could manage for two days on my own and reminding her that I could always call on Maurice or Oliver in the event of an emergency. For the final push, I'd read her my parents' most recent letter, which instructed me to ensure that Katie took a few days' well-deserved holiday, even if it meant locking her out of the house.

It was the letter, I think, that convinced her. The previous winter, Katie and I had watched with our hearts in our throats as my mother came slowly back to life, her long season of grief finally thawing under the warmth of Lucille Fiske's attentions. It had seemed nothing short of a miracle, in the months afterward, to hear her laugh and sing and joke again. As I read Mama's letter aloud, with its lively account of her adventures in the catacombs and teasing references to my father's run-ins with the Mediterranean temperament, I saw Katie's eyes fill with tears and immediately intuited the cause. "You see, Katie?" I'd said gently, putting the letter down. "Mama and I can both manage without you now, for a little while at least."

Although she'd never admit it, I knew she was looking forward to getting out of the steaming city and spending some time in the countryside with her favorite sister. But I also knew that, being an infrequent traveler, the thought of journeying by train unnerved her. I glanced at the hands of the dining room clock, which indicated it was not yet eight o'clock. "I thought your train left at eleven."

"That's right, it does, and I'm not going to risk missing it," she retorted, her tone daring me to argue.

"Fine. I'll buzz Maurice and have him drive you to the station."

"You'll do no such thing," she said with a wheeze, her soft cheeks flushing. "I can take the streetcar to the station, same as everybody else."

This strange reaction only fueled my recent suspicions that Katie, after all these years, had suddenly developed something more than collegial respect for our old chauffeur. "I'm sure Maurice would be happy to take you. He must be bored to tears, with my parents away and the motorcar under wraps."

"That man has more than enough to do, helping Oliver look after the horses and keeping the motorcar in working order, without having to worry about me. Now drink your tea before it gets cold."

I did as instructed, hiding a smile behind my cup.

While Katie fussed over the silver on the sideboard, wrapping everything in flannel as if preparing it for a ten-year hibernation, I opened the *Herald* and quickly perused the day's news. One of the nicest things about my parents' absence was having first crack at the newspaper. According to the front page headlines, Nikola Tesla was promising to demonstrate his new apparatus for signaling the Martians in the very near future, while the stock market had, for the moment at least, calmed down. More polio cases had been reported in the Brooklyn Italian colony, but the city's continuing street disinfection and home inspection campaigns had apparently averted the explosion of cases predicted on account of the street cleaners' strike.

Satisfied that nothing life-changing had occurred in the last twenty-four hours, I quickly scanned the back pages, where a small caption caught my eye: "Jilted Italian Murders in Revenge." An Italian man out west, the dispatch reported, had rigged a mine explosion to kill the brother of a woman who'd rejected his proposal of marriage, believing the brother was responsible for her refusal. According to the reporter, the incident illustrated "the medieval treachery of which the southern Italian is capable, and how little his manners or ideals have progressed in the last five hundred years." I laid the paper down. Remembering the many hardworking — and, to all appearances, law-abiding — Italians I had passed on the streets of Harlem, I found this last statement rather extreme. It was hard not to conclude, however, from this and other reports I'd read, that the Italian culture had molded a people little inclined to restrain their passions.

I was still thinking of the dispatch an hour later as I stood on the street in front of the Elm Street office of the Italian Legion. I'd been surprised to learn, upon arriving at police headquarters, that the Italian division was housed in an entirely separate building. I peered again at the number over the doorway in front of me, finding it hard to believe that this drab building, with its dirty windows and ground floor pawn shop, could be it. Joseph Petrosino was, after all, the closest thing we had to a living legend in the city. The man had worked his way up from street cleaner to first Italian detective sergeant on the force, earning the respect of such luminaries as Theodore Roosevelt and Enrico Caruso along the way. He was famous both for his extraordinary bravery and for his eagerness to make up with his fists for what he considered our overly liberal criminal laws; indeed, it was said that he had dislodged more teeth than a professional dentist.

After King Umberto I of Italy was assassinated by an Italian anarchist from New Jersey, Petrosino was recruited by the federal Secret Service to determine whether President McKinley might be in danger as well. The papers had recounted in glowing detail how the detective infiltrated radical groups in New York and New Jersey, posing as a sympathizer to gain their trust. After learning that McKinley was, in fact, on the target list, the detective had personally alerted him and urged him to avoid large crowds. He was said to have wept openly when the president was murdered at the Buffalo Exposition a few weeks later, after failing to heed his warning.

I pulled the door open and climbed the dim stairwell to the second floor, where I heard typewriters clacking on the other side of an unmarked door directly opposite the landing. I stepped toward it and tried the knob. It was locked.

The typewriters had stopped clacking. "Who is it?" called a gruff voice from inside.

"Dr. Genevieve Summerford," I called back, "here to see Detective Lieutenant Petrosino."

I heard the scrape of chair legs and the pounding of feet over the floor, and then the door opened partway. A short man with an oversized, square head and facial skin the texture of rough concrete peered out at me. "I'm Petrosino."

I gazed down at him — for he was several inches shorter than I was — surprised by his stature and the fact that he'd opened the door himself. I'd expected to have to work my way through several gatekeepers to get to him.

His gaze swept over me, sizing me up. He had a jutting brow over alert brown eyes and a full, determined-looking mouth. "You're the one Bugher called about."

"That's right."

He swung the door open and gestured me in.

The heart of the Italian Legion's operations was a small, bare room with four battered desks that faced each other in the center. Two of the desks were occupied. The men sitting in them looked up briefly as I entered and then immediately resumed their typing. End-to-end tables along the room's perimeter were heaped high with file folders, except for a section in one corner that held what appeared to be a pile of weapons. On the back wall, hundreds of blank-faced men stared out at me from rows of black-and-white photographs.

Petrosino gestured toward a chair in front of one of the empty desks. He perched on the edge of the desk as I sat down, hitching up his trousers in the process, which called my attention to his double-soled shoes. Apparently, the fearless detective was sensitive about his height.

"So what can I do for you, Dr. Summerford? The deputy commissioner left me a message, but he didn't give me many details."

"Thank you for seeing me, Detective. I know you're very busy, so I'll get straight to the point. I believe that someone may be preying on young Italian women who arrive in the city by boat, forcibly abducting them and compelling them into prostitution." I handed him an envelope containing Teresa's photograph along with both girls' names and other pertinent details. As he was perusing the contents, I told him everything we'd learned so far.

"And you think that because these girls are Italian, Italian criminals must be behind it, and that's why you have come to me," he finished.

"Precisely."

He sighed. "There are over a quarter of a million Italians in Manhattan, Doctor, and I have only twenty-five men. My wife will tell you, I'm a very busy man. We married in April and I have yet to take her on a honeymoon. Now, with the new deportation law, we are busier than ever." He gestured to the stacks of files on the tables. "What you see here is a catalog we're compiling of all the Italian immigrants in New York City whom we suspect have criminal records in Italy. Under the law that went into effect last week, if we can properly identify these men to the Italian authorities and get a copy of their penal certificates, we can send them back where they came from. But we can do this only if they have been in America for less than three years, which puts us in a constant race against the clock." He smiled faintly in apology. "I tell you this so you won't think me hard-hearted when I say that I cannot look into every crime in this city involving an Italian."

"I certainly appreciate the pressure you're under, Detective. But what crime could be more heinous than abducting innocent girls and forcing them into prostitution?"

"None, I agree. But may I suggest you are putting the cart before the horse? I understand why you might be inclined to be suspicious, with all the talk of white slave traders in the newspapers. But from what you've told me, all you know is that one woman who appears to have been a prostitute committed suicide, while another woman failed to meet her fiancé after her arrival."

"There are similarities between the cases."

"Perhaps. But that doesn't mean these women have fallen prey to traffickers. And even if they have been abducted, it was most likely not by Italians."

"Why do you say that?"

"Because there is no Italian network with the necessary capabilities."

I frowned at him. "What 'capabilities' would they require?"

"It is no easy feat to kidnap women from our ports, where the authorities are keeping an eye out for them," he explained. "For this reason, most cadets — or pimps, if you will excuse my language — would rather try to ensnare them at a dance hall or employment agency after they have taken up residence. Italian girls, however, are an exception, for they are rarely let out of their parents' sight and so cannot be found at the usual hunting grounds. It follows that if someone were intent on securing Italian girls in large numbers, they would have to have the organization and resources not only to elude the protections in place at Ellis Island and Hoboken, but to prevent the authorities from tracing girls abducted from the ports back to their dens. To my knowledge, there is no Italian network currently operating in New York with that ability."

"What about the criminals setting off all those bombs in Harlem? Perhaps they're expanding into prostitution as well."

Petrosino glanced at one of the men sitting at the other desks, who had stopped typing and was listening to our conversation. "Have you heard anything?"

The man shook his head. "Nothing."

"Three of my detectives have been working in Harlem for the last several months, investigating the bombings," Petrosino explained. He nodded at the seated man. "Including Butch Cassidy here."

I looked back in surprise at the slightly built, olive-complected man he was addressing.

"His real name is Ugo Cassidi," Petrosino said, with the closest thing to a smile I'd seen yet. "But he likes to be called Butch."

Detective Cassidi grinned at me. "Like the outlaw, yes?"

"If there was an Italian prostitution network operating out of Harlem," Petrosino went on, "my men would likely have heard about it."

"Well then, who else might it be?" I asked, thinking that the large number of single Italian men in the city would make a lucrative market for any resort offering Italian prostitutes, regardless of the operator's nationality. "What about the French?" I suggested, for growing up, I'd always associated bawdy houses with French-speaking madams and imported champagne. "Could they be behind it?"

"Highly unlikely," Petrosino replied. "The *maquereaux* brought in thousands of prostitutes from Paris during their heyday, it is true, but because few of them learned to speak English, they were unable to establish the political connections required to stay in business. The majority of the French houses were shut down during the reform administration, and the district attorney's raids this summer finished off most of the rest."

"Who else then?" I persisted. "Who has taken their place?"

He pursed his lips, considering. "Perhaps half of the remaining business is controlled by Jewish dealers, supported by the Jewish gangs. The rest is divided between smaller operators of various races and nationalities. It is becoming harder, you see, to make a living from crime in our city. The poolrooms and policy joints have been nearly wiped out, and racetrack gambling is under attack. Even burglary has become too risky, thanks to the new electric alarms. Prostitution is one of the few paying rackets left in town."

"I thought the Jewish syndicate was put out of business," I said, remembering press reports I'd read during the reform administration.

He shook his massive head. "They only relocated to Newark, where they've spent the last five years expanding their network from one end of the country to the other. And now, it seems they have decided to return. A few weeks ago, the district attorney raided a meeting of key members of their organization in a Bowery saloon. They were there to arrange new distribution lines out of New York."

"I remember reading about that raid," I said eagerly. "The group had an odd name . . ."

"The Independent Benevolent Association," Detective Cassidi said from behind his typewriter, his voice filled with contempt. "It pretends to be an ordinary benefit society, providing death benefits and burial plots for decent merchants, when in fact, it is an alliance of men who make their living from the flesh of women."

"Did the district attorney shut it down?"

"He was unable to produce sufficient evidence," Petrosino replied. "Still, there has been progress." He pushed off the desk and began to pace. "Last May, it was revealed that Newark's slum politicians were providing sanctuary for the exiled Jewish operators, in exchange for a cut of their business and the use of their cadets as repeaters at the polls. You may recall that the chief of police killed himself soon after, and a number of key operators went to jail. In Philadelphia too, the citizens rose up against Jake Edelman and his associates, after the Law and Order Society revealed the extent of the evil there. Unfortunately, so great is the filthy lucre of this enterprise that every time one arm is cut off, another grows in its place."

"Is this Benevolent Association known to traffic in foreigners?" I asked him.

"It has never needed to, with so many girls in the city tenements to prey on. Although I suppose it would have the manpower and the network to kidnap and transport new arrivals, if it chose to expand."

"And yet," I murmured, musing out loud, "if someone is snatching Italian women from the ports, I doubt they're dragging them away kicking and screaming. There has to be some element of deception involved. In which case, I still can't help thinking that an Italian procurer, who spoke the women's language and knew their customs, would have the best chance at gaining their trust."

He stopped pacing and frowned at me. "I never meant to suggest that there aren't Italian men in this city who live off the shame of women. You can see such men strutting like roosters on the lower Bowery and in Chatham Square, with their collars turned up and their hair cut in their own peculiar fashion. But these Jacks are all small-time players, with only two or three women under their control. They lack the business sense of the Jews. They're always fighting with each other, squabbling over territory. And the women they exploit are usually not

171

Italians but Poles or Slavs they find in the employment agency district north of Houston."

"But . . . if you *had* to name an Italian operator most likely to be involved, who would it be?"

He shrugged. "I suppose I would look first at those already practiced in kidnapping." Crossing to the photograph gallery on the back wall, he pinned a forefinger against a picture of a handsome man in his late twenties with a bandana tied around his neck. "If you'd asked me a few months ago, I would have suggested this man, Pietro Pampinella, a smooth-talking dandy of the worst sort. He made a living out of kidnapping children for ransom. But we arrested him and his gang in April, so he could not have been involved."

He moved to another picture. "We also know that this man, Enrico Alfano, ordered at least two kidnappings while he was in New York, although we could not get his victims to testify. We believe Alfano was the acting chief of the Camorra in Naples, a society similar to the Mafia in Sicily, until he was forced to flee here to escape murder charges. I wouldn't put it past him to dirty his hands with such a scheme as you suggest. But" — his lips twisted in satisfaction

— "I arrested him too, in April, and he is now awaiting trial for murder in Italy."

I stood and went over to join him by the photograph. It showed a well-dressed man in his prime with a lush mustache and a scar running from the base of his nose to his ear. Perhaps it was only the photograph, but his eyes looked dead to me. "How can someone charged with murder get into this country in the first place?"

"It's far easier than you might think," he said grimly. "A wanted criminal, or an ex-convict wishing to escape the *sorveglianza,* can buy a false passport, or use someone else's, or simply stow away on a steamer without one. The criminal societies keep men employed as stokers and stewards on all the lines to help their members escape. We know that Alfano traveled to New York disguised as a member of a ship's crew. Another fugitive was smuggled aboard sewn into a mattress. If we had a law requiring a person's picture to be on his passport, as I have repeatedly proposed," he added, his voice rising in agitation, "we could at least cut down their numbers. Instead, more of these undesirables arrive every day."

"What's the *sorveglianza?*" I asked, unable to locate the word in my limited Italian lexicon.

"The *sorveglianza speciale,*" Detective Cassidi answered. "In Italy, even after a criminal has served his sentence, the government keeps a hand on him. He may not leave his home at night, or take employment without police approval, or visit a saloon. He is not allowed to carry so much as a penknife in his pocket, and if he gets into a fight he will be assumed to be the guilty party. And of course, he is not supposed to leave the country, although one may wonder how diligently the authorities hold him back when failure to do so only relieves them of their lowest elements."

I nodded, glancing at the stacks of folders on the tables. Turning back to Detective Petrosino, I asked, "Are these Mafia and Camorra people who escape to America the same ones who operate here as the Black Hand?"

His eyes flashed with impatience. "The 'Black Hand' is a myth," he retorted, "created by the newspapers and fed by fear. The criminals we are tracking are nearly all small-time crooks without any ties to a larger organization. They are happy, though, to take advantage of the specter of a Black Hand octopus that has the whole city in its tentacles."

Drawing a breath, he continued more

calmly, "Perhaps, as more capos like Alfano seek to establish themselves here, one or two will gain sufficient power to control the rest. But for now, any petty crook can commit a crime in the name of *La Mano Nera* and profit from the association."

I looked again at the photograph of Alfano, chilled by the blankness of his expression. "That scar, on his cheek . . ."

"The *sfregio*. It's a sign of punishment among the Camorristi."

"The drowned girl had a cut on her cheek as well," I told him. "Could that mean her attacker was once part of this Camorra?"

He wagged his head noncommittally. "Many Italians are quick with a knife, Doctor. Here, let me show you something." Stepping toward the corner table, he rummaged through the assortment of knives, revolvers, razors, and scissors that were piled there, selecting a slim cylinder with a triangular blade on top and holding it up for my inspection.

I peered at it. "It looks like a pencil sharpener."

"It is a pencil sharpener. I took it from a man on Elizabeth Street who was using it to hold people up. He knew that by cutting their faces enough to draw blood, he could frighten them into giving him whatever he asked for." He grunted in contempt. "What American hold-up man would be so bold? The Italian criminal knows his countrymen will not call for help or report his actions to the authorities. Until decent Italians understand that American laws are meant to protect them, and not the people who oppress them, these criminals will continue to flourish."

I gazed at the hundreds of faces on the wall, daunted by the possibilities. I'd been sure the Italian Legion would know where to look for Lucia's abductor, but it was beginning to seem that they had no more idea than I did.

Petrosino glanced at the clock. "I'm sorry, Dr. Summerford, that we can't give you the easy answers you seek. But perhaps Detective Norton will come up with something. Meanwhile, I'll tell my men to keep their ears and eyes open. And now, if you'll excuse me, I have an appointment with the commissioner."

"Just one more question," I said quickly. "I still can't help thinking it's significant that Lucia Siavo was found in the river off Harlem, where we know from the recent bomb attacks that there's a growing criminal presence. Can you tell me if any one gang appears to be consolidating power up there?"

He turned to Detective Cassidi. "Detective? Perhaps you can answer that for me. I don't want to keep the commissioner waiting." He gave me a nod and headed for the door.

Detective Cassidi jumped to his feet. "I am at your service, Doctor," he said, coming around to take Petrosino's place in front of the desk. He was considerably younger than his superior, with a lively step and a decidedly flirtatious glint in his eye. "To answer your question: in Harlem, especially, there is no uniformity between the Black Hand threat letters or the methods of bombing that might suggest consolidation. The letters are written by different hands, in different dialects, and signed with different insignia. We've seen knives, skulls, coffins, open hands, and closed fists."

"Does any one group stand out from the rest?"

"There is, in fact, one newer gang that has been more active recently than the others. Its symbol first appeared two months ago: the picture of a spider, on a threat letter sent to the president of an Italian bank. The letter was followed by a bomb that destroyed the man's business. We have since traced four more dynamite bombings to the Spider gang."

Well, that sounds promising, I thought. "Have you been able to learn anything about them?"

"In fact, I have some personal knowledge of the Spider, as I told the chief when the symbol first appeared. You see, the Spider symbol is well known in Naples, where my family is from."

"Would you mind telling me what you told him?"

He flashed me another of his winning smiles, which I guessed had melted many a feminine heart in their day. "As I said, Doctor, I am at your service." He settled back against the desk and crossed his arms. With the easy rhythm of the born storyteller, he began, "Years ago, when he was young, my father's uncle was imprisoned for his political activities. While he was in prison, he met many members of the Camorra and, through long association, learned something of the Society's ways. Anyone who wanted to enter the Society, he told my father, first had to commit a series of crimes to prove his ability and obedience. Only then were the names of the members and their secret passwords and signals revealed to him. As part of his initiation ceremony, he was required to fight existing members with a dagger, one after another, until he succeeded in drawing first blood. Once he had tasted the blood of his vanquished adversary, he was ready for the final step: the tattoo that would seal his membership in the ancient order.

"Now usually," the detective went on, "this tattoo was of two hearts joined together with two keys, symbolizing the bond of brotherhood and secrecy between members. But in one district, initiates were tattooed with the picture of a spider, to symbolize the industry of the Camorristi and the silence with which they spun their webs around their victims. Because the Camorristi of this district were especially ruthless, my father told me, the symbol of *Il Ragno,* the spider, inspired much respect among the people of the city." The detective shrugged. "Of course, many of the old ways have fallen away now, except in the prisons. But according to the people who live there, the tradition of the tattoo continues."

"So . . . whoever ordered the bombing of the bank president was a member of the Camorra in Naples?" I asked.

"Perhaps," he said. "Or perhaps he is only using the Spider symbol to inspire fear among those who are familiar with it."

"What sort of criminal activity does the Camorra engage in, in Italy?"

"Smuggling, extortion, counterfeiting," he counted off. He tipped his head. "And prostitution."

"So it's not unreasonable to think that the transplanted Camorra in general, or this Spider gang in particular, might have taken up prostitution here as well?"

"It is certainly possible, although as I said before, I have seen no evidence of it."

"Maybe when you find the man behind the letters, you'll find such evidence," I said with mounting excitement. "How long do you expect it will be before you run him to the ground?"

He frowned. "You must understand, Doctor, that these brigands, although ignorant, are sly in their way. It is always the insignificant *picciot'*, or apprentice, who steals the child or delivers the letter or lights the bomb. An apprentice would rather go to jail than name his superior. He will rarely need to make such a sacrifice, however, because no witness will be willing to speak against him. This is one reason Italian criminals love this country. In Italy, no complaining witness is necessary; when an accused is brought before the court, nine times out of ten, he will go to prison. Here, the criminal knows that if he can reach the witness and call him off, he has nothing to worry about."

I sat back with a sigh.

"But do not despair," he said gallantly. "If there is such a scheme afoot as you suggest, and Italian girls are being snatched from the ports, I am sure we will soon catch wind of it."

I rose to go. "If you do hear anything, could you please let me know?" Pulling a calling card from the case in my bag, I used the pen on the desk to write down my phone number and slipped it under a corner of the blotter.

"I will be sure to do so," he said, bowing smartly before escorting me to the door.

A punishing sun was beating down when I exited onto the street a few minutes later, sapping the vigor from horses and pedestrians alike in the normally bustling district. Even the stoop and sidewalk sellers seemed subdued, hawking their candy and combs and chewing gum with only half their usual gusto. My mood was equally desultory. How naive I'd been to think that if I could just bring Teresa's disappearance to Petrosino's attention, he would somehow miraculously solve her case by dinnertime. I'd let myself be swayed by sensational newspaper reportage, seduced into believing that the powers of good, in the person of one Joseph Petrosino, could be sufficient shield against an alarming and little-understood menace. It was what all native New Yorkers wanted to believe, so that we could sleep soundly at night.

There had to be something more that could be done, I thought as I continued north toward the subway station. But short of searching for Teresa in the disorderly resorts myself, which would, of course, be patently dangerous, I couldn't think of what it was. I was approaching the Bleecker Street station, fuming in frustration, when I noticed two stout women in peaked caps collecting donations near the entrance. A placard identified them as workers for the Howard Home for Little Wanderers. I paused in front of them, struck by sudden inspiration. Perhaps I'd been going about my search from the wrong angle. I dug into my bag for some coins and dropped them into the bucket.

"Thank you, miss," they chorused.

"Thank *you*," I replied and hurried into the station.

CHAPTER NINE

Before I could put the next phase of my plan into action, I had a psychotherapy class to conduct. It had been seven months now since I began my class treatment program designed to help women suffering physical ailments that stemmed from chronic grief. It had proved to be an instructive time for me as well as for my patients. When I first started out, I'd been a strict adherent of the persuasion therapy technique, which relied largely on a doctor's ability to convince his patients that they could heal, an alternative to hypnosis that relied on a direct appeal to the patient's reason to eliminate faulty thinking, and the psychic and physical problems that it produced. Because the doctor's absolute authority was a key element in this approach, providing the forceful persuasion that convinced the patient of his ability to heal, I'd been taught to discourage my patients from interrupting me or trying to discuss their problems in class.

In our weekly sessions, however, I'd been intrigued to discover that contributions by class members, when they were allowed to occur, could be therapeutic in their own right. My patients seemed to gain a sense of safety and a relief from tension by sharing their stories with others who'd suffered similarly and were more able to view their experiences in a new, salutary light. I had, accordingly, been gradually deviating from my formal training, forging a new path dictated solely by the results in my classroom.

Today, as always, I arrived at the Holy Trinity Church complex a few minutes early so that I could rearrange the chairs and go over my notes in the basement space that Reverend Palmers had provided for me. As I started down the path to the parish house, I spotted one of my newest patients, Martha Crimmins, leaving the church at the end of the service, accompanied by her adolescent daughter. Martha stopped at the fork in the path and said a few words to the girl, who leaned forward to embrace her. To my surprise, Martha stiffened and pulled back, averting her face. The girl drew back in turn. Martha started briskly toward the parish hall as her daughter looked sadly after her.

I remembered this encounter twenty minutes later, after I'd finished my introductory lecture on fearing to love again — a fear expressed by many of my class members, who'd all experienced the death of someone close to them — and opened the floor for discussion.

"I'm not afraid to love my daughter," Mrs. Crimmins immediately volunteered. "My only fear is that she won't love me back." She glanced at the other women seated around her, who were all listening sympathetically. The youngest Crimmins girl had died from burns after setting her dress on fire, which left Mrs. Crimmins with only one surviving child.

"She seems to have withdrawn from me since her sister's death," Mrs. Crimmins went on. "It breaks my heart when she doesn't return my affection."

"Wasn't that Clara I saw coming out of church with you, just before class?" I asked.

"Why, yes. She always comes with me to the second service."

"It looked to me as though she tried to embrace you, but that you turned away."

She regarded me with frank astonishment. "Oh no, you're quite mistaken. She pulled away from me. She always does."

She clearly believed what she was saying. And yet, I was equally certain of what I'd seen. I regarded her in silence for a moment, trying to reconcile the two. Mrs. Crimmins had just told us that she wasn't afraid to love again . . . but I wondered. I remembered a journal article I'd read recently about forces that worked on an unconscious level to keep painful or unacceptable thoughts out of a person's awareness, forces that one of their main proponents, the Austrian Sigmund Freud, was calling "defences." What if fears outside of Mrs. Crimmins's conscious awareness were affecting her behavior? What if, without even realizing it, she was keeping Clara at a distance to protect herself from the pain she'd have to endure if she lost her as well? Dr. Freud had suggested that a person could project ideas that were unacceptable to his conscious mind onto someone else. Perhaps this was what Mrs. Crimmins was doing when she assigned her own desire for distance to her daughter.

I was awestruck by the possibility, amazed once again by the lengths to which the human mind might go in its attempt to avoid pain and psychic disequilibrium. And yet, unfortunately, by holding Clara at a distance, Mrs. Crimmins seemed to be creating the very loss of connection with her daughter that she so feared. My mind reeled at the irony.

"Perhaps," I said to her gently, "we should talk a little more about how you and your daughter have been getting along."

I emerged from the cool basement thirty minutes later into another scorching day. The heat rose up in waves from the pavement, carrying manure dust and the smell of burning asphalt with it. My successful class had buoyed my spirits, and the withering heat could not dispel the sense of optimism I felt as I pulled my veil down against the dust and struck out uptown on foot, determined to discover something useful on Teresa Casoria's behalf.

I'd spent a good part of the previous evening poring over the charity directories in my father's library, looking for an institution that might suit my purposes. My plan was to search for other Italian women who'd been abducted into prostitution but had escaped or been rescued, and try to learn what I could about the man or men who had taken them. I'd assumed there would be a large number of shelters for former prostitutes where I might find such a woman, and hoped I might be able to locate one near the Harlem Italian colony.

My assumption, however, had proved incorrect. There were plenty of charities dedicated to helping destitute women "of good character," or girls "still innocent" who'd been saved from the jaws of evil, or even women recently liberated from prison — but only a handful seemed interested in helping the fallen. And of these, only two were anywhere near the uptown colony.

I was familiar with one of them: the House of the Good Shepherd at the foot of Ninetieth Street, by the East River. Run by Roman Catholic nuns, this "home" had accommodations for eight hundred inmates and was a primary city depository for women who'd been arrested for disorderly conduct or been committed by their parents for incorrigibility. Although I had no doubt that excellent work was being carried out there, with so many girls arriving through involuntary channels I suspected it must be operated more as a reformatory than a refuge. There had been newspaper reports of escape attempts over the years, and of at least one accidental death after a girl attempting to climb down from her room on a rope of knotted sheets fell to the court below. I doubted that either the management or the inmates of such an establishment would be eager to speak with me.

I was looking for a different sort of place, where the girls had come willingly in search of a new life and might therefore be open to telling me about their start in the old one. I was hoping I'd found just such an establishment in the Goldstein Women's Home. Located on 102nd Street on the approximate border between Jewish and Italian Harlem, the twenty-four-bed refuge billed itself as "open to friendless and fallen women of all religions, space permitting, no questions asked or references required." It sounded like a good place to start.

There was no shade on the sidewalk, and I'd only walked a few blocks before my shirtwaist was sticking to my back and my collar was rubbing against my clammy skin. I eyed some children licking a giant block of ice on the corner, coveting a lick of my own. Even the free horse shower at the stable across the street looked enticing. I was more than ready to get out of the sun when I finally reached my destination, a four-story building with "Goldstein Women's Home" painted in white across the top of the brick facade. Through the yellow gingham curtains that framed the window front on the bottom floor, I could see an earnest-faced young man folding pamphlets at a desk. I pushed the door open and walked in.

The man looked up at my entrance. He had long, disheveled hair and wore a threadbare waistcoat. "Can I help you?"

"I'd like to speak with Mrs. Goldstein, if she's available."

"She's handing out pamphlets down the street." Looking me up and down, he added, "If you're here to make a donation, I can get her for you."

"Oh no, I don't want to interrupt her work. I'll just go speak to her outside."

"You can't miss her. She'll be standing in front of the Swann Hotel." He held out a handful of the pamphlets. "Could you give her these for me? She ought to be nearly out by now."

I took the pamphlets, glancing down at one as I walked out the door. BLINDNESS! INSANITY! DEATH! *FOR YOU, YOUR WIFE, AND YOUR UNBORN CHILDREN.* IS THIS WHAT YOU WANT? I opened it up and sucked in my breath. An extremely lifelike sketch of a phallus took up the entire left page, with a red, hand-painted syphilis chancre on its head. I looked furtively up and down the street before scanning the rest. On the right side was a smaller sketch of a crying infant with a full-body rash, and below it a list of the symptoms of syphilis and gonorrhea, ending with the warning, THERE IS NO CURE — ONLY PREVENTION! A telephone number followed, with instructions to call for more information.

I closed the leaflet and peered down the sidewalk. A sign for the Swann Hotel hung from a pole over the sidewalk three doors down. Half of the tiny incandescent bulbs that rimmed it were burned out, while the other half still glowed feebly in the bright light of midday. A short young woman with a scuffed leather bag at her feet stood below it, holding a thin stack of pamphlets. She had an arresting, angular face under a mass of wiry copper curls shoved haphazardly under a nurse's cap. She stood with her shoulders squared and her head lifted, like someone expecting trouble and ready to meet it head on. She was a far cry from the prim, middle-aged, vaguely saintly woman I'd been expecting.

As I started toward her, a man came out of the hotel with a cigar between his teeth and a walking stick hooked over one arm. The woman stepped into his path, holding up a copy of the pamphlet. He stepped left, then right, while she deftly mirrored his moves, making it impossible for him to avoid her. Finally, with a growl that even I could hear, he grabbed the pamphlet and jammed it into his pocket.

Although it was a Sunday, raucous voices and music from an out-of-tune piano wafted out of the bottom-floor windows of the hotel, suggesting that liquor was being served inside. I glanced at the upper stories. After the Raines law went into effect, prohibiting Sunday liquor sales except at hotels, hundreds of saloon owners had rushed to add upstairs bedrooms and kitchen space to their establishments. Since these accommodations were generally of the roughest sort, and since there was no legitimate demand for the sudden influx of space, the great majority of these new "hotels" had quickly become venues for prostitution, where pimps arranged assignations with customers from the downstairs saloon. If that's what was going on inside the Swann, it would explain why Miss Goldstein was distributing tracts about venereal disease at the door.

Her eyes brightened on sight of me. "Are you the new volunteer?" Her voice held the inflection of the Russian Jewess, softened by at least one generation in America.

"No, sorry. The man inside just asked me to give these to you." I handed her the pamphlets. "I'm Dr. Genevieve Summerford. I was hoping to speak to you about the women in your care."

Her keen brown eyes searched mine. "What's your interest?" she asked, her manner as forthright as one might expect of a woman who could hand out pictures of diseased phalluses in broad daylight.

"I'm trying to find an Italian girl who I think may have been abducted and sold into prostitution. I'm checking asylums like yours, looking for any girls who may have —"

"Just a minute," she interrupted, pushing past me as a pair of young men approached the hotel entrance. "Gentlemen," she called out, "a moment of your time." Pressing a leaflet into each of their hands, she launched into a condensed version of the message it contained. As they sidled, horrified, toward the door, she pulled two small tins from a bag around her waist and thrust one into each man's pant pocket. "Call the number on the leaflet to get more!" she shouted after them as they escaped into the hotel.

She turned back to me, pushing a curly wisp of hair from her eyes. "You were saying?"

"What was that you put in their pockets?"

I asked in disbelief, pretty sure I knew the answer.

"Rubber cots," she confirmed, wiping the sheen from her brow with the back of her hand. "The pimps won't make the customers wear them, so I must try to convince them myself."

I glanced up and down the street again. "What about the police?" The leaflets were bad enough; if the police caught her handing out contraception devices, they would certainly throw her in jail.

"The police?" she repeated with a smirk. "The police on this beat are regular customers here, and they're happy for the free goods."

It took me a moment to digest this. "And the owner? He doesn't consider you bad for business?"

She shrugged. "We have an understanding. He lets me stand here on Sundays, and I don't tell his wife what goes on upstairs."

She elbowed me in the ribs, nodding toward two more men who were coming up the sidewalk. "Here," she said, handing back some of the leaflets. "Help me give these out, and then I'll answer whatever questions you want."

My dismay must have been apparent, for her amber eyes flashed with impatience.

"A doctor of medicine you say you are?" she demanded.

"That's right."

"And eliminating disease is your calling?"

I made no reply, seeing where this was going.

Stooping to unclasp the bag at her feet, she pulled out a handful of tinned condoms and thrust them toward me.

I threw up my hands. "Oh no. I'm sorry, Mrs. Goldstein, but I wouldn't have the nerve."

Her shrewd eyes assessed me. "It's *Miss* Goldstein, but you can call me Pauline. And if you want information about my girls, you'll find the nerve." She grasped one of my hands and folded it over the tins.

I glanced toward the approaching men. "But . . . how do I know which ones are here to see the women?"

"I know, and I will tell you." She jerked her chin toward the second of the two men coming toward us. "Starting with that one there. In the checkered cap."

I drew a bracing breath. *For Teresa,* I told myself and prepared to accost him.

Over the next thirty minutes, we had the opportunity to impress our message on some dozen or more men. I found it dif-

195

ficult to believe at first that they could really all be here for assignations — but a furtive something in their gaze at our approach seemed to confirm it. I gradually warmed to my task, inspired by Miss Goldstein's zeal. It was for their own good, after all. The only way to prevent the transmission of venereal disease, apart from abstention, was to use a protective sheath, but since the dissemination not only of contraception devices themselves, but also of information about their use had been illegal for the last several decades, many young men weren't aware of this. Even if they were, they were frequently so ignorant of the ravages inflicted by the disease that they chose to engage in unprotected relations regardless. All too often, it wasn't until their wives or newborn children exhibited symptoms that they even realized they'd been infected.

"Where did you receive your nurse's training?" I asked Pauline during a lull in traffic.

She looked puzzled. "Oh, you mean this?" she asked, touching her cap. "It belongs to a friend of mine. I just wear it when I'm handing out leaflets so people will listen."

Before I could express an opinion on this unorthodox conduct, she elbowed me in the ribs again to alert me to an approaching customer.

When we had exhausted our leaflet supply, we returned to the shelter, where the earnest young man at the front desk was now painting the finishing touches on a placard.

"This is Jacob," Pauline told me. "A true friend of our cause. When he isn't writing articles for the daily *Forverts,* he's here, helping me and my girls."

I introduced myself and shook his hand, tilting my head sideways to read the words on the placard. VOTES FOR WOMEN! MEETING TONIGHT AT COOPER UNION, 7:00 P.M. I smiled up at Pauline. "So you're a suffragette, as well as a savior of lost women?"

Her eyes flashed reproachfully, in a way that was becoming all too familiar. "Tell me only, how is it possible to be one and not the other? Without power, women will never be treated with respect!" She gestured toward the only two chairs in the narrow vestibule. "Now come, sit," she said, her temper abating as quickly as it had flared, "and tell me more about why you're here."

I sat beside her and told her about Lucia and Teresa and what I'd learned so far. "If someone *is* abducting Italian women and forcing them into prostitution, I thought I might find a clue to their identity by trying to interview some of their prior victims."

"Most certainly, these abductions are taking place," she said.

I blinked at her. "What makes you say that?"

"Because three of their victims have been sent to me in just the last four months."

"Sent here, to your shelter?"

"The Chicago Law and Order Society asked me to house them, after the state's attorney's office conducted raids on some of the worst dens in that city. According to the Society, all three girls were taken captive upon their arrival in New York by Italians who were strangers to them."

Three of them. I could hardly believe my luck. "Could I speak to them?"

She shook her head. "These girls I keep only until they are healthy enough to travel. The Society gives me the steamship fare to send them home. The first one left a month ago, and the second one last week."

"But the third one? She's still here?"

She hesitated. "Her body is here. As for her mind, I cannot say. She has been with us for over a month but still refuses to leave her room. She never talks about what happened to her. I know only because of the Law and Order Society's report."

I sank back in my chair. If the girl was still in shock, I wasn't going to be able to question her about her abduction. Trying to force her to talk about it before she was ready would not only be unproductive, but might even worsen her distress. "What's her name?"

"Caterina Bressi."

"How old is she?"

"Seventeen, and fragile as an eggshell. Frankly, I've been wondering what to do with her. Her refusal to leave her room has been making things difficult for our cooking and cleaning staff."

I'd still like to see her, even if I couldn't ask about her captors. "Perhaps I could help. My specialty is medical psychology."

Her eyebrows rose. "A doctor of the mind?" She nodded. "This, I think, is exactly what she needs."

"I'm not saying I can affect any immediate improvement," I added hastily. "But I have had some experience with people suffering from psychic shock. I might be able to suggest ways to help her move forward."

"Then certainly, you must try. I should warn you though, she doesn't speak much English. We'll need to have our cook, Angela, translate for you." She glanced at the wall clock. "Angela will be finished cleaning up from lunch soon. Why don't I show you around the place, and then we'll go fetch her?"

The bottom floor of the building, she explained, had been converted to a theater by its former occupant in hopes of cashing in on the moving picture craze. When that scheme failed, the desperate owner agreed to let out the entire building to Pauline's enterprise for slightly less than market rate. The cheap rent allowed her to provide beds, food, and training space for twenty-four women at a time.

Leaving behind the gated vestibule — once used for ticket collection, she explained, and now a handy barrier to the occasional angry pimp — we entered the former seating area, where the shelter's sewing and ironing operations were housed. Some two dozen young women sat at four long tables, wielding irons, practicing stitching on sheets of newspaper, or bent over sewing machines. Several open windows in the rear provided ventilation, while a generous scattering of hanging incandescent lamps cast an even light over the work space. Scratchy music played on a phonograph in the corner.

Pauline led me up a side stairwell to a narrow balcony that hung over the work area. "This is my office," she said, indicating a battered desk and chair in the middle of the open space. "And these," she added, turning and gesturing over the balcony rail, "are my girls."

I joined her at the rail, from where we could easily observe the industry below.

"The shirtwaists the women sew and the bread they bake in the basement ovens are sold directly to stores and hotels," she told me proudly. "We don't do piecework for garment manufacturers, paying the women a pittance for their labor, as other shelters do. Here, the women keep all the profits from their work, minus only the cost of materials. Even after they've moved out, they may continue to work for our established customers, without paying us any commission." She gave me a probing look. "Which is why we depend so heavily on outsiders for support. We wouldn't be able to carry on our work without donations."

"Of course. I understand," I said, resigned to the fact that I wouldn't be leaving without making a sizeable one.

"Look, Miss G!" one of the youngest girls called from the floor, holding up a nearly finished shirtwaist.

"Molly! How smart you are! Two weeks only you have been here, and already you sew like a Paris seamstress!"

The girl grinned and went back to her hemming.

"She's one of the lucky ones," Pauline said with satisfaction. "We got to her before the vultures could, when she ran away from home. She is eager to learn and make something of herself."

"And the rest of them? The unlucky ones?"

She shrugged. "Some will take up a new life, once they have the skills. But many will not. Often, these girls are so filled with shame that they can't be convinced they deserve another chance and decide to go back to the streets. Others simply tire of the monotony of honest labor."

"That must be a bitter pill for you to swallow, after all you do for them."

She gave me a stern look. "I don't judge. I wish only to give them a choice. What they do with it is up to them."

I gazed at the sea of bent heads below me, trying to imagine the paths that had led them here. "Could you tell me some of their stories? What about that woman in blue there, filling the water bowls on the ironing tables?"

"Sarah," she said with a nod. "She came to New York from Austria three years ago to make money to send back to her family.

Because she didn't have the dollars to prove she wouldn't become a public charge, she was told she must either go back home, or be committed to the Austrian Society's guardianship for a year. She chose the second, of course, and was bonded to the home of a jeweler as a servant by her 'guardians.' After a week, the husband began to make advances. The wife caught him trying to pull up her skirts in the kitchen and chased her out of the house."

"Good Lord! Did her guardians have the man arrested?"

She turned to me with a grimace. "They told her she had to go back."

I stared at her. "And did she?"

"Would you?" She looked back out over the railing. "It was winter, and after two days of wandering without finding employment, she took a job as a waitress in a saloon. They paid her just enough for her to split the cost of a boardinghouse room with three other girls. There was barely enough money to eat, let alone send anything home to her family, and she was constantly propositioned by rough men in the saloon. One night, one of the regular customers, a big spender who'd always been kind to her, offered to pay her two dollars to go behind the curtain with him in the back." She glanced at me. "Two dollars, you understand, is nearly half of a waitress's weekly wages." She shrugged. "So she went. And kept on going after that, one or two times a week."

I thought of what I'd said to Simon, about there always being other choices. But what if your only other choice was to toil twelve hours a day in a low-wage shop or saloon or factory, with nothing to look forward to but another week, another year, of the same soul-draining tedium? For the first time, I wondered if I'd be able to resist the lure of an easier life if that was the lot I'd been given.

"And then, one day, she was arrested by an undercover detective and sentenced to two weeks in the workhouse," Pauline went on. "When she was released, there was a man waiting outside who told her she'd need police protection if she didn't want to be arrested again and offered her his services. Before she knew what was happening, this man had taken control of her life, forcing her to have sex whenever and with whomever he wanted. When she tried to run away one time too many, he sold her to one of the worst resorts in the Tenderloin, where she was kept prisoner for over a year. On Christmas Day, a customer started a fire when he kicked over a candle, and in the confusion, she managed to escape. But not before she had been infected with syphilis."

"Dear God" was all I could manage.

She frowned at me. "God, I think, has nothing to do with such things."

I looked back out over the room. "Is that how it usually begins?" I asked after a moment. "I mean, the girls enter more or less willingly into the enterprise?"

She shrugged. "Of the women who have come to my shelter, perhaps two-thirds have entered willingly. The rest were either tricked or forced into the trade. The macks are everywhere these days, masquerading as employment agents and theater managers and boardinghouse representatives. I know of one man out west who gained entry into homes in the guise of a Graphophone salesman, pretending to fall in love with any pretty young woman who lived inside. They talk the girls into leaving home by promising to marry them or find them employment. Sometimes, they actually do marry them; there are pimps who have married dozens of times over."

"How can there be so many young men willing to engage in such deceit?" I exclaimed. "Don't these men have mothers and sisters? How can they be so cruel?"

205

She gave me a sidelong glance. "You're the doctor of psychology. You tell me."

I shook my head. "They must be masterful liars."

"And of course," she said with a sigh, "the girls are eager to believe. Here in the city, the men find the easiest pickings at the dance halls, where the factory and shopgirls go on their night off to forget their misery for a few hours. The greatest dream these girls have is to find a man who will take care of them, and that is what these wolves falsely offer."

A clock struck the hour somewhere below. "Angela should be finished by now," she said, turning away from the railing.

"Miss Goldstein —"

"Pauline," she insisted.

"Pauline, do you think you could tell me a little about Caterina's history before I meet with her? It might help me decide how to proceed."

She shrugged. "Why don't you read the report for yourself?" Crossing the three steps to her "office," she pulled a two-page document from a stack of papers on her desk and held it out to me.

The Chicago Law and Order Society was engraved across the top of the first sheet. The caption below read simply *Case No.*

"You might want to sit down," Pauline suggested, nodding toward the single chair. She leaned against the desk with her arms crossed, watching me with an inscrutable expression.

Stomach fluttering with apprehension, I lowered myself onto the chair and began to read.

CHAPTER TEN

According to the report, Caterina Bressi had been found "in a state of abject terror" during a brothel raid conducted by Assistant State's Attorney Clifford Roe. She had insisted at first that she was working at the brothel by choice, apparently fearing she'd be recaptured and punished by the brothel owner. Only after Roe convinced her she was under the protection of the U.S. government did she break down and confess the true story.

One year earlier, she told her interrogators, an Italian-born American lady wearing beautiful clothes had visited her village just outside Naples. The lady met Caterina and her mother at their market stand, striking up a conversation with the two of them after buying some of their figs and apricots. After remarking on Caterina's modesty and uncommon beauty, she introduced the possibility that the girl might come to America to work as her companion. Excited by the woman's attention, the family invited her to come to their humble home for supper, where she spoke about her grand house in New York City and her many carriages and all the other fine things she owned. Shrewdly, the report suggested, she didn't attempt to take the girl with her when she left. A few weeks later, however, just as the family was beginning to fear the offer of employment had only been a dream, a letter arrived renewing her invitation and including money for the girl's New York passage.

Caterina's parents sent her off by the next boat, celebrating the family's good fortune. At Ellis Island, the girl was met by her sponsor, who attended to her entrance papers and rode the barge with her to Manhattan. At the Barge Office, the woman handed her into a carriage with two men, explaining that she had errands to attend to but that the men would take her to her new home. Exactly where these men took Caterina, she didn't know — but they quickly accomplished her ruin, by violent and brutal means. The next day, she was moved to a place with other Italian girls, also recently arrived, where for two weeks she was subjected to "the most unspeakable treatment" until made to feel that her degradation was complete. "And here let it be said," the report's author noted, "that the breaking of spirit, the crushing of all hope for any future save that of shame, is always a part of the initiation of the white slave."

The girl was then shipped to Chicago and sold to a dive resort holding exclusively Italian women, where she was locked in a room without food or light until she became thoroughly submissive. Having been deprived of everything but her undergarments in New York, she was then supplied with gaudy new apparel, which, she was told, she must pay for with six hundred dollars of her earnings before she could leave her keeper's employ. From that day on, she lived in a locked room with barred windows, servicing anywhere from eight to fifteen men each night.

As soon as she had earned six hundred dollars, Caterina tried to pay off her account, only to be told that she had since incurred an additional four hundred dollars for room and board. Realizing she would never be let go, she made a frantic dash for escape but was caught at the door by her captors. They dragged her back inside and slashed her cheek, ear, and eyelid with a razor, explaining that she'd brought this punishment on herself by failing to appreciate her keeper's care and protection. A doctor came and crudely stitched her up, but her face was now badly scarred, and her right eye remained permanently open. The resort owner had been about to transport her to a mining camp farther west, where some profit might yet be squeezed from her, when the den was raided and Caterina was set free.

I lowered the papers slowly to my lap. "No wonder she doesn't want to leave her room."

"There's another page," Pauline said.

I flipped to page two. It was titled "Disposition of Case" and contained just two short paragraphs:

Caterina Bressi refused to testify. She was remanded to the care of the Chicago Law and Order Society for safe transport to the port of New York and eventual return to her family in Italy.

As a result of the raid at 407 Clark Street, charges were brought against the brothel owner, Battisti Pizzi, and the procurers, Frank Romano and Antonio Colufiore. Based on the testimony of Santina Bomba, one of six other women rescued in the raid, all three men were convicted and fined the maximum penalty of two hundred dollars.

I reread the final sentence in disbelief. "A fine? That's all?"

"There are no laws in Illinois applying specifically to procurers," Pauline explained. "They can only be charged with crimes against public morals, which is a misdemeanor."

"That's . . ." I groped for a word big enough to express my outrage. "What about in New York?"

"Here, the worst a pimp usually has to worry about is being charged as a vagrant, which carries a maximum six-month penalty. But he needn't worry overly much, since the women under his thumb know better than to testify against him."

I looked back at the report. "Did they at least get the names of the men who sold the girls to the resort?"

"It's always the same: the pimps claim they bought the girls at the stockades, the markets where new girls are put on display. Why should they reveal their suppliers' names, when the most they are threatened with is a two-hundred-dollar fine? A big house can make that up in a few nights."

"What about the other girls who were

rescued?" I asked, thinking they might have revealed something that could help trace the supply line back to New York. "Were they all enticed in the same way?"

"I only know about the other two who came here. One was also tricked with a false promise of employment. The other answered an ad from a marriage broker who claimed to be seeking a wife for a man working in the Colorado mines."

"And none of the girls could give the authorities any useful information about their abductors?"

"What could they give? They know nothing real about the people who deceived them. The procurers all use false names, and the employment and marriage brokers, even if they could be found, can always claim they believed their client was an honest customer."

I tossed the report on her desk. "How do you do it? How can you work day after day under such discouraging conditions without going mad?"

"Who says I haven't?" she asked, returning the report to the stack.

I smiled and shook my head. "How did you get involved in this line of work, anyway?"

Her face was turned away from me, but I

213

still saw the shadow that moved across it. She laid her hand on top of the pile, resting it there for a moment. "Come," she said finally, moving away from the desk without answering me. "Let's go see just how good a doctor you are."

Our first stop was the basement kitchen, where the shelter's cook, Angela, was hanging pots on an overhead rack when we arrived. She was a middle-aged woman with voluptuous curves, a full mouth, and liquid eyes as deep as the Adriatic.

"Checking up on me, eh, Boss?" she said to Pauline. She winked at me. "She's worried I'm going to use too much butter in the sauce tonight."

"I *know* you'll use too much butter, Angela," Pauline replied. "That's why I pay you so little; to make up for all the extra money you cost me. Just don't try to bake that cheesecake of yours for the girls behind my back, when I leave for my meeting. That special cheese you order costs more than I pay you altogether."

"Boss!" she protested, affecting a hurt expression. "I would never!"

Pauline rolled her eyes. "Angela Marino," she said, "meet Dr. Genevieve Summerford."

Angela wiped her hand on her apron and held it out. Her grasp was firm and welcoming.

"Angela showed up here the day we opened to ask if we needed help," Pauline told me. "That's not the usual reaction from our neighbors, I can tell you. One local minister threatened to burn us down."

Angela grimaced. *"Stronzo di asino."*

I raised an eyebrow. "I beg your pardon?"

"I said he is a" — she rolled her hand back and forth in the air as she worked out the translation — "a donkey's turd. What man of God turns his back on unfortunates?"

"But now we have Angela," Pauline said, "and she is worth three ministers."

Angela eyed me curiously. "Have you come in Dr. Burnham's place?"

I looked blankly at Pauline.

"Burnham is the doctor who looks after my girls," she explained. "He has a heart as big as a horse and treats the girls for free. But unfortunately, his thirst is even bigger than his heart, and he is drunk more often than not. He hasn't shown up at all this week." Turning to Angela, she added, "But we must hope that he sobers up soon, for Dr. Summerford has come here for reasons of her own." She repeated the gist of our earlier conversation.

215

"She wants to talk to Caterina?" Angela asked with a frown when she was done.

"Yes, I know. I told her." Paulina turned back to me. "Angela has made some headway with the girl, but she still refuses to join in any of our activities. We can't get her down to meals or out to the water closet, which means she has to use a slop pail and take sponge baths in her own room. I'm letting her have the room to herself for now, but I hate to let the other bed go to waste."

"Has she ever spoken with you about her captivity?" I asked Angela.

"Never. We speak only of simple things."

"What about her physical health? Has she had a medical exam?"

"According to the Society's cover letter," Pauline answered, "she was examined immediately after her rescue. She was very thin and had burn marks on her thighs and breasts —"

"Burn marks?" I broke in, remembering the coroner's report on Lucia.

"Courtesy of her abductor in New York apparently," she said with a frown. "But the most immediate problem is her eye. It's very red and painful. I was able to convince her to let Dr. Burnham look at it when she arrived, but he told us there was nothing to be done."

"Perhaps I could take a look when I meet with her and give you another opinion." Though the slashed eyelid might be beyond repair, it seemed to me it ought at least be possible to reduce the pain it was causing.

Pauline turned to Angela. "What do you think? We can't let her stay in that room forever."

"I think," Angela said, "that it's a good thing I used some of your precious butter to make a batch of biscotti this morning. They're Caterina's favorite." She lifted a tray of oblong-shaped cookies from the table behind me. "Come on, Doctor. I'll take you upstairs."

She led me up the back stairs and down a narrow hallway to the last room on the right. Propping one side of the pan on her generous hip, she knocked softly on the door. *"È Angela, cara, con un'amica,"* she crooned. *"Possiamo entrare?"*

Several seconds ticked by. "If she doesn't want to open her door, we can't force her," Angela told me quietly. "Every room in this shelter has a lock, and only the girls who live there have the key. It's one of the promises Pauline makes to them when they come here."

She knocked again, singing, *"Ho biscotti . . ."*

Nearly half a minute passed before a key scraped in the lock and the door opened a few inches. A dark eye gazed out at us from behind the crack.

"There you are!" Angela said in Italian, giving the specter inside an encouraging smile. Turning sideways so the girl could see me, she added, "I've brought a doctor friend of Pauline's who wanted specially to meet with you."

The eye turned toward me.

"*Buongiorno,* Caterina," I said.

"*Lei è un dottore?*" asked a wispy voice.

"Yes, dearest, a lady doctor, and a very nice one," Angela assured her. "Now will you please open the door, so I can put down this heavy tray?"

The girl opened the door and stepped back. Because I'd been expecting the scarring on her face, I was able to maintain a neutral expression — but it took some doing. A puckered seam ran from her eyebrow down the middle of her right eyelid, pulling the lid away from the eye and preventing it from closing when she blinked. Doubtless because of the dryness this caused, the eye beneath it was red and inflamed. Another, longer scar ran from the base of her ear to the corner of her mouth.

She backed toward the bed on the right

side of the room and sat down, watching me warily.

"You did better today!" Angela exclaimed, nodding at a tray on the floor near the door that held a crust of bread and a half-eaten bowl of soup. "But there is always room for biscotti, yes?" She lowered the cookies onto a plank-topped barrel between the beds. Except for the beds, the barrel table, and two pine shelves holding folded clothes and toiletries, the room was devoid of furniture. Light poured in through the clean window, however, and a red-and-yellow rag rug added a patch of cheerful color.

"Please, Doctor, sit," said Angela, indicating the unoccupied bed.

"May I?" I asked Caterina in Italian.

Her eyes slid rapidly between me and Angela, her body tense as a spring-loaded mousetrap.

Angela settled onto the bed beside her and wrapped an arm around her shoulders. I noticed that the girl didn't flinch or otherwise object to her close proximity. "She's here to help you," Angela murmured to her in Italian.

Some of the tension seemed to leave the girl's frame under the older woman's touch. She gave me an almost imperceptible nod.

I sat down across from her, folding my

hands loosely in my lap, trying to make myself as unthreatening as possible. I was dying to ask her about the men who'd taken her in New York, for identifying them could well be the key to finding Teresa. But the poor child was clearly still far too disturbed for me to broach the subject. "Pauline tells me your eye has been bothering you," I said instead.

Angela translated. Caterina leaned against her, murmuring into her ear.

"She says the other doctor told her nothing can be done for it," Angela told me.

I bent forward slightly, peering across the space between us at the weeping eye. "Ask her if it feels like there's sand in it all the time."

The question drew a nod from Caterina.

"And if it hurts when she looks into the light."

She answered again in the affirmative.

"It sounds like a scratched cornea," I concluded. "I'll have the druggist deliver some eye drops to clear up the redness and some ointment to take the scratchiness away. Perhaps a cotton eye patch as well that she can wear while she sleeps to help keep it from drying out."

A look of wonder came over the girl's face as Angela translated. She stared at me for a long moment, blinking repeatedly, whether because her eyes were hurting or were damp with tears of relief, I couldn't be certain. *"Grazie,"* she said finally.

I smiled. "You're welcome."

"Time for biscotti!" Angela said, offering up the tray.

We each took a cookie, Caterina using her left hand to lift hers from the platter. Her right hand, I noticed now, was curled around a terra-cotta doll that was wedged between her hip and the bed pillow. I curiously perused the doll as we nibbled our cookies. It had a young woman's face, with lifelike glass eyes and painted pink cheeks and chipped lips parted in a half smile. The blue silk dress it wore must have been elegant once, but was now torn at the bottom and streaked with grime. "How do you say 'doll' in Italian?" I asked Angela.

"Bambola."

"Che bella bambola," I said to Caterina.

She stopped chewing, her hand tightening on the doll's midriff.

"It's a crèche doll," Angela explained to me. "Italian mothers give them to their daughters when they leave home, to place in the crèche at their new residence at Christmas time."

"You mean it came with her from Italy?" I

221

asked. "And she managed to keep it with her through . . . through everything?"

"Oh yes, she keeps the doll with her always. She calls her Isabella, and takes great care of her, combing her hair and singing her to sleep."

I looked at the doll with heightened interest. Though I knew little about crèche dolls, I doubted it was customary to give them names. "Isabella," I repeated. In Italian, I said to Caterina, "It' a beautiful name, for a beautiful doll."

"Lei non è bella," the girl retorted. *"È sporca."*

I paused with my cookie halfway to my mouth, startled by her declaration.

"She says she isn't beautiful," Angela began. "She's —"

"Dirty. Yes, I understood," I said, feeling a frisson of recognition.

A few minutes later, we took our leave and returned to the kitchen, where we found Pauline waiting with a fresh pot of coffee.

She gestured toward three mismatched cups on the table. "Sit, and tell me how it went."

"This doctor, she's all right," Angela said, patting my shoulder as we all sat down. "She's going to get some medicine to make Caterina's eye better."

222

"The medicine will help, but of course, it's not a cure," I said. "Once she's more comfortable with strangers, I'd like to have her examined by a surgeon friend of mine — a woman I went to medical school with, who lives here in the city. There's a chance she could flatten out the lid so that it closes properly. I can ask her to take a look, if Caterina is willing."

"I will speak to her and see," Angela said.

"And her mind, Doctor?" Pauline asked as I took a sip of the coffee. "Will she recover?"

"Considering what she's gone through, I'd say her behavior is entirely understandable. It's going to be a long time, if ever, before she regains the basic trust required to function normally. But . . . there might be a way you can help her."

They eyed me over the rims of their coffee cups, waiting for me to go on.

I hesitated, wondering how best to convey the half-baked idea that had come to me when I saw Caterina interacting with her doll. "In my work, I've seen the mind do some extraordinary things," I began. "I've seen how, when it's subjected to a terrible shock, it can develop an alternate personality to hold and remember the shocking event, relieving the original personality of

223

the burden. Just today, I saw how a feeling that's too painful or shameful to experience can be projected onto someone else. In both cases, the individual seems to be taking the unbearable thought or feeling or memory and placing it outside of himself, either into a new, separate personality, or onto another person entirely."

I paused, searching their faces, wondering if they could even entertain an idea that sounded so far-fetched. Seeing only thoughtful concentration, I continued, "When I saw Caterina with her doll, it occurred to me that something similar might have happened in her case. The doll might be acting as a sort of external personality, bizarre as that may sound, protecting her from having to remember the horrible things she endured in captivity. Or maybe she's projecting her intolerable feelings of shame and degradation onto the doll. I'm not clear on the exact mechanism, but if something similar is going on, then when she speaks about the doll, she may actually be speaking about herself. When she says that Isabella is dirty, for example, she may really be saying that she thinks she herself is filthy and unacceptable."

"Like a child who blames his dog for eating the cake?" Angela suggested.

"Something like that, only she isn't aware that she's doing it."

She nodded thoughtfully. "So her mind plays tricks on her, to make her feel better."

"Exactly! And if I'm right, and the doll has been instrumental in helping her cope with her ordeal, then it seems to me you might be able to use it as a tool in her recovery as well."

"You mean, we can find out how she's feeling by asking her about the doll," Angela said.

"Yes. You might even be able to get her to talk about her experiences in captivity eventually."

"It's worth a try," Pauline said, looking at Angela.

"I will ask her tonight," Angela agreed, "when I bring up her dinner." She turned to me. "And will you come again, to see how we're doing?"

I hadn't meant to become personally involved in the girl's case; I'd only come to the shelter to find information that might help locate Teresa. But once again, after what I'd seen and heard, I didn't see how I could refuse. "You can count on it," I told her. I didn't know if I, or anyone, had the skills to heal Caterina's psychic injuries. But

I would do what I could to help restore her trust in a world that didn't deserve it.

CHAPTER ELEVEN

Hearing Caterina's story and witnessing her present condition left me in a state of extreme agitation. As usual, when confronted with something utterly outside of my experience, I felt an urgent need to comprehend it — and except for a brief stop at the druggist's to order Caterina's medicines, I spent the entire walk home pondering the psychological makeup of the men in the prostitution trade.

From what Pauline and Detective Petrosino had told me, there were hundreds, perhaps even thousands, of pimps in New York City alone who made a living from selling women's bodies. Since it was unlikely that all of these people could be mentally abnormal, I had to conclude that the average pimp was simply a particularly vile version of the common street tough, hardened by life and funneled into a parasitic existence. But the men and women involved in the more vicious aspects of the white slave trade struck me as another breed altogether. To mercilessly "break in" an abductee, to starve and deprive her into daily submission, to burn her for pleasure, and beat, cut, or kill her if she disobeyed — surely, these were not the actions of a normal mind.

When I was in medical school, we'd read about a new category of criminality receiving scrutiny from social scientists: a type that Richard von Krafft-Ebing called "the morally insane" and that Emil Kraepelin referred to as "the psychopathic personality." It had occurred to me that this might be the type of man or men responsible for the girls' abductions. As soon as I got home, I ran upstairs to my room and pulled out the trunk of old textbooks from under my bed. Selecting tomes by Kraepelin and Havelock Ellis, I carried them to the reading chair by the window and settled in to read.

Moral insanity, the authors explained, was the inability to feel or act in accordance with the normal, moral standards of society. Just as some people were born blind to colors, in the morally insane, the psychic retina was insensitive to the rights and feelings of others. These people typically exhibited acts of cruelty from an early age, usually toward their siblings or whatever unlucky animals crossed their path. Cunning, hypocritical, and delighting in falsehood, they could commit atrocious crimes without the slightest remorse, justifying them as necessary to their egotistic ends or even blaming them on their victims. Interestingly, despite a tendency to laziness, they often ran successful organizations thanks to their ability to terrorize their employees.

I turned and gazed out the window. A successful white slave trader would have to have complete disregard for social and legal norms. He'd need to be a masterful liar and manipulator — capable of both gaining a stranger's trust and breaking a captive's will — and impervious to his victim's distress. He would also have to be able to ruthlessly enforce loyalty and obedience among his subordinates. The psychopathic personality seemed perfectly suited to the job.

But there was another trait that struck me as intrinsic to the white slave trader: a particularly disturbing trait that these books only touched on. Returning to the trunk, I dug out my copy of Krafft-Ebing's *Psychopathia Sexualis* and found it in the table of contents. *Sadism. The Association of Active Cruelty and Violence with Lust.* I knelt on the floor and began to read.

In the normal intercourse of the sexes, the active or aggressive role belongs to the man, while woman remains passive and defensive . . . This aggressive character, however, under pathological conditions may be excessively developed, and express itself in an impulse to subdue absolutely the object of desire, even to destroy it.

While the impulse to inflict small amounts of pain while in the throes of lust, as by biting or scratching, was not in itself abnormal, the author asserted, arising from the intense excitation of the entire psychomotor sphere, in the psychopathic individual "the impulse to cruelty which may accompany the emotion of lust becomes unbounded; and at the same time, owing to defect of moral feeling, all inhibitory ideas are absent or weakened."

In other words, there was nothing to stop the psychopathic personality from acting on his most primitive impulses, or to keep those impulses from becoming abnormally intensified. I sat back on my heels. This was not a man I'd like to meet in a blind alley. And yet, the deeper I dug into Teresa's disappearance, the closer I came to putting myself in such a person's orbit. I put the book down and stood up. I needed a cup of tea.

I was halfway down the stairs to the basement when I heard people talking in the kitchen and stopped short. It took me a moment to recognize Katie's voice, for it sounded unusually breathy and high-pitched. I continued to the door and peeked around the doorframe. Maurice sat next to Katie at the kitchen table with his hand over hers on the tabletop. Katie's cheeks were flushed, and her eyes were lowered to the table. I watched Maurice lean closer and murmur something that made her laugh — then stifled a gasp as he drew her toward him into a kiss.

I pulled back behind the doorframe. *Well done, Katie,* I thought, delighted that she'd found love and companionship after all these years. The sight of her bliss, however, triggered a fresh ripple of discontent over my own predicament. How pathetic it seemed that I couldn't enjoy the gentle intimacy that even gray-haired old Katie had managed to elicit. I must have made a sound, because Katie called out, "Genna? Is that you?"

I walked briskly around the doorframe into the kitchen. "Katie! I didn't realize you were back. I just came down to fix myself a cup of tea."

"Well, have a seat, and I'll put on the kettle," she said, starting up from her chair.

I laid a hand on her shoulder. "You stay put, and I'll put on the kettle. You're not even officially back until tonight."

I brewed the tea, poured three cups, and joined them at the table, sampling slices of ripe peaches that Katie had already laid out, while she regaled us with stories of the county fair she'd gone to with her sister, whose health was apparently much improved.

"It sounds like you had a wonderful time," I said when she was done, wiping peach juice from my chin.

"Oh, I did, but it's good to be home." She blushed again, glancing at the chauffeur. "Maurice was kind enough to pick me up when the train came in. And it's a good thing too, or I never would have managed all those bags of peaches!"

They smiled at each other across the table, causing me a fresh pang of envy. Love seemed to be such a simple thing for other people. Why did it have to be so complicated for Simon and me?

Deciding I had intruded on their budding romance long enough, I headed back up to my bedroom to get changed for the evening's big event. Simon had taken the boys to see a magic show a few weeks before, followed by a visit to the Martinka Brothers workshop, and they'd been working up their own acts ever since. They were putting on a performance at the Wieran clubhouse tonight, and I'd promised Frankie I would be there to act as his "volunteer."

I picked up the scattered textbooks, and was returning them to the trunk, when the Krafft-Ebing fell out of my grasp and splayed open on the floor. As I picked it up, some lines at the bottom of the open page caught my eye:

Among animals, it is always the male who pursues the female with proffers of love. Playful or actual flight of the female is not infrequently observed; and then the relation is like that between the beast of prey and the victim.

I allowed myself an unladylike snort. I could say without reservation that Simon had been woefully underperforming in his duties as beast of prey. I thought again of Katie and Maurice, reenacting the ancient rites of courtship. Wasn't intimacy a natural part of the wooing process? Why was Simon being so obstinate? It wasn't as if I was asking him to drag me into the bushes and consummate our relationship on the spot. Why should he deprive himself — and me — of the thrill and implicit promise of smaller, intimate exchanges?

I read a few more lines, hoping to find an answer.

It affords a man great pleasure to win a woman, to conquer her; and in the arts of love, the modesty of a woman who keeps herself on the defensive until the moment of surrender is an element of great psychological significance and importance.

I felt my cheeks growing warm, as I remembered how I'd practically served myself to Simon on a platter. Perhaps that was where I'd gone wrong. But if a man wasn't looking for an honest and equal partner, what was he looking for? I read on.

As a result of a powerful natural instinct, at a certain age, a man is drawn toward a woman. He loves sensually, and is influenced in his choice by physical beauty.

I frowned down at the words.

Like Kitty, Krafft-Ebing seemed to be saying it was a woman's physical, "sensual" attributes that counted most in attracting a man. I tried to consider this with an open mind. Instead of fighting it, perhaps I should try to take advantage of this apparent weakness in male psychology. Simon was, I knew, a master of self-control. But apparently, I had instinct on my side. If there was a beast of prey lurking within Simon's breast, it might be possible for me to draw it out, if only I used the proper lure.

I crossed to the wardrobe and eyed the contents. Far to the right, among my seldom-worn apparel, was a blouse Aunt Margaret had bought me on one of our trips to Europe. Although she was a conscientious chaperone, my aunt tended to fret over my lack of suitable marriage prospects and had bought me the blouse to help me "develop my flirtatious side." I pulled it out of the wardrobe. Similar to the gypsy bodice Kitty had worn, it had a very low, gathered neckline, with a sheer lace inset that covered but didn't conceal. I had only worn it once, in France. At my aunt's insistence, I had paired it with my highest corset to enhance my bust line and then felt uncomfortable the entire evening because of all the attention I received. Although I'd never been one to flaunt it, I knew I had nothing to be ashamed of in the bosom department, something I presumed Simon remembered from our brief mutual exploration in the hay. If I wanted to rouse his inner beast, perhaps a visual reminder would be just the thing.

But no, I thought, hanging it up again. For one thing, the boys' club was hardly a suitable venue for such a display. More importantly, I just didn't have it in me to play the come-hither seductress. I was what I was, and if that wasn't good enough to make me irresistible to Simon, then so be it. I pulled out a fresh shirtwaist and buttoned it on.

An hour later, I was seated beside the object of my frustration in the second row of seats the boys had set up in the Wieran Club's meeting room — or what tonight was being billed as the "Wieran Palace of Mystery," according to the hand-painted banner hanging between the windows. The rest of the seats were occupied by club members not taking part in the show, plus assorted friends and saloon regulars.

It was the first time I'd seen Simon since his astonishing revelation two days prior, and I was glad the event gave us little opportunity to interact, for I found myself feeling uncharacteristically ill at ease in his presence. I didn't know how I was supposed to behave or what I was supposed to say, now that our cards had been laid on the table. Simon, on the other hand, had not appeared the slightest bit uncomfortable to see me, crossing his arms over his chest when I sat beside him and giving me a self-satisfied smile. Indeed, he was acting far too smug for my liking. I had the feeling he rather enjoyed having me in his thrall, with the power to give or withhold his affections.

The magic had been moving forward in fits and starts for the past ten minutes, some of the acts more successfully than others, many accompanied by jeers and catcalls from the audience. "Can I have a nickel from the audience?" asked the boy currently onstage. Simon dug into his pockets but came up empty.

I tried my own pocket, pulling out a handful of loose change along with a button, a ticket stub, and other bric-a-brac. "Here you are, Tommy," I called out, holding up a nickel with my other hand. From the corner of my eye, I saw Simon stiffen. He was staring at my open palm. Following his gaze, I saw that it was locked onto one of Pauline's condom tins, nestled among the detritus.

"Thanks, Doc," said Tommy, wresting the coin from my suddenly frozen fingers.

Simon's stunned gaze rose to mine. I was

about to explain, horrified by what he must be thinking — when I suddenly thought better of it. Simon had called me a "red-blooded woman." Why not let him wonder what a red-blooded woman might do if the man she wanted denied her all satisfaction of her natural desires? "Oh! I forgot that was in there," I said. I slid the tin back into my pocket and returned my attention to the stage.

I could feel unspoken questions radiating off Simon as Tommy proceeded to make the coin disappear. Without turning my gaze from the performance, I leaned toward him and whispered, "It belongs to a friend."

"What friend?" he sputtered loudly.

Two boys in the row ahead of us turned and, doing their best imitation of the Webster branch librarian, gleefully shushed him.

Simon scowled at them, circling his finger in the air, and they turned back around with a snicker.

Tommy bowed to tepid applause and gave up the stage to Frankie Dolan.

"I have here an empty hat," Frankie squeaked, removing the junkshop find from his head and turning it over to reveal the interior. "See? It's empty. Can I have a volunteer?"

That was my cue. I got up and made my

way to the stage, taking up position beside him.

"Lady, would you be so kind as to look this hat over and make sure I ain't trying to pull a fast one?"

I peered inside the hat and patted the sides, feeling for hidden compartments. "The hat is empty."

"OK." Frankie laid the hat brim-side down on the cloth-covered table in front of him and fluttered his left hand over the top. From where I stood, I could see his other hand reach into a small black bag that was nailed to the inside edge of the table and rummage around inside. As he flipped the hat over with his left hand, he pulled something gray and squirming out of the bag with his right, shoving it into the hat as he turned it over. He held the hat up at chest level. "It ain't empty now!" he squeaked, pulling a rat out of the hat by its tail.

There was a moment's stunned silence from the audience before the rat, clearly unhappy with this state of affairs, curled up and bit the thumb that held it. "Ow!" Frankie howled, releasing the tail. The rat dropped to the table, ran down the side, and scampered across my foot toward the wall.

The room exploded into applause. Frankie

beamed and took a bow while I turned and stared after the rat, watching anxiously for its return.

A few moments later, I was in the kitchen with Frankie, applying a point of caustic to the bite. Simon had followed us out of the meeting room and was leaning against the doorframe with his arms crossed, observing us in stony silence. I ignored him, heartily enjoying his reaction. He might not want to make love to me, but he obviously didn't want anyone else to either. "All right, Frankie, that should do it," I said.

He scampered out to see the rest of the show.

"What friend?" Simon asked again the minute he was gone.

"A new one," I said over my shoulder, returning the stick of caustic to the kit I kept in the cupboard.

A strangled sound escaped him. "Does he have a name?"

I turned to face him. The tips of his ears, I noticed, had turned an interesting shade of pink. "*Her* name is Pauline Goldstein," I told him, deciding he'd stewed long enough.

His jaw sagged open.

"Oh dear," I said. "You didn't think . . ."

He shut his mouth, frowning in chagrin.

"She operates a refuge for former prostitutes that I visited today. I was helping her distribute condoms as part of a campaign against venereal disease."

"Correct me if I'm wrong but isn't handing out condoms a jailable offense?"

"Only if you're caught."

His frown deepened. "So now you're not only visiting with ex-prostitutes, you're thumbing your nose at the law? How far are you planning to take this, Genna?"

I propped my hands on my hips. "You know, you sounded exactly like my father just then."

He bristled. "I suppose every once in a blue moon, even your father gets things right."

I dropped my hands to my sides with a sigh. "I was just trying to find out more information for the police." I told him everything I'd discovered at the Goldstein home, including the fact that Caterina bore the same burn marks as Lucia. "First thing tomorrow, I intend to call Detective Petrosino and pass along what I learned. I'm hopeful that once he hears that other Italian women have been abducted in New York City, quite possibly by the same man, he'll launch a real investigation, and that Teresa, if she has fallen into their hands, will be rescued before she ends up like the others."

"I just don't get why you care so much," Simon said, shaking his head. "You've never even met the woman."

"I know, but I still feel a responsibility for her welfare."

He studied me for a moment, looking genuinely puzzled. "Why is that, do you suppose? You don't think it could have something to do with your brother, do you?"

A reflexive denial rose to my lips but made it no further, as his question set off ripples of recognition inside me. After my brother died while under my care, I'd been beset by new imperatives: to try to make my parents happy again; to take up the space, somehow, that Conrad had been meant to occupy; and perhaps most importantly, to never, ever fail again in my responsibilities toward another. Over the years, I'd come to recognize the psychic forces at play within me and had worked to consciously override them. I thought I'd managed to put my guilt and remorse behind me, and that my past no longer dictated my present. But could it be that this last imperative was driving me still? Was that why I couldn't get Teresa out of my mind?

Perhaps, I conceded. Or perhaps it was a combination of motives. All I knew for certain was that once the awful sense of responsibility had been triggered, the only relief I could find was in taking action. "You may be right," I answered at last. "I hadn't even realized. But that doesn't mean that trying to help Teresa isn't the right thing to do."

He sighed. "There's no way I can make you let this go then."

"I hope I'm wrong about her, Simon. Really, I do. I hope she just got cold feet or met someone more interesting on the boat. But until we find out more, I can't forget about her." I shrugged. "I just can't."

We left it at that, although I sensed he would have liked to say more, and went back in to watch the show.

CHAPTER TWELVE

Detective Petrosino wasn't available when I telephoned the Legion the next morning, but I was able to catch Detective Cassidi on his way out of the office and related what I'd learned about Caterina's abduction. "And she wasn't the only one," I finished. "There were at least two other Italian girls in that same resort who were captured in New York and sent on to Chicago."

"Suggesting that there's a regular distribution channel," Cassidi mused.

"And in all three cases, the men who met the women when they got off the boat were of Italian extraction. Unfortunately, the Chicago authorities weren't able to learn anything more about them."

"I may have come up with something on my end," he surprised me by saying. "I heard about an Italian clothes peddler a while back, over on West Thirty-Fourth street, who specializes in used women's clothing. Plain clothes, you understand, nothing fancy. The kind the owners would normally keep until they were threadbare and past repairing. Thing is, these clothes are always relatively new, which made my informant think the peddler might be fencing stolen goods. You follow?"

"I follow, Detective. Please go on."

"After you told me Teresa Casoria got off the boat at the Thirty-Fourth Street pier, I got to thinking: if somebody was kidnapping women off the boat, maybe they were selling the women's street clothes and other belongings for extra cash somewhere nearby. Yesterday, I tracked the peddler down, and we had a little chat. He told me a man drops off a load of clothes every few weeks, and the peddler pays him on consignment. He swears he doesn't know the man's name or where the clothes come from. The last time he saw him was a week ago.

"I had a look through the peddler's cart and found a valise with the initials TMCF monogrammed across the top. It was in very good condition — practically brand-new. The peddler said it originally contained what looked like a wedding dress, along with a small paint and brush set, a shirtwaist, and some undergarments, all of which had already been sold. I'm wondering if the valise might have belonged to Miss Casoria."

"It must have!" I cried. "The *T, C,* and *F* all match, if she included her married name, which she would have done if she'd purchased the valise for her trousseau. And the wedding dress! What more proof could we ask for?"

"Just to be sure, is there any way of finding out what her middle initial is?"

"Her friend Rosa might know. I can ask her."

"I'd appreciate that. In the meantime, we've got a man shadowing the peddler in case his supplier comes back with more merchandise. Assuming Miss Casoria is still being held somewhere near the pier, he may lead us to her."

At last, we had something tangible to go on. "Thank you, Detective. I know how busy you are. I deeply appreciate your taking this on."

"There's no need to thank me. If someone is preying on innocent women, they deserve to burn in hell, and I'd be pleased to be the one to send them there."

I let out my breath, feeling a great weight lift from my shoulders. Now that the police were on the abductors' trail, I could rest a little easier.

"I also contacted Detective Norton," Cassidi went on, "to see if he'd learned anything more about the girl in the river. He told me he'd located an uncle of hers on Elizabeth Street. The uncle told him that when the girl didn't come to visit as expected, he went to look for her at the address the fiancé had given to her and her family. Nobody there had ever heard of him. The uncle tried the fiancé's supposed place of employment too, with the same result."

"Are you suggesting the fiancé was in on her abduction?"

"Could have been."

I didn't want to believe it, for it struck me as the ultimate betrayal. But from what Pauline had told me, the vultures were everywhere, and false proposals were a frequently used tool of their trade.

"Detective Norton had some other news to report. Apparently, the night watchman at the ferry pier on 116th Street saw a young woman run to the end of the dock and jump into the water the night before they found Lucia Siavo's body. He says he shouted to her, but she didn't answer. He couldn't see much with his lantern, and by the time he grabbed his searchlight and returned to the river, she was gone. He called the harbor police, but they couldn't find anything in the water."

"Was the watchman able to give a description?"

"He could see that she was wearing a coat, which is of course unusual for July, and that she was barefoot. Taking the timing of the tides that night into account, Detective Norton believes there's a high likelihood it was Lucia Siavo."

I chewed the inside of my lip, considering. "But the watchman didn't see anyone in pursuit?"

"No, and the streets are well lit around the pier. He said she came running down 116th Street alone and continued headlong across the dock. She didn't even stop at the end, just went right over."

I closed my eyes, not wanting to imagine the desperation that could prompt such a flight. "Does Detective Norton still believe she jumped out of a carriage while being transported?" I asked, opening them again.

"If that were true," Cassidi observed, "someone would probably have been chasing her. My guess is she was being kept somewhere nearby and managed to escape undetected."

"Which suggests that whoever is abducting these girls has a den in the uptown colony, possibly in addition to a place near the pier."

"Exactly. That being the case, and in light of what we know about the drowned girl's false engagement, I think we have to consider Antonio Fabroni a possible suspect in Miss Casoria's disappearance."

Although it was a logical conclusion, I didn't think the evidence quite added up. "Mr. Fabroni has a successful, legitimate business," I pointed out. "He has no need to stoop to crime, let alone such a vile crime. But more importantly, he told his mother all about his engagement. I can't imagine he would have done so if he was intending to sell Teresa into prostitution."

"I must ask you to give him a wide berth, all the same, until we've had a chance to question him. I would have talked to him already, but there's been another dynamite bombing in Harlem that has required my attention."

"Who was the target this time?"

"A fruit merchant on 105th Street, who'd already paid two times. According to the fire commissioner, there were actually two blasts: the first from the dynamite, the second caused by gas from the lighting fixtures. The combined force blew out the front of the man's home, as well as the windows across the street, and cut a lamp-post on the street in two."

"Was anyone hurt?"

"Unfortunately, the merchant lost his wife in the blast. His despair made him co-operative, and he showed us the threat letter. It was signed with the mark of *Il Ragno.*"

The Spider again. "But you still have no clue as to the Spider's identity?"

"We might have a lead on the bomber. A woman across the street says she saw a policeman enter the building shortly before the blast. We think he may have been tipped off ahead of time."

I sat up straighter. "Really? You think he knows who the bomber is?"

"That's what we're trying to find out. If a precinct officer has managed to acquire an informant, we certainly want to know. Unfortunately, we haven't been able to identify the officer yet. The patrolman assigned to that beat says he was at the other end of his post at the time. But we've put the word out, and we're hoping whoever it was will contact us soon. Meanwhile, we're still sifting through the rubble, looking for clues."

I thanked the detective for the information, promising to get back to him as soon as I'd spoken to Rosa about the initials on the valise, then hung up the phone and hurried out the door. I had a patient at my Madison Avenue office at eleven, and I wanted to get there early to review my notes from our last appointment. As soon as the session was over, I decided, I'd go up to Harlem to see Rosa.

To my surprise, when I locked the door to my office behind me at twelve o'clock, Simon was waiting on the sidewalk with a lunch pail. "Roast veal sandwiches and Saratoga chips," he said, holding up the pail. "Your favorite. I thought we could eat them in the park."

Simon was usually tied up in court on Mondays; it couldn't have been easy for him to clear his schedule to meet me. I wondered if he might be hoping to melt some of the frost that had built up between us over the last few days. "How sweet," I said, my stomach rumbling at the thought of the sandwiches. "But I was just on my way uptown." I filled him in on Detective Cassidi's discoveries.

"I'll come with you then," he said, "and we can eat on the way."

"Are you sure you have the time?"

"I'll make the time."

A few minutes later, we were bouncing uptown in a hansom cab, eating our sandwiches and chips and speculating on Detective Cassidi's discoveries. "It does seem odd that the policeman seen entering the building before the bombing never reported in," I mused. "Do you suppose the bomber might have disguised himself as a policeman, to gain easy access to the building?"

"Police are a pretty close fraternity," Simon said, offering me a chip. "An imposter wouldn't last long on the street."

I considered this as I nibbled on the chip. With all the betrayal I'd been privy to over the last few days, perhaps my next thought wasn't all that surprising. "What if the bomber actually *was* a policeman then?"

"Now there's a devious idea," Simon said, looking at me askance. "But as far as I know, there aren't any Italian policemen working out of the 104th Street Station."

"Maybe he was a non-Italian, just using the Spider name," I countered.

"I don't reckon an Irishman or German would have much luck strong-arming Italians. He'd probably be knifed in his sleep for his trouble."

I supposed it was true that someone ignorant of the language and lacking the clout of a criminal organization behind him wouldn't last very long in the Italian extortion game.

"Can't you just see Patrick," Simon went

on with a chuckle, "trying to work out the Italian words for 'pay or die.' "

I stiffened beside him on the hansom seat, beset by a memory of Patrick directing a boy to pick up an old Italian man's satchel. "Oh, Simon . . ." I gasped.

He swiveled toward me. "What?"

"I saw something the other day, something that didn't make sense at the time . . ." I thought of the beautiful dress Kitty had been wearing at dinner — a present from Patrick, she'd said — and of his plans to set her up in her own shop . . .

"Well, out with it," he urged.

Reluctantly, knowing that Patrick was one of his oldest friends, I told him what I'd seen at the cafe. "What if he was forcing that old man to pay him?" I finished. "What if Patrick's been making extra money by extorting on the side?"

To my surprise, Simon burst out laughing. "If there's one person on the police force whose honesty you don't have to question, it's Patrick."

"Where did he get the money to buy Kitty that dress then?" I asked, a bit miffed by his response.

"He got a promotion, remember? Patrick's always been generous with his jack. He'd be happy to spend whatever he could on Kitty."

"And what do you suppose was in the old man's bag?"

"I don't know. Fabric samples for Kitty? Or maybe the man was just turning over lost property." He frowned at me. "Why don't you ask Patrick, if you're so concerned?"

"I'm sorry," I said, seeing that I'd offended him. "I suppose I was letting my imagination run away with me."

"It wouldn't be the first time," he said with a strained smile. "Although I wish you'd have a little more faith in my friends."

We rode in silence the remainder of the way.

Fortunately, Simon was familiar with the location of the Church of Our Lady of Mount Carmel on 115th Street, which turned out to be on the north side of the street near the corner of Pleasant Avenue. He asked the driver to drop us off in front, then had me wait while he went inside, having cleverly thought to ask the priest if he knew the Velloca family's whereabouts.

"Two buildings down on the north side," he said when he reemerged, saving us the necessity of canvassing the block. Continuing to the building in question, we located the Vellocas' name on the letter box and climbed the steps to the third floor.

The old woman who'd been with Rosa in the park answered my knock. *"Sí?"* she said, regarding us with a frown. A table was set for lunch in the kitchen behind her. A pot simmered on the stove, and the smell of baking bread filled the air.

"Good afternoon," I said, not sure if she remembered me.

Three young boys of varying ages raced across the kitchen area behind her, the last and smallest brandishing a wooden sword.

"Calmati!" the woman cried after them, throwing her hands in the air. She turned back to us, shaking her head.

"I met you and Rosa in Jefferson Park a few days ago," I reminded her. "I'm afraid we weren't properly introduced at the time. My name is Genevieve Summerford, and this is Simon Shaw."

She heard me out with a frown, then turned and called over her shoulder. Peering around her, I saw Rosa on a sofa in the front room with a book in her lap. "Hello, Rosa!" I hailed.

The girl's face lit up. Tossing her book aside, she jumped off the sofa and bounded toward me. "Have you found her?" she asked breathlessly, coming to a stop two feet away. "Have you found Teresa?"

"Not yet, but the police are working on it."

The boys raced back through the kitchen, the oldest one now in possession of the sword. The old woman made a grab for him, but he slipped out of her hands and disappeared into one of the bedrooms off the hallway. She turned wearily back to us. *"Entri, entri,"* she muttered, waving us inside.

"Please, will you join us for lunch?" Rosa asked prettily, gesturing toward the table.

"Thank you, but no," I answered. "We've only come to tell you what we've learned about Teresa."

"Then come, let us sit," she said and led us back into the front room.

This was filled with an abundance of mismatched furniture, much of it showing considerable wear, presumably inflicted by the flat's young male inhabitants. Doilies covered nearly every horizontal surface, while paintings of lush country vistas adorned the walls. Rosa jumped back onto the sagging sofa, tucking her legs beneath her, while Simon and I perched on two rickety chairs.

"I knew you would help," she said, hugging herself. "I've been praying every night, asking God to guide your way."

"I wish we had more to tell you," I said.

"We have confirmed that Teresa arrived in New York as scheduled and that she had left the pier by the time her fiancé came to collect her. Mr. Fabroni told me that he hasn't seen her since and that she hasn't been in touch with her relatives back home."

"So she is still missing?" Rosa asked, her face falling.

"Yes, but the good news is that the police are looking for her. And not just the regular police: the Italian Legion."

She nodded somberly, taking this in. "Where do they think she might be?" she asked, looking from me to Simon.

"It's really too early to say," I hedged, "but they have found a clue: a valise they think might belong to her. It's monogrammed with the initials TMCF."

"Yes, that must be hers!" Counting off on her fingers, she recited, "Teresa Maria Casoria Fabroni!" Her face clouded over. "But . . . how could she have lost her valise? Do you think someone stole it from her?"

"That's what the police are trying to find out. We know the valise contained a wedding dress and other items of women's clothing, as well as a small paint and brush set."

Her hand flew to her mouth. "She told me she was bringing me a birthday present!

She knows how much I love to paint."

I glanced at Simon. It seemed we had all the confirmation we needed.

The front door opened and closed, followed by the sound of voices in the kitchen. A moment later, a middle-aged, clean-shaven man with a sizable paunch entered the room and took in the gathering with a frown. "I'm Rosa's father, Tommaso Velloca," he said. "Is my daughter in some sort of trouble?"

Simon stood. "Not at all, Mr. Velloca." He extended his hand. "I'm Simon Shaw, and this is Dr. Summerford. Your daughter asked us to look into the disappearance of a friend of hers. We're just here to bring her up to date."

"Ah, of course," he said, comprehension erasing the tension from his face. He shook each of our hands in turn. "Rosa has been quite distraught. I understand that she and this girl were friends at school, in Italy. I hope you have brought her good news?"

"The police are on her trail," I answered, "but we have nothing solid to report yet."

"They found her valise, Papa," Rosa told him.

"I see." His brow furrowed as he considered this piece of news. "Rosa, would you tell your brothers it's time for lunch and help Nonna at the table?" The girl got up to do as she was told.

When she was gone, he said in a low voice, "I think this cannot be good, if they have found the girl's valise. What do the police suspect has happened to her?"

"The current thinking is that she may have been abducted," Simon told him bluntly.

Mr. Velloca stiffened. "So now the Black Hand is preying on young women? Have they no honor at all?"

"We're not sure yet that it was a kidnapping for ransom," I said.

"Oh, you can be sure of it, signorina," he retorted, his voice vibrating with emotion. "There is nothing these men would not stoop to! They are nothing but cowardly brigands, and a disgrace to all decent, law-abiding Italians. I can tell you this with some authority, for I myself have been a target of their operations! Here — let me show you." Storming to a desk in the corner, he pulled out a piece of paper from the lower drawer and waved it in the air. "They dared to demand that I pay them two thousand dollars for the privilege of conducting my business! The business that my partner and I built from nothing, out of our own sweat and blood! We had to move to Harlem to escape them. And now they have spread up here like a disease, bombing and killing more innocent people." He thrust the letter into Simon's hand.

Peering over Simon's shoulder, I saw several scrawled lines of handwriting followed by a crudely drawn black hand.

"Find out who is behind these letters," Mr. Velloca urged, "and perhaps you will find Rosa's missing friend!"

Rosa rushed back into the room. "What is it, Papa?"

Her father calmed himself, laying a hand on her shoulder. "It's nothing, Rosa. I'm only concerned for your friend. But now the police are looking for her, eh? So perhaps they will find her soon."

I heard Rosa's grandmother in the kitchen, imploring the boys to eat their lunch.

"It's too salty!" One of the boys whined.

"Gennaro!" shouted Mr. Velloca. "Do as Nonna says!" He sighed, meeting our eyes over Rosa's head. "It has been hard for my children, since my wife died. Rosa especially. If there is anything I can do to help in your search, I trust you will let me know."

"Thank you, Mr. Velloca," I said. "We're hopeful that with the Italian Legion working on her case, she'll be located soon."

"You hear that, Rosa?" he said, ruffling

his daughter's hair. He glanced at the wall clock. "And now, I must get back to work." He gestured to me and Simon. "May I walk you out?"

We started for the door.

"But Papa, your lunch!" Rosa protested, following us into the kitchen.

He nodded at her grandmother. "Add it to my supper pail," he told her. To Rosa, he said, "Now be a good girl, Rosina, and help Nonna with your brothers."

Simon and I bid Rosa good-bye, promising to let her know if there was any more news, and then Mr. Velloca walked us down to the sidewalk, where he shook our hands before heading off toward Pleasant Avenue.

"I just couldn't bring myself to tell him we think white slavers took Teresa," I said, watching him trudge around the corner with an old lard pail at his side.

"Well, we don't really know what's happened to her," Simon reminded me. "Might as well let him believe she was kidnapped for ransom, for now."

"I'm going to have to tell Antonio though," I said with a sigh, "now that we know the valise belonged to Teresa. I suppose this is as good a time as any."

"What if he's in on her disappearance, like Cassidi suggested?"

"I have to say, I'm having trouble believing that he could be. He seemed so distraught when I spoke with him . . . although, of course, I realize he could have been pretending. I can use the news about the valise as an excuse to ask him more questions and gauge his response. Why was he late meeting Teresa's boat, for example? That's something that's always bothered me. You'd think he'd make a point of being there when she arrived. His reaction to the news they've found her valise could also be revealing."

"All right then," he said, turning toward First Avenue. "Let's get this over with."

I smiled up at him. "You mean you're coming with me?"

"Only because it's easier than trying to talk you out of it."

"You're a very wise man, Mr. Shaw," I said, taking his arm in mine.

CHAPTER THIRTEEN

An adolescent boy was seated behind the desk at the Fabroni Painting company office, entering numbers into a ledger. He informed us that Antonio and his crew were on a job in Jefferson Park, painting a shrine that had been erected for the upcoming *festa* of Our Lady of Mount Carmel. We retraced our steps uptown, arriving hot and sticky fifteen minutes later at the 114th Street entrance to the park, where the project in question was in clear view.

Approached through an ornate arch, the shrine rose at least forty feet into the air, supported by columns of elaborately carved wood topped with fanciful, multitiered spires. Two angels with doll-like faces looked down from its apex, smiling at our approach. Some of the columns had already been loosely wrapped in gold cloth, while others still waited to be dressed. Two men on ladders were painting the decorative top of the arch, while three more worked on the shrine's unfinished columns. Antonio stood on the rearmost ladder, his shirtsleeves rolled up and a red bandana tied around his forehead.

We followed a raised walkway under the arch and came to a stop at the bottom of his ladder. I squinted up at him, watching him fill one fluted section of the column's capital with a few quick, efficient strokes before moving on to another. Antonio Fabroni might be selling women on the side, I mused, but his proficiency as a painter was indisputable.

"Mr. Fabroni?" I called up to him.

He looked down, holding his brush in midair. I wasn't sure at first if he recognized me.

"Miss . . . Summerford?" he asked after a moment.

"Yes, and this is my friend, Simon Shaw. I was wondering if we might have a word with you."

He glanced at his loaded brush. "Now?"

"We have some news."

He dropped the brush into a tin pail hooked to the ladder and climbed nimbly down the rungs. "What news?" he asked, pulling off his kerchief and using it to wipe his brow.

The other men had paused in their work and were listening to our exchange. Their silent watchfulness gave me the willies. "Perhaps we could speak in the shade," I suggested and started into the shrine.

It was several degrees cooler inside. A plaster figure of the patron saint rested in a niche in the back, framed by little green, blue, and red oil lamps that I imagined would glow prettily on their shelves when alight. Narrow benches had been built into the sidewalls, presumably to hold candles and other offerings but presently unoccupied.

I sank onto one of the benches under a painting of the Holy Family, glad to be off my feet and out of the sun. Simon sat beside me while Antonio took the bench opposite.

"Your news?" Antonio prompted, scanning our faces.

"After I spoke with you last time," I began, "I met with detectives in the Italian Legion and asked them to look into Teresa's disappearance." I put up a hand to forestall his protest. "I know you asked me not to, but I believed it would be in Teresa's best interests, and I just couldn't see how it would hurt. Yesterday, Detective Cassidi of the Legion found a valise in a peddler's cart, not far from the Thirty-Fourth Street pier, monogrammed with Teresa's initials. It contained a wedding dress and a paint kit that was likely intended as a birthday present for her friend Rosa. The valise was included with a batch of used clothing that was sold to the peddler a week ago. The police suspect the clothes may all have been taken from abducted women."

Antonio raked a hand through his hair, muttering under his breath. I watched him closely, trying to gauge the sincerity of his reaction.

"I'm sorry to bring you such disturbing news," I went on, "but at least now the police have something to go on."

"I told you before, the more people who become involved, the more dangerous it is for Teresa," he hissed, his dark eyes blazing. "You should have listened to me, signorina!"

Simon shifted beside me. "Easy there, now, Mr. Fabroni," he said. "She's only trying to help." Although his attitude was pleasant enough, something in his tone suggested that that could change in an instant.

Antonio stared at him, clenching his fists, while Simon held his gaze.

Finally, Antonio turned to me and tipped his head. "You must excuse me if my concern for Teresa makes me thoughtless. I meant no disrespect. I am sure you have her interests at heart."

"I assure you that I do, Mr. Fabroni," I said. "And to that end, I was wondering if you might clear up a few things for me. I've been trying to put together a timeline of events for the morning Teresa's boat came in. According to the officials at the Barge Office, the boat docked at approximately 10:00 a.m. Do you remember what time it was when you got to the pier?"

"I remember very well. It was a quarter to eleven."

"What was it that detained you, if I may ask?"

"I was held up."

I hesitated, not sure if he was being intentionally unforthcoming or simply hadn't understood my question. "Yes, but what was it, exactly, that held you up?"

The corner of his mouth twisted downward. "Three men, as I was leaving the bank."

I blinked at him in surprise. "You mean to say that you were robbed?"

"Saturday is payday," he answered in a clipped tone. "Since I planned to spend it with Teresa, I had to go to the bank before I met the boat, to get the money to give my foreman to pay the men. We went to the bank early, as soon as it opened, so that I could get to the pier in plenty of time. But as we were leaving, we were attacked by three men hoping to relieve me of my money. We were able to fight them off, but my foreman was hurt, and I had to bring him home. By the time I got to the pier, Teresa was gone."

It was either an outrageous lie, or the perfect alibi. "Did anyone at the bank come to your aid?" I asked.

"The robbers waited until we were around the corner to strike, so nobody saw them. But fortunately, my foreman is a bull, and two men are no match for him."

"Did you report the incident to the police?" Simon asked.

"I saw their faces," he answered with a smirk. "I had no need of the police."

Simon glanced at me, no doubt thinking as I was that with no bank witnesses and no police report, there was no way to corroborate Antonio's story.

"And have you, in fact, been able to locate these men?" I asked after a moment.

His expression darkened. "I'm working on it."

"What about Teresa?" I pressed, remembering how determined he was to solve her disappearance by himself. "Have you been able to learn anything new?"

He leaned back and folded his arms across his chest. "Nothing that I wish to share."

I shook my head. "I'm sorry, Mr. Fabroni, but I simply don't understand why you won't cooperate with the police. If you know something — anything at all — you should tell them!"

"You are wrong," he shot back. "If someone is holding Teresa and becomes aware that the police are in pursuit, he might move her someplace we will never be able to find her."

I tried to read his face. Did he suspect a Black Hand gang? Might he actually have some idea where she was, and be planning his own rescue? "Are you that close to finding her, then?" I asked.

"I pray to God that I am." He stood. "And now, I must get back to work." He lifted his bandana to slide it back over his forehead. As he did so, his rolled shirtsleeve moved further up his arm, revealing the untanned top of his shoulder.

I made a hiccuping noise as I attempted to stifle a gasp.

Eying me curiously, he followed my gaze. The tattoo of a spider stood out clearly against the pale skin of his upper arm. His eyes darted back to me, then to the men on the ladders, then up the walkway, where a group of children and their minders were just entering the park.

He slowly lowered his arms, regarding me with new interest. "Good day, Dr. Summerford," he said coolly, inclining his head. "I trust you have all the answers you came for." With a curt nod to Simon, he left the shrine.

"You're sure it was a spider?" Detective Cassidi asked me an hour later, rubbing his thumb over his lower lip.

"I'm positive."

He looked at Simon, who was seated beside me. "Did you see it?"

"I was on his wrong side. But if Genna says she saw it, I'm sure she did."

Detective Cassidi pulled a sheet of blank paper from a drawer in the desk and slid it toward me. "Could you draw it for me?" he asked, handing me a pencil.

"It was a classic spider silhouette, like you see in picture books," I said, setting pencil to paper. "With two round body parts, like this . . ." I drew two ovals, one on top of the other. "And the legs coming out of the middle."

"How many legs?"

I tried to remember. "Four on each side, I think?" I drew them in, some curving up, some curving down, the right and left sides symmetrical. "Parts of the legs were covered by his shirtsleeve, but I saw more than enough to recognize the whole."

The detective opened a file on his desk and drew out a paper. "So it looked something like this."

It was a letter, handwritten in Italian. At the bottom was an ink version of the same figure I'd just drawn, except that the two oval body parts were connected by a short, thick line, and the legs were attached to the bottom of the top oval. "Exactly like that, actually. I forgot about that little piece in the middle."

"Well, this is interesting," Cassidi said.

"You think Antonio has been setting the dynamite bombs?" I asked.

"It's a possibility I intend to explore."

"What about Teresa? Do you think he was in on her abduction as well?"

"If he is behind the bombings, then the fact that his fiancée has also mysteriously disappeared is the first real evidence we have suggesting a link between a Black Hand extortion gang and the white slave trade. But of course, a suggestion is not a fact. You have spoken to this man face to face, Doctor, as I have not. What do you believe?"

I shook my head. "I just don't know. Part of me wants him to be the abductor, because that would mean we're that much closer to finding Teresa. But another part refuses to believe it. Are you going to arrest him?"

"If we arrested him on the basis of a tattoo alone, we'd be laughed out of court. We need some proof connecting him with illegal activity. Besides, if our experience with other Black Hand operators is any indication, arresting him won't help us find Miss Casoria if he has abducted her. He won't talk, and no one else will come forward with information."

"What can you do then?"

"Have him followed, for starters. Although of course, if he saw you react to the tattoo, as you say, he will expect you to inform us of it. Which means he will likely be on his best behavior from now on and looking for a tail."

"Or he could be innocent," I murmured, gazing down at the spider picture, "and we'd be following the wrong man while the right one got away." I looked back up at the detective. "What if you contacted the Italian authorities for information? If Antonio was a member of the Camorra in Italy, as his tattoo seems to indicate, he might have a history of criminal activity there. He might even have been involved in prostitution. If so, we could be more confident that he's the man we're after."

"I can try," Cassidi said, "but to obtain information from the department of penal records in Italy, we are required to supply the suspect's date and place of birth, along with the name of his parents. We have people who can help us find that information in Italy, but before they can do so, we must at least provide them with the suspect's real name. Unfortunately, it is not uncommon for criminals to take an alias when they come to America. If Fabroni is an assumed name, they will be able to tell us nothing."

We fell silent, pondering this potential obstacle. "What if we provide them with some other identifying information?" I asked after a moment.

"Like what?" Simon asked.

"Like a photograph," I said, turning toward him. "If we sent them a picture of Antonio, they could compare it to their own photographic records to see if there's a match."

Cassidi grunted. "It's a good idea, Doctor, but I doubt that Mr. Fabroni will oblige us by sitting for a photograph."

"He doesn't have to," I said, swiveling

back toward him. "There's a picture of him and his mother on the table in his parlor; I saw it while I was there. If I could smuggle that picture out of his flat, you could send it on to the Italian authorities."

"And just how are you going to do that?" Simon demanded.

"Well, I don't know yet . . . I have to think about it."

"Forget it, Genna," he said. "It's too dangerous."

"I agree," said the detective. "If Fabroni is the Spider behind the bombings, he won't want to hurt you if he doesn't have to, knowing that we will suspect him. But if he catches you trespassing in his flat you might never come back out. You have been most helpful, Dr. Summerford, but I must insist that you let the police handle this from now on."

I resolved to do exactly as Simon and the detective had instructed: leave the rest of the investigation to the professionals and get on with my own life. As it happened, I'd been contacted the previous afternoon by a certain Dr. Heff, who'd been given my name by a colleague of my father on the Mount Pleasant Hospital board. Dr. Heff, who was currently on holiday, had received a frantic telegram over the weekend from the mother of one of his patients and was hoping I might step in during his absence. I'd readily agreed, encouraged that my diligent trolling of family and social connections was beginning to yield results.

Dr. Heff described his patient to me as a "delicate" girl who, being an only child, was the subject of her parents' abundant and undivided concern. Although she'd been a healthy infant and toddler, in recent years she'd begun to suffer recurring episodes of neurasthenia that often left her too weak to bathe or dress. Hydrotherapy, electrotherapy, and hypodermic injection had all proved ineffective. For the past four months, the doctor had been overseeing a modified version of the Weir Mitchell rest cure at the girl's home, restricting her physical activity, removing all mental stimulation, and feeding her a high-protein diet of milk and eggs.

Despite the doctor's biweekly visits, improvement was sporadic. According to the telegram, the girl had suffered yet another attack over the weekend, leaving her so fatigued that she was now unable to get out of bed or even lift her arms. Although Dr. Heff didn't say so, I presumed our mutual acquaintance on the Mount Pleasant Hospital board had recommended me in the belief that mental therapy might have a place in her treatment.

I arrived, energized and alert, for my appointment. My examination of the girl revealed a strong and regular pulse, normal respiration and color, and well-developed muscle with no apparent paralysis, despite her statement that she couldn't lift her arms. During our lengthy interview, it became clear to me that her recurring fatigue had been inspired by her well-meaning but overly fretful parents — aided unintentionally, perhaps, by the solicitous Dr. Heff — who'd managed to make her believe that she was cursed with a weak constitution. Over the years, this belief had apparently developed into a learned helplessness that made the child prone to collapse at the mere hint of a challenge.

It was, I decided, a perfect case for persuasion therapy in its purest form. I did not think, as her governess had implied when she brought me up to the child's room, that her fatigue was merely a ruse to avoid her lessons. I believed, rather, that it was a very real product of autosuggestion — and as such was amenable to opposing suggestions, which I was fully prepared to supply. Following the protocol I'd been taught by Dr. Cassell, I explained to her in the most gentle but insistent way that it was her false beliefs that were making her weak. I told her that fatigue such as hers, though truly experienced, had psychic origins and could be cured simply by replacing her false beliefs with more accurate ones. I asked her to describe the life she'd like to lead if she wasn't so confined and, after she'd described it in glowing detail, told her quite forcefully that it could be hers; that it was within her reach; that it was, in fact, already in her hands. When she admired my hat, I invited her to try it on, then pointed out the ease with which she'd lifted her arms to do so. By the end of our session, she was, as the great persuasion therapist Paul Dubois had described it, "like one under a spell of kindly thought, exhibiting a hopefulness akin to euphoria," and sufficiently improved to get out of bed and walk me to her door. Although I would need to confer with Dr. Heff regarding future sessions, I told the girl's mother I believed a full recovery was possible with continuing mental therapy, suggesting that she allow the child to do more for herself in the meantime and reward her for carrying things through.

Dr. Cassell would have been pleased, I thought as I started up the sidewalk toward home. Although persuasion therapy wasn't a panacea, in the right cases it could yield dramatic results, and I was delighted to have been able to employ it successfully in this one. It was telling of how absorbing I found the work that I hadn't thought once about Teresa during the consultation.

As soon as I returned home, I telephoned Dr. Heff at his hotel to report on the results of my examination. He was glad to hear that the "crisis" had passed and that the patient's mother could rest easy until his return. But when I told him I believed a complete resolution of the girl's symptoms could be achieved with just a month or two of persuasion therapy, he laughed rather unpleasantly and said, "Good heavens, Doctor, at that rate you'll put us all out of business." He rebuffed my offer to meet with her again, telling me he'd be back in the city shortly and that his "usual nurse" would be available then to assist him, saying nothing at all about compensation for my consultation or about recommending me to his colleagues. It was all I could do not to swear at him before I hung up the phone.

My professional aspirations thus temporarily thwarted, and with little else to divert me, Teresa once again took center stage in my mind. Although I was relieved that her fate was no longer in my hands, I'd become too deeply invested in the outcome of the case to be comfortably relegated to the sidelines. I ate some lunch, sorted through the mail, and tried to finish Morton Prince's article on hysterical amnesia in the latest *Journal of Abnormal Psychology* — but my thoughts kept returning unproductively to Detective Cassidi and the investigation. I was considering returning a book to the library, just to break my mind from its restless circling, when the telephone rang. I trotted to the closet and lifted the receiver to my ear, my heart skipping when I heard Simon's voice on the line.

"What are you doing?" he asked.

"Nothing important. Why?"

"It's haircut day."

I smiled into the transmitter. A month ago, Simon had instituted a new rule requiring all club members to keep their hair in decent trim. Most of the older boys, being eager to impress the neighborhood girls and adhering to an athletic aesthetic, were happy to comply, but the younger boys had proved less acquiescent. Simon had accordingly taken it upon himself to round up the miscreants every few weeks and deliver them to the owner of a local stable, who was happy to provide, in exchange for free beer at the saloon, a cut for each lad with the horse shears, followed by a quick rinse in his trough.

"And you need help," I guessed, more than ready to give it if it meant getting away from my thoughts for a while. "How many are in for it this time?"

"Five. But I've got a treat in store for them."

"A treat? You mean something better than a dunk in a horse trough?" I teased. "I can't imagine what that would be."

"Why don't you come with us and find out?"

An hour later, Simon, five shaggy Wieran members, and I were seated on one end of a long wooden bench that lined the wall of the Ellington Barber College. The rest of the bench was occupied by a dozen or so unshaven, unshorn men who looked as though they'd come straight from a Bowery street mission — or more likely, from one of the local lodging houses — each clutching a ticket entitling him to a free cut and/or shave.

Twenty hydraulic barber chairs took up the opposite side of the room, each manned by a student barber in a white duck coat. The students hunched earnestly over their customers, combing and clipping at a frenzied pace, while a sharp-eyed instructor paced behind them, barking out cautions and corrections.

We had been there for some fifteen minutes, watching the students work through different styles on each customer's head — starting with a lofty pompadour, followed by a businessman's fringe, and finishing with a short sailor's cut. As tufts of hair piled up on the floor, patches of scalp began to appear on some of the heads where the shears had gone too close. One customer howled as a comb caught on a tangled knot; another swore as the scissors stabbed his ear.

I glanced at the boys, who were watching the proceedings with expressions of horror. "This is your treat?" I murmured to Simon.

"It's better than the horse shears," he said with a frown, although even he looked doubtful.

One of the students ejected a customer from his chair and called, "Next!"

Frankie Dolan was next in line.

"You're up, Frankie," Simon said.

Frankie shook his head. "I ain't gettin' in one of those chairs."

"Come on, now," Simon cajoled. "It's just a haircut. There's nothing to be afraid of."

Frankie eyed him reproachfully. "If you

think it's such a good idea, why don't you let 'em take a whack at you?"

"Well, I would, Frankie, but I'm not in need of a haircut at the moment."

"How about a shave then?" I suggested.

Simon looked at me askance.

"Since it's such a treat," I added innocently.

"Next!" the student called more loudly.

The Wieran boys were all watching Simon expectantly.

"Fine," he said, pushing up from the bench. He strolled over to the vacant chair. "What's your name?" he asked the student, who looked only a few years older than Frankie.

"Albert," the student told him, his voice breaking on the first syllable.

"Well, give me a shave, Albert, and make it a close one," Simon said loudly, glancing back at the boys. He settled into the chair.

"Yessir!" Albert scurried to the sink, where he soaked a towel under a stream of steaming water. Carrying the towel gingerly back by the fingertips, he dropped it onto Simon's upturned face. I heard a muffled oath and saw Simon's hands tighten on the armrests. Albert glanced nervously at the instructor, who was occupied further down the line.

Taking a razor from his tool kit, Albert ran its edge up and down a horsehide strop that was attached to the chair, flipping it awkwardly from side to side and dropping it once in the process. Loading a brush with shaving soap, he removed the towel and applied the lather to Simon's red face, managing to fill both nostrils as he did so. As Simon snorted in distress, he set the edge of the razor against his cheek, pulled the skin taut, and scraped the blade across the stubble, his tongue protruding in concentration. I saw Simon flinch as the blade dug in.

"Sorry," Albert croaked, adjusting his angle.

He had just finished both of Simon's cheeks, and was starting on his chin, when the instructor came to a halt behind him and barked, "*Up* under the lip, Mr. Mayers, not down!"

"But I ain't learned up yet!" Albert protested.

"Hmm. Well, carry on then," the instructor said, "but go easy on him." He moved on down the line.

Simon was bleeding in several places by the time Albert slapped some Bay Rum on his broken skin and pronounced him finished. He staggered back to the bench, his eyes moist and his cheeks red, and gave us all a limp smile. "Well, that wasn't so bad," he said. "Who's next?"

CHAPTER FOURTEEN

I was indulging in a long soak in the bathtub two hours later, still smiling at the thought of the barber college outing, when the telephone rang downstairs. Thinking it might be Simon again, I jumped out of the tub and hurried downstairs in my robe and slippers, tamping my wet hair with a towel. "This is Genevieve," I answered breathlessly.

"Dr. Summerford, it's Pauline Goldstein," a familiar voice shouted on the other end. "Can you hear me?"

I moved the receiver away from my ear. People who used telephones infrequently, I'd found, tended to distrust the ability of the wires to carry their voices the full distance. "Good evening, Miss Goldstein. I can hear you very well."

"It's Pauline, remember?" she shouted. "Anyway, listen, I need your help. Dr. Burnham still hasn't shown up, and one of my girls is sick."

I frowned at the telephone box. Although I was happy to advise Pauline concerning Caterina's psychological care, I wasn't prepared to act as general physician for her girls. "I'm sorry, Pauline, but as I told you, my practice is in psychotherapy, not general medicine. Isn't there someone else you can call?"

"I've tried, but no one else can come out tonight, and it can't wait. I think she may have polio."

I pulled the towel off my head. "What makes you think that?"

"She stumbled on her way upstairs after dinner tonight and could hardly get up again. And she told me she's been feeling pins and needles in her feet and legs for days."

"Has she had any fever or headache?"

"No, I don't think so . . . but the visiting nurses were on our block just a few days ago, looking for new polio cases, and they took two girls from the tenement next door. Can you please come? If she does have it, I'll need to move her somewhere else before she can give it to the others."

Although the exact method of polio transmission hadn't been identified, we did know that it spread from person to person and was therefore apt to break out wherever people were in close proximity. While in the past, the vast majority of polio victims had been children, for some unknown reason, more and more young adults had been contracting the illness in recent years, most often in the paralytic form. She was right to be concerned.

"I'm on my way," I told her and hung up the phone.

It was dark outside by the time I arrived at the shelter. Angela was waiting for me in the entry, her face creased with worry. "Come on, Doc, this way." She led me up to the second floor and three doors down the hall to the sickroom. Sarah, the Austrian girl who'd been bonded to the lecherous jeweler, was lying in the bed inside. Pauline was sitting in a chair beside her, holding a thermometer under the girl's arm.

Pauline looked up as I entered. She withdrew the thermometer from Sarah's armpit and squinted at it in the light from the bedside lamp. "No fever," she told me, pushing back her chair so I could get by.

I laid my hand on the girl's forehead, confirming what Pauline had told me. "Hello, Sarah. I understand you're having trouble walking?"

"I can't seem to keep my balance," she

said, her voice slurring. "It's the strangest thing."

Her breath, I noticed, had a faintly metallic smell. "Pauline said you've been feeling pins and needles in your feet and legs."

She swallowed. "In my hands too." She lifted one of her hands a few inches before dropping it listlessly back on the bed.

I glanced at the upturned palm. Dark spots were scattered all across it. "What are those marks?"

"Those are left over from the rash she had when she first came here," Pauline answered.

I remembered Pauline had told me Sarah was infected with syphilis by the time she escaped from her handler. The rash must have been a symptom of the secondary stage of the disease. "Did Dr. Burnham treat your rash?" I asked the girl.

She nodded, looking toward the plank-topped barrel beside her bed.

I followed her gaze. The plank held a pitcher of water, a glass, and a small amber bottle. I lifted the bottle and read the label. *100 Tablets, Calomel, 1 grain.* "This is what he gave you for it?"

She nodded again.

"What dose did he prescribe?"

"Two grains, three times a day."

"And how long have you been taking it?"

"Three or four months. Ever since I came here. Why?"

I put the bottle down. "That's a long time to be taking mercurous chloride at such a high dose."

She swallowed again.

"Do you find you're salivating more than usual?"

"Why yes, I do."

"I'm guessing your bowels have been loose as well."

She frowned. "Dr. Burnham said not to worry about that."

"What about your gums? Are they sore?"

She nodded, her frown deepening. "Yes — and I can feel my teeth move if I push against them with my tongue."

I suppressed a sigh. "I suppose Dr. Burnham told you not to worry about that either."

"I haven't had a chance to tell him. He hasn't been here for ages." Her pale eyes peered into mine. "Do you think the medicine is making me sick?"

"Let me examine you first, and then I'll tell you what I think."

Several minutes later, I lowered my medical bag to the floor. "Well, you don't have polio. But I'm afraid you are showing clear symptoms of mercury poisoning. We're going to have to take you off the tablets for a few weeks to give your body a rest and then start you on something else." There was, of course, no "safe" treatment for syphilis, but a combination of mercury and sodium iodide would at least be less muscularly debilitating and less irritating to her gums.

"Will I be all right, then?"

I felt my chest constrict as I gazed into her upturned face. The truth was she would never be all right. If she stopped taking the mercury completely, the syphilis would develop unimpeded; but if she kept taking it, even in a more tolerable form, it would most likely lead to kidney failure and death eventually. Laying my hand lightly against her cheek, I gave her the only true piece of encouragement I could. "You should start feeling a little better in a week or two."

After I'd given her some Veronal to help her sleep, Angela tucked her in and turned out the light, and we retreated into the hallway.

"Thank you, Doctor," Pauline said when we were outside.

"Please, don't thank me," I said, sickened by the fact there was so little I could do.

She studied my face with a frown. "You need some cheering up, I think. You must come to the kitchen with us and try some of Angela's cake."

"Thank you, but I really should be getting home . . ."

She wrapped her hand around my arm and turned me toward the stairs. "Now you listen to Nurse Pauline. For sickness of the heart, Angela's cake is the best medicine there is. Besides, we have some news for you."

I didn't resist any further, for seeing Sarah's condition had indeed left me dispirited, and I found the company of these two women strangely comforting.

Back in the kitchen, Angela set out plates of cake and forks while Pauline poured steaming coffee into mismatched cups and I found some napkins in the cupboard. "You said you have news?" I prompted as we all sat down to eat.

"Cake first," Pauline said, lifting a forkful to her mouth.

Angela's cake turned out to be an inspired amalgam of ladyfingers, chocolate cream, nuts, jam, and lord knew what other precious ingredients that must, I thought as I crammed a second bite into my mouth, have set the shelter's budget back a pretty penny. Pauline was right; this was medicine at its finest. For a moment, I forgot all about

Sarah and Teresa and just concentrated on the sensory experience. Pauline and Angela appeared to be equally absorbed, and we ate in silence for several minutes, emitting only the occasional groan of satisfaction.

After washing down the last of my cake with several swallows of the excellent coffee, I asked them how Caterina was faring.

"That's what I wanted to tell you," Pauline said. "Her eye is already much improved from the drops you sent. She's practicing stitch work now too, in her room — and Angela even got her to go out to the water closet!"

I swiveled toward Angela. "How did you manage that?"

"I told her I thought Isabella would be happier if we took her to the sink to wash her dress. After all," she added with a wink, "no lady likes to wear dirty clothes."

"And that worked?" I asked, delighted — and a little surprised — to hear that my idea of using the doll to communicate had actually born fruit.

She nodded happily. "She has started telling me about her life in Naples too. About gathering hazelnut and olive branches for the oven, and collecting snails after the rain."

I shook my head in amazement. "You're a

miracle worker."

"Maybe I'll learn to be a doctor of psychology like you, eh?" she asked with a grin.

"The profession would be better for it," I readily replied.

"But there's more," Pauline said. "Go on, Angela, tell her the rest."

"Well," Angela said, pouring me more coffee, "the first time I suggested we go to the water closet, the night after you met with her, she refused. I didn't press her, but the next morning, I brought up some borax to clean the doll's dress with and asked again. Caterina became agitated then, saying she couldn't take the doll out of the room because 'Un-Occhio' might see her. Although she didn't say so, I guessed from the way she spoke the name that this Un-Occhio was one of the men who had hurt her."

"Un-Occhio," I repeated with a frown. "That means 'One-Eye,' doesn't it?"

She nodded. "When I tried to reassure her by telling her that the bad men were far away in Chicago, she said that no, Un-Occhio was here, in New York. Only after I convinced her that no bad men were allowed inside the shelter, and that Pauline and I would make sure that Isabella was safe, would she agree to take her out."

I looked from Angela to Pauline in excitement. "Do you think Un-Occhio is the man who abducted Caterina in New York?"

"He must have been at least one of the men involved," Pauline answered.

So now we had a name, or at least a description, that might lead us to the New York ring. My mind raced about, trying to make sense of this new information as Angela refilled our cups. Antonio had two functioning eyes, so he couldn't have been the Un-Occhio Caterina was referring to. But of course, he could still be part of a gang in which someone else fit that description. Or there could be more than one group of Italians in New York preying on their countrywomen. Either way, if the man wore an eye patch, he should be relatively easy to identify . . .

"What about your missing Italian girl?" Pauline asked me. "Have you learned anything new?"

They listened with interest while I related the events of the past two days.

"So you need the picture of the fiancé to find out if he has a history of dealing in women," Pauline summed up when I was done.

"Especially now that you've told me about this Un-Occhio," I confirmed. "I'd hate to think the police were concentrating their attention on the wrong man. But I can't think of a way to get the photograph out of his flat."

She thought for a moment. "What if you went to his flat while he was gone, pretending to be a visiting nurse searching for cases of polio?"

I gazed at her in admiration. "That's a brilliant idea! But unfortunately, his mother saw me when I was there last time. She'd be sure to remember me."

She shrugged. "Someone else could do it then."

"I can't very well ask someone to enter a home under false pretenses and make off with stolen property," I said, taking another sip of my coffee.

"I'll go."

I stared at her over my coffee cup. She appeared to be serious. "No."

"Why not? I already have the nurse's cap. I even have the brochures that the real nurses gave me when they were making their rounds."

I put down my cup. "It wouldn't work. From what I've seen of Mrs. Fabroni, she'd slam the door right in your face."

"I'll tell her the Department of Health sent me and that she has to let me in," she countered.

I shook my head. "It's too dangerous."

"But not too dangerous for you?"

"That's different. I'm already involved. You're not, and you have no reason to be."

Her amber eyes narrowed. "Now that, Doctor, you are wrong about."

I saw the kaleidoscope of emotions play across her face, and waited for her to say more.

"You asked me why I opened this shelter," she said finally. "So now I will tell you."

Angela slid a hand across the table and laid it over hers. Pauline's face softened for a moment as she glanced at her, then hardened again. "I opened it because of my sister," she continued. "Rebecca was two years older than me, and the oldest girl in our family. Being a girl, she was expected to help support the family while my brothers received their education. She worked in a garment factory from the time she was eight, and brought home piecework as well, besides helping with the cleaning and cooking. I also worked in the factory, of course, but my parents expected more of Rebecca. She was never allowed a moment to herself."

I nodded, seeing the pain in her eyes and dreading what was to come.

"When my sister was just fourteen, a man

offered to buy her an ice-cream soda after work. She'd never had one before." She shook her head in wonder. "Such a simple thing, an ice-cream soda! She told me that night when she came home that it was the best thing she'd ever tasted. The next day, she was gone. We discovered later she was working in a brothel on Hester Street."

"You mean the man abducted her?"

"No." Her mouth tightened. "She chose to work for him."

"She chose to be a prostitute?"

I jumped as her palm struck the table. "Is it so hard to understand that she might succumb? Our men pride themselves on the purity of their women, but they fail to consider just how we are to maintain this purity when so much is expected of us, and so little given! Should a girl be blamed for wanting some small comfort for herself in life? Even a stone yearns to feel the rain, at times!"

Drawing a calming breath, she continued, "When my parents found out what she'd done, they cast her off as if she were dead, slashing their clothes and sitting out seven days of mourning." She stared into the distance, as if seeing it all again in her mind's eye. "They forbade me to see or speak to her, and I obeyed, angry at her for leaving us and for bringing disgrace on our family. She wrote to me, but . . ." She drew another, sharper breath. "I didn't reply. Two years later, in the winter, my sister was found dead in a rear yard, along with her frozen newborn baby." Her eyes met mine. "I didn't help my sister, to my eternal shame. But there are other girls in trouble, and I have sworn to do whatever I can, whenever I can, to help them. So don't tell me I have no reason."

"Oh, Pauline. I'm so sorry." I shook my head. "But I still can't let you do it. I'd never forgive myself if you were hurt."

She leaned toward me across the table. "It isn't up to you." Sitting back, she added, "Besides, if you want this done right, you need somebody capable, and I'm the most capable person I know."

Gazing at the woman in front of me, with her formidable intelligence, energy, and conviction, I found myself actually contemplating her offer. "But you'd need to convince his mother of your purpose for coming," I pointed out, "and you don't even speak Italian . . ."

"But I do," Angela offered. She smiled at Pauline, who smiled back.

"Oh no, now that's not fair," I protested.

"I don't stand a chance against the two of you!"

"Just tell us where he lives," Pauline said, crossing her arms, "and we'll take care of the rest."

Chapter Fifteen

I was a bundle of nerves the next morning as I waited to hear from Pauline and Angela, who'd promised to call me the minute they got back from the Fabronis'. Although I could, in fact, think of no one more capable of getting the job done, I already regretted involving them. I'd thought about calling the whole thing off, but suspected that once Pauline had been set in motion, there could be no stopping her. At least she'd agreed to abandon the mission if Antonio's van was at the curb when they arrived. I was terrified that he'd see through their disguise and suspect them of an ulterior motive.

I passed the time by helping put up several jars of peach preserves, one of my father's favorite winter indulgences. It had been years since I last helped with the preserving, and Katie had to constantly refresh my memory on the finer points of temperature and paraffin seals, making me more of a hindrance than a help, but I appreciated the distraction. I made sure to leave the kitchen and stairwell doors open so that I could hear the telephone upstairs, just in case Pauline called earlier than expected, and ran to the steps more than once thinking I'd heard it ring.

It wasn't until eleven o'clock, however, when the jars had been cooling in the pantry for nearly an hour and I was pacing a hole in the sitting room carpet, that the call finally came. I lunged toward the closet and grabbed the receiver. "Yes?"

"You didn't tell me he was such a handsome scoundrel," Pauline said on the other end.

I let out the breath I'd been holding all morning. "You got it?"

"I'm looking at it as we speak."

Antonio's van had been gone when they arrived, she told me, and they'd found Mrs. Fabroni alone at home. As I'd predicted, she hadn't been eager to let them in, but had acceded when Pauline flashed a makeshift badge. The photograph was exactly where I'd told them it would be, and as Angela took Mrs. Fabroni by the arm and guided her into the parlor, chattering all the while, Pauline followed behind and simply lifted it into her bag.

I told her I'd come retrieve it immediately. I was leaving the house a few minutes later, shutting the front door behind me, when I saw Simon walking up the street with a satchel over his shoulder.

He smiled in greeting. "Katie called and offered to give me some jam for the boys."

"Aren't you supposed to be at the shape-up?" I asked. Usually on Wednesdays, Simon took the unemployed male residents of his district down to the South Street docks, in the hope the hiring bosses would select them from the scores of other long-shoremen who assembled there, looking for work. As he was not the only person peddling Tammany influence at these events, however, and as his men were not always the most impressive of physical specimens, he usually had a few left over from the morning selection. Often, he remained at the docks through the early afternoon on the chance that another tramp steamer or coastwise boat might arrive and trigger a second round of hiring.

"I only had one man left after the morning pick, and I got him a job as a watchman on a coal barge." He looked me quizzically up and down. "Where are you off to?"

Somewhat reluctantly, I told him about the successful mission, unsure how he would react. "I'm on my way to pick up the picture now," I finished, "to deliver to Detective Cassidi."

"I thought we agreed you were going to let the police handle things from now on."

"I was. That is, I am. But Pauline insisted on doing this one thing."

His shoulders rose with a deep inhale, but perhaps afraid of being compared to my father again, he said only, "I'll go with you then. Just let me get the jam first. The boys'll tar and feather me if I come back without it."

We arrived at the Goldstein home some twenty minutes later to find Pauline waiting in the entry. I rushed toward her and gave her a hug. "Thank you! For the picture, and for not getting caught. I never would have forgiven myself."

"Psh," she said, pulling awkwardly from my embrace. "I owed you, for Sarah." She lifted the photograph from her bag and handed it to me.

Simon stepped up behind me, peering at it over my shoulder. "He wasn't much more than a kid when they took that."

"This is Simon Shaw," I told Pauline. "He's a Tammany captain in Yorkville. He's been helping me look into Teresa's disappearance."

The two nodded, sizing each other up.

I returned my attention to the photograph, which I'd only glimpsed before. A girl who strongly resembled Antonio, and who I guessed was his sister, stood in the center, wearing a white dress and veil and smiling shyly at the camera. Mrs. Fabroni stood to one side of her and Antonio to the other. They in turn were flanked by two men who looked about the same age as Mrs. Fabroni, dressed in formal clothing.

"Angela says it's a confirmation picture," Pauline told us.

"What happens when they realize it's missing?" Simon asked.

Pauline and I looked at each other.

"Did you leave anything at the flat that could identify you?" I asked her.

"Nothing but the brochures, and they're handing those out all over the city. Don't worry. We left no trail."

Angela came into the entry, wiping her hands on her apron. "Hey, Doc! We did good, huh?"

"More than good. Thank you so much for your help." I introduced her to Simon, and the two shook hands.

"So now you have what you need, yes?" Angela asked me. "To find your girl and put this man in jail?"

"It's a start."

"It will take time, though, to hear back from Italy?"

This was unfortunately true. Even with the faster mail boats to Europe, it would be several days before the authorities could receive the photograph and respond via telegraph. "The police have put a tail on him in the meantime," I told her. "If he's got Teresa holed up somewhere, he may lead them to her."

"Why doesn't Mr. Shaw try looking for her in the disorderly resorts near Italian Harlem?" Pauline asked coolly. "In case her abductor has already sold her to one, or is holding her there."

I frowned at her, puzzled by her tone. "I wish that were possible. But I don't suppose we're going to find a list of suspected disorderly resorts at the public library."

"Mr. Shaw?" Pauline said. "Maybe you would know where to find such a list."

"Why on earth would he know?" I asked.

"He's a Tammany man, isn't he?"

They regarded each other in stony silence.

I looked from her to Simon. "I'm not sure why —"

Simon glanced at me. "Some assembly leaders allow disorderly resorts in their districts," he explained, "in return for a cut of the protection money. But there's no such thing as a master list, as far as I know. And even if there was, I wouldn't be privy to it."

"Maybe you've got friends in the police who could tell you," Pauline said.

"Look, Miss Goldstein," he said, "I don't have a hand in the disorderly till, if that's what you're suggesting."

"Pauline!" I protested. "I can assure you, Simon would never take advantage of women in such a way."

She pursed her lips, her amber eyes appraising him. "I'm glad to hear it," she said finally.

A few moments later, Simon and I were back out on the sidewalk on our way to the Italian Legion's office, the precious photograph in my bag.

"So that's Pauline," Simon mused.

"Mmm."

"She doesn't pull any punches, does she?"

I made no reply.

"Somethin' troubling you?" he asked when I'd said nothing more for several moments.

I stopped and faced him. "What Pauline said in there . . ." I shook my head. "I was under the impression that Tammany had changed its ways." The election of 1901 had been a turning point for the city, when citizens fed up with Tammany's profitable connections with criminal enterprise in general, and prostitution in particular, had voted a reform candidate into the mayor's office. I wasn't so naive as to believe that corruption would ever disappear entirely, but from what Pauline had said, it sounded as though the current ties between Tammany and prostitution were still far more extensive than I'd realized.

"It's a big organization, Genna," he said with a sigh. "Different members have different ways of doing things. I can only tell you that it's not as bad as it used to be."

I frowned at him, unable to understand why it was allowed to persist at all. "How can you work for an organization that supports the victimization of women?"

"It doesn't sit well with me."

"And yet you continue to work for them."

"If I were to quit, someone worse might take my place. Besides, Rush doesn't allow profiting from prostitution in his assembly district," he said, referring to the Tammany man he reported to, "and even if he did, I would never take a nickel of that sort of graft, you must know that."

I did know that, and so didn't press him further. But my hazy notions of his employer's essential magnanimity had been abruptly dispelled. How could you applaud the Tammany organization for giving free coal to a needy family with one hand when, with the other, it took a cut from the ruin of that family's daughter? Clearly, the intricate web of interactions I'd perceived as benign had a far more sinister side.

Detective Petrosino was once again out on a case when we arrived at the Legion's office, but Detective Cassidi was eating lunch at his desk and greeted us warmly. Or more accurately, he greeted me warmly, jumping up from his desk to pull a chair around for me before returning to his seat, leaving Simon to fend for himself.

"You remember Simon Shaw," I said as Simon dragged a chair over from one of the other desks.

"Yes, of course. Mr. Shaw," he said with a brief nod in Simon's direction. He turned back to me, his eyes aglow. "I have news."

"What is it?" I asked.

"Yesterday, I sent a telegram to my contact in Italy, asking for information on the Fabroni family. This morning, I heard back from him."

"And?" I asked, leaning toward him.

"There is no Italian ex-convict or wanted criminal by the name of Antonio Fabroni," he said gravely.

"Oh," I said, sitting back again.

Lifting his forefinger in the air, he added with a mischievous grin, "Fabroni *is,* however, the maiden name of the wife of Micello Gagliere, a former capo in Naples and one of the twelve chiefs who ran the Camorra before the crackdown of 1901."

I gasped. "Are you telling me that Antonio's mother was married to a Camorrist?"

"So it appears. Serafina Fabroni married Micello Gagliere in 1882. Her husband was imprisoned in 1901 at the age of forty-six, convicted on counts of prostitution, counterfeiting, and extortion. She had one daughter with him, who died at the age of twelve, and a son, named Antonio, who was eighteen at the time of his father's arrest. Gagliere's organization remained active during his imprisonment, which caused the police to suspect he was conveying orders to his subordinates through his son. They arrested the son on suspicion but were never able to build a case against him."

I did a quick calculation: if Antonio Gagliere was eighteen in 1901, he would be twenty-four now — right about the same age as Antonio Fabroni.

"Micello Gagliere was stabbed to death on the day he was released from prison, in

November of 1904," Cassidi continued. "His murderer was never apprehended. His wife and son disappeared from Italy shortly thereafter, although there is no official record of their departure."

"It all fits!" I exclaimed. "Antonio is the right age, and if he ran the business while his father was in prison, he would have learned the ins and outs of the prostitution trade and be prepared to take it up here. He must have used a false passport to leave the country."

"You can make it fit; but you can't be sure you're right," Simon interjected. "There are plenty of twenty-four-year-old men in the world, and probably more than one named Antonio Fabroni."

"Then let's make sure," I said. I pulled the photograph out of my bag and slid it over the desk to Cassidi.

The detective's eyes widened. "How did you get this?" he asked, then immediately put up a hand to silence me. "No, don't tell me, or I might have to arrest you." He flashed me a smile. "Either that, or make you an honorary member of the Legion."

I blushed at the compliment and heard Simon mutter under his breath.

Cassidi looked back at the photograph. "I'll send this to the Italian authorities on the next mail boat. We know Antonio Gagliere was arrested at least once, so there should be a picture of him in their police files."

"I've received some interesting information as well," I told the detective. "I'm not sure how it fits in, but the Italian girl who was rescued in Chicago named one of the men who abducted her here in New York. She called him 'One-Eye.' If Antonio is, in fact, the ring leader, then perhaps this One-Eye is working for him." I glanced at the rogues' gallery on the back wall, looking for anyone who might fit the description.

Cassidi frowned. "The only one-eyed Italian criminal I know of is a gambler, not a procurer. But I'll ask the other detectives if anyone comes to mind. I will ask the Italian authorities, as well, if they've heard of such a man. Perhaps Fabroni had a one-eyed confederate in Italy who traveled here with him."

We smiled happily at each other.

Simon sat back, stretching his legs out in front of him. "You still need to find where he's put the girl," he said, introducing a sour note into our celebratory spirit.

Cassidi turned to him. "As Dr. Summerford is aware, we already have one man watching the peddler we found with Miss

Casoria's valise, and another is following Mr. Fabroni. But I agree, more is needed." He turned back to me. "Which is why," he added, "I have asked for more men to help me carry out the next phase of my investigation."

I clapped my hands together. "What are you planning to do?"

"The next passenger steamer from Italy is scheduled to arrive here tomorrow afternoon. I intend to post detectives at Ellis Island, the Barge Office, and the Thirty-Fourth Street pier to keep an eye on all disembarking passengers. If anyone attempts to take a single girl in hand, whether she comes in steerage or in cabin class, we'll be ready for him. The men will be instructed not to apprehend any suspects but to follow them to their destination, where, if we are lucky, we might find other women already in captivity, including Miss Casoria."

"Oh, that's a wonderful idea!" I cried, feeling a surge of gratitude for this spry little detective who, unlike so many people in power in the city, seemed to have no other agenda but to see that justice was done, and had treated my concerns with respect from the first.

"I only wish we could spare more men," he added, "but unfortunately, most of them are already tied up with other cases."

"I could help," I said. "I could go to the Thirty-Fourth Street pier and be another pair of eyes."

"No, you couldn't," Simon snapped. "Fabroni has already seen you. As have the men from his painting crew. They could all be in on this."

"I could keep a veil over my face and wear simple clothes," I suggested, reluctant to give up a chance to help with Teresa's rescue.

"I've got a better idea," Simon said.

"What?" I asked.

"*I'll* go to the pier."

"But Antonio and his men have seen you too!" I protested.

"That's why I'll watch from the hay exchange across the street," he said smugly. "No one will see me, but I'll have a full view of anyone who gets in or out of any vehicle at the foot of the pier."

It was a perfect solution. "And I'll watch with you," I said. "That way, we'll both be safe."

"All right," Cassidi said before Simon had a chance to object. "You two will watch from inside the hay exchange and use the telephone there to call headquarters if you see anything suspicious. But that must be the extent of your involvement. Are we all agreed?"

"Agreed!" I said, jumping to my feet before Simon could argue otherwise.

CHAPTER SIXTEEN

According to the Italian line's Whitehall Street office, the boat from Naples was expected to arrive at the pier at approximately three o'clock. I arrived at the hay exchange an hour beforehand, to be sure I was in place before any would-be abductors arrived. Simon had wanted to come fetch me, but as he had a mandatory noon meeting at Tammany headquarters on Fourteenth Street, and I was afraid we'd be late if he came all the way back uptown, we agreed to meet at the exchange instead.

This, I discovered, was a three-story brick structure that took up the entire block between Thirty-Third and Thirty-Fourth Streets. Entering through the storage shed end at Twelfth Avenue, I found the place packed with buyers poking and sniffing huge stacks of sweet-scented hay. The men moved down the aisles with an air of practiced efficiency, scratching notes on their order pads as they checked for signs of mold or beetles, taking no notice of me as I crossed to the northwest corner and took up position by the plate-glass window.

From here, I could easily see the Italian line pier, diagonally across the street. Although it was presently unoccupied, the piers on either side of it were bustling with activity, their slips filled with railroad cars that had been floated over from New Jersey. Husky longshoremen with ropes and hand trucks swarmed through the pier sheds and over the floats, transferring inbound cargo onto wagons and moving outbound freight into the empty cars. The street that ran along the waterfront was equally congested: to my left, a caravan of wagons carried hay from the New York Central pier to hoists outside the storage shed, while to my right, a locomotive rolled out of the West Shore yard, cutting a swath through the jumble of express trucks and butcher carts that were jockeying for space on the avenue. It was a scene of barely organized chaos, and I was glad I'd offered my services as an extra pair of eyes. Our work would be cut out for us once the boat arrived.

I gazed out at the river, imagining the pretty young Italian girl who might be steaming even now into the harbor, unaware of the trap that had been laid for her. But had a trap in fact been laid? As the moments ticked by, I found myself alternating between optimism that the detectives would break the case, and anxiety that the day's exercise would come to naught and we'd be no closer to finding Teresa than before.

I longed for Simon's reassuring presence. Not even the mesmerizing choreography of crane operators, hatch tenders, and sack turners at work on the pier could keep me from glancing at the exchange's door every few minutes, hoping to see his familiar figure. When I finally heard footsteps moving up behind me some twenty minutes later, I pivoted around with a smile.

It was not Simon coming toward me, however, but Patrick Branagan, dressed in police uniform.

"Patrick! What are you doing here?"

"Simon's meeting went on longer than expected," he said, unstrapping his helmet to wipe the perspiration from his forehead. "He can't leave until they take the vote, so he called the station house and asked me to wait with you until he gets here."

"Oh, I see," I said, trying to hide my disappointment, wishing Simon hadn't felt the need to send someone just to stand with me by the window. "It was good of you to come. But I'm sorry you were interrupted at work on my account."

"I'm on the reserve shift," he said with a grin. "The only thing he interrupted was my beauty sleep."

I smiled back awkwardly, wondering if Simon had conveyed my suspicions about Patrick's dealings with the elderly Italian man in Harlem. "You must be wondering what this is all about."

"Simon painted the big picture, but he didn't have time to give me the details."

"Then let me fill you in," I said, glad to have something to talk about while we waited.

By the time I'd finished bringing him up to date, a small crowd had assembled at the foot of the pier and along the adjoining street, waiting for the boat to come in. Many of the men, I noted, wore the peaked cap and collarless shirt of the recent Italian immigrant. They stood in small groups, talking and gesticulating, or paced along the water's edge, fanning themselves with their caps as they stared expectantly down the river. "I can't tell which one is the man from the Italian Legion," I said.

"That's kind of the point, isn't it?" Patrick asked.

It was, of course, but I couldn't help worrying that if we did see something untoward, we'd have no way to know if the detective had seen it too.

At least I needn't worry about uncomfortable silences with Patrick, for he proved to have the policeman's knack for whiling away time, regaling me with amusing tales about his early years on the force while we waited for the boat to arrive. He gave no indication that he resented me for suspecting him of unsavory conduct. Indeed, he was such pleasant company, and I was so absorbed in our conversation, that it was with some surprise I glanced out the window fifteen minutes later to see that the steamship was warping in. "There she is!" I cried.

We turned and watched the behemoth ease into the slip. It was several more minutes before the gangplank was dropped into place and the passengers began to disembark, trailed by porters hauling hatboxes and trunks and baskets. I waited on tenterhooks for the first travelers to come out of the shed, training my eyes on the open doors.

A young man was first to emerge ten minutes later, carrying a valise and consulting his pocket watch.

"Here we go," said Patrick.

A solitary woman in an elegant French

suit came next, blinking into the sunlight, surrounded by porters carrying cartfuls of luggage. She hardly had time to open her parasol before she was whisked into a carriage by two liveried servants and trotted off across town.

Several families straggled out after her, followed by a group of men with blackened faces whom I guessed were coal stokers on shore leave. Soon, the trickle of passengers became a steady stream, one group blending into another so that it was difficult to tell at first glance which women were traveling alone. My gaze jumped from one colorful hat or shawl to another as I struggled to keep track of a growing number of moving targets.

A middle-aged, thickset woman broke out of the pack and walked alone toward the curb. A balding man of similar age and girth hurried over to meet her and walked arm in arm with her toward a waiting carriage. My gaze moved to the dark-haired young man striding past the couple in the opposite direction. His hair was oiled back over his head, and he wore what for someone of modest means would constitute Sunday best. He hurried to the shed and disappeared inside.

A few moments later, I was watching a

young boy chase his windblown boater across the pier when I heard Patrick murmur, "Looky there." Returning my attention to the shed, I saw that the man with the oiled hair had reemerged with a woman in tow. The woman wore a striped shawl over her head and was pulling an overstuffed sack behind her.

"Is that Fabroni?" Patrick asked me.

"No," I said, peering through the window, straining to keep them in view amid the surrounding swirl of commotion. "But I suppose it could be someone working for him." The young man reached for the woman's sack and hoisted it over his shoulder. "She's older than the others we know about," I noted.

"Still a good looker though," said Patrick.

She was indeed a handsome woman. I scanned the crowd around her, searching for the Legion's man. No one appeared to be paying the slightest attention to the couple.

The two had started toward the street. "Where's the detective?" I fretted.

"Give him a minute," Patrick said. "He won't want to crowd them."

The couple reached the end of the pier and turned south, continuing on foot along Twelfth Avenue. Just as I thought they were going to get away without a tail, I saw a slouch-shouldered man peel away from a crane at the foot of the pier and start briskly after them. I sagged in relief, recognizing one of the men I'd seen in Petrosino's office, the first time I visited. "That's the Legion's man," I told Patrick.

I flattened my cheek against the window to keep the trio in sight until a cab pulled out from the pier curb and blocked my view.

I straightened. "Now what?" I asked, every nerve aflutter.

"Now you go home, and I get back to work," Patrick said.

It wasn't what I wanted to hear. I was bursting to know where the couple was headed, and if the detective would find Teresa when they arrived. But I supposed I would just have to wait to speak with Detective Cassidi to find out what transpired.

Patrick had already started for the door. Taking a last look out the window, I noticed that a closed carriage had rolled into the spot just vacated by the cab on the opposite curb. I paused, watching a dark-haired young man with a trim, wiry build hop out of it, clothed in a purple shirt and ill-fitting sack suit, and start up the pier. Glancing toward the shed, I saw that a solitary woman, considerably younger than the one who'd just walked away, was now standing by the entrance next to a plain valise. Although her head was partially covered by a scarf, I could see the glossy black hair beneath it and the pretty face it framed. She waved to the man, smiling shyly at his approach.

"Patrick!" I called.

"What?" he said, returning to my side.

I nodded toward the shed.

The man was lifting the young woman's hands to his lips, eliciting another bashful smile. Picking up her valise in one hand, he grasped her arm in the other and started leading her back to the carriage.

Patrick frowned. "How many detectives are here?"

"I think that might have been the only one."

As the couple approached the carriage, the driver turned and climbed down from his perch to attend to the woman's valise. I gasped, catching sight of his full mustache and disfigured ear. "I know that man! I saw him at the Fabronis' flat!"

"Which one?" Patrick asked.

"There." I pointed. "The carriage driver."

"You sure?" he asked, peering through the glass.

"I'm positive!"

The driver tossed the valise up onto his seat while the young man lifted the woman into the carriage and, with a decidedly furtive look over his shoulder, climbed in after her.

I groaned. "The detective went after the wrong man!"

"Maybe both women were targets," Patrick said.

Perhaps. There was no way to know. But the appearance of Antonio's acquaintance was all I needed to convince me that the girl in the carriage across from us was in grave danger. "What do we do?" I asked, bouncing up and down on my toes in agitation.

"We just sit tight for a minute," Patrick said, "and see if they've got a tail."

It was one of the longest minutes of my life. The driver snapped the reins and turned the carriage out of the loading area, waiting for a truck to rumble past before he started across the avenue. I frantically scanned the pier behind him. A dark-haired man in a collarless shirt and suspenders appeared at first to be following, but as the carriage continued across the avenue onto the side street, he turned back toward the shed.

I grabbed Patrick's sleeve. "They're getting away!"

"All right," he said grimly. "I'm going after them."

I followed him to the door.

"You stay here," he tossed back over his shoulder, pushing through it to the street.

"But you're in uniform," I protested, stepping out behind him. "If they see you coming after them, they may not carry through with their plan, and if the other woman wasn't a target we'll have nothing!"

"I'll be careful. Now go on back inside." Continuing to the end of the street, he removed his helmet and peered around the corner to gauge the carriage's progress.

Even if he was careful, I thought, he'd stick out like a sore thumb. Gliding up behind him, I said into his ear, "What if I follow the carriage at a slight distance, and then you follow me? That way, you'll be too far back for them to spot you."

He pulled back from the corner and swiveled toward me. "And what do you suppose Simon would say if I agreed to that?"

I stared back at him, fairly vibrating with frustration. "You're right," I said finally. "He wouldn't like it." I tried to stop myself. Truly, I did. But we were too close to finding Teresa to let things fall apart now. "So I won't ask you to agree." Pulling my hat brim low over my face, I stepped around him onto Thirty-Fourth Street.

I heard furious muttering behind me but walked on anyway. The carriage was nearly at the other end of the street, slowing to a stop behind a loaded wagon. I moved toward it at an unhurried pace, swinging my arms in what I hoped was a natural manner, fixing my gaze on the sidewalk a few yards ahead of me. Another wagon lumbered up the street from the pier and pulled up behind the carriage, temporarily blocking it from view. By the time I came alongside it, the carriage was turning north onto Eleventh Avenue. Glancing over my shoulder, I saw Patrick striding up the sidewalk behind me with his helmet squashed against his chest.

I crossed the intersection and hurried up the sidewalk after the carriage. Eleventh Avenue was an unusually wide thorough-fare, built to accommodate freight trains up and down its length, and the traffic was moving at a good clip. I lengthened my stride to cover more ground without appearing to be rushing. A number of women were straggling up the sidewalk on both sides of the street, carrying heaps of wilted produce in their aprons or in overflowing gunnysacks. I guessed that they'd been down to the

Thirtieth Street yard, gathering discards left by the vendors who filled their carts from the trains. By positioning myself strategically behind them, I found I was able to keep myself out of the carriage's line of sight. Glancing over my shoulder, I saw Patrick doing the same thing farther back.

When the carriage stopped at the next intersection, I stopped as well, turning to admire the donkey engine in the nearest storefront until it had started up again. In this halting fashion, I continued up the avenue, first speeding up and then slowing down, all the time attempting to keep some physical barrier between myself and the back window of the carriage.

I wondered, while I walked, where we were heading. The avenue here was lined with machine shops, breweries, and small factories, with very little residential housing in evidence, making it an ideal locale for concealing unsavory activities. As I approached the next corner, I caught a whiff of decaying flesh from the slaughterhouse district three blocks north. I resisted the impulse to cover my nose, for none of the others on the sidewalk seemed offended by it, and I didn't wish to stand out. As I continued up the block, the caramel notes from a condensed milk factory joined the smells of putrid flesh and rendered fat, sweetening but by no means improving the olfactory experience. No wonder no one lived here, I thought, trying not to breathe.

After Thirty-Seventh Street, the traffic thinned for a block, allowing the carriage to make even more rapid progress and forcing me to adopt a pace that had me panting and sweating by the time I reached the corner. I hurried after it through the Thirty-Eighth Street intersection, then came to an abrupt halt when it stopped midway up the next block. A long line of vehicles was waiting in front of it, all the way up to Thirty-Ninth Street. I didn't want to get any closer, but I couldn't just stand in place on the sidewalk either, so I ducked into a steam laundry and watched from inside, waiting for the traffic to start up again.

A minute later, the door opened, and Patrick slipped inside. I braced myself for a lecture, but to his credit, he didn't waste his breath scolding me. "You all right?" he asked.

"I'm fine. What's the holdup?"

"It's the sheep. They float them across to the Thirty-Ninth Street pier and herd them over to the abattoir. They've closed off the avenue up ahead to keep them from turning the wrong way."

I pushed the door open slightly for a wider view. "I don't see any sheep."

"You will."

I heard it first: the distant clinking of what sounded like a cowbell, mixed with a steady bleating and the rumble of hooves. A moment later, a white ram with gorgeous, spiraling horns and a bell around its neck trotted around the corner and turned up the avenue.

"That's the Judas," Patrick said behind my shoulder.

Before I could ask him what he meant, a bobbing, bleating mass of sheep came dashing around the corner after the ram, bumping into each other in their haste to stay close as they made the turn and reconfigured behind their leader. The ram started up the incline into the slaughterhouse, his cheerful bell urging the flock on. The sheep followed trustingly, baaing in excitement, ears flapping and tails wagging as they scampered up the ramps to the pens. The last one crossed the threshold and the door slammed shut, leaving the street eerily quiet.

"Do they kill the ram too?" I asked, a bit crossly, in the silence.

"Nah," Patrick answered, "he'll go back across the river, to lead the next group in."

A man swung open the gate that was

blocking the avenue, and the traffic began to move again. I reached for the door.

"Let's wait until the carriage is across the intersection," Patrick said.

I watched the carriage start up again and jockey for position among the surrounding vehicles, shifting toward the midline of the street. Instead of continuing up the avenue, however, it turned left at the intersection onto Thirty-Ninth Street and drove out of view.

I pushed the door open and hurried after it, followed closely by Patrick. At the corner, I stopped and peered down the side street. The abattoir of the New York Butchers Dressed Meat Company and its adjacent powerhouse occupied the right side of the street. On the left side, end-to-end wagons holding crates of live chickens were parked in front of what I deduced was a poultry processing plant. The wagons were double-parked in places, clogging the travel lane. The carriage was threading its way down the narrow strip that remained.

"We'll have cover," I said, turning back to Patrick. "There are wagons parked all along the curb, and stacks of empty crates on the sidewalk."

I eased around the corner and started down the street. There were no tarpaulins shading the wagons, and as I walked past I could see that the crowded birds inside the crates were in considerable distress. Some had already succumbed to the heat and lay in an exhausted layer on the bottom of their crates, while others stood on top of them, sticking their heads through the slats and gasping for air.

I dragged my gaze away from the pitiful creatures — just in time to see the carriage turning into an alley some twenty feet up ahead, on the near side of the processing plant. I lunged sideways, taking cover behind a head-high stack of empty crates as the horses clattered across the sidewalk. Through the slats of the crate, I could clearly see the carriage as it crossed in front of me. Only a solitary, male head was now visible through the window.

I leaned back against the wall, my breath catching in my throat. We would have seen the woman if she'd gotten out earlier. The most likely explanation was that she'd been drugged or otherwise subdued and was lying unconscious inside the carriage. It was really happening, right here in front of me.

"You all right?" Patrick asked again, moving quietly up behind me.

"I couldn't see her through the window," I said, my voice sounding high and strained to my ears. "I think they may have chloro-formed her so she wouldn't make a fuss when she saw where they were taking her."

Patrick continued cautiously to the alley and looked around the corner. Returning a moment later, he informed me, "They carried her through a side door into the building. I'm going to see if I can get inside and scout things out."

I swallowed down a lump of fear. "But you'll be outnumbered. Shouldn't you call for help?"

He glanced back toward the alleyway with a frown. "I don't think I should leave her alone in there with them."

"No, you're right," I said, remembering how quickly and brutally Caterina Bressi's ruin had been accomplished.

"If it looks like more than I can handle, I'll come back and call for help. You sit tight and stay out of sight. If the carriage comes back out while I'm gone, don't follow it by yourself. Just see which way it turns onto the avenue so you can tell me. Got it?"

I nodded.

He unhooked a key from a chain on his belt and handed it to me. "If I'm not back in ten minutes, or if anyone so much as looks at you twice, go to the nearest call box and send for the reserves." Drawing his revolver from his hip, he took off down the sidewalk.

I watched him disappear down the alley, already feeling his absence acutely. My hands were trembling as I reached for my pendant watch. I noted the time and settled in to wait.

Each second that ticked past seemed an eternity. The stench of chicken manure from the empty crates assaulted my nostrils, while the pitiful gasping of the birds in the wagons played havoc with my nerves. I held my breath, freezing in place as two men in aprons emerged from an open door in the front of the plant. They grabbed some more crates from the wagons and returned inside without noticing me.

Two minutes crawled past, then three. Through the open plant door, I could hear the low hum of machinery and the relentless squawking of birds inside. This must be where they killed and plucked the chickens before sending them off to butcher stores throughout the city. I supposed that if girls were being held on an upper floor, the constant noise from below would obscure their calls for help, making it possible to conceal their presence. Or did the workers downstairs know what was going on above them? Perhaps even participate in the girls' undoing? After what I'd learned of human nature in the past few days, I feared anything was possible.

Four minutes had passed when I suddenly heard voices and looked up to see the two men from the carriage coming out of the alleyway. They stopped and looked both ways as if searching for something. My heart stopped as they turned up the sidewalk in my direction. I shrank back against the wall, unsure whether to stay or bolt. Deciding that they were going to see me in either case, I turned on my heel and started briskly back toward Eleventh Avenue, trying to act as though my sudden emergence from behind a crate was the most natural thing in the world.

"Hey!" one of them shouted.

I picked up my pace.

The next instant, a hand grabbed my arm from behind and swung me around. It was the young man who'd met the woman at the pier. "What you doin' there, heh?"

"Let go of me!" I said, trying to pull my arm away.

"You lookin' for something?"

"I was waiting for a friend."

He leered at me. "That copper, he your friend?" He looked at the older man, the one I'd seen at Antonio's, and said something in rapid Italian that I couldn't understand.

The older man grunted and stepped forward, grabbing me by both arms.

I tried to pull away, but he was too strong for me. "You'd better let me go," I rasped, terror strangling my voice. "The police know who you are. I already told them I saw you at —"

His fist crashed into my face. I staggered backward and fell, blinded by shock and pain. Together, they hauled me to my feet and started pulling me backward toward the alley. I tried to scream, but to my dismay, nothing came out. I tried again, with only slightly more success. They paused, and I thought for a moment that I'd made enough noise to frighten them into releasing me. But they'd only stopped so that the younger man could shove a handkerchief into my mouth before continuing toward the alley. I bucked and writhed, gagging on the handkerchief, fearing that if I let them drag me into the building, I was done for. Their hands were like iron bands on my wrists, however, and no matter how hard I tried, I couldn't break free.

The light suddenly dimmed as we entered the alleyway. I released a muffled, heartsick wail as they dragged me in a dozen yards, away from the street and anyone who might come to my aid. I heard a door open behind me and felt a gush of fetid air. I was yanked over the threshold and into the building, my shoes scraping over the concrete floor. The door slammed shut and they dropped me onto my back.

I scrabbled away from them on my heels and elbows. As the younger man reached for me again, I kicked at his midriff, catching him in his solar plexus. He grunted and took half a step back. Before I could get to my feet, however, he dropped on top of me with a snarl, straddling my chest with his knees and crushing my throat with his forearm.

"Gallo!" The older man put a restraining hand on the younger man's shoulder, muttering something in Italian.

The man on top of me sat back, lifting his arm from my throat with obvious reluctance. Pulling the handkerchief from my mouth, he doused it with liquid from a vial he withdrew from his trouser pocket. My blood ran cold as I caught a whiff of the sickly sweet scent. "Help!" I tried to scream through my aching throat, hoping against hope that Patrick or one of the workers on the other side of the wall might yet come to my aid. "Somebody, help me!"

The man Gallo flattened the handkerchief over my mouth and nose, grinding my lips against my teeth. I held my breath but could still feel the icy vapor seeping up my nostrils and down my throat.

Gallo shouted in Italian to someone behind me. "Nucci! Bring down the other one, then get the van." He looked back down at me, holding the cloth with an iron hand, waiting until my lungs were screaming for air and I had no choice but to breathe. I began to weep as I took in the undiluted chloroform, knowing it would only be a minute or so before I passed into the stage of active intoxication and another minute or two after that before I became insensible. I coughed and struggled against the harsh vapor, but it was no use. I couldn't keep myself from breathing it in. Soon, with my captor's cold eyes bearing down on me, I started feeling the disorienting symptoms. My jaw grew heavy, and my head began to swim as the sounds of voices and machinery undulated weirdly in my ears. I felt my arms and legs begin to tingle and gradually go numb. Eventually, I stopped struggling and relaxed against the floor, my fear receding along with everything else in my awareness. The face above me grew hazier and my senses duller, until finally, darkness overtook me.

CHAPTER SEVENTEEN

When I came to, the floor was moving underneath me. I opened my eyes to find that I was lying on my stomach in the back of a delivery van, with my mouth gagged, my feet bound, and my hands tied behind me. Turning my head, I saw the girl from the boat sitting against the opposite side of the van, similarly bound and gagged, watching me with huge eyes. The memory of my capture returned, along with a wave of nausea from the chloroform. I turned over and struggled into a sitting position, breathing deeply through my nose until the nausea had passed.

My arrival with Patrick must have upset the abductors' normal operations, forcing them to move me and the girl immediately in case more policemen were on their trail. Although there were no windows in the horse-drawn van, I could feel it moving in fits and starts, suggesting we were driving through areas of congestion. I strained to make out the chatter up front, wondering where they were taking us and how long we'd been traveling. Although chloroform as normally applied was not a long-acting agent, if it wasn't properly diluted, it could have a far more stupefying effect, which meant I might have been unconscious for as long as twenty or thirty minutes. If Italian Harlem was our destination, we could be arriving at any moment.

I felt a fresh explosion of panic, realizing that no one knew where I was. Even if Patrick was still alive, he wouldn't be able to tell anyone where the men had taken me. Maybe, I told myself, they didn't intend to keep me, but only to hold me until they could decide how to return me. I wasn't a friendless immigrant who could vanish without consequences. Abducting a well-to-do young woman from the city's native population would presumably create more headaches for them than it was worth. I clung to this idea, for doing so was the only way I could keep the breath moving through my lungs and my mind from seizing in fear.

The other girl made a whimpering sound. I nodded and mumbled through my gag, wishing I could explain to her what was happening. She was fully dressed and showed no outward signs of injury. I mentally surveyed my own condition. A sore jaw and some irritation of the skin around my mouth from the chloroform seemed to be the only record of my captors' brutality. But of course, that could change very soon . . .

Five minutes later, the van turned hard left and rattled over some wooden planking before coming to a stop. I stiffened as I heard hands working the rear latch, deciding on the spot that despite my bonds, I would make a break for it when the door opened and try to get the attention of some passerby. When the back of the van swung open, however, I saw that we were already inside a three-bay carriage house and that the doors to the street were closed tight. A full-breasted woman well past her prime, with a powdered face and rouged lips, stood at the foot of the van between me and the doors, wearing a green dress with a soiled hem. Two men stood behind her: the false bridegroom, Gallo, who had chloroformed me, and a second man I'd never seen before, but who I guessed was the "Nucci" who'd been behind me in the poultry plant, and who had presumably been sitting up front with Gallo in the van.

The woman eyed me with a frown. "Who is this?"

Gallo answered her in Italian too rapid for me to understand.

Her frown deepened. "Get them out." She turned to the man I'd recognized from Antonio's flat, who was just climbing down from the carriage they'd used to collect the girl from the pier. "Donato, take care of the horses."

The two younger men climbed into the van, yanking off our gags and cutting our ankle bonds before pulling us out and dropping us onto our feet in front of her. I quickly scanned the room. Two other vans were crowded into the adjoining bays beyond the carriage, along with a severed dashboard and a stack of brightly painted wheels. "Elmwood Butchers" was emblazoned across one of the vans, while "Ludwig Bauman & Co." had been partially sanded off the side of the other, leaving only a shadow of the name behind. Scrapers, brushes, and paint cans were scattered on the floor around the vans.

The woman brought her face within inches of mine. The lines around her eyes and over her red lips were caked with powder, and she smelled faintly of gin. "My name is Claudia," she told me in English. "You do what I tell you to, and we'll get along fine. You make any trouble, you'll have to deal with Gallo and Nucci here." She jerked her thumb over her shoulder at the two young men. The one called Nucci snickered, saying something I was glad I didn't understand.

I searched the woman's eyes, hoping but failing to detect the slightest trace of feminine sympathy. "If you're smart, you'll let me go," I said, my voice scratchy from fear and chloroform. "People are going to be looking for me. If you keep me here, they're going to find me, and when they do, they'll find you too."

She stepped back. "Take them up," she ordered the men, as if I hadn't spoken.

Nucci grabbed my shoulder as Gallo reached for the girl from the boat. The girl backed away from her erstwhile bridegroom, shaking her head. *"Non capisco, Alessandro! Perché stai facendo questo?"* I don't understand! Why are you doing this?

"*Cara* Francesca," he said, cupping her chin in his hand. "You will still be my girl! And you are in America, yes? Now be happy, and give me a smile!"

The older man, Donato, had unhitched the horses from the van and was leading them up a ramp on the left side of the room. Nucci pushed me up the ramp after him while Gallo followed, dragging Francesca.

The next floor contained a long corridor lit by hanging electric lights, with horse stalls on either side. As Donato started leading the horses into empty stalls, Nucci pushed me past him down the hallway.

Collars and harnesses and other tack were piled onto large hooks on the stall doors, narrowing the corridor and making passage difficult. My mind registered, without comprehending, the distinct smell of shoe polish wafting from the horses inside. At the far end of the hall, where the tack room should have been, was a closed door.

Nucci propelled me roughly toward it. I knew it was pointless to resist, with my arms still tied behind my back and the two men right behind me. But when I saw the locked bolt on the door, my feet took root of their own accord. As Nucci put his hand on my back to give me another push, I arched backward, trying to hit his nose with my head. He mustn't have been directly behind me, however, because I could feel the blow glance off his cheekbone. The next minute, he had me in a headlock, crushing my Adam's apple with his elbow as he pulled me, cursing, toward the door. He slid the bolt, opened the door, and threw me in.

I staggered inside with Francesca close on my heels, and the door slammed shut behind us. The room was in deep shadow, the only light entering through cracks between some boards that were nailed across a window in the back wall. I stood in the silence, gasping for breath, and waited while my eyes adjusted.

Eight straw pallets lay on the floor, four on each side of the room, with their narrow ends to the wall. Five of these were occupied by dark-haired, barefoot girls wearing nothing but thin chemises. The girls sat with their backs against the walls, staring up at me and Francesca, their faces ghostly ovals in the gloom. A tin candle holder on the floor beside each cot and two slop basins under the window were the only other furnishings.

Francesca swayed on her feet and sank to the floor. The girl nearest to her stood and helped her onto an empty cot, while another moved behind me and began to untie the rags around my wrists. The knots in the rags had been tightened by my struggles, and it took my helper some time to work them free. My legs were shaking with delayed shock by the time she threw the rag to the ground. "Sit," she said in Italian, lowering me onto an empty cot.

I turned to say thank you, and had my first good look at her face. I felt a jolt of recognition. "Teresa! You're Teresa Casoria, aren't you?"

She took a step back. "How do you know my name?" she asked in English.

"Rosa showed me your picture; she asked me to look for you."

She stared at me. "You know Rosa?"

"She was sure something bad had happened to you when you didn't come visit as you'd promised."

She dropped to her knees beside me on the cot, pressing her hands against her cheeks. "Rosa," she said again, whispering the name as if it came from another world.

She listened, slack-jawed and wide-eyed, as I explained how I'd come to be there. Fortunately, she had a good grasp of English, so I didn't have to rely on my rusty Italian.

"But if the police know you were taken, they will be looking for us, yes?" she asked when I was done. "They will come find us?"

I hesitated, ashamed that I'd made such a mess of things. "They'll know I'm missing, yes. But no one saw the men bring me here. I don't know if they'll be able to find this place."

She sank back onto her heels, her eyes losing their momentary luster. I looked around the room at the other girls. If any of them had understood my conversation with Teresa, they gave no sign of it. The one who'd helped Francesca had moved soundlessly back to her cot and sat propped against the wall again, clutching her knees to her chest. They all appeared to be in shock, their bodies tense, their eyes staring blankly or darting toward the door whenever a noise floated up from downstairs. I wondered how long they had been here.

"I'm sorry," Teresa said.

"For what?" I asked, turning back to her.

"That you are here, because of me."

On the adjacent cot, Francesca started to cry, hugging herself and rocking back and forth. Teresa scuttled over and put an arm around her shoulders, shushing her softly. As she moved off my cot, I noticed the overlapping reddish-brown stains on the center of the ticking. Virgin blood, I realized with a twist of my stomach.

Francesca was speaking in a dialect I couldn't understand. "What's she saying?" I asked Teresa.

"She says she doesn't understand why she is here," Teresa answered, stroking a lock of hair back behind the girl's ear.

Of course she didn't, I thought bitterly. "That man downstairs — Gallo — tricked her into coming here with a promise of marriage," I told Teresa, "just as Antonio tricked you."

She stiffened, dropping her arm from Francesca's shoulders. "Antonio? Antonio didn't trick me! Why would you think such a thing?"

I frowned at her. "Didn't he bring you here from the boat?"

"No!"

"Then . . . who did?"

She seemed to suddenly deflate, her face turning even grayer in the dim light. "Un-Occhio."

Un-Occhio — the same man Caterina had spoken of. A murmur of unease rippled through the room at the sound of his name. "How did he get you to go with him?"

"I thought he was a friend of Antonio's," she said, her voice bitter with self-reproach. "I had been waiting at the pier a long time. When he called my name from the carriage, I thought Antonio must have sent him for me."

"But you didn't recognize him?"

She shook her head.

Apparently, she'd managed to keep believing in her fiancé's sincerity throughout her ordeal. I hated to have to disillusion her. "How do you suppose the man at the pier knew your name?"

"I don't know. I have asked myself that question a thousand times."

"You never wondered if Antonio might have told him? If he might, perhaps, be working with Un-Occhio?"

"No!" she cried, her eyes ablaze. "You don't know Antonio. He could never do such a thing!"

"I know his father was a capo with the Camorra in Naples," I told her bluntly. "And that he ran a prostitution business there."

She clamped her lips together, taking this in but apparently unwilling to follow it to its natural conclusion.

"And I know that the man downstairs with the deformed ear is a friend of his."

"What man?" she demanded.

"The one called Donato, who drove the carriage to the pier to pick up Francesca."

"There is no man here with an ear like that!"

"Ask her," I said, indicating Francesca.

She swiveled toward Francesca, questioning her rapidly in Italian. The girl nodded dully in response.

Teresa turned back to me, thrusting out her chin. "Well, then, I am sure he is no friend of Antonio's."

"I've seen them together, Teresa."

Her mouth dropped open. "You've seen Antonio?"

"I went to his home to ask him if he knew where you were."

She pressed her hands to her chest. "Then you must have seen that he is a good man! Whatever this Donato has done, it can have nothing to do with Antonio." She leaned toward me, fairly vibrating with intensity. "There are many things I do not know, but of this, I am certain: Antonio's love for me was real."

I studied her face, struck by her conviction. Despite the evidence against him, I'd never been wholly satisfied with the notion of Antonio as our white slaver, based on my own observations. Nor did Teresa strike me as someone who would be easily taken in. If she was still convinced of her fiancé's integrity, after everything she'd been through, perhaps I shouldn't be so quick to condemn him. "I'm sorry if I jumped to the wrong conclusion," I told her. "Please forgive me."

She peered into my eyes a moment longer, as if to be sure I really was sorry, before sitting back with a curt nod.

Although I regretted that I'd upset her with my questions, I was glad to see that she could still be angry. Anger was good;

anger meant that they hadn't broken her yet. Perhaps together, we could still find some way out of this hellhole. "The man who took you from the pier . . . Why is he called Un-Occhio? Does he wear an eye patch?"

She shook her head.

"Why then?"

She bit her lip, dropping her gaze to the cot. "Because he has only one" — she gestured toward her lap — *"testicolo."*

"Testicle?" I blinked at her in surprise as an unwelcome image of her discovering this fact flashed grotesquely across my mind. "I . . . see. Well, do you have any idea what his real name is? Or any clue as to his identity?"

"I can tell you only that he is the son of the devil, for he knows things that only God or the devil could know."

"What sort of things?" I probed.

She looked back up at me. "He calls me Reza," she said, her voice full of wonder. "The special name that only Antonio uses for me. How could he know that, unless he is the devil himself?"

The most obvious explanation, of course, was that Antonio had told him, but I was determined to remain open to other possibilities.

"And he knows the special ways to hurt us," she went on, "to make us do what he wants. Some, he burns. Others, he cuts. Me, he hurts with words."

"With words?"

Her dark eyes clouded with despair. "He tells me that Antonio will suffer because of me. That I will be his instrument of revenge."

"I don't understand. Why would he want to hurt Antonio?"

"I don't know! I only know that he hates him, as the devil hates an angel. I can see it in his eyes when he speaks of him."

I digested this for a moment. If the men were enemies, they most certainly couldn't be working together, suggesting that Teresa's faith in her fiancé had been well placed. "And he hoped to make Antonio suffer by stealing you away?"

"Even . . . even worse than that," she said, lowering her gaze again.

"What do you mean?"

In a strained voice, she answered, "He wanted to make Antonio watch."

I sat back. "You mean, watch him violate you?"

She nodded, her cheeks aflame. "When he took me to the chicken house, from the boat, he told me all the terrible things he was going to do to me when Antonio arrived. There was a chair in the room, and pieces of rope. He said they were for Antonio. He said —" Her voice broke. "He said that Antonio would have the best seat in the house." She drew a deep breath, and a little of the fire returned to her eyes. "But then his men returned and told him Antonio had escaped. For this one thing, at least, I thank God."

I remembered Antonio's story of being accosted by thieves outside the bank the morning Teresa's boat arrived. It must have been Un-Occhio's men, I realized now, trying to spirit him away. "Did Un-Occhio tell you how Antonio escaped?"

"No. But . . ." She blanched. "He was very angry."

And took it out on her, I guessed. I reached over and laid my hand on her shoulder.

The bolt suddenly rattled on the other side of the door. I felt Teresa stiffen, and saw the other girls shrink back on their cots as if trying to disappear into the walls.

The door swung open to reveal Claudia on the threshold. "Let's go," she barked. "It's time to eat."

The girls seemed to hesitate, looking at each other in confusion before they pushed themselves to their feet and started for the door.

"Usually, the men come before supper," Teresa whispered to me as we joined the back of the line. "That way, if the girls resist, they can refuse to let them eat. Your coming must have upset things."

"The girls," I repeated as I stumbled along beside her. "But not you?"

"No. Not me," she said, her voice clipped. "I am for Un-Occhio only."

Claudia ushered us down the ramp to the main floor and then down another ramp into the basement. This was one large, dirt-floored room with hay bales around the perimeter and a long, battered table in the middle. Donato was eating with Nucci at a smaller table near the door.

"That's him," I whispered as we walked past, nudging Teresa. "The man I saw with Antonio. Have you seen him before?"

Following my gaze, she shook her head.

A ladle and bucket of soup were waiting on the main table, along with a pile of spoons and a stack of chipped bowls. The girls eagerly took their seats. They were all very thin, I noticed now, probably half-starved to keep them compliant. Claudia walked around the table with a shallow basket, distributing rolls so hard they bounced on the table, while the girls ladled the soup into bowls. They dunked the rolls into the broth and gnawed at the moistened ends, pulling off chunks with their teeth.

"Eat up, ladies," Claudia drawled, before going to join the men at the other table.

I made no move for the ladle, hollow with fear and nauseated by the thought of food. My mind kept churning over the question of One-Eye's identity and his relationship with Antonio. If I could just solve that puzzle, my predicament would feel less hopeless. For if I could figure it out, there was a chance that Simon and Detective Cassidi could as well.

"Eat," Teresa said, sloshing a ladleful of soup into my bowl.

"I couldn't," I said, shaking my head.

"You must keep up your strength!"

I supposed she was right. Whatever happened from here on in, I was going to need every ounce of physical and mental strength I could muster. I filled my spoon with the greenish gruel and lifted it into my mouth. It was even worse than it looked, cold and watery and . . .

I swung my gaze toward the soup bucket as the broth washed over my taste buds, staring at it for several paralyzed seconds. I swallowed and swiveled back to Teresa.

"What does Un-Occhio look like?"

She paused with her spoon halfway to her mouth. "Older, about the age of that one there," she said, tipping her head toward Donato. "With shorter hair and small eyes, close together."

"Heavy or thin?"

"Not heavy everywhere, but thick around the middle."

"Does he have a beard or mustache?"

"No."

"What about jewelry?"

She frowned, searching my face. "He wears a silver ring on his little finger."

I put down my spoon. "Which hand?"

She thought a moment. "The right."

My breath left me in a ragged exhale. He'd been there under our noses, all the time. I was about to tell Teresa what I'd just realized, when Gallo came running down the ramp and burst into the room.

"We go tonight, at midnight," he announced to the others.

"But the vans aren't finished," Nucci protested.

"He said we have to finish them now." He turned to Claudia. "He wants you to get the new girls ready."

"What about her?" Claudia asked, pointing to me.

His eyes skimmed over me. "Especially her."

Claudia walked toward us, clapping her hands. "All right, everybody up, *fai presto.* Nucci and Gallo, you take the girls back up while Donato gets started on the vans." She shook a finger at the younger men. "But no dawdling! We don't have much time."

"What's happening?" I asked Teresa as we were herded back up the ramp.

"They must be moving us out."

My feet faltered beneath me as reality sank in. I'd been fooling myself, thinking they might let me go to save their own necks. The truth hit me now like a powerful paralytic. Of course they weren't going to let me go. Whatever threat my discovery posed to them could be easily eliminated by transporting me out of the city.

"Get moving," Nucci growled, shoving me from behind.

This time, the men followed us into the tack room and closed the door behind them. Nucci removed a toothpick from his mouth and pointed it at me and Francesca. "You two. Take off your clothes."

The rest of the girls slunk back onto their cots, leaving the two of us alone in the middle of the room. Nucci and Gallo stood with their legs spread and their thumbs hooked in their pockets, watching us hun-grily.

I realized that Francesca was looking at me for guidance, and struggled to think rationally through the haze of my fear. Most likely, they didn't intend to rape us on the spot, since they were expected downstairs to help with the vans. Taking away a captive's street clothes was, I had learned, simply the first step in the breaking-in process. If we resisted, we'd only give them the pleasure of overpowering us. It might be better to go along with them now and save our energy for a battle we could win.

Though it sickened me to do so, I nodded to Francesca, signaling her to obey their command. Methodically, I stripped off my skirt, shirtwaist, stockings, corset, and drawers, folding each item and laying it on the floor at my feet, until I was wearing nothing but my chemise. It took all my willpower not to cringe or try to cover myself as their eyes raked my thinly veiled body. Francesca followed my example, although her fingers were trembling so badly it took her longer to comply.

Nucci swaggered toward me, coming to a stop just inches away. "What you got under there?" he asked with a grin, his rancid breath fanning my face as he flicked the top of my chemise with his finger. "You got something nice for Nucci?"

I fought to keep my expression blank.

His grin turned into a sneer. He grabbed the placket of my chemise and pulled it toward him, thrusting his other hand inside.

I gasped as his hand roughly squeezed my breast. Without stopping to think, I raised the call box key I'd removed from my skirt pocket as I was undressing and jabbed it into his face. He turned away reflexively, so that the point of the key dug into the corner of his eye. He jerked back with a howl, ripping the front of my chemise as he did so.

I started for the door. Within two seconds, he had grabbed me from behind and thrown me onto my back on a cot. He dropped on top of me, loosing a stream of invective as he trapped my wrist against the cot with his forearm and dug the key from my fist. Pinning my legs with his knees, he started unbuttoning his trousers with his free hand.

I raised my left arm and scratched at his face, forcing him to pull back his head, but he was still sitting on top of me, making quick work of the buttons. His hand moved up the outside of my thigh, pushing up my chemise, then slid around the top of my leg and groped for my crotch. I groaned in helpless protest, trying to twist away from his prying fingers — but it was like trying to get out from under a slab of cement. I squeezed my eyes shut, desperate to distance myself from my body and the inevitability of what was happening.

And then, suddenly, the door swung open and Claudia was behind him, pulling him off of me. "Are you crazy?" she shrieked.

He stumbled backward across the floor.

"Un-Occhio will kill you!" Claudia cried, swatting at him with her open hand.

He straightened, pulling up his trousers. His right eye was half-shut and watering profusely.

"Go on, get out!" Claudia said, stepping between us. "Go help with the vans!"

He backed toward the door, holding his eye with one hand and pointing at me with the other. "I'll be back for you," he promised, spittle flying from his lips, before he staggered out of the room.

Claudia turned to me with a frown. "Give me your hairpins," she ordered, holding out her hand.

I stared at her, too dazed to make immediate sense of her request. She bent over me with an oath and started plucking the pins out one by one, yanking out strands of hair with each pin. Scooping up my clothes from the floor, she followed the others out, then closed the door behind her and slammed the bolt home.

CHAPTER EIGHTEEN

I sat on the cot, hugging myself, waiting for the shaking to subside.

"Are you all right?" Teresa asked.

I turned to her. "Why did she stop him?"

"Un-Occhio must be the first to have each girl. It's the rule."

Another shudder wracked my spine. I couldn't believe this was really happening. I squeezed my temples, trying to pull myself together. "I think I know who he is."

"Un-Occhio?"

I drew a deep breath, knowing that what I was going to say would upset her. "I think it's Mr. Velloca. Rosa's father."

She just blinked at me.

"You never met him in Italy, did you?"

"Well, no, but . . . *Rosa's father?*" She shook her head.

"So you wouldn't have recognized him. He probably knew about your coming here, though. Rosa was very excited about it. She would almost certainly have talked about it with her family."

"It cannot be! Rosa is a sweet, wonderful girl. She can have nothing to do with a monster like Un-Occhio."

"There are men in this world who are capable of both great charm, and great cruelty and deceit," I said bitterly. "I suspect that Velloca is one of them. For self-protection, he's probably hidden his activities well from his family. I'm sure Rosa has no idea what he's involved in."

"But why would Rosa's father wish to hurt me?"

"You told me yourself, Un-Occhio is using you to get revenge on Antonio for something that happened in their past. If Velloca is in fact Un-Occhio, he'd jump at the chance to hurt Antonio by stealing his bride."

"But . . . what reason do you have to believe that it *is* him?"

"I went to Rosa's house two days ago to see if she recognized a valise the police had found with your initials on it. Mr. Velloca came home for lunch while we were there. His mother filled a lard tin full of soup for him to take when he left. He called it his supper pail, but it was awfully large for one person. It looked exactly like the tin on the table downstairs. And Rosa's brother complained that the soup was too salty. That soup tonight was so salty, it was almost inedible."

"And because of this, you accuse him?" she asked with a frown.

"And the fact that he looks exactly as you described. Right down to the silver ring on the little finger of his right hand."

She digested this, her brow puckering.

"Did you tell Rosa about Antonio's special name for you?"

Her eyes widened. *"Dio mio,"* she whispered.

I nodded. "It all adds up."

"But if he knows that you are aware of his true identity . . ."

We stared at each other, contemplating what a man like Un-Occhio might do to a woman in a position to give him away.

I swallowed down a brick of fear. "Do you think he'll come tonight? Before they move us?"

She shrugged helplessly. "I don't know. He comes most nights, but everything is different today."

My terror must have been plain on my face, for she reached out her hand in sympathy. I grabbed onto it, holding on as if to a lifeline.

The sounds of scraping and sanding had been wafting up for some time from the floor below. Now I heard stall doors creak open and shut in the corridor outside, followed by the nickers and snorts of horses. "What are they doing?"

"The vans and horses are all stolen," she explained. "They repaint the vans and cover the horses' . . ." She hesitated, circling her free palm over her forehead.

"Markings?"

"Yes, cover them with shoe polish. Then they take the girls away in the vans. All of them except me."

"How many times have you seen this happen?"

"Just once, a week after they brought me here. There were different girls here then."

I rubbed my hand over my eyes. So Un-Occhio traded not only in human flesh, but in horse flesh and stolen vehicles as well. Perhaps he even used the same distribution routes, selling the girls, horses, and vehicles to established customers in each location. I supposed to him it was all of a piece. Like a true psychopathic personality, he would see only the advantages in diversifying his offerings.

As darkness gradually descended outside the crack in the boards, one of the girls lit a candle. I followed her example, lighting the candle next to my own cot with shaking fingers and watching the shadows jump over the bare walls. Most of the other girls were lying curled on their sides or hunched on the ends of their cots. Even Teresa had fallen silent.

Every time I heard footsteps on the ramps, my lungs forgot how to breathe. How was it possible I had come to this? I thought of Simon and my heart seized with regret. I should have remembered that life could change in the blink of an eye, and accepted his proposal on the spot. How petty my reasons for waiting seemed now.

The world out there, my old world, felt like another universe, and the woman I once was, a stranger. As one moment bled into the next, I could almost feel my old self leaking away, leaving nothing to fill the shell of my body but fear. Perhaps, though, there was only so much fear a person could take. Because as I thought about what these men were stealing from me, and had already stolen from so many others, something else began to flicker to life inside of me. I consciously fanned the ember of anger, feeling it grow hotter and brighter until it burst into welcome flame.

I wasn't going to be like those sheep on

the street, going meekly to slaughter, I decided. I would at least put up a fight, in whatever way I could. Yes, they would hurt me if I resisted, but they were going to hurt me anyway — and possibly worse.

I rose stiffly to my feet. Crossing to the window on shaky legs, I slid my fingers into the crack and pulled on the bottom board. It was nailed on tight. I put my foot on the sill and threw all my weight into my next try, but it still wouldn't budge. I looked around for something to lever or break it with, but our captors had been careful to remove anything so useful.

Putting my eye to the crack, I saw tenement fronts directly across the street, their windows lit dimly from within. Looking to the left, I was surprised to see a brightly lit pier jutting into a river, with a ferry docked on one side. Sliding my eye further along the crack, I recognized the lights of the House of Refuge on Randall's Island. I felt a quiver of excitement, knowing at last where I was: at the foot of 116th Street, less than a block from the Randall's Island ferry. Lucia Siavo had fled down this very same street on the night she drowned. The hairs on the back of my neck bristled at the thought. Had she once stood where I stood now, staring at the river and dreaming of a watery end to her misery?

Two women in black shawls suddenly came into view on the sidewalk below. They were walking arm in arm, their heads bent in conversation. This was my chance. I put my mouth to the crack and shouted, "Help! I'm being held prisoner! Call the police!"

They continued up the sidewalk without pausing.

Teresa pulled on my arm. "No, you mustn't! They will punish you!"

I shook her off. Putting my mouth back to the crack, I tried again in Italian. *"Aiutami, per favore!"*

One of the women stopped and glanced over her shoulder, forcing the other to stop as well.

"Aiutami! Help! I'm up here!" I cried.

Her gaze swept across the building facade and continued past it.

I heard footsteps thundering up the stairs. *"Qui! Qui!"* I screamed. *"Polizia! Fai presto!"*

I heard cursing as someone fumbled with the bolt. The door opened, and Claudia burst in. She ran across the room and spun me around, slapping me hard across the face. "You want the police?" she asked, her chest heaving. "I'd be happy to bring them here and introduce them to you. I know one in particular who likes his girls pale and skinny, just like you."

"I don't believe you," I spat back at her.

She brought her face within inches of mine. "Scream again, and I'll prove it."

Nucci and Gallo ran in behind her, paintbrushes in hand.

"Get some rags," she ordered, her face flushed beneath its powder.

Gallo hurried out of the room.

I swiveled back toward the crack in the boards, praying I would see the women running for help. But they were ambling on up the street, heads bent again in conversation, my cries already forgotten.

Nucci grabbed me by the waist and swung me around, holding me in a stinking embrace in front of Claudia. She clucked at me and shook her head. "Oh, you're a frisky one. Un-Occhio is going to like you."

Gallo ran back in with a fistful of rags. He tied my wrists at Claudia's direction, then pushed me to my knees and secured my wrists to the side of the radiator beneath the window. Meanwhile, Nucci wrapped one of the wider strips around my mouth and nose, pulling it tight with a vicious tug. The fabric obstructed my nostrils, making it difficult to breathe. I started to panic, making it even harder to draw a full breath. I grunted in protest, working my jaw to try to free my nose, assuming he'd adjust it if he realized it was suffocating me — but he only watched me struggle with a smirk.

Claudia swept her arm around the room, pointing at each girl in turn. "No one helps her, *capite*?" With that she left the room, taking the men with her.

As soon as the bolt had slid into the lock, Teresa scuttled over and pulled the rag down to my chin. "You mustn't give them reason to hurt you!"

I sucked in a deep breath. "And you mustn't help me," I wheezed, "or they'll hurt you too."

"I'll put it back when they return."

I wasn't sorry for what I had done, even though I was even more helpless now than before. If things went the worst for me, at least I'd know that I had tried. "Was there a girl here before named Lucia?" I asked her.

She sat back on her heels. "Yes, there was a Lucia here when I arrived. How do you know of her?"

"Her body was found in the East River last week. She drowned herself."

She frowned. "But I thought . . ."

"What?"

"When Un-Occhio couldn't capture Antonio he was very angry. I was sure he was going to hurt me, but he didn't. Instead, he hurt Lucia." She shook her head. "I think he must have still been hoping to make Antonio watch, the first time he took me. I know he sent his men to try to capture Antonio at least one other time."

"Why did he choose Lucia, do you suppose?"

"I don't know. Perhaps because she looked a little like me? But there were other times he hurt her that had nothing to do with Antonio. The last time, he took her into an empty stall down the hall. He had her there for a long time. We could hear her cries, but there was nothing we could do. And then suddenly, the cries stopped. I thought he must have killed her, because we never saw her again."

"No, he didn't kill her," I said, remembering the bruises on the girl's throat, "but he may have choked her badly enough to render her unconscious. She must have recovered after he left and managed to get out somehow."

We fell silent, Teresa staying beside me, keeping me company on the floor as we strained to interpret the sounds and smells from below. The scraping and sanding had stopped and the smell of paint was now strong in the air. We heard a stall door creak open again down the corridor, followed by the sound of hooves clopping down a ramp. "What time do you think it is?" I asked.

She shrugged. "I didn't hear the bell from the last ferry yet. But if they are bringing the horses down, they must be planning to leave soon."

Time stretched interminably as I waited for the sound of approaching footsteps. I had been reduced to a creature of instinct, my senses hyperalert, my energy focused solely on anticipating and repelling the next attack. Indeed, so attuned had I become to the pattern of sounds from downstairs that I was instantly aware when something changed. It started with a thump and a scuffling noise. Then a man shouted, followed by footsteps moving quickly up the ramp. There were more shouts, and the sound of something heavy falling somewhere nearby.

I sat up, my ears twitching and my eyes straining in the candlelight. "What's happening?"

Teresa's hand was gripping my arm. "I don't know."

"Pull up my gag."

No sooner had she done so than the footsteps thundered up the hallway and stopped outside the door. "Genna! Are you in there?" The bolt rattled in its slide, and the door swung open.

Simon stood on the threshold, his chest heaving and his shirt askew. His gaze took in the cots on the left, swept past me to the cots on the right, then snapped back to me in the middle.

I blinked hard, unable to believe what I was seeing. But yes, it really was Simon, looking like an avenging warrior with his hair disheveled and a lethal blackjack in his raised fist.

"Simom!" I cried into my gag, straining toward him against my bonds.

He stood oddly transfixed, his gaze fastened on my gaping chemise.

I heard more footsteps racing up the ramp. "Simom, hully!"

Finally, like a man coming out of a trance, he started toward me. But it was too late; before he'd completed a single step, Nucci rushed up behind him and smashed him over the head with a board. He collapsed into a heap on the floor.

"No!" I wailed as Nucci grabbed him by the ankles and dragged him out of sight.

I stared in horror at the empty doorframe.

Teresa tugged down my gag. "Who was that?"

I shook my head, unable to speak.

"He is your man?" she guessed. "Your *adorato*?"

I turned to her in a daze. "Yes," I said faintly, "my *adorato.*" And now, I thought as my eyes brimmed with tears, he was either dead or soon would be.

I had barely grasped the enormity of what had just occurred when there were more footsteps in the hallway, and Donato strode through the door.

"Everybody up," he ordered.

The girls began pushing themselves up and straggling toward the door. Donato's gaze turned to Teresa, who was still crouched by my side. "Quickly," he ordered, jerking his head toward the door.

She rose reluctantly and joined the others.

Drawing a knife from his waistband, he pulled the cork off the tip and strode toward me, bending to cut my wrists free. I scrambled to my feet and sidled away from him.

"Come," he barked, reaching for my arm.

In a moment of utter clarity, I realized that I would rather die than get into one of the vans downstairs. I punched his chest as he closed in on me and kicked blindly at his shins — but it was like attacking an ancient redwood, my blows as effective as the flapping of gnat wings against his unyielding bulk. He spun me around and pushed me ahead of him toward the door.

The board that had felled Simon lay just

beyond the threshold. With a surge of desperate energy, I lunged toward it and lifted it from the floor. Before Donato had time to react, I turned and swung it at his head, seeing him blink in surprise the second before it made contact. I held my breath, waiting for him to drop to the floor.

He shook his head with a grunt and started after me.

I turned to run but immediately tripped over a body that was splayed across the hall. It was Gallo, I saw as I fell to my knees, and his head was bleeding. Simon must have knocked him out with the blackjack on his way to me. I started pushing myself up, and was almost back on my feet when Donato reached around from behind me and pressed a damp cloth to my face. Despair washed through me when I smelled the familiar scent. I clawed futilely at his hand as my eyes began to tear and my ears to thrum. I couldn't go yet, I thought, not before I knew if Simon was dead or alive. It was the last thought I would have for some time.

CHAPTER NINETEEN

I came slowly to consciousness, holding on to the tail of a dream unlike any I'd had before. A delicious dream, in which Simon and I were together at last, lost in the delectable pleasure of each other's bodies. The images were rich and detailed, the sensations so intense that they still pulsed in the deepest parts of me, leaving me in a state of languorous desire. I opened my eyes reluctantly, loath to leave the blissful cocoon behind.

I blinked at the ceiling above me. This was not my bedroom. Reality suddenly came flooding back, swamping the lingering images from my dream. I felt a fresh, stabbing sense of loss at the memory of Simon's capture and my own inability to escape the monstrous Donato. It must have been the anesthetic, I realized, that had produced my erotic dream — a dream of a future now forever out of reach.

I pushed myself up on rubbery elbows and looked around me. What I saw didn't make sense. I was lying on the sofa in the Fabronis' parlor, covered by a large, fringed shawl. Mrs. Fabroni was sitting in a wing chair on the opposite side of the room, watching me.

"You're awake," she said in perfectly adequate English.

I struggled to sit up, my mind and body still sluggish from the drug. "What am I doing here?"

"It's all right. You are safe now."

I pulled the shawl around my shoulders, clutching it in front of my torn chemise. "Where's Simon?"

"He's fine. You'll see him shortly. He wanted to be here when you woke up, but I asked to see you alone first."

"He's here?"

"He was here. He went back to the stable with Antonio and Donato to help the police bring in Carulo's men."

I dropped my head to my knees. I didn't understand half of what she was saying, but all that mattered was that Simon was safe. "And Teresa?"

"She and the other girls are with Felisa, in the flat at the end of the hall." Pushing herself to her feet, she walked to a table behind the sofa and filled a small glass from a bottle containing an amber liquid. "Here," she said, holding it out to me. "Drink this. It will make you feel stronger."

I eyed it suspiciously.

"I am not your enemy, Miss Summerford."

"Until I understand what's going on, everyone's my enemy."

"Of course, you are confused," she said, setting the glass on the table beside me. "Please allow me to explain." Pouring herself a glass, she returned to the wing chair and sat down. "I was seventeen when I married," she began, her back straight and her voice devoid of emotion. "Ten years younger than my husband, who was already the *capo paranza* — the chief — of the Camorra in our quarter. At that time, my husband's main interests were money lending, gambling, and fixing elections. Like the *capo* before him, he was known as *Il Ragno,* the Spider, and was one of the most respected men in *Napoli.* But he wanted more."

She paused, taking a sip from her glass. "A few years after we married, my husband decided to enter the prostitution business to increase his profits. It sickened me to see him making money off the poor young girls in our quarter, but I had no say in his affairs. By this time, I had given him two children: Antonio, who you know, and a daughter, named Bianca. A short time after my husband starting selling women, my daughter became gravely ill. Fearing God was punishing us for my husband's deeds, I promised Him I would persuade my husband to stop the terrible business if only He would save my daughter's life. Miraculously, Bianca recovered. But my husband would not stop, no matter how much I begged him, and I was unable to keep my promise. Two months later my daughter's illness returned, and this time, she died."

She got up and crossed to the window, gazing down at the street. "In 1901 my husband was sent to prison during the uprising against the Camorra, after someone betrayed him. He had many loyal *picciotti,* but because I was the only one who was allowed to visit him, I became his eyes and ears and voice on the outside. At first, I delivered his orders exactly as he gave them to me. But once my role was secure, I began to make changes. I ordered the members of the organization to stop their prostitution activity and return their attention to other business, dividing my husband's share of the *paranza*'s proceeds between them to help make up for their losses. But of course, many resisted, and I was forced to impose a penalty for failure to obey. The first time, the price was a fine. The second time, the loss of a testicle." She turned back to me with a thin smile. "There never was a third time."

"So . . . Velloca was one of the men who worked for your husband's organization?" I asked, rubbing my aching head.

"Vittorio Carulo, the man you know as Velloca, was my husband's younger cousin, a *picciotto* with several years of service in the society. He was a cruel man with a bad temper, eager to reap the fruits from seeds that others had planted. I always suspected it was he who betrayed my husband, but I had no proof. When he refused to stop selling women, I sent four novices to remove his testicle with a wire garrote. He believed the order for the attack had come from my husband, and murdered him in revenge on the day he was released from prison. Fearing for my own life and that of my son, I left Italy and came to New York, determined to start a new life in which my son would have nothing to do with the Camorra. The last we heard of Carulo, he had joined a rival organization."

"So you didn't know he'd come to America."

"Not until you told us about the girl, Rosa, who had knowledge of Teresa's betrothal to Antonio. Until then, we thought Teresa might have been the victim of a Black Hand gang operating near the pier, and that was where Antonio was searching for her. But when you told us about Rosa, we became suspicious and sent one of Antonio's workers to investigate. He followed the girl's father from his home to the stable on 116th Street. Based on his description, I was nearly certain that Velloca was Carulo. And from the comings and goings Antonio's man saw at the stable, I guessed that Carulo had taken up horse theft again, his main business in Naples after prostitution."

"But why would Carulo want to hurt your son? His grudge was against your husband, not Antonio."

"There were many who believed that Antonio was running things while his father was in prison, even though he was only eighteen at the time. I let them think it, for it gave me more freedom to do what I needed to. Carulo must have believed that Antonio relayed the order for the attack against him. Once we knew he was in New

York, we suspected he had taken Teresa for revenge. Especially after my son was attacked."

"At the bank, you mean."

She shook her head. "That was the first time, which we believed was a simple robbery attempt. But a few days later, after we discovered that Carulo was in the city, two men threw a bag over Antonio's head and tried to push him into a van. My son has been careful to keep some friends by his side ever since." She sipped again from her glass.

I tentatively lifted my own glass and tasted the liqueur inside. It was sweet and syrupy, tasting of hazelnuts, and left a comforting trail of warmth behind.

"We couldn't confront Carulo until we knew where he was hiding Teresa," she continued, "so I sent a trusted friend to infiltrate his operation."

"Donato," I said, as the pieces started coming together.

"Yes. He approached Carulo's man, Nucci, suggesting he had experience stealing horses, and was hired to help with the stable operation. On his first day of employment he brought in a rig that he told them was stolen, thereby earning their trust. Yesterday, after we'd made sure their regular driver was indisposed, they asked him to drive the carriage to pick up the newest girl from the pier."

"Why was he still playing along if he knew where Teresa was?"

"He didn't know. He'd learned that they were holding girls in at least one other place, and he'd never seen the girls at the stable because he had no reason to be there at night when they came down. Until to-night, when he was ordered to stay and help repaint the stolen vehicles."

"Yes, that's right; Donato was in the base-ment when they brought us down to eat. He must have seen Teresa then."

"He was supposed to come back for help, once he'd confirmed Teresa's presence. But it had become clear that they intended to move the girls out tonight, and he was afraid Teresa might be gone by the time he re-turned. So he stayed, hoping for a chance to escape with her when the others were oc-cupied. And then your Mr. Shaw arrived." A faint smile curved her lips. "Donato is not easily impressed, but he told me Mr. Shaw fought as fiercely as any Redshirt, breaking through the door, felling one of Carulo's men and rushing up to find you before anyone could lift a hand. Donato took care of the other man, and the woman, and after convincing Mr. Shaw that they were on the same side, he drove you all back here in one of the stolen vans. Once they'd delivered the women safely, they went back to meet the police at the stable."

"Simon — Mr. Shaw — wasn't badly hurt then?"

"I saw him only briefly, but he did not appear to be. He was well enough to go back to the stable with the others."

A wave of relief swept through me, turning my overstrung muscles to custard. I took a long sip of the liqueur, glad for its bracing warmth.

There was a knock on the hall door. *"Permesso?"* a man's voice called.

"Entra," Mrs. Fabroni replied.

The door opened, and Donato strode through to the parlor. There followed a rapid exchange in Italian with Mrs. Fabroni, which caused the creases in her forehead to deepen.

"What's the matter?" I asked her.

"Carulo's men were gone when the police arrived at the stable," she told me.

She spoke a few more words to Donato. He nodded and started toward the door, but stopped, as if remembering something. Turning to face me, he removed his hat and held it sheepishly between his hands. He glanced from me to Mrs. Fabroni, muttering something I couldn't understand.

"Donato's English is not so good," she said. "He asks me to tell you he is sorry for giving you the *cloroformio,* but there was no time to explain. He was afraid Carulo might be on his way to the stable or might be sending more men to finish the vans."

"Tell him I understand," I said, meeting Donato's gaze.

Donato said something else that caused Mrs. Fabroni to raise an eyebrow. "It seems he must also apologize for striking you in the face," she said as her eyes flicked to my swollen jaw. "He says it was necessary to keep you from giving him away, and he hopes you can forgive him."

I thought back to when Gallo and Donato first discovered me on the sidewalk outside the poultry plant. I'd been about to reveal that I'd seen Donato with Antonio when he punched me. I also remembered that it had been Donato who urged Gallo to subdue me with chloroform when I resisted, instead of throttling me half to death. "Please tell him that I accept his apology." I paused, then added, "And that I'm sorry for hitting him on the head with the board."

Mrs. Fabroni's other eyebrow rose, but she conveyed my apology without comment.

385

Donato grunted in response, looking even more sheepish than before, and continued out the door.

"Where are Antonio and Simon now?" I asked Mrs. Fabroni.

"They have gone to Carulo's home." Seeing me stiffen, she added, "Have no fear. The police went with them."

I let out my breath, relieved to know that the police were on the case, and that Velloca — or Carulo — would soon be locked away where he could no longer be a threat to anyone. "Why wouldn't Antonio speak to the police before?" I asked. "Was he afraid they'd discover you'd been involved with the Camorra? Or was he, perhaps, involved as well? You suggested that he wasn't, and yet he bears the Spider tattoo."

"Of course, his father wished him to be initiated, and believing it would make him a man in other people's eyes, Antonio was eager to comply," she told me. "He had listened to his grandfather's stories about the honorable ways of the old Camorra and had no appreciation of how things had changed. But once he came to truly understand what his father did to make his living, he wanted no part of it."

I didn't know if it was because of the passage of time, or the liqueur, or the remarkable self-possession of the woman before me, but I had stopped trembling and was finally beginning to believe that I was safe. Safe enough that I dared to ask, "So Antonio isn't the one who's been sending threat letters in the name of the Spider, here in America?"

She appraised me over the rim of her glass, swirling the liqueur within. "The Spider has bitten only once in this country," she said finally. "And it was not my son who inflicted the bite. It was me."

I stared at her in dismay. I'd been ready to forgive her the criminal past that had apparently been thrust upon her, in light of her attempts to repair the damage done by her husband and to start a new life in America. But if she was still engaging in extortion, she was no better than any other Black Hand operator.

"I vowed I would have nothing to do with the old ways when I came here," she added, watching my face, "but honor required me to break that pledge."

"How can it ever be honorable to make anonymous threats?" I demanded, pulling the shawl more tightly around my shoulders.

She put down her glass and sat back. "For two years after I came to this country, I led a quiet life, helping my son build his business. I wanted nothing to do with the Camorra or its ways. But then, one day last spring, Donato came to see me. Donato, whom I have known since childhood, and who is the man I would have married had my parents not chosen for me." She waited a moment for this to sink in, then continued, "Donato came to New York on the same boat I did, and found work here as a laborer. Two months ago he sponsored his niece and nephew, who were hoping to find work in the city as well. His nephew was hired as a digger in the subway tunnels, while his niece, Felisa, found a job as a chambermaid through an employment agency. You may remember Felisa, for she was here the first time you came to the flat."

I nodded, remembering the young woman who'd been having supper with Antonio and Donato.

"The head of the family who hired her was a man of some distinction, a banker with much influence among the *Napolitani* here. One day, while his wife and children were out of the house, he attacked and violated Felisa, telling her afterward that he was protected by important men and warning her that if she told anyone what he had done, things would go badly for her. Knowing that her brother and uncle would try to avenge her, she said nothing of what had happened, fearing that they would be killed by her employer's protectors. But she refused to go back to work, and Donato, sensing a change in her, eventually prevailed on her to tell him what was wrong."

She crossed her arms over her chest, her face hardening, and for a moment, I glimpsed the woman who'd been capable of forcing an entire organization to come to heel. "Knowing of my past, Donato came to me seeking justice. Using the Spider insignia, I sent a letter to the banker demanding ten thousand dollars in penance, which I intended to use to set the girl up in business, as no man would want her now for his wife. When he chose not to pay, we set off a bomb in his bank after hours. Then we sent a second letter, threatening his life. This time, he complied."

"Who set the bomb?"

She shrugged. "A friend from the old days. He repairs watches now in Brooklyn, but he owed me a favor."

I had to admit, there was a rough justice in what she had done. "But what about the other bombings? The police told me there have been several connected to Spider threat letters."

"That is the only time the real Spider has

spun a web in America," she said firmly. "On this, I give you my word."

The door flew open, and Antonio barged into the room, red faced and panting, with Simon at his heels. "Carulo denied everything!" he shouted. "The police left without arresting him."

Simon hurried toward me, looking ten years older than the last time I'd seen him. "Genna!" He crouched in front of me, clasping my shoulders and scouring my face with his eyes. "Are you all right?"

I could only nod, suddenly incapable of speech.

He gingerly touched my swollen jaw.

"It doesn't hurt anymore," I assured him.

He looked so miserable that I felt compelled to assume a lightheartedness I was far from feeling. "What about your head?" I asked, lifting my hand to his scalp, where I encountered an egg-sized lump. "Does it hurt?"

"No more than I deserve," he said with disgust, "letting him sneak up on me like that."

I didn't recall any sneaking being involved, but I wasn't about to chide him for finally being mesmerized by me, even if the timing had been less than ideal. "Have you seen Patrick? Is he all right?"

"He's fine. He was just tied up for a while."

I heaved a sigh of relief, hardly able to believe we'd all emerged relatively unscathed. Glancing at Antonio, I asked, "So why hasn't Velloca been arrested?"

"Cassidi said he needs to get affidavits from the girls first, as a basis for the arrest warrant. He should be here soon."

"But he did question him?"

"He did, hoping Velloca might give something away, but the man is too slick. He came to the door in his nightclothes, as if we'd just awakened him from a deep sleep. Said he knew nothing about the stable and swore he hadn't been visited by anyone at his home tonight. His mother backed him up."

"What if he runs before Cassidi can get the warrant?"

"He could." He frowned. "But I don't think he will. He's too cocky. I could see it in his eyes. He thinks he's going to get away with it."

"And the other men? Gallo and Nucci?"

"I gave the detective a good description. Every cop in the city will be on the lookout for them. They'll probably be in custody by tomorrow."

Antonio and his mother were arguing on

the other side of the room. "I did not come all the way to America to see you go to prison!" I heard Mrs. Fabroni say.

"But he has to pay!"

"Leave this to the police, Antonio," his mother urged.

All Teresa needed, I thought, was to see her fiancé go to jail for murder, after everything she'd already been through. "Mr. Fabroni," I broke in, in hopes of diverting him. "Have you been to see Teresa yet?"

At the sound of her name, he seemed to freeze. He slowly turned to me, the anger leaching from his face, replaced by something I couldn't quite read. "No."

"You should go to her," his mother said.

He glanced toward the door, raking a hand through his hair. I couldn't tell if it was fear or disgust I saw moving through his features.

"You have seen her?" he asked his mother.

"Only for a moment, when she arrived."

"How is she?"

"I cannot tell you how she is, Antonio. I can only tell you where she is. Down the hall, with Felisa and the others."

He nodded, but made no move for the door.

"Antonio . . ." his mother began.

"I can't face her!" He threw himself onto

the chair beside her, dropping his head into his hands.

It was fear then, I decided, hoping that I was right. I stood. "Do you think I could see her?" I asked Mrs. Fabroni.

"Of course," she said, getting up from her chair. "I will take you."

Simon's hand landed lightly on my shoulder. "Are you sure you don't just want me to bring you home?"

"I won't be long," I told him. "Wait for me here, all right?"

I followed Mrs. Fabroni out of the flat. As soon as the door had closed behind us, I asked, "Do you think Antonio still intends to marry her?"

She shot me a penetrating look. "That, only Antonio can tell you."

"I suppose it's a lot for him to come to terms with."

"It will be a test of his heart," she agreed. "A test I hope he will not fail."

At the door of the rear flat, she stopped and turned to me. "I have seen that you have courage, Miss Summerford. I trust that you are also capable of discretion. Tonight, I have spoken to you woman to woman so that you might understand the circumstances in which you find yourself. But I must ask that you not repeat what I have told you to anyone. Not even your Mr. Shaw."

It was strange, but I did feel an odd sort of sisterhood with this woman, born, I supposed, of the peculiarly female terror that I had endured over the last several hours, and of my knowledge of her anonymous crusade to help the victims of rape and prostitution. I felt no compulsion to tell the police about actions in her past that I couldn't bring myself to condemn. "All right," I agreed. "But you can trust Mr. Shaw."

"Trust is not something we give easily," she replied. "The less he knows, the better. For him as well." Her dark eyes probed mine for a moment longer until, apparently satisfied with what she'd seen, she lifted her hand and rapped on the door.

The reticent young woman I'd seen in Antonio's kitchen on my first visit answered her knock. Her gaze swung from Mrs. Fabroni to me, taking in my state of dishabille.

"Felisa," Mrs. Fabroni told her, "Miss Summerford is here to see Teresa."

"You were with them?" she asked me.

"As you see," Mrs. Fabroni answered, gesturing toward my torn chemise. "Perhaps you can lend her some clothes to wear home."

Felisa beckoned me into the flat.

"Tell Teresa I will visit her later," Mrs. Fabroni said and started back down the hall.

Francesca and four of the other girls from the stable were sitting at a large worktable covered with ostrich feathers in the front room, drinking from steaming metal cups and talking quietly among themselves. Felisa led me in the opposite direction, to the kitchen. "Teresa, the American lady is here to see you," she announced. Turning to me, she murmured, "I'll get you some clothes," and continued down the hall toward the bedrooms.

Teresa was sitting in a tin washtub in the middle of the kitchen floor, surrounded by a cloud of steam, scouring her bruised arms and chest with a dishcloth. She looked up briefly when I entered. "I don't know your name," she said as I took a seat at the small kitchen table.

"It's Genevieve."

A pot was simmering on the stove, adding more steam to the already saturated air. I let the shawl drop from my shoulders, feeling the damp heat penetrate my corded neck muscles.

"Genevieve," she repeated with a nod, moving the cloth to her other arm. She was scrubbing herself so roughly that it was leaving red streaks across her skin.

"I've just seen Antonio," I told her.

She paused for an instant, her gaze trained on a blotchy arm, then started scrubbing again.

"You should let him know that you want to see him, Teresa."

"Teresa is dead."

I sighed. "What happened to you wasn't your fault."

"I thought I was something special," she said as if I hadn't spoken, dragging the cloth around her neck. "But I am just a stupid, selfish girl. I will buy a ticket back to Italy as soon as I can get the money. He'll be better off without me."

"At least give him a chance," I implored. "If he's half the man you believe he is, he'll do right by you."

Finally, she stopped scrubbing and looked up at me, her eyes brimming with tears. "How can I ask him to marry me, when every time he looks at me, he will imagine me with Un-Occhio?"

"Oh, Teresa." I shook my head. "You are more than what happened to you in that stable. Of course, I can't know what Antonio will do, but whatever he loved about you is still there, waiting to be loved again."

She pressed her quivering lips together. "You don't understand." She scooped up some steaming water in the cloth and poured it over her head, turning her face into the stream.

"What don't I understand?" I asked, sitting back.

She dropped the cloth into her lap and stared down at it as water dripped from her hair. "There are . . . pictures. Of him, and me."

"Pictures?" It took me a moment to comprehend. "You don't mean . . ."

She looked up. "After Antonio escaped from Un-Occhio's men the first time, Un-Occhio brought a man with a camera to the stable. He wanted the man to take pictures while he forced himself on me. He told me he was going to send the pictures to Antonio. But he . . . he couldn't do it."

"Couldn't send them?"

Her steam-reddened cheeks turned even redder. "Couldn't . . . enter me. Not then."

I thought of Krafft-Ebing's sexual psychopath, aroused more by suffering and humiliation than by the sex act itself. Perhaps, foiled by Antonio's absence, Velloca had lacked the stimulus he needed to attain an erection.

"But he kept trying, at other times," she went on in a ragged voice, "and finally . . . he was able." She drew in a breath. "Then last night, the photographer came back and got his pictures."

"And this photographer made no protest, when he saw that you were being held captive?"

"Protest?" she spat out. "He was enjoying himself. Un-Occhio told him he could have one of the other girls when he was finished."

After everything else I'd seen and heard in the last week, I supposed this shouldn't have shocked me, but I was still sickened to my core.

"Once Antonio sees the pictures," she said faintly, shaking her head, "he will never be able to forget."

I was afraid she might be right, and that Velloca would succeed in his hateful mission. I chewed on the inside of my lip, trying to think of some way to keep that from happening.

"What kind of camera was it?" I asked after a moment.

"I don't know," she answered with a helpless shrug.

"Big or small?" I asked, spacing my hands first at the approximate width of a view camera, and then at the width of the smaller, box variety.

"Big."

"Was it on a tripod?"

"A what?"

"On legs."

She nodded.

It was a view camera then, the kind professionals used. "Do you know what the photographer's name was?"

Her lips twisted in disgust. "He called him Steemitz."

If the pictures were only taken the night before, there was a good chance they'd still be at the photographer's studio. "What if I tried to locate Mr. Steemitz and relieve him of the pictures before he delivered them to Velloca?"

She straightened, a glimmer of hope in her eyes. "You would do this?"

"If I promise to try, will you agree not to buy a ticket back home just yet?"

She frowned at me.

"Please? Just take a little time to think things over." I held my breath, watching the struggle take place across her features.

"All right," she said finally. "But I will not see Antonio."

Felisa returned with clothes for us both, and I dressed and left the flat. As I walked back down the hall to the Fabronis', I felt a pang of unease, worrying that I may have unduly raised Teresa's hopes. I had no idea if I'd even be able to locate the photographer, let alone convince him to give me the photographs. But I felt I had to at least attempt it, for if I could return the pictures to Teresa, it seemed to me, I'd be returning a little piece of her soul, as well.

CHAPTER TWENTY

"You sure you're all right?" Simon asked me for the dozenth time as we were riding back to my house in a hansom cab. He hadn't taken his eyes off of me for a second, ever since we'd sat down.

"I'll be fine," I snapped. "You don't need to treat me like an eggshell that's going to break at any moment."

He pulled back with a frown. "Sorry. I'll try not to."

I bit my lip, blinking back tears. The fact was, I did feel like an eggshell, and I didn't like the feeling one bit. But I had no cause to take it out on Simon. I was sure he was anxious to hear the details of my captivity, but I just couldn't bring myself to talk about it. Not yet. "How did you find out where I was?" I asked instead.

When he arrived at the pier and no one was there, he told me, he tried contacting Patrick and Detective Cassidi to find out what was going on. When that failed, he called Katie, who informed him that I wasn't at home. At that point, he returned to the saloon, reasoning that if anyone was trying to reach him, they'd call him there. At five thirty, Patrick telephoned and told him what had happened, explaining that he'd been discovered as he was following the suspects up a side stairwell to the second floor of the poultry plant. The men had tied him up and left him in a machine room at the foot of the stairs, where he wasn't found until a plant worker came in to shut down the equipment for the night.

"You're sure he wasn't hurt?" I asked.

"The only thing injured was his pride. They came up behind him, threw a bag over his head, and wrestled him to the floor. He never even saw their faces. But he heard a woman scream, soon after he was locked up, and figured they'd gotten you too. He called Detective Cassidi as soon as he was released, and between them, they questioned the workers at the plant, but the men claimed to have seen nothing and to have no knowledge of what went on upstairs."

"What was upstairs, exactly?"

"A room a lot like the one in the stable, where girls had obviously been held, but no clue as to where they might have taken you."

I shivered, despite the balmy night air. "So how did you figure it out?"

"It occurred to me that if I could find out who owned the poultry plant, it might lead me to the men in the carriage, and hopefully to you. The city offices were closed by that time, but I was able to pull a clerk I know away from his dinner to open up the tax bureau and help me locate the property in the records. I discovered it was purchased by a man named Bruno Pardello nine months ago. As soon as I saw that, things started falling into place."

I looked at him blankly, for the name meant nothing to me.

"Pardello was the other name on the threat letter Velloca showed us, that day at his flat. He told us the letter was written to him and his partner, remember? I couldn't read much of the letter, since it was in Italian. But the name of his partner stuck in my head, because Pardello is also the name of the wrestler who beat Tom Sharkey for the heavyweight championship two years ago." He grimaced. "I lost a pile on that match.

"Anyway, when I asked Cassidi if he'd ever heard of him, he told me the Legion sent Bruno Pardello to Sing Sing over a year ago for horse theft. Apparently, he and his gang did a big business stealing untended butcher and grocer wagons in the downtown Italian colony. They'd drive the rigs right into their own stable on Elizabeth Street, then cut the horses manes and tails, or tie false hair to tails that were already bobbed, and cover up their markings. They drove the repainted wagons to regular buyers upstate in Centreville or down in Philadelphia and Elizabethport.

"It was a good racket while it lasted, but unfortunately for Pardello, there was another horse thief gang already operating in the downtown colony that didn't like him encroaching on its territory. The letter Velloca showed us was probably from the rival gang, telling him to bugger off. Apparently, it didn't have the desired effect, because a while later, the Italian Legion received some anonymous information, presumably from the rival gang, revealing the stable's location and activities and leading to Pardello's arrest."

"So knowing that Velloca had some association with Pardello, you concluded he was a partner in the horse theft business."

He nodded. "Using Pardello as his front man, most likely, since he himself wasn't sent to prison."

I frowned at him. "Why do you suppose

Velloca showed us that threat letter?"

"To cast suspicion on someone else, I suppose, and make himself look like a victim. Or maybe just to toy with us. He was probably laughing at us the whole time."

I shivered again, reminded of the malevolent intellect we were dealing with. "But how did any of this lead you to the stable on 116th Street?"

"That's where things get interesting. Like I said, the poultry plant was sold to Pardello nine months ago — *after* he went to prison. When I looked for additional Pardello holdings, I discovered that he owned a stable on 116th Street as well. That property was also purchased after he went to Sing Sing, presumably by someone who had power of attorney to act for him. I found it interesting that the stable was located right around the corner from Velloca's flat."

"And you concluded that Velloca might still be using Pardello as a front?"

"The way I figured it, after their downtown operation was broken up and Pardello went to prison, Velloca must have moved the horse theft business up to Harlem, where he could graze in less crowded pastures. Either the business was less profitable there, or he just got greedy, but at some point he saw the value of expanding his operations to include prostitution. He already had distribution lines in place for the stolen rigs. All he had to do was switch from open wagons to vans and fill the vans with girls to substantially increase his profits. It seemed even more likely when I realized that Velloca was one of the few people who would have known that Teresa Casoria was coming to New York, thanks to her friendship with his daughter."

"So then you came charging up to the stable to save me," I said, my heart swelling at the thought, "without even waiting for help from the police."

He smiled wryly. "I was pretty much out of my mind, it's true, but I wasn't quite that far gone. I called the 104th Street Station before I left and asked them to send up the reserves in half an hour. I just wanted to get there first, to try to make sure you were safe before any shooting started." He grimaced. "A lot of good it did you."

He looked so mortified that I reached for his hand and gave it a squeeze. "If you hadn't come when you did and knocked out Gallo, Donato could never have gotten us out of there in time."

The hansom swayed as the horses turned right onto Ninety-Second Street. I gazed out the side window at the empty sidewalks and darkened buildings rolling past. Although I'd traveled down this street hundreds of times, the buildings all looked strangely unfamiliar, their dark windows peering back at me like hostile eyes from their pale facades. I turned my gaze forward, trying to concentrate on things that would need doing when I returned home. But unwanted images kept flashing into my mind, pulling me back to the stable and the terror and degradation I'd known there. I knew it wasn't my fault that I'd been gagged and pawed and treated like chattel — but I still felt dirty and humiliated all the same.

It was long past midnight by the time we stepped out of the cab. I stiffened at the sight of a policeman standing next to our stoop, fearing that some new calamity had befallen my household.

"It's all right," Simon said, taking my elbow and guiding me forward. "I asked for an officer to be posted at your house until Velloca and his thugs are in custody."

I nodded mutely to the officer and climbed up the steps, where I had to ring the bell, since I no longer had my key.

"Thank the Lord," Katie cried as she pulled open the door. Her skirt seams were crooked, and her hair was falling from its pins. "Where on earth have you been? I've been thinking the worst since Simon called."

"I'm sorry, Katie," I said. "I was just . . ." For once, I could think of no little white lie to soothe her.

"Come on," said Simon. "You'd better sit down." He led me into the sitting room and lowered me onto the chaise longue. "Is there any whiskey in the house, Katie?"

Though she was obviously bursting with questions, she shuffled off to retrieve the bottle from my father's study.

"I don't know what I'm going to tell her," I said as her footsteps clicked down the hall.

"How about the truth?" Simon suggested.

Instead, when she returned with the whiskey and three glasses, I gave her a modified version of the truth, telling her I'd been swept up by a kidnapping gang rather than a white slavery ring, omitting any mention of chloroform or attempted rape. I also told her I'd been hit by an elbow in all the commotion when the policemen came to our rescue, to explain the bruise on my jaw. "But the good news," I finished with a brightness I was far from feeling, "is that we found the girl I was searching for, so it was all for a good cause."

Katie drained her glass and dropped it onto the tray table with a crack. "And what was I supposed to tell your parents if things *hadn't* worked out?"

Her hand, I saw, was trembling on the glass. "I'm sorry, Katie," I said, my false smile evaporating. "I never meant for things to get so out of hand."

"Well, it's over now," Simon said with a pointed look at Katie.

"If it's over," she asked, "why is there a policeman standing on our stoop?"

"He's just here to protect us until they round up all the gang members," I told her.

"Come on now, Katie," Simon cajoled. "We all had a good scare, but things turned out all right in the end. And thanks to Genna, some very bad people are going to get their comeuppance."

Katie let out her breath. "I suppose you're right," she said as some of the starch went out of her shoulders. "What's done is done. There's no point going on about it." Her pale-blue eyes searched mine. "I just hope you've learned your lesson!"

I nodded, eager to wipe the anxiety from her face, although I wasn't sure exactly what the lesson was.

She clapped her hands against her thighs. "All right, then. Let's get you to bed." She hoisted herself up from the chair.

"Wait! Not yet," I protested as Simon rose to leave. I wasn't ready to be alone with my thoughts. "I'd like Simon to stay a little longer. Please, Katie."

She looked from me to Simon, and her shoulders heaved with another long-suffering sigh. "Fine," she muttered. She crossed to the windows and pulled down the shades. Returning to collect the whiskey bottle and empty glasses, she added, "But I'll be listening!" She glared at each of us before disappearing into the hall.

Simon sat back down, studying me with a frown. "I don't suppose you want to tell me what really happened."

"I will, later. But I'm trying not to think about it at the moment."

Mercifully, he didn't press me. "All right," he said. "Then what else can I do to help?"

Unexpected tears suddenly blurred my vision. "Do you think you could just . . . hold me?"

I saw the breath go out of him. Crossing to the chaise, he lifted me carefully to one side, then lowered himself next to me and took me in his arms.

This was not how I had envisioned our first real adult embrace — but it was exactly what I needed at the moment. I closed my eyes and laid my ear against his chest, listening to the steady beat of his heart. "I didn't think I'd ever see you again," I whispered.

"I would have found you, no matter where they took you. Or died trying."

His voice vibrated through his chest like a solid thing, holding me together as I struggled not to fall apart. "I wasn't raped," I said into his shoulder.

I felt his breath stop for a moment before he slowly exhaled. "I'm glad to hear it. But it wouldn't matter if you had been. Not to me, I mean."

The wonderful thing was, I believed him. How lucky I was, I thought as the tears finally escaped from my eyes: lucky to be back in my own home, safe and sound; lucky to have Simon to love me, no matter what. I searched for his hand, clinging to it as my body gradually unwound. The whiskey and fatigue had caught up with me and were tugging on my eyelids. I caught myself drifting off and started fighting back to wakefulness, sensing dark shapes lurking just beneath my consciousness.

"It's all right," Simon murmured, pressing his lips to the top of my head. Only then did I let myself succumb, knowing it was safe to let go.

When I woke several hours later, I was wrapped snugly in a quilt and bright light was streaming in around the window shades.

A note lay in the space where Simon had been, telling me he'd gone to see Detective Cassidi but would be back soon.

I rolled off the chaise and climbed upstairs to take a bath. As the tub was filling, I assessed myself in the mirror. My ribs and larynx still hurt, but the swelling had gone down in my jaw, leaving only a bruise behind. Although I suspected it would be some time before I could walk down the street without looking over my shoulder, I was beginning to feel human again.

My own good fortune in escaping intact, however, only made me feel worse about Teresa. If I had been shaken to the roots by my experience, how must she be feeling? I'd been a captive for less than ten hours, while she'd been terrorized for thirteen days, subjected to rape and psychological torture. I had Simon's love to see me through — but Teresa? Would Antonio be with her, to help her recover from her ordeal?

The newspaper was waiting for me on the dining room table when I went downstairs. Katie bustled in from the pantry the moment she heard me, carrying a tray bearing tea, toast, and a boiled egg. She seemed to have decided that carrying on as normal was the best strategy, making no mention of the previous day's events as she poured my tea and cut the top of my egg with the egg scissors. I did my best to act normal as well, even managing a second piece of toast — not only to reassure Katie, but because I desperately wanted to *feel* normal, like someone who was in control of herself and the world around her, rather than the nervous creature who seemed to have taken up residence inside me.

As soon as I'd finished breakfast, I went up to my father's office and pulled the Trow's business directory from its shelf. There was no Steemitz listed in its pages. There was, however, a listing for "Stimitz, Morris, photographer" at 438 East 102nd Street. I sank onto my father's reading chair, staring down at the listing. I now had a name and an address. I also had a plan of sorts. But did I have the courage to carry it out? Doubts suddenly assailed me. What if the photographer saw through my ruse? What if I somehow ended up back in Velloca's hands?

Whatever composure I'd regained in the last few hours deserted me at the thought. What on earth had made me think I could do this? My heart was pounding in my chest again, and my throat was stopped up with dread. I couldn't do it. I couldn't put myself back in harm's way. I started to stand, but immediately sank down again, dropping my head into my hands.

I didn't want fear to take over my life. And I sensed that it would take over, if I let it, coloring my every decision, changing the way I moved in the world. I forced myself to wait for the panic to pass, for my body to grow quiet again. In the silence that followed, I heard the voice of the person I used to be, before life took such an unexpected turn. *You can do this,* it urged. *You have to do this, for yourself as much as for Teresa.*

I looked at the bottle of whiskey on the table beside Father's chair, remembering the relief it had brought me the previous evening. I uncorked the bottle and took a swig. The liquid burned down my throat, making me gasp. I took another, larger swallow for good measure, coughing as it went down.

A few minutes later, I was in my bedroom, putting together my costume. I started with the blouse Aunt Margaret had bought me, cutting out the lace inset so that nothing would be left to the imagination and then pairing it with a slim-fitting, dark-red skirt. I retrieved a fringed table runner from the linen pantry, wrapping it around my shoulders like a shawl, and an abandoned hat from the wardrobe in the maid's room — a gaudy, overblown affair sporting a waterfall of arching feathers. A thin red ribbon around my neck completed the ensemble.

Proceeding to my mother's boudoir, I covered the bruise on my jaw with several layers of powder and stained my lips and cheeks with rouge from the pot in the dressing table drawer. It was the same pot Mama had brought home with her from France fifteen-odd years ago, used so sparingly that I found it still three-quarters full. By the time I was done, only half remained.

I leaned back and stared at my reflection in the mirror, repulsed and weirdly fascinated by the painted woman I saw there. The woman I could have become. *Maybe this wasn't such a good idea,* I thought, breaking into a sweat beneath the powder. But I could think of no other way to get my hands on the pictures.

As soon as Katie had left to do her morning shopping, I draped a gauzy veil over my hat and face, wrapped the "shawl" around my bare shoulders and décolleté and — after looking through the front window to be sure no neighbors were about — let myself out of the house.

I turned off the stoop and plunged down the street, scurrying past the officer on watch with my face lowered, praying I wouldn't pass anyone I knew. I was nearly to the intersection when I heard someone call my name.

I cringed. Looking up, I saw Simon coming toward me up the avenue.

"Genna?" he called again as he drew closer. "Is that you?"

"Shh," I replied, glancing over my shoulder.

He came to a stop in front of me and peered through my veil. "What's that on your face?"

"Rouge," I said, stepping around him and starting across the intersection.

He grabbed my arm. "Hold on."

"We can't stop here," I said, dragging him with me across the street.

He fell into step beside me, his jaw muscles jumping. "Are you going to tell me what's going on before I do something I regret?"

Reluctantly, my face hot inside the veil, I told him about the photographs and my promise to Teresa to try to retrieve them. "The only way I can think of to do it is to pretend that Velloca sent me to pick them up," I finished. "And the only way someone is going to believe he sent me is if I look like this."

He groaned. "Sweet suffering Jesus,

haven't you had enough excitement? Why would you want to put yourself in more danger?"

I stopped and swiveled toward him. "I don't *want* to," I practically shouted at him as my eyes swarmed again with tears. "I *have* to."

"All right," he said, putting up his hands. "All right." He studied me for several long moments. "I think I understand."

I blinked the tears away, embarrassed by my new inability to control my emotions. My doctor's brain understood that this was to be expected after what I'd been through, but I was going to have to get a grip on myself if I was to be of any use to Teresa.

He handed me a handkerchief. "So let me help you."

I nodded at him, blowing my nose, and we started together toward East Harlem.

I stood on the corner of 102nd Street, eyeing the dreary shop a dozen yards down the block. "Stimitz Photography," read the chipped and fading gold letters on the window front. The glass was grimy, and the door hadn't been painted in some time. I straightened my shoulders, working up my courage.

"Having second thoughts?" Simon asked me.

"No. Well, yes, but . . . no. I can do this."

"Just remember, you can turn around and walk out anytime. I'm going to be standing two feet outside that door, and if I hear so much as a peep from you, Mr. Stimitz is going to wish he'd never been born."

I blew out my breath. "All right, here goes." I peeled off my veil, handing it to Simon, and dropped the shawl to my elbows, revealing my low décolleté.

"Jesus, Mary, and Joseph," he muttered.

For once, I didn't care that I was blushing, for I was wearing so much rouge I knew he wouldn't be able to tell.

We crossed to the opposite side of the street, Simon a few paces behind me, and continued down the sidewalk toward the studio. Simon stopped in front of the adjacent harness shop, pretending to peruse the inventory, while I pulled open the studio door and went inside.

There was no one at the counter. I paused inside the door, breathing in the scent of chemicals and something faintly putrid, like days-old food. The shelves along the walls were littered with empty plate crates and stacks of dusty magazines, and the floor looked as though it hadn't been swept in some time. I approached the bell on the counter, which was wedged between a glass funnel and a broken bulb-and-tube assembly, and gave it a tap. A moment later I heard answering footsteps in the back room.

A scrawny, middle-aged man with slumping shoulders, a long neck, and a prominent Adam's apple walked through the door behind the counter. "May I help you?"

I relaxed slightly at the sight of his unimposing physique. This was not someone who could easily subdue me. I tipped my head and looked him slowly up and down. *"Buongiorno,"* I said in a sultry drawl, doing my best imitation of the keeper at the stable. "Claudia sent me to see if the pictures for your customer at 116th Street are ready." Since I didn't know what name Velloca had used when he hired the photographer, I had decided this would be the best approach. I held my breath, wondering if he would take exception.

His gaze swept over my scanty costume, pupils dilating in response. "I haven't seen you before."

I leaned over the counter, propping my chin on my hand and placing my cleavage directly under his nose. "Well, you're seeing me now."

He swallowed, making the Adam's apple

bob in his scrawny neck as his eyes darted between my face and my breasts. "I told him I'd have them by tonight. I haven't mounted them yet, and I've got other orders ahead of him."

"But he wants them now."

"Eager, ain't he?" He snickered. "Not that I can blame him."

I felt a flash of anger at the thought of this miserable excuse for a man taking vicarious pleasure from Teresa's suffering. But I needed to manipulate him, not rebuke him — so I reined my anger in, channeling it into an acting performance I hoped even Maude Adams would be proud of. "He says he will pay you more if you can give them to me now," I said, infusing the words with a seductive lilt.

"How much more?"

"Double," I answered promptly. And then, just to make sure there would be no further haggling, I added, "Plus an hour with one of the girls."

He licked his lips, his gaze returning to my cleavage. "How about an hour with you?"

I repressed a shiver of revulsion. "I'm sure that could be arranged."

He nodded. "Give me twenty minutes."

As soon as he'd disappeared into the back

room, I ran to the door and stuck out my head. Simon swiveled toward me, his eyes questioning. "Everything's fine," I whispered. "He's finishing the photographs now." I went back inside to wait.

When Stimitz returned, he had a large manila envelope in his hand. He also had a new swagger in his step and a decidedly nasty gleam in his eye — whether incited by thoughts of me, or the images he'd just been handling, I didn't want to know.

"Here they are," he said. He laid the envelope on the counter. It was thick with photographs and smelled of mounting paste.

"He wants the plates too."

"What does he want those for?"

I shrugged one shoulder. "This girl, he doesn't like to share."

Grumbling, he went into the back again and returned with a stack of glass plate negatives, housed in thin yellow envelopes and tied together with a piece of string. He dropped his hand over the stack when I reached for it. "How about a little kiss, as prepayment?" he asked, his Adam's apple bobbing.

"How about you give me my change first?" I countered, sliding a five-dollar bill on the counter to be sure I was covering the agreed-upon price.

He quickly made the change and handed it over.

"These are all of the negatives?" I asked.

"That's all of 'em." He leered at me. "You want a box to carry them in, it's going to cost you extra."

I smiled thinly. "I don't need a box." Taking the stack in both hands, I turned away from the counter, lifted the plates to my chin, and dropped them onto the floor. The thin glass sheets made a satisfying *crunch* on impact. I stomped on the top of the stack with my heel, then flipped it over and stomped some more, until the envelopes' contents felt like gravel under my shoe.

I turned back to the gaping Stimitz with a shrug. "Like I said, the customer doesn't like to share." I scooped up the envelope of photographs and started for the door.

"Hey, what about my kiss?" he called after me.

"I'd rather kiss a donkey's turd," I replied over my shoulder in Italian, and hurried out of the store.

CHAPTER TWENTY-ONE

Though it hadn't been easy facing Stimitz, I felt stronger for having done so. Now I just needed to convince Teresa that without the pictures, she and Antonio stood a chance of putting the past behind them. I let Simon walk me home, but declined his offer to accompany me back up to Harlem, knowing that he had work to tend to and that I would need to speak with Teresa alone. Instead, I promised to have Maurice drive me up and wait for me.

As I'd hoped, Katie was down in the kitchen when I entered the foyer, eliminating the need for sartorial explanations. She'd left a message for me on the console table, telling me that Detective Cassidi had paid a call while I was out. The detective had requested that I come to his office between the hours of two and four so that he could take my deposition. I glanced at the hallway clock on my way upstairs; it was just after noon now. I had plenty of time to return the pictures to Teresa first.

Half an hour later, after I'd scrubbed my face, changed my clothes, and eaten a light lunch of toast and sardines, I set out in the motorcar with Maurice. Before Father purchased our motorcar, Maurice had served as our groom and coachman. He was a compctcnt whip and skilled rider, and had a marvelous rapport with the horses. He'd been getting on in years, however, and my parents were concerned that the physical requirements of the job were becoming too much for him. They'd "promoted" him to the position of chauffeur to solve the problem with the least possible injury to his dignity.

Unfortunately, Maurice had never achieved the same affinity for the mechanical conveyance as he had for its flesh-and-blood counterparts. The drive up to 109th Street was no exception. He always drove well under the eight-mile-an-hour speed limit, but traversing the streets of Italian Harlem took even longer than usual because he kept slowing to a crawl to stare and mutter at the unfamiliar sights. Although born in England, he'd lived in New York for over fifty years and was as suspicious as any Knickerbocker blueblood when it came to our more recent immigrants.

"Do you want me to go up with you, Miss Genna?" he asked when we finally pulled up in front of the Fabronis' building, frowning up at the windows as if he suspected armed hoodlums were waiting on every landing. I deduced that Katie had thoroughly briefed him on my recent trials.

"I don't think that will be necessary, Maurice, but thank you."

Carrying the borrowed skirt and shirtwaist that Katie had cleaned for me, I proceeded directly to the rear apartment, where Felisa once again opened the door. She was holding a threaded needle between her lips and a bunch of ostrich feathers in her hand. "Come in," she mumbled around the needle, leading me into the front room.

All the girls from the stable except Teresa were seated at the large table, each working a needle clumsily through a stack of feathers. Pieces of snipped quill lay scattered around their feet and feather particles floated around their bent heads. They appeared to be tying the stalks of the feathers together to create single, fatter plumes, of the type seen on fashionable ladies' hats.

Returning to her seat at the table, Felisa plucked the needle from her mouth to explain, "I'm teaching them to willow feathers for the hat manufacturers. If they learn well, they can earn fifteen cents for every knotted inch."

I watched Francesca struggle to tie a knot around two stems. "Are they all going to stay, then?"

"What else can they do?" Felisa asked, putting her needle down to help Francesca. "If they go back to their families the shame will always hang over them. Better to make a life for themselves here, among strangers." She nodded toward the clothing in my arms. "You can put that anywhere."

I glanced around the room. Every horizontal surface was covered in feathers or feather fragments. I brushed off a stool near the window and set the clothes on top. "Thank you for the loan. Is Teresa here?"

"She's in the back, ironing laundry."

Nodding to Felisa and the girls, I proceeded through the kitchen into the hall that led to the bedrooms. "Teresa?" I called.

The door to the rear room opened and Teresa stepped out, holding an iron. Her face was flushed and beaded with perspiration. I saw her gaze flick to my empty hands. She frowned, wiping the back of her hand across her forehead.

"Could I speak with you for a moment?" I asked.

She bobbed her head and disappeared into the room, reappearing a moment later without the iron and leading me into the kitchen. A loaf of bread and a half-eaten chunk of cheese lay on the middle of the table, along with some empty cups. She pushed these aside and sat down, gesturing to me to sit across from her.

I searched her face. She looked even more drawn than she had the previous evening. "How are you?"

She shrugged.

"Have the police been here?"

"They came last night after you left. They wanted us to tell them our stories, and agree to be witnesses against the men who took us."

Something in her expression made me ask, "And did you?"

Her lips twitched. "I wanted to."

"But?"

She looked down at her hands. "But I couldn't. If there was only me to think of, I would have." She looked up again, her eyes pleading. "But I can't bear to bring Antonio further shame by telling all the world what they did."

"I see," I said, struggling to hide my disappointment, galled that Velloca had managed to infect her with such self-loathing that she

427

couldn't even seek justice against him. "What about the others?"

"Francesca talked to them. She said she would speak in court as well. But the others . . ." She shook her head. "They are too afraid Un-Occhio and his men will come after them."

"Well, it's all right," I told her. "Francesca and I will testify against Velloca. The rest of you have been through enough already."

"I don't wish you to think me a coward."

"I could never think you a coward. I think you're one of the strongest, most courageous women I've ever met."

She recoiled at my words. "I'm not strong! If I was strong, I would have killed myself like Lucia."

"Please don't say that, Teresa. It takes tremendous strength to go on living after life has dealt you such a blow." It wasn't uncommon, I knew, for victims of violent crime to blame themselves for what had happened to them. At school, we'd been taught that this was a side effect of our need to believe we exerted control over our lives. Few of us would have the courage to get out of bed in the morning, after all, if we didn't fundamentally believe that the world was an orderly and predictable place, where following the rules would ensure that we were treated fairly. An unfortunate corollary of this belief was that if the world treated us unfairly, we must have done something to deserve it.

"What reason do I have to go on living, now that I have lost everything?" Teresa asked. "I live only because I haven't the courage to die."

"You still have a great deal to live for. Including, perhaps, a marriage with Antonio. You can't know unless you give him a chance."

"It isn't possible," she said, staring stubbornly at the table top.

"Would it help you to know that Antonio will never see the photographs?"

She looked up sharply.

I pulled the envelope from my bag and laid it on the table between us.

"You found them?" she whispered, making no move to take it.

I nodded, noting the glimmer of hope in her eyes. "I haven't looked at them."

She reached slowly for the envelope and pulled it toward her. Opening it with stiff fingers, she peered into the packet for half a heartbeat — then shut the flap and dropped it back onto the table.

"Antonio will never see them, Teresa," I said. "Un-Occhio has failed."

She shook her head, her face pale. "It doesn't matter. Antonio and I both know I am no longer fit to be the wife of any man."

"Because someone violated you against your will? How can you be held accountable for that?"

"Because . . . I let it happen," she rasped, the words catching in her throat.

"It wasn't your fault! What if it had been your friend or your sister who was taken instead? Would you blame her for what some wicked man forced her to do?"

She frowned, registering surprise and confusion at my question.

"Well, would you?" I pressed.

"But if I hadn't gone with him into the carriage —"

"Antonio was late! It was entirely reasonable for you to believe he'd sent someone to fetch you. Good Lord, if you have to blame someone, between the two of you, blame Antonio."

"I could never blame Antonio!"

I slapped my hands against the tabletop. "Then blame Un-Occhio! Blame the monster who did this to you!"

Her eyes fixed on mine, wide and unblinking.

"Oh, Teresa," I implored. "Be angry! Be angry at him for what he did."

Her breath left her in a long exhale. She looked down at the envelope, her lips compressing into a thin line. Opening the flap once more, she drew out one of the mounted photographs. Her nostrils flared as her gaze jumped around the image. She looked up at me, then back at the photograph. I held my breath, watching as a storm gathered across her features. Suddenly, she grasped the photograph by its top edge and started twisting it in both hands, until a rip appeared in the middle. She pulled harder, ripping it several more inches. Frustrated by the stiff backing, she snatched the knife from the cheese plate and stabbed and sliced at the image, tearing off pieces and crushing them in her fingers, until all that remained was a pile of mangled strips on the table. She put down the knife and stared, panting, at the wreckage.

I could hear the steady murmur of the women willowing out in the front room, and the muted din of horns and engines on the street outside. Inside the kitchen, however, time seemed to have stopped for a moment, as if to settle and cool. I imagined I could see Teresa growing lighter, steadier, as the hatred she'd been aiming toward herself began to turn like a lumbering sea vessel and point in a new direction.

"What do you say to burning the rest?" I asked after a moment.

She looked up at me, eyes shining at the prospect.

I opened the stove's firebox and threw some more coal on the grate. She waited until the flames were roaring and then slid the pictures in, one by one. I caught only glimpses of what they contained, but it was enough to make me thankful that Antonio would never set eyes on them. We listened in silence to the crackle of burning card stock, breathing in acrid chemicals as the photographs were reduced to ash.

"Burn in hell," Teresa whispered as the last one was consumed.

I was tired by the time I arrived at the Italian Legion thirty minutes later — bone-tired, despite the fact that Maurice had delivered me directly to the door. If I'd been my own patient, I would have chastised myself for taking on too much too soon. But I couldn't stop now, with Velloca's comeuppance so close at hand.

To my surprise, Simon was sitting with Detective Cassidi in the Legion's office when I arrived. Both men stood as I entered.

"Thank you for coming, Dr. Summerford," Cassidi said, pulling another chair in front of his desk. "I asked Mr. Shaw to come by as well, to provide us with corroborating evidence for the arraignment."

"Have you rounded up Velloca's men?" I asked Cassidi as we all sat down.

"Two of our detectives started canvassing the neighbors around the stable early this morning. They were able to identify the men who worked there as Marco Nucci and Pietro "Gallo" Gaspari. Based on Francesca Ragusa's deposition, we obtained arrest warrants for both men. We also contacted the police in Centreville and Elizabethport, on the chance they'd try to sell the stolen vans to Pardello's known buyers there. A few hours ago, we heard from the Centreville police. They have apprehended Nucci and are returning him to the city. He should be arriving at any moment." ·

"Oh, well done, Detective," I said.

"What about the other one? Gallo?" Simon asked.

"Nothing yet. We haven't been able to locate the woman, Claudia, either. But it's only a matter of time."

"And Velloca?" I prompted. "I assume he's been arrested by now?"

The detective pursed his lips. "There, we have a problem, I'm afraid."

"What do you mean?"

"Miss Ragusa confirmed that Nucci, Gallo, and Claudia were all involved in her abduction from the pier and subsequent confinement. But she wasn't able to provide any evidence against Velloca. In fact, she'd never even heard of him. I'm hoping that you may be able to give us what we need."

I frowned, not sure what I could tell him that Francesca already hadn't. "Like what?"

"Why don't you just tell me your version of events, from the time you left the pier," he said, pulling his memorandum book toward him.

I glanced at Simon. I would have preferred not to rehash the sordid details of my experience in his presence. But I supposed he'd have to hear them sooner or later, and if providing them to the detective would ensure Velloca's arrest, it might as well be sooner. "Well, as I believe Officer Branagan already told you, we decided to follow the carriage when it looked as though none of your men were tailing it," I began.

"For that, I must apologize," the detective broke in. "With Ellis Island and the Barge Office to cover as well, we could post only one man at the Thirty-Fourth Street pier. The couple Detective Silva followed turned out to be brother and sister. The detective was most distraught when he learned what had happened."

I shook my head. "It's not his fault. There were simply too many people to keep track of. In any event, when we didn't see a tail we followed the carriage ourselves, up to the plant on Thirty-Ninth Street, where Officer Branagan went inside to investigate and was captured. I was discovered shortly afterward and taken through a side door into the building."

"By Donato and Gallo," Cassidi said.

"That's correct."

"Did you see anyone else inside the building?" Cassidi asked.

"I heard someone behind me, but I couldn't see him."

"Why is that?"

With another glance at Simon, I answered reluctantly, "Because I was dragged backward into the building and then held down on the floor. So I was never able to look behind me. But I know it was Nucci, because Gallo called to him by name to get the van."

"And as far as you know, there was no one else but Nucci behind you?"

"As far as I know. Then Gallo put a chloroformed rag over my face, and when I came to, I was in the van with Francesca. I could hear Nucci and Gallo talking up front."

I told him about being brought up to the tack room at the stable, and everything I'd seen and heard there, and explained how I'd come to suspect Velloca. "And then, when we were finishing supper, we learned that they'd been ordered to move us out at midnight."

"Who gave this order?"

"Gallo. He came running in while we were eating and relayed the information to the others. I assumed he'd been to see Velloca."

"But Velloca didn't come himself."

I shook my head.

"And in the entire time you were there, no one mentioned Velloca by name?"

"No."

"All right," he said with a frown. "What happened next?"

"Then Nucci and Gallo took us all back upstairs . . ." I hesitated.

"Yes?"

"And told Francesca and me to take off our clothes."

A strangled oath escaped Simon.

Cassidi looked from Simon to me. "I'm sorry, Doctor. This must be uncomfortable for you. Perhaps you'd like Mr. Shaw to wait outside?"

"No, it's all right." I lifted my chin, reminding myself that I had no reason to feel ashamed. "Then the man Nucci attempted some unwanted familiarity, and I dissuaded him by stabbing him in the eye with Officer Branagan's call box key. When he took exception, Claudia pulled him off of me, reminding him that Velloca was entitled to first crack at all the new girls."

The detective paused in his scribbling to look at me askance.

"Pardon me if I've shocked you."

"Not at all," he said stiffly. "I appreciate your directness."

Simon's jaw appeared to have turned to stone. "I'd like to have a little chat with Mr. Nucci when he arrives," he told Cassidi.

"I'm sure you would," the detective replied, eying him warily. "But you're going to have to leave the questioning to the police." He turned back to me. "Now, Dr. Summerford, if you would continue?"

"There isn't much more to tell. We could hear the men working on the carriages and bringing down the horses. At one point, I tried to call out the window to some passersby and was tied to the radiator for my trouble. A short time later, I heard a great commotion, and then Simon burst through the door, followed by Donato a few minutes later. I believe you know the rest."

"So you never saw Velloca at any time during your captivity," the detective concluded.

"No, but I met him before, and I can tell you that he matches Teresa's description perfectly, right down to his silver ring."

He dropped his pencil onto the notebook. "I'm afraid that's not good enough."

"Good enough for what?"

"To obtain a warrant for his arrest."

I gaped at him. "How can that be?"

"To obtain a warrant, we need to show both that a crime was committed and that there are reasonable grounds to believe Velloca committed it. Without an affidavit from one of his victims, we can do neither."

"But you know exactly what he did! Teresa told me, and I've told you!"

"We need to hear it from the victim herself, or at least from someone who witnessed the crime. And unfortunately, neither Miss Casoria or any of the others who were there before you are willing to speak to us."

"But Francesca and I have testified that we were abducted by Nucci and Gallo, who we know were working for Velloca . . ."

He shook his head, cutting me off. "We don't as yet have any proof establishing a connection between Velloca and the others."

"The stable is in Pardello's name," Simon reminded me, "and we've got nothing else proving that he was involved with what was going on there."

I wracked my brain, trying to think of what proof we did have. One of Antonio's workmen had followed Velloca from his home to the stable, I remembered; that would constitute firsthand knowledge. But he hadn't witnessed any crime, and in any event, it was clear from my conversation with Antonio's mother that no one in the Fabroni coterie was going to confirm anything for the police. "Teresa told me the reason her abductor was called Un-Occhio was because he only had a single testicle," I told them. "It should be simple enough to ascertain whether Velloca is similarly deficient."

"Not if he hasn't been arrested," Cassidi said. "We can't drag anyone we want off the street and strip him of his clothes. Besides, as I said, Miss Casoria won't testify — as to her attacker's 'deficiency' or anything else."

"What about the soup then?" I tried. "I told you, his son complained that it was too salty at his flat. The soup they fed us at the stable was salty too. And it was in exactly the same type of lard pail."

"I'm sorry, Doctor," Cassidi said wearily, "but if I attempt to get an arrest warrant based on some salty soup . . ." He shook his head.

I sat back, crossing my arms. "You did question him last night?"

"I did."

"Then tell me, how does he claim to make a living if he has no involvement with the stable?"

"He told me he's a real estate agent. I looked into it. He has an office on 116th Street, three doors down from the stable."

"Well, isn't that convenient," I scoffed. "Did you ask to see a history of his recent transactions?"

"Unfortunately, it's not against the law to be a poor salesman."

I sighed in frustration. "Maybe you could arrest him for something else then. Have you considered that he might be the man behind the Spider bombings?"

"It's possible, but we've seen nothing to suggest he is. We searched the stable from top to bottom and found no evidence of bomb making or any other illegal activity."

"So Velloca is going to remain at large," I said in disbelief. "That's what you're telling me."

"I understand your frustration, Doctor. It's something I must deal with every day. But don't worry; it's only a matter of time before we find the evidence we need."

I rubbed my face, horrified to think that Velloca could still go free. And then it came to me. "Wait," I said, raising my head. "You said before that you needed testimony from one of his victims or from someone who'd seen him carrying out the crime, is that correct?"

"That's right."

I nodded with satisfaction. "Then you need to speak to Morris Stimitz."

Cassidi cocked an eyebrow.

"Velloca hired Stimitz to take pictures of him and Teresa, in flagrante delicto."

"In what?" the detective asked with a frown.

"The sexual act," Simon answered.

"Which was clearly against her will," I added.

"And you know this how?" Cassidi asked me.

"Teresa told me. She remembered his name, and I looked him up in the business directory. He has a studio on 102nd Street."

Cassidi stroked his chin. "If this is true, we can arrest him for taking pornographic photographs and then offer him a reduced sentence for his testimony against Velloca."

I sat back in relief.

"And of course," he went on, "we can use the photographs themselves as evidence, assuming he still has them in his possession."

"I'm afraid that's not possible," I said. "The photographs are gone."

"Gone? Gone where?"

I explained how I'd tricked Stimitz into giving me the images and that Teresa and I had burned them shortly after.

"But there will still be the negatives," the detective said.

"I'm afraid not. I destroyed those as well." Seeing his obvious disappointment, I said, "It didn't occur to me you'd need them as evidence. I thought the testimony from Francesca and me would be more than sufficient. And knowing that the images existed was driving Teresa mad."

"Did you at least look at them before you burned them?"

"I caught a few glimpses. But I didn't want to invade Teresa's privacy."

"You saw him though? You saw Velloca in the pictures?"

"Not . . . not his face," I answered, my cheeks flushing.

He leaned back in his chair.

"You don't need the pictures so long as

you can get Stimitz to tell you what he saw," Simon interjected. "And he shouldn't put up much of a fight if you threaten him with prison time."

Cassidi nodded. "Very well. I will pay Mr. Stimitz a visit as soon as we are done here."

I had just finished signing the prepared affidavits when the telephone rang.

The detective lifted the receiver to his ear. "Cassidi." He nodded. "I'll be right over." He hung up the phone. "Nucci's here. They just brought him in." His eyes met mine over the desktop. "If I may ask one more thing of you, Doctor?"

"Yes?"

"Will you walk with me over to headquarters to identify him?"

An odd paralysis suddenly overcame me as an all-too-vivid memory of Nucci's terrifying attack flooded my mind. I stared dumbly at the detective, my tongue refusing to respond.

"I could bring Miss Ragusa down instead," he said slowly, watching my face. "But since you're already here . . ."

I drew a shaky breath. "No, it's all right, Detective," I managed to say, forcing myself to my feet. "Please, lead the way."

Chapter Twenty-Two

"Are you sure you're up to this?" Simon asked as we climbed the steps to the imposing gray stone edifice that was police headquarters.

Cassidi glanced over his shoulder at me as he reached for the door. "You don't have to talk to him. If you want, I can get you one of the masks the detectives use when they look over the morning lineup."

"Oh yes, I'd like that," I said as he ushered us through the door. I doubted a mask would do much to conceal my identity from Nucci, but at least it would keep him from seeing the fear he still invoked in me when I faced him again.

After the bright light of outdoors, traversing the hallway that stretched between the Mulberry and Mott Street entrances of headquarters felt like walking through an underground tunnel. In the first room to my left, I caught a glimpse of Commissioner

Bingham sitting before an open window, speaking into a telephone with such military precision and volume that I suspected his words could be directly transcribed by the newspapermen in the offices across the street. The detective bureau's offices came next, followed by a rogues' gallery and a room for officers on reserve. The last door was marked "Museum of Criminal Relics." Glancing through it, I saw two large display cases, one containing nooses and hoods from the hanging days of the old Tombs prison, the other full of faro boxes and other gambling implements from the more recent past.

Detective Cassidi stopped to speak to an officer who'd emerged from a stairwell at the end of the hall. "They've got Nucci in a holding cell downstairs," he said, turning back to us. He pointed to a bench across from the reserves room. "Why don't you two wait there while I go upstairs and get Dr. Summerford a mask." He disappeared into the stairwell.

I sat on the bench while Simon stood at my shoulder, surveying the comings and goings in the corridor. Although I tried to think of other things, memories of my encounters with Nucci kept intruding into my mind, forcing my body into a state of extreme agitation. My heart was beating too hard and too fast, and it was a struggle to draw a full breath. Perhaps the Italian girls had been right not to testify, I thought in dismay. It seemed that doing so was only going to make me keep reliving the terror I'd experienced, when all I wanted to do was forget.

Two uniformed officers were sitting inside the door of the reserves room across the hall. One of them looked out and caught sight of us. "Hey, Simon!" he called. "What brings you to the block?"

Simon strolled over to chat with him, leaning against the doorframe with his shoulders at ease and his hands in his pockets. I tried to feel as relaxed as he looked, smoothing my facial muscles and breathing the tension from my neck and shoulders. I wasn't helpless anymore, I reminded myself. Nucci was the prisoner now.

I was almost feeling calm again when I heard footsteps to my right and glanced in their direction. Nucci was walking toward me down the hall, his wrists in handcuffs and his elbow in the grip of a burly officer. He saw me a second after I saw him. His feet slowed as recognition swept across his face.

I stared at him as a rabbit stares at a hawk

diving in for the kill, unable either to move or to look away.

His walk turned into a saunter as he continued toward me, his gaze moving deliberately down my body, bold as brass and revoltingly familiar. As he drew abreast, he slowed even more and, turning his face so that only I could see, wet his lips with his tongue.

"Go on, get moving," the officer growled, shoving him along. They continued farther up the hall and turned into one of the detective bureau's rooms.

I propped myself up on the bench with both hands, shaking uncontrollably and angry with myself for my reaction.

Across the hall, Simon laughed and slapped the officer on the shoulder before ambling back to the bench. His smile evaporated on sight of my face. "Are you all right?"

I could only nod in response.

Detective Cassidi reemerged from the stairwell, holding a black cloth mask. "Got it," he said, holding up the mask. "Let's head on downstairs." He gestured to us to come with him.

"I believe Mr. Nucci is in there," I said, pointing in the opposite direction, toward the office.

The detective looked at the office door and back at me. "You saw him?"

I nodded.

"When?" Simon asked.

"An officer took him past in handcuffs just a moment ago."

Cassidi muttered under his breath. "I'm sorry, Doctor. I told them I was bringing someone in for an ID. They must have thought I wanted to use the standup room."

"Well, I can tell you it was definitely him," I said with an attempt at a smile.

"That's good enough for me," he said. "There's no need for you to go in there if you've already seen him."

"Actually, I think it might be best if I do," I told him, for I was alarmed by the near paralysis the sight of my attacker had provoked. I needed to prove to myself that I wouldn't fall apart when it came time to testify, or let fear make me appear uncertain of my story.

The detective scratched his head. "If that's what you want."

"It is," I said and got to my feet.

He led us to the door of the standup room and pushed it open. Nucci was seated on the far side of the room with his knees splayed and his head cocked to one side. The officer stood behind him with his arms crossed.

I walked a few feet into the room and stopped, flanked by Simon and the detective.

"Get up," the officer ordered Nucci.

Nucci slowly gathered himself and rose from the chair.

"Do you recognize this man?" Cassidi asked me.

"I never seen her before," Nucci said.

"Shut up," the officer said, slapping the back of his head.

Nucci jerked his head away from the officer, then looked back at me, his mouth twisting into a lewd smirk — the same smirk he'd worn as he'd watched me undress and then helped himself to my body. For a sickening moment, I was back on the floor beneath him in the tack room. I willed myself to breathe.

"Dr. Summerford?" Cassidi prompted.

Nucci's eyes bore into mine, full of malice. He raised his bound hands to his throat and drew his forefinger slowly across it.

I heard a low growl beside me. "Son of a . . ." Simon sprang across the room and grabbed Nucci by the shirtfront, pulling back his fist.

"Hey!" Cassidi shouted, seizing Simon's

arm from behind before he could punch him.

"You ever come near her again, you're a dead man," Simon told Nucci.

"Are you going to restrain yourself, Mr. Shaw," Cassidi demanded, still struggling to contain him, "or do I need to ask you to leave?"

Simon let go of Nucci and threw up his hands. "Just making a few things clear, for the record." He returned to my side, wrapping an arm around my shoulders.

"All right, Doctor, let's try this again," Cassidi said, smoothing his rumpled shirt. "Do you recognize the prisoner?"

"Yes," I said hoarsely, holding Nucci's gaze. "That's one of the men who kept us prisoner at the stable on 116th Street. They called him Nucci. He thinks he's a big man, but he's not. He's just a little puppet who did whatever his bosses told him to."

Nucci stiffened, his eyes narrowing. *"Stupida vacca,"* he muttered, spitting on the floor.

Cassidi threw up a hand to ward off Simon, who had started back across the floor. "Thank you, Doctor." Glancing at the uniformed man, he jerked his head toward Nucci. "Get him out of here."

The officer grabbed Nucci's arm and

pulled him out of the room.

"What happens now?" I asked in the silence that followed.

"The courts are closed for the day," the detective said, "but he'll be arraigned first thing in the morning."

"When will he go before the grand jury?"

"Within a week or so. You'll receive a summons when the time comes."

I nodded. "The sooner the better. I won't sleep soundly until he's locked up."

"He probably won't be locked up after his indictment," the detective said, looking uncomfortable. "Most likely, he'll be admitted to bail."

I stared at him. "You mean to tell me he'll be out on the street until the trial?"

"You saw him threaten her just now," Simon said.

Cassidi raised his palms in supplication. "The DA can ask to raise the amount of his bail, of course. But bail is almost never denied, except in homicide cases."

"So Velloca and Nucci — not to mention Gallo, wherever he may be — will all be at large and free to attempt to persuade me not to testify," I summed up.

"These thugs know you're not some Italian peasant who can be easily intimidated," the detective replied. "They'd be fools to resort to the usual tricks. But we'll continue to post a man in front of your house, just in case, until Nucci's trial."

So now I was to become a prisoner in my own home. I drew a deep breath. I supposed I could tolerate my own company for a couple of weeks, in the interest of seeing justice served. "And how long will it be, do you think, until the trial?"

He met my gaze with difficulty. "Well, unfortunately, the courts are on summer schedule right now . . ."

"What does that mean?"

"It means that defendants released on bail won't be tried until the normal court schedule resumes in October," Simon said flatly.

I stared at the detective in disbelief. "You mean to tell me I'll be looking over my shoulder for the next three months?"

"As I said, an officer will be guarding your house day and night," he stiffly replied.

"What about when I leave my house?"

"I would suggest you do so only in the company of others."

Once again, I questioned the wisdom of my decision to testify. "Tell me, at least, that Nucci will go to prison for a long time once this is all over. Because I've been told that abductors and procurers often get only a six-month sentence under the vagrancy laws."

"In many cases that is true," he conceded. "But only because a man can't be convicted of abduction or compulsory prostitution on the testimony of his female victim alone. These crimes require corroborating evidence from another, which is often impossible to obtain. The prosecution must therefore resort to the lesser charges, if it hopes to win a conviction."

"Well, fortunately, we have corroborating evidence in my case," I said sourly. "Simon saw me tied to the radiator in that stable."

"Exactly so. And if Mr. Nucci is convicted of abduction, he will face up to ten years in prison."

I rubbed a hand over my forehead as a wave of exhaustion overtook me. "Very well, Detective. If you don't mind, I'd like to go home now. It's been a very, very long day."

Although Simon had remained silent during much of my exchange with the detective, I could sense him brooding beside me as we walked toward the subway station.

"Come with me to the boys' club," he said suddenly.

"What, now?"

"I have a present for you."

"A present! What is it?"

"You need to come with me to find out."

I was sufficiently intrigued — and sufficiently eager for something else to think about besides having my throat slit — that I ignored the ache that had been building behind my eyes for the last several hours and promptly agreed.

Thirty minutes later, we were climbing the stairs toward the clubhouse. Simon accompanied me inside and lit the lamps, then invited me to sit down. "Here," he said, handing me a copy of *Popular Mechanics* magazine.

"That's my present?" I asked, frowning down at the cover.

"That's to keep you busy while I go get it. I should be back in half an hour."

"Half an hour! I could have gone home and taken a nap if I'd known."

He reached down and tucked a loose lock of hair behind my ear. Though he was smiling, his eyes were warm with concern. "Why don't you try to catch a few winks here? I'll lock the door when I go so no one disturbs you."

A moment later, he was gone, his steps moving purposefully down the hallway. I opened the magazine and flipped through it, but the articles proved beyond my current capacity for concentration, and I soon put it down. Deciding to take Simon's suggestion, I went into the dark back room and lay down on the cot. Although I didn't really expect my restless mind to allow it, I must have fallen asleep, because it seemed only minutes after I closed my eyes that I heard the sound of knocking and Simon's voice, calling my name. I rose from the cot and went to open the hallway door.

"Where's my present?" I asked with a yawn, seeing his empty hands.

"Come on, I'll show you." He took me by the elbow and led me down the hall to the stairwell, where he surprised me by turning left instead of right.

"Where are we going?"

"You'll see." He guided me up two more flights and through a door at the top, onto the roof. I stepped out beside him and looked around. The roof was empty except for a laundry line on the left and an old wooden target on a stand on the right. "Which one's my present?" I asked with a frown.

"Neither." Unbuttoning his waistcoat, he pulled a revolver from beneath his waistband and held it out to me, grip first. "This is your present."

I stared at it, now fully awake. "Where did

you get it?"

"From a friend. Go ahead, see how it feels."

I removed my gloves and took it gingerly in my hand. It was lighter than it looked and fit snugly into my palm.

"It's a single-action revolver," he told me, "which means you'll have to cock the hammer before each shot, but I figured it would be easier for you to get the hang of the trigger pull on this one than on a double-action model."

"Is it loaded?" I asked, pointing it nervously toward the ground.

"Not yet." Removing a box of ammunition from his pocket, he showed me how to load the cartridges through a gate in the side, instructing me to leave the top chamber under the hammer empty so the gun wouldn't go off accidentally if I dropped it. "Of course, that only leaves you with five shots before you have to reload," he added, "so you'll want to make each one count."

"The last time I relied on a gun to keep me safe," I fretted, "I dropped it into the gutter."

"Then we'd better be sure you're so familiar with it that that can't happen."

I must have been looking queasy, because he added, "Look, chances are you'll never need to use it. But if you do have to shoot, I want you to shoot straight."

Leading me to a point several yards from the target, he showed me how to stand with my knees bent and my weight slightly forward to resist the recoil when I fired. "Now raise your arms with your elbows locked, and support your right hand with your left."

I did as he instructed, wrapping my left hand over the fingers on the grip.

"You don't want to crowd your gun hand," he cautioned. "Your left hand is only there to hold the gun steady and cock the hammer. Here, let me show you." Moving around to stand behind me, he raised his arms alongside mine and adjusted my fingers. "Now, when you shoot," he said, his words rustling against my cheek, "the barrel is going to want to jerk up, so you'll need to keep a firm grip on it."

I closed my eyes, soaking in the touch of his hands and the feel of his chest against my back.

"Not too firm though," he added. "About the same as if you were shaking someone's hand."

I obligingly slackened my grip. It was much easier to imagine shooting someone, I found, while cocooned within Simon's sheltering body.

"Now relax your shoulders," he murmured, "and lift your chin."

I softened my shoulders and tilted back my head, acutely aware of his lips just inches from my ear. Of its own accord, my cheek turned toward them, craving more than the warmth of his breath.

I felt, as much as heard, his ragged exhale.

"Is that right?" I asked thickly when he'd said nothing more for several moments.

He let go of my hands and stepped back. "Yeah, that's it," he said gruffly. "Now go ahead and give it a try."

Returning reluctantly to the task at hand, I settled my gaze on the target, but hesitated as I heard voices waft up from the street below. "Won't the police come running if they hear shots?" I asked.

"I've already cleared it with Patrolman Flaherty."

Of course he had. "What if the bullet goes astray and hits someone?"

"There's nothing to hit behind that target but the party wall, and it will forgive you," he answered drily.

Balancing my weight evenly between the balls of my feet, I relaxed my shoulders, lifted my chin, and raised my arms to line up the sight with the bull's-eye.

"Now just breathe out nice and easy, and at the end of the exhale, pull the trigger all the way through."

I did as he said. The revolver kicked up in my hand when I fired, forcing me backward. Simon caught me by the shoulders and set me upright.

I swivelled toward him. "Did I hit it?"

"No, but you put a good scare into the party wall," he said, his eyes twinkling. "Go ahead, try it again."

It took me a while to get the hang of it, but thirty minutes later, I was hitting the target every time, and had come close to the bull's-eye more than once.

"Nice work," Simon said when we finally called it quits.

I gave the gun an affectionate pat. My headache was gone, I realized, and for an entire half hour, I'd forgotten to be afraid. "I think I'll call her Calamity," I said, "after Calamity Jane, the shootist."

Simon cocked an eyebrow. "That doesn't sound very promising."

"No, I suppose you're right. Annie then, after Annie Oakley, 'sure shot of the west.' Where should I keep her, do you think?"

"I couldn't get a holster that would fit you on short notice, but I'll keep working on it. In the meantime, keep it somewhere you can get to it in a hurry."

I opened my bag and tucked the gun carefully into the inner pocket along with a box of ammunition, feeling better than I had in some time. The only thing Velloca and his men really had over me, when you thought about it, was their sheer physical strength and the willingness to use it — and that imbalance, it seemed to me, had just been corrected.

Simon took me home in a hansom cab and saw me safely to my door, introducing me to Officer McNulty, the new man on watch, and instructing me to call him at the saloon if I needed anything. I let myself into the house, and had barely taken off my hat and gloves, when Katie emerged from the sitting room with a feather duster in hand and planted herself in front of me.

"So you've been to see the detective," she said.

"Why, yes," I said, wondering what had put such a scowl on her face. "He needed to take my statement about the kidnappers."

Her scowl deepened. "White slavers, the officer told me. Not kidnappers."

I silently released my breath. "You spoke to Officer McNulty."

"Who was kind enough to tell me the

truth. Unlike some people."

I dropped my bag onto the console table. "I'm sorry, Katie," I said, feeling ten years old all over again under her reproachful gaze. "I should have told you everything."

"You know, I do worry about you, Miss Genna," she said stiffly. "Like I'd worry about a child of my own, if I had one."

"I know you do; that's why I didn't tell you. I didn't want to upset you."

. "I can always tell when you're keeping something from me," she went on, as if I hadn't spoken. "It makes me sad to think you can't trust me enough to confide in me."

"It's not that I don't trust you! I just don't want to burden you with my problems."

She pressed her lips together, unmoved by this response. "The people who care about you deserve to know when you're in trouble."

"You're right," I said, now thoroughly contrite, "so let me tell you now." Leading her into the sitting room, I sat beside her and told her all the frightening and unsavory details I'd omitted earlier. She took it like a soldier, making no comment, although I knew she must be turning somersaults inside.

"All this for some girl you'd never even

met," she said when I was done, shaking her head. "And a foreign girl at that."

I studied her face, wishing there was some way to make her understand. "How old were you when came to America, Katie?"

"Fourteen."

"What if someone had abducted you right off the boat and sold you into slavery? Wouldn't you hope and pray that some stranger might come along to help you?"

She crossed her arms. "I wouldn't be so foolish as to get kidnapped in the first place."

"No, I suppose you wouldn't," I said with a sigh. "Well, I'm sorry it's all come so close to home, in any event. Can you forgive me?"

She sniffed. "I just thank the Lord the neighbors are all gone so I don't have to explain why there's a policeman standing at our door."

The day had thoroughly drained me, and after a light supper, I retired to my room and crawled into bed in relief. But although I desperately needed it, I was not blessed with restful sleep. Instead, I had a terrible dream — a dream of cruel hands pushing me into a pit, deeper and deeper into the earth, their steely grasp inescapable. When I tried to scream, the hands moved to my face, clamping over my mouth and nose and cutting off my air. I woke with a sob and sat up in bed as the first rays of the new day's light entered my window.

CHAPTER TWENTY-THREE

Detective Cassidi telephoned me the next morning as promised, just as I was finishing breakfast. "Stimitz denied ever taking photographs for Velloca," he told me, "and a search of the premises didn't turn up any other pornographic materials. The strange thing is, I got the distinct impression he was expecting us. Do you think he might have suspected you weren't who you said you were?"

"No, I don't think so," I said, wiping crumbs of buttered toast from my lips. "Why would he have given me the pictures if he had?"

"Maybe he got suspicious afterward and contacted Velloca to check."

I considered this. "He did say he'd promised to have the prints ready by late yesterday afternoon. I suppose if Velloca tried to collect them then, he would have discovered that someone had already been there."

"That would explain Stimitz's emotional state. He seemed terrified, but not of us."

Velloca would have realized, of course, that Stimitz could link him to the girls in the stable. Even if he didn't know who'd taken the pictures, he'd want to make sure the photographer never revealed his identify. "You think Velloca threatened him?"

"If he did, it did the trick, because Stimitz refused to cooperate, even when we told him he'd be spending considerable time in jail if he didn't."

"Did you arrest him?"

The detective sighed. "We did, but since we don't actually have the pornographic pictures in our possession" — he paused to let the silent rebuke sink in — "I doubt the district attorney will decide to prosecute."

I bit back an apology for destroying the evidence, for I didn't see how I could have done things any differently. Showing the pictures in open court would have devastated Teresa. Even if Antonio never saw them, knowing that they existed and what they captured would have been just as bad — and possibly worse — for it would have left too much to his imagination. "What about Nucci? Has he shown any inclination to bargain with you?"

"To the contrary, he baits us with insults

at every opportunity." He hesitated, then added, "And I'm afraid I have some more bad news. Francesca Ragusa has changed her mind. She's not going to testify against Gallo."

I sank onto the closet seat.

"She received an anonymous letter threatening harm to her sister in Italy if she testifies. We told her it's most likely just a bluff, but she said unless we could guarantee that her sister would be safe, she couldn't risk it. Of course, we could give her no such guarantee."

"Can she do that? Back out now, when things are already in motion?"

"The DA could always commit her to the House of Detention as a hostile witness, and hold her in contempt until she talks. But I don't think he'll want to do that."

"And I wouldn't want him to," I said with a sigh. "She's been through enough already."

"You understand what this means?" the detective asked. "The entire case against Nucci now rests on you. I think you need to prepare yourself for the likelihood that he and Velloca will be threatening you as well."

So we'd gone from slight chance to probability in just a few hours. "Fortunately, I don't have any sisters," I muttered.

"Brava, Doctor," he said, sounding relieved. "I knew we could count on you. Rest assured that we will continue to guard your house around the clock. In light of the circumstances, I will ask again, as a personal favor, that you stay indoors as much as possible."

"All right, Detective. But you will you do me a favor as well?"

"Of course. Anything you wish."

"Don't call me again unless you have good news."

In my new spirit of honesty, I brought Katie up to date on the latest developments, telling her I'd be taking all my meals at home for the foreseeable future and helping her write up a more extensive weekly shopping list than usual, since I wouldn't be able to run errands for myself. I caught her looking at me more than once as we worked on the list, her forehead creased with concern.

"Try not to worry too much, Katie," I said finally. "I've got Simon and Maurice to look out for me, and we'll have a policeman standing guard around the clock."

She snorted. "Fat lot of good the police will do you, if they're all three sheets to the wind."

I frowned at her. "What do you mean?"

She jerked her head toward the front

stoop. "I saw that one takin' a tipple out of his flask before the sun was barely up in the sky."

"Good heavens! You mean to say he's drunk on the job?"

"No more than usual, I expect," she answered darkly.

From what I'd seen of the New York police, I guessed this was a fair conclusion. "Well, bring him a strong cup of coffee, will you? And tell him to pour out his flask immediately, or I'll have to report him."

I was at the desk in my bedroom, trying to prepare for my therapy class the following day, when the telephone rang for the second time that morning. I trotted down to answer it, remembering my words to Cassidi and praying that he was, indeed, calling me with good news.

"Genevieve Summerford," I announced.

"Good morning, Miss Summerford," a male voice replied.

The hairs on the back of my neck prickled at the Italian inflection. "Who is this?" I asked, although I was pretty sure I already knew.

"A great admirer of yours."

Velloca. It took all my willpower not to drop the earpiece like a venomous scorpion.

468

"I believe you have something of mine," he said.

"I don't know what you're talking about," I managed to reply.

"Mr. Stimitz has an eye for the ladies. I recognized you immediately from his description."

I said nothing, my mind racing.

"I can only assume that our mutual friend is as eager to preserve the mementos of our time together as I am, and prevailed on you to intervene. But alas, I find I cannot live without them. I do hope, for your sake, that they are still in your possession?"

What was the best answer? Should I tell him that the photographs had already been destroyed? Or perhaps pretend that I'd given them to the police? Either might keep him from coming after me to try to recover them. But then again, he might not believe me, or he might discover that the police actually didn't have them and come after me anyway. If he thought they were still in my possession, on the other hand, I could threaten to give them to the police unless he and his thugs stayed far away from me, now and throughout the trial.

He was waiting for my answer. "Yes," I said. "I still have them."

"I'm glad to hear it. You have caused me

much inconvenience, Miss Summerford, but if you bring them to my office right now, I am prepared to put the past behind us."

"Why would I do something as stupid as that?"

He chuckled. "It pains me to think that the pleasure of my company is not a sufficient reason. But let me give you another. Your housekeeper. She is with my man Gallo as we speak."

Katie. I swiveled toward the hall clock. She had left to do the marketing forty minutes ago.

"Perhaps you remember Gallo from your stay with us?" he was saying. "I'm afraid that he is not the most patient of men. If you don't meet me at my office with the photographs in twenty minutes, there's no saying what he might do."

Katie, with Gallo. My mind went suddenly blank, wiped clean by fear. I squeezed my eyes shut. *Think.* I wasn't defenseless; I had a gun. I could bring the patrolman outside up with me and have him wait nearby while I . . .

"She's being held where she will never be found, to be released only when I give the word," he continued, as if I'd been speaking out loud. "If you bring anyone with you, I'm afraid I will not be able to keep her from suffering badly."

"Well, I'm not going to come alone," I said, my voice cracking like a dry twig. "If I do, you'll only take us both."

"So much pluck," he said with a sigh. "I truly am sorry we didn't have a chance to become better acquainted while you were enjoying my hospitality." He was silent for a moment. "Very well, we will meet at a public place. Say, the café at 105th Street and Third Avenue? If you leave now, you can be there by eleven. Don't be late, or your housekeeper will pay for it." He hung up the phone.

I stood paralyzed with the receiver in my hand, random thoughts careening through my mind. Gallo wouldn't care that the arthritis in Katie's knees made it hard for her to go up steps, or that she needed to call her sister every Sunday, or that she'd been like a mother to a frightened and lonely young girl. He'd hurt her without a moment's hesitation and enjoy doing it. I swayed on my feet, undone by the knowledge that once again, I'd put someone I loved in mortal danger.

I braced myself against the telephone box, struggling to think clearly. I had to meet with Velloca and try to get him to reveal Katie's location. That much was clear. But I had no guarantee that he wouldn't try to abduct me as well, even if our meeting was in a public place. Which meant that despite his warning, I'd have to bring someone to protect me.

But not the patrolman outside. I needed someone stealthy on his feet and quick-witted enough to avoid detection, not someone stupified by alcohol. I tapped the telephone hook and told the operator to put me through to the Italian Legion.

Detective Silva answered the call.

"I need to speak to Detective Cassidi," I told him. "It's an emergency."

"He's already on his way to court."

Of course, I remembered belatedly; he was taking Nucci to his arraignment. I quickly explained my predicament.

"Lieutenant Petrosino is at the Harlem station house, interrogating a prisoner," Silva told me. "That's only a few blocks from the café. Maybe he could go over and take up surveillance."

"Could you ask him to?" I pleaded, gripping the receiver cord.

"I'll call the station house right now. If I can't reach him, I'll tell them to send one of the precinct detectives."

I thanked him and hung up, glancing again at the wall clock. Three minutes had elapsed. Tapping the hook again, I put a call through to Simon's saloon.

"No one answers, ma'am," the operator said after several rings.

I supposed Billie hadn't arrived yet to open up. And Simon didn't have a telephone in his private quarters, so I couldn't reach him there. I tried to tell myself that Petrosino would be enough, but my self wasn't convinced. It was suddenly very clear to me that I needed Simon to go with me. I simply couldn't do this without him.

I dashed out of the phone closet and up the stairs to my bedroom. Pulling the revolver from my handbag, I grabbed a handful of garters from the bureau, pulled them over my stockings onto my thigh, and slid the gun underneath them, distributing the garters evenly along its length to hold it secure. Continuing to my father's study, I took a large manila envelope from the desk drawer and wrote "Stimitz Studio" with a fountain pen on the top left corner. I carried this down to the pantry, where I pulled two boxes of Malt-Too Flakes off the shelves. Dumping out their contents, I sliced the boxes into pieces with a paring knife and slid the pieces into the envelope.

A moment later, I descended the front steps with the envelope under my arm. Waving to the officer so as not to alarm him into following, I continued up the block and around the corner at a brisk pace, then ran the remaining distance to the carriage house. Our groom, Oliver, was mucking out the stalls when I arrived.

"Where's Maurice?" I asked, pushing my hair out of my eyes as I glanced around the building. I'd forgotten my hat, and chunks of hair had escaped their pins in my mad dash to the stable.

He straightened, resting his shovel blade on the ground. "In the park, exercising the carriage horses, miss," he said, disapproval of my breathless and disheveled condition written clearly across his face. Although he was at least two decades younger than Maurice, Oliver often acted much older, and was averse to excitement or impropriety of any sort.

"Damn!" I cried, slapping the stall gate, which only caused Oliver's frown to deepen. With my parents away, Maurice had taken it upon himself to exercise the carriage horses in his spare time. I had hoped that by having him drive me in the motorcar — ignoring the speed limit, for once — I could pick Simon up at the Isle of Plenty and still get to the café on time. I strode to the side of the motorcar and peered over the door at the controls. "Do you know how to drive this thing?"

"No, miss," he said with a sniff. "I never saw the need to learn."

"Do you think you could help me get it started?"

He shrugged. "I've helped Maurice often enough."

"All right then, grab the crank." I opened the door and climbed into the driver's seat. I'd watched Father and Maurice operate the machine on countless occasions. Once I got the thing going, I thought I ought to be able to manage. I flipped the switch I'd seen Maurice throw before he cranked the engine. "Give it a turn," I called.

He frowned at me over the hood. "You'll want to bring the spark down first, miss, so she don't take my arm off."

I peered at the two levers attached to the column below the steering wheel. The one on the right was already as far forward as it could go, so I pushed up the one on the left. "All right, go ahead."

He grasped the crank handle and pulled it upward. The car bucked as the handle jerked back counterclockwise in his hand. He yelped and let go of it, shaking his wrist. "*All* the way down, miss," he said, eyeing me with misgiving.

"Sorry." This time, I moved the lever as far as it would go. "Try again."

Warily, he grasped the crank and gave it another turn. The engine started up but sputtered out again almost immediately.

I closed my eyes, envisioning Maurice at the controls. After he spun the crank, he always hurried back and pulled both levers partway toward him. "Once more, please." This time, the moment the engine started, I eased both of the levers toward me. The vehicle shook and coughed, spewing out a cloud of exhaust, and then settled into a steady clatter.

"Open the doors!" I cried, sliding closer to the wheel.

Oliver scratched his head. "Are you sure, miss?"

"Now, Oliver, please!"

While he was swinging the carriage house doors open I grabbed hold of the gear stick, envisioning Maurice as he worked the stick in concert with the clutch pedal. With a silent prayer, I stepped on the pedal and pushed the stick into the low position. As I cautiously lifted my foot from the pedal, the car started to move forward. I gave a silent prayer of thanks and steered toward the open doors. I'd gone only a few feet, however, before the car bucked and stalled once more.

I smacked my palms against the wheel. At this rate, I'd never get out of the carriage house, let alone up to Simon's and to the cafe. But I'd already wasted too much time to find another conveyance. I gestured impatiently to Oliver to spin the crank. This time, as I let out the clutch I pulled the gas lever all the way toward me. The car lurched toward the door. "Watch out!" I shouted, searching frantically with my foot for the brake pedal. I was halfway across the sidewalk before I found it. I stamped down hard, terrified I might hit a pedestrian, and the engine cut out once more.

I gritted my teeth. All right then; no more braking. "Again!"

Rubbing his shoulder in silent rebuke, Oliver returned to the crank. The car started up, and I cleared the rest of the sidewalk. I veered hard right, afraid to use the brake lest I stall out again, and plunged into the traffic on Madison Avenue. Fortunately, it was Saturday, so traffic was light, but weaving through the vehicles that were on the road, using only the throttle for control, was still a knuckle-whitening exercise. I swerved around a street car, then squeezed between a surrey and an ice wagon, constantly searching the road up ahead for the path of least resistance. As I came to an empty stretch, I tried advancing both levers and felt the car respond with a surge of speed. Spotting a rig approaching the next intersection from the right, I advanced them even more to beat it.

I was now going well over the speed limit and, from the noise the machine was making, guessed I ought to be changing gears, but I was too worried I'd stall out again to try it. And so I weaved on down the avenue and across Eighty-Third Street with the motorcar straining and vibrating in protest, shouting at the occasional pedestrian to get out of my way, until the Isle of Plenty came into view.

A handful of the youngest Wieran boys were clustered under the canopy on the sidewalk. They all turned and stared as I roared up the street and pulled abreast of them. I stomped on the brakes, bringing the engine to an abrupt stop, and leaped out of the car. "Is Simon here?"

Frankie Dolan shook his head. "He's picking up the tools for carpentry class. He told us to meet him here at eleven o'clock to help him unload."

My heart sank. I couldn't wait until eleven; I had to be at the cafe by then.

"What about Billie?" I asked, peering into the dark saloon.

"He ain't here yet," Frankie told me.

"All right, I need you boys to give Simon a message when he comes," I told them. "Can you do that for me? It's extremely important."

Four heads bobbed in reply.

"Tell him I'm meeting Velloca in a café at eleven o'clock, on the corner of 105th Street and Third Avenue. Have you got that? Tell him they've got Katie."

"Velloca, eleven o'clock, 105th and Third, Katie," Tommy Farrell repeated. "Got it."

"And tell him to come as soon as he can!" By the time he arrived, I reasoned, I'd either know where Katie was, or know that Velloca wasn't going to tell me, so there'd be no need for Simon to stay under cover. I jumped back into the car.

"Frankie," I called, retarding the spark, "could you turn the crank for me?"

He trotted around to the front to spin the crank, bringing the engine to sputtering life. I pushed out the clutch and threw the gear lever into position, but forgot to advance the spark and gas levers, putting the engine once more through its death throes. I strangled a curse, my eyes tearing in frustration. I shouldn't have wasted the time trying to bring Simon on board. I was going to fail Katie before I'd even begun . . .

"Say, Doc, maybe I should drive." Frankie stood beside my door, watching me with a frown.

I looked up at him, feeling a spark of hope, remembering his ease at the controls of his father's van. But I was on my way to meet with a vicious criminal, who wouldn't think twice about hurting anyone who got in his way. It would be inexcusable to introduce a child into such a situation . . .

He reached across me to adjust the lever then went back to crank the engine. I was still debating as he returned to my side and tweaked the levers with a practiced hand, coaxing the engine from a grumble to a purr. He pulled the door open. "Shove over, Doc," he said, with the authority of someone three times his age. "I'll get you where you need to go."

To my eternal discredit, I moved over and let him drive.

Exactly ten minutes later, at two minutes before the hour, we pulled up to the curb a block away and around the corner from my destination. "You stay here with the motorcar," I told Frankie. I had given him a rough explanation of the situation on the way up, not so much as to inspire him to heroics, but enough so he'd know I was serious about him not coming after me. "The man I'm going to meet will not be pleased if he sees I've brought someone with me."

For once, he didn't protest. I gave him a smile meant to suggest that all was well, although it didn't quite reach its intended span, and set out toward the café. I saw no sign of Detective Petrosino, who I could only hope was watching from inside one of the storefronts, ready to intervene should Velloca try to spirit me away. I did notice a swarthy-skinned man sitting in an idle wagon halfway down the block, however, who watched me with interest as I walked past. I gave him a wide berth, ready to grab my gun if he climbed out of the wagon.

Reaching the café on the corner unmolested, I wiped my damp palms on my skirt and walked through the open door. Velloca was seated at a table near the back, facing the street. Only two other tables were occupied: one by a couple of young men in dungarees, the other by an older, bearded man near the window. The young men looked up when I entered, but registered no particular interest in my presence and quickly resumed their conversation. A waiter stood behind a counter in the back, making coffee.

"My dear," Velloca greeted me without getting up, motioning to the seat across from him. "How wonderful to see you again."

I lowered myself onto the chair on quaking knees.

"*Due caffè,* Marco," he called to the waiter.

"Where's my housekeeper?" I asked, willing my voice to be strong.

He settled back in his chair. "In my country, we have a custom of breaking bread before conducting business."

"Well, you're in America now. We prefer to get to the point."

He gave me a chilly smile. "As you wish." He held out his hand, tipping his head toward the envelope.

"Tell me where Katie is first."

"You are in no position to bargain."

"You're in no position not to. If I give these photographs to the police, they'll have proof that you're a rapist and a white slave trader."

He raised his eyebrows. "I think not. The photographs merely show a man and woman engaged in one of life's most pleasurable activities. Surely, there is nothing wrong with that? They do, however, have a certain sentimental value, which is why I must insist on their return."

The waiter arrived with two coffees and set them in front of us. I couldn't be sure Velloca would tell me where Katie was once I handed the envelope over. But since the pictures weren't actually in the envelope, I really had nothing to lose. I laid it on the table between us. "Now tell me where she is."

He pulled the envelope toward him. "All in good time," he said with a contented sigh, tucking it under his arm. "I know you'll understand when I tell you we must keep her close until Nucci's trial, to make sure you remember where your loyalty lies." He pushed back his chair and stood up.

"Wait! We're not finished."

His eyebrows rose in mock surprise. "I find your desire to spend more time with me touching," he said, his gaze raking my body. "Perhaps, at some future date . . . ? But I'm afraid that now, I must go share these photographs with an old acquaintance."

"Look in the envelope," I said, easing my skirt up under the table.

Uncertainty flickered across his face. He turned the envelope over and pried it open.

As he was doing so, I slid the gun out from under my garters.

He reached into the envelope and pulled out the pieces of paperboard. He stared down at them and then at me, his face flushing. "Where are they?"

"Somewhere you'll never find them until Katie is returned."

His eyes narrowed into calculating slits, and for a moment, I glimpsed the reptile behind the smooth facade. He threw the envelope and its contents onto the table. "I regret, for your housekeeper's sake, that we were unable to come to terms." He turned and started for the door.

He was calling my bluff. I jumped to my feet, pointing the revolver at his back. "Tell me where she is, or I'll shoot."

He stopped, and slowly turned.

All other movement had ceased in the café. The distant cry of a newsboy was the only sound that penetrated the silence as Velloca coolly took my measure.

"Somebody call the police," I rasped, cocking the hammer with shaking fingers.

Nobody moved.

"Put the gun away, Miss Summerford," Velloca said, "before you hurt somebody."

"If you don't want to get hurt, you'll tell me where she is."

He shook his head. "Such big talk, for such a little woman."

Sweat trickled down my back as we held each other's gaze. He didn't think I would shoot, I realized. He was so used to dominating women, he didn't believe that one could ever best him. For a moment, unnerved by his utter lack of concern, I wasn't sure I could either.

But then I thought of Lucia's limp body, and Caterina's ruined eye, and Teresa's broken heart. I thought of all the women who were even now lying on a filthy bed in some mining camp or barred up in a brothel against their will. And I thought of Katie, cowering in terror when she should be at home, having her tea. My hands stopped shaking as a strange calm descended over me. I lowered the gun, aiming at his crotch, and fired.

Velloca stared down at the red spot that appeared on the inside of his thigh, then back up at me in astonishment.

"Where is she?" I asked again.

Helpless rage spread across his face.

I aimed higher, at his chest, cocking the hammer again. "Tell me, or I'll kill you."

"That won't be necessary!" The old man by the window leaped to his feet, yanking a false beard off his face and throwing it onto the table. His other hand aimed a revolver at Velloca. "I'm Detective Lieutenant Joseph Petrosino, and you are under arrest."

Not a fly buzzed in the stunned silence that followed.

Velloca recovered first. "You're arresting *me*?" he protested, clutching his bleeding leg. "You should be arresting her! She's the one with the gun!"

"Put your hands in the air." Without moving his eyes from Velloca, the detective added, "Please, Dr. Summerford, put away your gun."

"But what have I done?" Velloca asked. "Surely, it is no crime for an old widower to have coffee with a young woman who has befriended his daughter? A woman who, I have only now discovered, is mentally deranged?"

"You're charged with unlawfully entering this country to avoid arrest for murder in Italy," the detective said. "Under Section 21 of the Immigration Act of 1907, you will accordingly be arraigned in federal court and, upon conviction, turned over to the authorities for immediate deportation."

For the first time in my experience, Velloca seemed to be at a loss for words.

"I said hands up," Petrosino repeated.

"Very well, detective," he sputtered, "but

at least allow me to tie my wound. I would not wish to bleed to death on the way to the station." He started limping back toward the table.

"Keep your hands where I can —"

Before the detective could finish his sentence, Velloca had grabbed me and swung me around in front of him. The next second, I felt a knife blade pressing against my throat. "I'll take that," he snarled in my ear, wresting the revolver from my hand. I felt him thrust it under his waistband. "Slide your gun toward me on the floor," he ordered Petrosino.

"You can't escape, Carulo," the detective said. "You'll only make things worse for yourself."

"I appreciate your concern," Velloca said with a sneer, "but I'll take my chances. Now give me the gun."

Petrosino lowered the gun to the floor and slid it toward him. Velloca shoved it under his waistband as well, then started pulling me backward toward the open door.

His arm was tight as a barrel hoop around my chest and shoulders. I locked eyes with Petrosino, praying that he would do something — but he was as helpless as I was. Velloca couldn't take me far, I told myself. As soon as we were on the street, Petrosino could summon help from nearby patrolmen, who would quickly chase us down . . .

Then I remembered the man in the wagon, waiting at the curb down the street. If he was one of Velloca's men, he could drive us away before help arrived. Ignoring the bite of the knife, I dug in my heels and flailed frantically for the doorframe as Velloca started to pull me through. He might slit my throat, but that would be better than ending up alone with him and at his mercy. No matter what he did to me here, I was not going to go through that door.

CHAPTER TWENTY-FOUR

Before I could grab hold of the doorframe, I heard Velloca grunt in surprise and felt him topple backward, pulling me with him. He threw up his arms to catch his balance, releasing his hold on me. I rolled to one side and landed on all fours on the sidewalk.

As I was scrambling to my feet, I saw a young boy crouched on elbows and knees on the café threshold, his head down and body tucked, with Velloca's legs sprawled over him. I lunged toward Velloca's knife hand as it landed on the sidewalk and stepped hard on his wrist, holding it there until Petrosino could run up beside me. The detective leaned over Velloca and smashed the butt of his gun over his head. "Be advised that you are also charged with resisting arrest and assault," he muttered.

I pulled Frankie out from under the legs of the now unconscious Velloca — for of course it was Frankie on the sidewalk, who had ignored my instructions and come to my aid — and helped him to his feet. "Are you hurt?"

"Nah," he said, brushing off his pants. He pointed to my throat. "But you're bleedin'."

I pulled my handkerchief from my skirt pocket and pressed it against the cut. "It's just a nick," I said, "although it could have been much worse. How did you know I was in trouble?"

He shrugged. "I could tell something was dodgy, the way you were acting, so I decided to follow you and keep cases on things." Warily, he added, "I nicked a newspaper from the stand down the block and started hawking it near the corner, where I could see you through the window. When I saw this monkey start pulling you out the door, I figured it was a good time for a jelly roll."

I shook my head. "You wonderful, wonderful boy."

He frowned. "You ain't mad at me then, for nicking the newspaper?"

"Mad at you! I'm forever in your debt, Frankie Dolan."

"Say," he said, his face brightening, "does that mean you might buy me another one of them ice-cream sandwiches?"

"Oh, Frankie." I grabbed him in a breath-defying hug. "I'm going to buy you a whole cartful."

I heard an engine start and looked up to see the wagon I'd noted earlier do a U-turn and race to the other end of the street, disappearing onto Lexington Avenue. "I think that might be Velloca's man," I told the detective, who was clapping a pair of handcuffs onto Velloca.

Petrosino grunted. "Don't worry, I saw him on my way here. I'll be sure to recognize him again." Rifling through Velloca's pockets, he extracted a handkerchief and used it to make a tourniquet around the prisoner's injured thigh, using a club from his hip pocket to tighten it. He glanced up at me, raising an eyebrow. "An inch farther over, and he'd probably be dead by now," he said, apparently knowing his femoral artery from his elbow.

I hugged myself as the full implications of my actions sank in. I had shot a man, with no physical provocation, in full view of a policeman. Petrosino might not be a criminal coddler, but from what I'd seen, he wasn't the sort who would let a felony go unpunished either. I had acted on impulse, but of course, that was no excuse — especially because I knew that I would do it again in a heartbeat. "Are you going to have to arrest me?"

He sat back on his haunches. "Arrest you? To the contrary, I congratulate you on a successful citizen's arrest."

"A citizen's arrest?" I repeated.

"The laws of our state provide that a private citizen may not only arrest a wanted felon," he cheerfully advised me, "but may use all necessary means to effect said arrest — even killing him — if he resists or flees and cannot otherwise be taken." He looked down at the injured man. "Carulo is just lucky you didn't fire a second time."

Arresting Velloca, I thought to myself, had been the last thing on my mind when I'd pulled the trigger. But I wasn't about to argue.

I would have liked to ask the detective how he'd learned of Velloca's true identity, and about the disguise he'd been wearing in the café, but those questions were going to have to wait. "What are you going to do about my housekeeper?"

"I've already sent men to check the stable and the poultry plant," he told me, rising from his crouch, "just in case Gallo was foolish enough to take her there. I'll have someone speak with the officer on watch at your house as well, to see if he witnessed anything."

I feared that wouldn't be enough. "Do you

492

think you can get Velloca to talk?" I asked, staring down at the unconscious man on the sidewalk.

"I'll do my best. But now that he's being sent back to Italy, he has little reason to cooperate."

I heard someone shout my name and turned to see Simon running up the avenue.

"I got here as soon as I heard," he said, pulling up panting in front of me. From the sound of it, I guessed he'd run the whole way.

"Who are you?" asked Petrosino.

"He's a friend," I said. "He's been helping Detective Cassidi and me look for Teresa."

Petrosino handed me back my gun. "You two keep an eye on him," he said, nodding toward Velloca. "I'm going to call for a wagon." He set off for the nearest call box.

"What happened?" Simon asked me.

"I'll tell you later. I couldn't find out where they're keeping her, Simon. All I know is that she's with Gallo. We've got to find her!"

He nodded, his face taut. "All right then, we will. When did you see her last?"

"We had breakfast together, and then she went out to do the shopping. Gallo must have snatched her right off the street."

He thought for a moment. "If he was waiting for her to leave the house, he probably parked around the corner on Madison so the watchman at your stoop wouldn't notice him loitering."

"You think he grabbed her somewhere along the avenue? It is very quiet there on Saturdays. I suppose if he timed it right, he could have taken her without being noticed by a passing vehicle."

"On the other hand," Simon mused, "there would have been policemen directing traffic at every other intersection. With traffic so sparse, they might have noticed a van pulling up to the curb on a residential block and pulling a woman in."

"Where then?" I asked.

"My guess is he'd wait to grab her until she started crosstown, on Eighty-Sixth Street."

"But it's so busy there, with all the shops and street vendors . . ."

"Exactly. With so many express wagons and delivery vans regularly servicing the shops, no one would think twice about another van pulling up to the curb."

I nodded. "Or take note of an altercation, most likely, with all the noise and bustle on the street."

"Do you know the shops she frequents in Yorkville?"

"I think so; most of them are either on or just off of Eighty-Sixth Street, between Third and First Avenues."

"Then I'd suggest we start there. Someone may have seen something that could prove useful." He turned to Frankie. "I understand you drove Dr. Summerford up here in the motorcar."

"And then knocked Velloca on his backside with a jelly roll," I added, "just as he was about to make off with me."

Simon nodded in approval. "We'll need a lad with sand to be our driver. Go get the car, will you, Frankie?"

"Yes sir!" Frankie said and took off like a shot.

Detective Petrosino had returned by the time the motorcar rolled smoothly up to the curb a few minutes later. We told him what we were planning to do, and he promised to let us know if he learned anything. As I stepped into the passenger seat, I tried not to think what would happen if our combined attempts to find Katie's trail proved futile. For I suspected that if we didn't find her soon, we wouldn't find her at all.

"Eighty-Sixth Street, Frankie," Simon said, climbing into the back. "And pull out all the stops."

A smile of pure joy spread across the boy's

face. "You got it!" he said, and threw the car into gear.

We started at Liebhoff's Bakery, where Mrs. Liebhoff confirmed that Katie had been in to buy her usual bag of rolls and buns that morning. "So you were right that she made it down to Eighty-Sixth Street," I said to Simon. "How do we find out where he accosted her?"

"I suppose we'll just have to try to follow in her footsteps and see where the trail ends. Where would she normally go after the bakery?"

I led him half a block down Third Avenue to Schlutzki's Quality Meats, where Mr. Schlutzki reported that Katie had been there as well. "How could I forget?" he groused when I asked if he was certain. "That one is always looking for a bargain. I had to practically give her my chops at cost." Knowing Katie's penchant for bargaining, I trusted that he was remembering correctly.

"Where next?" Simon asked when we were back on the sidewalk.

"We talked about putting in an ice order," I told him, nodding toward Hoffman's Ice and Coal across the street. We cut through the traffic and descended the steps to the cellar, where we found *Summerford, 7 E. 92nd* scrawled near the bottom of the order pad. "So she got this far," I said as we climbed back up to the sidewalk. "What do you think Gallo was waiting for?"

"Maybe he still felt too exposed here. He'd want a place where there were plenty of delivery vehicles clogging the curb so no one could see what he was up to." He looked up and down the street, scratching his head.

"The dry goods store!" I said, remembering the chamois cloth Katie had added to her list that morning. "They're always unloading boxes in the street and sending out clothing and linens for express delivery."

Simon whistled to Frankie in the motorcar, signaling him to follow us back up to the corner. Once there, we turned right onto Eighty-Sixth Street and hurried down the half block to Muller & Sons. Vans and wagons in various stages of loading and unloading were parked all along the curb out front, two or three deep in places. I followed Simon past them into the shop.

I didn't recognize the woman working behind the counter, but when I described Katie, she gestured toward her own corpulent figure and asked in a thick German accent, "A big lady? In a dark dress and felt hat?"

"Yes," I said, "and probably carrying several parcels by the time she got here."

She nodded. "I saw a lady like that arguing with a man in the street this morning while I was waiting on a customer. I called to my son to see what was the matter, but they drove off in a carriage before he could speak to her."

"They drove off?" I clutched Simon's arm, feeling a fresh jolt of despair at this confirmation that Katie really had been abducted, which a part of my mind had apparently been refusing to accept.

"Which way did the carriage go?" Simon asked.

"Helmut!" she called to a young man in the back of the store.

The man looked up from the dish towels he was stacking.

"Those people arguing in the street this morning: Which way did the carriage go when it left here?"

"That way," he said, pointing east.

"Did it turn onto Second Avenue?" Simon asked.

He put down the towels and walked toward us, looking curiously from Simon to me. "I don't know; I didn't watch for long.

I had work to do."

"But it was a carriage, not a van?" I asked him.

"That's right."

"Did it have any unusual carving or trim work?" Simon asked.

He shrugged. "It was parked on the other side of a delivery wagon. I didn't even see it until it drove away. I don't remember anything unusual."

"What about the man she was arguing with?" I asked. "What did he look like?"

He stuck out his lower lip out, considering. "About thirty years old, with dark hair. On the smaller side but wiry."

I glanced at Simon. That was Gallo, to a T.

"He was holding her by the arm," the young man went on, "waving a handkerchief near her face like he was trying to wipe something off her mouth. She kept swatting at his hand and cussing at him."

I nodded sickly, remembering my own struggle to avoid the noxious chloroform vapor.

"Then he pulled her around the back of the delivery wagon," he went on, "and I lost sight of them. I was about to follow when a customer stopped me at the door. By the time I came around the wagon, they were driving off in the carriage. That's when I saw the second man."

"There was another man?" I asked.

"He was the one driving."

Whatever small hope I'd entertained that Katie might have escaped was crushed by this revelation. By bringing another man to drive, Gallo would have been able to ensure that she remained insensible in the back of the carriage until they arrived at their destination.

Simon questioned the young man and his mother for several more minutes, but they were unable to remember anything else of value. I followed him out of the store and listened with bated breath as he made inquiries at the neighboring shops, but no one there had noticed the altercation.

"What do we do now?" I asked, stumbling over my feet as we returned to the motorcar, nearly blinded by anxiety.

He grasped my arm to steady me, his own eyes clouded with worry. "Let's get back to your house," he said, helping me into the vehicle. "Petrosino's man should be there by now. Hopefully he'll have learned something useful."

The stoop and sidewalk were empty and the front door was unlocked when we arrived at my home. I led Simon and Frankie inside, cocking my head to listen. The main floor was silent. Continuing to the top of the basement stairs, I heard Detective Cassidi's voice waft faintly up from below.

"Down here!" I called to the others, starting down the stairs.

I followed the voice to the open kitchen door. There I stopped, so abruptly that Simon and Frankie piled into me from behind.

Katie and Maurice were sitting at the kitchen table, drinking tea with Detective Cassidi and the officer from the stoop. A body lay on the floor by Maurice's feet, wrapped in a gingham sheet and tied from head to foot with butcher's twine.

"There she is!" Katie said on sight of me, pushing up from the table. "And Simon too, and one of your lads, looks like. Come on in then, and have some tea. I was just telling the officers here how Maurice saved me from that brute's clutches." She thrust her chin toward the bound and gagged form on the floor.

I collapsed onto a chair as Simon and Frankie took the seats on either side of me. Katie brought over three more cups and poured us tea, then passed a plate of cookies that Simon and I declined but Frankie quickly depleted, stuffing several into his pockets for some future date.

"Go on, dear," Katie said to Maurice, settling back in her chair. "Tell them how you did it."

Maurice put down his cup and commenced his tale. Before he'd taken the carriage horses out for their exercise that morning, he explained, he'd arranged to pick Katie up at Eighty-Sixth Street when she was done shopping. Knowing that she was picking up extra supplies, however, and fearing they might be too heavy for her to carry, he'd decided to cut his drive short and meet her earlier. He had just caught sight of her on the sidewalk in front of the dry goods store, and was pulling up behind a van already parked at the curb, when Gallo grabbed her by the arm, shoving what looked like a wet cloth in her face, and started pulling her toward the back of the van.

"You should have seen him," Katie said, clapping her hand to her chest. "He drove right up alongside and snapped his whip, catching that fiend's wrist in the lash. Reeled him in like a fish, he did. I've never seen anything like it."

"Not that you needed the help," Maurice said with a chuckle. "You already had him licked, giving him what-for with that cauli-flower." He winked at me. "I'd try to stay on this one's good side if I were you. She's a devil when her hackles are up."

"But how did you subdue him?" I asked.

He shrugged. "I did a bit of boxing and wrestling in my day. It's surprising how much you remember."

"First, he stunned him with a haymaker," Katie elaborated, eyes shining as she swung her fist sideways through the air. "Then we gave him a taste of his own medicine."

"A whiff, more like," Maurice said with a grin.

"Oh, you," Katie said, giving his arm a playful shove.

The heap on the floor wriggled and jerked, emitting muffled sounds of protest from behind his gag. But apparently, Maurice's skills included hog-tying as well, for Gallo's feet were bent up behind him and tied by a triple length of twine to his neck, making any movement, let alone escape, impossible.

"More tea, officers?" Katie asked, lifting the teapot. She refilled their dainty cups, taking no notice of Gallo as he grunted and squirmed on the floor near her feet.

"Genna, dear?" she asked, lifting the pot toward me.

I sank slowly back in my seat, shaking my

head, and started to laugh.

Detective Petrosino arrived with the paddy wagon a few minutes later. He informed us that Velloca/Carulo would be held in custody while the immigration authorities and the Italian Consulate General arranged his return to Italy where, Petrosino's sources had assured him, he was certain to be convicted and sent to prison for a very long time.

"How did you find out he was wanted for murder in Italy?" I finally had a chance to ask.

Petrosino looked at Detective Cassidi. "Detective? Perhaps you should explain, while I tend to our prisoner." He started around the table toward Gallo.

Cassidi turned to me. "I had the feeling I'd seen Velloca before when I questioned him at his home, but I couldn't put my finger on where. Only later, as I was retrieving the photograph you'd given me of Antonio Fabroni from the mail pile, did I realize that Velloca was one of the men in the picture. Younger and leaner and wearing a mustache, but most certainly Velloca "

"I looked at that picture very closely," I marveled, "and I had no idea that it was him."

"You must understand, Doctor," he said gravely, "that we detectives are trained to pay attention to the slightest of details, which makes such identifications possible even after a considerable lapse of time."

I heard a stifled snort and glanced to my right to see Simon rolling his eyes. On the other side of the table, Petrosino and the uniformed man were untying the string from Gallo's neck, while Frankie "assisted" by tickling the captive's nose with a feather duster. "Simon," I suggested, "why don't you help bring the prisoner out to the wagon?"

"Gladly," he said with a grimace, pushing back his chair.

"In any event," Cassidi continued, "when I told Lieutenant Petrosino what I had discovered, he immediately arranged to have the photograph hand-delivered to our man in Sing Sing."

"Your 'man' in Sing Sing?" I repeated.

He smiled smugly. "You see, while it is true that Italian criminals would rather die than talk to the police, it is also true that they love to brag among themselves. For this reason, the lieutenant rotates one of our men into Sing Sing every few months, to listen in on their chatter. You'd be amazed how much information we have gathered in this way. Our man showed the picture to some inmates there, pretending it was of his niece's confirmation. One of them recognized Velloca, calling him Vittorio Carulo and referring to him as a member of the Neapolitan Camorra. As soon as I heard, I telegraphed the authorities in Italy, who informed me that Vittorio Carulo spent a year in prison for horse theft before fleeing to America to avoid a murder charge."

Petrosino called to Cassidi for a pair of handcuffs, and then he, Simon, and the other officers pulled Gallo to his feet and walked him out to the patrol wagon. I followed them out, for there was one more thing I needed to know. I waited until Detective Petrosino had slammed the back door shut and then pulled him aside. "That was you I saw in Harlem last week, wasn't it, Detective? Giving that boy a satchel for Patrick Branagan? You were wearing the same false beard and hat that you wore in the café today."

He raised an eyebrow. "It seems you have a detective's eye for detail after all, Doctor."

"What exactly were you doing?"

"I'm afraid I'm not at liberty to say just yet. But if you read tomorrow's paper, I believe all your questions will be answered." He jumped into the passenger side of the patrol wagon as Cassidi cranked the engine. "We'll leave Officer McNulty here to stand watch," he said, nodding toward the uniformed man, who had already returned to the stoop. "But with Velloca on his way back to Italy, I don't think you'll have any more trouble. The magistrate fixed Nucci's bail at five thousand dollars this morning, and will likely do the same for this one. Without Velloca to pay for the bail bond, I expect both men will be enjoying a long summer vacation in jail." He saluted me as the wagon rolled away from the curb.

Simon came and stood beside me, reaching for my hand as we watched the wagon drive off. I closed my eyes, focusing all my attention on that one simple connection, feeling no need to speak or to move. After the commotion of the last few days, it felt like heaven.

"So, what did happen with Velloca at the café?" he asked finally, turning toward me.

I opened my eyes reluctantly. "Well, let's see. I tried to trick him, and to reason with him, and to threaten him." I shrugged. "And when none of those worked, I shot him."

"*You* shot him? It wasn't Petrosino?"

"Apparently, I was making a citizen's arrest, although I didn't know it at the time."

He was looking at me with a strange

expression. "You're a marvel, Genna Summerford."

I felt myself blush.

His gaze drifted over my flushed cheeks to my half-parted lips and lingered there. Was it possible, I wondered, that the thought of a woman shooting someone could have a passion-rousing effect? If so, I did hope it wasn't the only thing that could put that glint in his eye.

"Hey, Doc, watch this!"

I turned to see that Frankie had persuaded Officer McNulty to let him borrow his baton and was practicing twirling it, policeman style, by its thong.

"I'd better get him home," Simon said. "His father will have been expecting him back after carpentry class."

"Oh, yes, you'd better then."

He released my hand. "See you for lunch tomorrow?"

Lunch at his saloon after my Sunday class had become something of a ritual in prior months. "I'll be there."

He turned toward the stoop. "Come on, Frankie. Let's go."

Reluctantly, the boy relinquished the baton, and the two started off down the street.

I watched them walk away, still hardly able

to believe that the nightmare was over. For me at least. But there were thousands of other women, I now knew, who would likely never waken from theirs.

There was something terribly wrong, I mused as I started back inside, with a world where so many women could be treated so abominably with such near impunity. And it wasn't just the Vellocas who were the problem. I thought of the quote I'd seen on the kitchen wall at the Goldstein Home, by the reformer George William Curtis: *The test of civilization is the estimate of woman. Among savages she is a slave. In the dark ages of Christendom, she is a toy and a sentimental goddess. With increasing moral light, and greater liberty, and more universal justice, she begins to develop as an equal human being.* Would we ever have a society, I wondered wearily, where women were given the same respect as the sons they brought into the world?

I returned to the kitchen to find Maurice and Katie still seated at the table, finishing their tea. After being assured that Maurice had suffered no ill effects from his run-in with Gallo, I asked him to drive me up to 109th Street so that I could tell Teresa and the others about Velloca's capture, suggesting he take a look at the motorcar first to make sure I hadn't inflicted any damage. He went to do as I asked, leaving me alone in the kitchen with Katie.

She got up from the table and carried some teacups and saucers to the sink. I watched her wash and rinse and rack as I had watched a hundred times before, feeling an after-tremor of fear as I thought of how close I'd come to losing her. On impulse, I walked up behind her and wrapped my arms around her shoulders. "I'm so sorry," I said, laying my cheek on her back.

She turned around and grasped my hands, pushing me back as she did so and looking me sternly in the eye. "Now none of that, Miss Genna. You've got nothing to be sorry for."

"I almost got you killed! I should have listened when you warned me not to get involved —"

"Don't you waste another breath apologizing," she ordered, giving my hands a shake. "I understand now why you got involved! Good lord, what's the world coming to when a man can steal a woman right off the street? Somebody's got to stop those devils."

She released my hands and returned to the table for more cups. I shook my head in wonder. I must have done something right, if I'd earned even Katie's approval.

I followed her to the table and reached for the remaining cups. "We're going to have quite a story to tell Mother and Father when they get back.".

She dropped the saucers she was holding back onto the table and swiveled toward me. "Not a word to your parents, about any of this!"

"But . . . I thought you said the people who care for us deserve to know the truth!"

"Oh sure, sure," she said, wagging her head, "but not your mother and father! It would kill them."

I bit back a smile. "Won't they know we're keeping something from them? You did tell me I was a terrible liar."

"Psh," she replied, waving her hand in the air. "Don't you worry on that account. I'm a much better liar than you are. Now you go do what you have to do, and let me clean up my kitchen."

CHAPTER TWENTY-FIVE

Nobody answered the door when I knocked at Felisa's flat. "It's Genevieve Summerford," I called, knocking again. "Is anyone home?"

Several more moments ticked by before the key turned in the lock and the door opened. Teresa gazed out at me, her gaze stony.

"I have news."

She stepped back, and I walked into the foyer, glancing to my right and left. The flat was quiet, the kitchen and the front room abandoned. "Where is everyone?"

"At church, making a novena. *Per la remissione dei loro peccati.*"

For the remission of their sins, I silently translated. I searched her face. "Why didn't you go with them?"

"There is no place for me in God's house."

"But, Teresa, if God is all merciful, surely —"

She turned away. "You said you have news?" She led me into the kitchen and took a seat at the table.

"The police have taken Velloca into custody," I told her, sitting across from her. "They're sending him back to Italy to stand trial for a murder he committed there. They tell me he is certain to be convicted and sent to prison for a very, very long time."

A muscle in her cheek twitched, but she evidenced none of the relief — or the sense of vindication — that I'd been hoping for. "I will tell the others."

I studied her with concern. There was a new hardness in her demeanor, a deadness in her eyes that hadn't been there in the stable. I feared she was walling herself up in punishment, cutting herself off from anything that might bring happiness into her life. "Will you tell Antonio and his mother too?"

For the first time, a flicker of emotion crossed her face. "Felisa will tell them."

"Teresa," I implored, "have you spoken to Antonio at all?"

"I have no reason to speak to him," she said flatly.

I sat back. "What are your plans then?"

"As soon as I make enough money from the feathers, I will move into a boardinghouse on Elizabeth Street that Felisa knows. I hope to give lessons in English to Italian women who wish to learn."

"That sounds like a good plan."

"But there is one thing that troubles me."

"Yes?"

She clasped her hands on the table. "Rosa. What will become of her?"

I had been wondering the same thing myself. "Perhaps there are relatives, here or in Italy, who can help care for her and her family after her father goes to prison."

"Will she be told of his crimes?"

"I don't know. I would hope that her grandmother would keep the whole truth from her and her brothers."

"I want to see her."

I blinked in surprise. "Are you sure?"

"She has already lost her mother. I don't wish her to think I have forgotten her."

Well, that was something, I supposed. At least she wasn't cutting herself off from everyone she'd ever cared for. I reached for a scrap of butcher's paper and a pencil from the center of the table. "This is her address," I said, scribbling it down and handing it to her.

She slipped it into her pocket.

"You're a good woman, Teresa."

Her lips compressed into a hard line.

Without another word, she got up and showed me to the door.

Mrs. Fabroni was holding what appeared to be a snail in her hand when she answered my knock a minute later. "Miss Summerford!" She stepped aside so I could enter. "I am making Antonio's favorite recipe to celebrate. Won't you join me?" She gestured toward a work table positioned near the sink. A wicker basket sat on one end with its lid open, next to a bucket of water. I took a seat next to the basket as Mrs. Fabroni crossed to the bucket, plunged the snail briefly into the water, and started scrubbing it with a nail brush.

"What are you celebrating?" I asked, staring at the horned creature in her hand as it pulled back into its shell.

She dropped the cleaned snail into a bowl and lifted another one from the basket. "Carulo's arrest, of course."

I looked up at her. "You already know about it?"

"I've had a man following him since the night I last saw you. He told me what happened at the café today."

I thought of the man I'd seen in the wagon near the café. "You've been following Carulo all this time?"

She cocked an eyebrow at me. "Why else do you suppose he is still alive? I had to have him followed, to make sure Antonio did nothing foolish."

It took me a moment to digest this. "You think Antonio wants to kill him?"

She paused in her brushing, locking eyes with me. "My son is a decent, law-abiding man who wishes only to be a good American. But there are some things a man cannot ignore if he wishes to keep his honor."

I shook my head. "Then why have you been protecting Carulo?"

"I am not protecting him," she said, resuming her brushing. "I told Antonio I would see to him if the American authorities did not. I made my son promise that he would not sacrifice his own life by killing Carulo and ending up in prison." Her lips curved into a wry smile. "Even a good son needs help sometimes, keeping his promises."

"And . . . will he be satisfied, do you think, to see Carulo in prison?"

"That is not the question," she said, dropping another snail into the bowl. "The question is whether Carulo will go to prison. He has escaped from the Italian authorities before."

"But not from custody, as far as I know.

He came to America before they could apprehend him. Besides, I expect he'll be very closely guarded."

"Perhaps," she said. "Let us hope so." She pushed back a snail that was trying to climb out of the bowl.

"What will you do if he does somehow evade prison?" I asked uneasily.

She regarded me for a moment in silence, her dark eyes unreadable. Gesturing toward the basket of snails, she said, "My son brought these home for me from the park. They like the damp earth beneath the benches near the shower baths."

"Is that right?" I asked queasily. "And they're safe to eat?"

"Oh yes, quite safe. And delicious too. But of course, you already know that, for you have eaten them before."

"Oh no," I said, suppressing a shudder. "I don't believe I've had the pleasure."

"Oh, but you have! I remember you enjoyed them very much, the first time you came to my home."

I blanched, recalling the stew I'd tasted during my visit. "I was eating snails?"

She eyed me ruefully. "You see, Miss Summerford, sometimes it is better not to know too much."

A few minutes later, she walked me to the door.

"Please say good-bye to Antonio for me," I said, "and tell him that I wish him well."

"Why don't you stop at the shop on your way out and tell him yourself? He'll be in the back, washing out his equipment. I am sure he would like to thank you for all you have done on Teresa's behalf."

"Perhaps I will," I said, for there were things I'd like to say to Antonio as well. I held out my hand. "Good luck, Mrs. Fabroni."

She took my hand in a firm grip. "And to you."

Since it was Sunday, the bar was empty when I arrived at the Isle of Plenty for lunch the next day, but the dining room was filled with families enjoying bowls of creamed oysters with thick slices of buttered bread. I caught Billie's eye as he came through the doors from the kitchen, carrying a loaded tray over his shoulder. He jerked his head toward Simon's office, mouthing, "In the back."

I waved my thanks and cut across the room, pausing at the door to pinch my cheeks and bite my lips for color.

"Come in," Simon called at my knock.

He was sitting at the table with his sleeves rolled up, staring down at a number of documents spread out before him. "Genna!" he exclaimed with a glance at the wall clock. "I didn't realize what time it was."

I went to stand beside him, peering over his shoulder. "What are those?"

"Job applications. I'm trying to get some men hired on at the Ninety-Sixth Street power house."

There must have been at least a dozen of them. "Shouldn't they be filling out the applications themselves?" I asked.

"I'm just giving them my endorsement," he said, stretching his neck. "They'll stand a better chance that way."

I longed to knead his neck for him, but I wasn't sure how he would react. In fact, I wasn't sure quite where things stood between us, now that the crisis was past. "I could come back later, if you'd like."

"No," he said, "I wouldn't like." He stacked the papers and pushed them away.

"Well then, shall we go see what Billie's cooked up for today?"

"In a minute," he said, getting to his feet. "There's something I want to say to you first."

I caught my breath. This sounded serious. Before he could continue, there was a loud knock and the office door flew open. A burly man in dungarees rushed into the room, waving a paper in his hand. His frantic gaze swept over me and landed on Simon. "Sorry to interrupt, Mr. Shaw, but Billie told me you were in here. I got another notice letter from the landlord; it was under the door when I got home. He says if I don't pay him his back rent by tomorrow, he's going to evict me."

"Let's see it," Simon said. He scanned the paper with a frown. "This isn't a legal notice. He can't kick you out yet. Tell him you're going to pay off a quarter of the back rent each month. You can do that, can't you? Now that you're working the extra shift?"

The man nodded. "That's what I was planning to do."

"Well, make sure he knows it, and tell him I'll guarantee the payments. I know Fiedler. He'll agree."

The man's shoulders slumped in relief. "Thanks, Mr. Shaw. I swear to you, I've never been late on the rent before. It's just that I fell behind during the strike . . ."

"No need to explain, Max," Simon said, laying a hand on his back and propelling him irresistibly toward the door. "I wouldn't guarantee the payment if I didn't think you were good for it."

He practically pushed the man out of the room before turning back to face me. "As I was saying. I've been doing some thinking. About you and me."

"You have?" Definitely serious, then. But was it good serious, or bad?

"About us getting married," he added.

My heart sank. Bad, then. He'd changed his mind about marrying me; he didn't want to wait, or he'd decided I was too reckless or uncontrollable or under my father's thumb to make a suitable wife . . .

The door flew open again and two young men barged in, one wearing a bandage around his head. "Simon," demanded the uninjured one, "will you tell this pigheaded brother of mine he's got to save his fighting for the ring? He won't be in shape for Saturday if he keeps going after every bum who rubs him the wrong way."

"Do I look like a baby minder?" Simon growled. He put a hand on each of their shoulders and turned them around. "Try to work it out between yourselves, will you, boys? And if you can't do that, come back and see me on Monday. The office is closed."

He shut the door firmly behind them and turned to face me. "Remind me to tell Billie

I'm not to be disturbed, the next time you visit."

"You can't do that," I said, trying to keep my voice light. "People might think something improper was going on."

He started toward me, his eyes gleaming. "Maybe they'd be right."

Hmm. Perhaps not bad serious, after all . . .

He came to a stop a foot away, so close I had to tilt back my head to look up at him. "I thought for a while that I might have lost you, when you disappeared from that poultry plant," he said, his voice husky with the memory. He shook his head. "I never want to feel that way again. But it made me think about what's important. In fact, I've been doing a lot of thinking over the last few days." His gaze drifted over my face, certain and determined. "I know I told you before that I couldn't be all in while you were still deciding. But the truth is, I'm already all in. I'm in so deep, I can't tell which way is up and which is down anymore. I do know, though, that I'm not doing myself any good drawing a line in the sand, when the one thing I want most in the world is standing on the other side of it."

I held my breath, searching the depths of his eyes. For the first time in a long time, I could see no hesitation or stubborn self-denial there. "Does this mean —"

"Yeah, it does," he said gruffly, and took me into his arms.

CHAPTER TWENTY-SIX

I was sure my lips must be swollen and my eyes too bright when we entered the dining room several minutes later, but I didn't give a whit. I'd waited far too long for Simon's kisses to have any regrets. I had to say, it had been worth the wait.

Billie had reserved our usual table near the front window. Simon pulled my chair out with unusual alacrity and then sat down across from me, his own eyes shining with a new, almost predatory attentiveness as he watched me smooth my hair and dab my lips with my napkin. I felt a shiver of exquisite apprehension. I wasn't sure just what I had unleashed, but I was looking forward to finding out.

Billie arrived with two steaming bowls of oyster chowder and placed them before us. The chowder was flecked with bacon and green onions and smelled divine. "This looks wonderful." I bent over to inhale the aroma, my senses all still heightened from their recent engagement. Before I could lift my spoon to my mouth, the saloon door opened, and Patrick and Kitty blew in on a cloud of street dust.

"Hey, Billie, is Simon here?" Patrick called.

Billie pointed to us with his chin.

They hurried over, pulling up two chairs to the side of the table.

"Have you seen the paper?" Kitty asked, waving a copy of the Sunday edition.

"Haven't had a chance," Simon said.

I shook my head as well, only now remembering, through the haze of my sensory overload, Petrosino's cryptic comment of the day before.

She held the paper up so we could read the headline:

CAPTAIN HURLEY IDENTIFIED
AS SPIDER BOMBER;
Captain of Twenty-Ninth Precinct
Extorting from Those He Swore
to Protect.

My mouth dropped open.

"Hurley? He was setting off the bombs?" Simon asked.

"That's your captain, isn't it, Patrick?" I asked.

"Here, I'll read it to you," Kitty said. Clearing her throat, she began, " 'Little Pietro Spinelli had a terrible tale to tell when he walked into Commissioner Bingham's office two weeks ago. His father was leaving the family flat to go to his bakery that morning, Pietro recounted, when he spied a policeman lighting a stick of dynamite in the tenement entry, the friction match still in his hand. His father had recently received a Black Hand letter, the boy explained, but had chosen to ignore it. Mr. Spinelli hurried down to stamp out the fuse and then turned on the intruder, who shot him in the heart and ran from the premises. Little Pietro, who had been sent to bring in the milk by his mother, watched his father's murder from the stairwell.' "

"Poor little fella," Kitty said lowering the paper. "Seeing his own father murdered. Did you ever?" Returning to the article, she continued, " 'Little Pietro was wise for his years. He had seen the police uniform on his father's assailant and suspected that all was not as it should be. But he had also heard his father speak well of Commissioner Bingham. Against the wishes of his mother, who feared further violence, Pietro took the threat letter from his dead father's pocket and carried it to police headquarters, where he demanded to see the great man who had vowed to wipe out corruption and extortion in the city.'"

"So Hurley was the policeman in the entry?" I asked.

Patrick shook his head. "It was Eugene Fox, Hurley's collector."

"Wait a minute now," Kitty went on, raising her voice. "This is the good part: 'General Bingham immediately launched a top-secret investigation, putting his best secret service man on the case.'" She put down the paper and beamed up at us. "His best secret service man," she repeated, elbowing Patrick in the ribs. "That's Patrick!"

Simon swiveled toward Patrick. "Secret service?"

"Not so secret anymore, I guess," Patrick said wryly.

"When did this happen?"

"Last fall, when Bingham transferred the captains to new precincts, he put together a secret squad to shadow the most corrupt ones and report back only to him. Deputy Commissioner Hanson recommended me for the job because I'd tipped him off on some shady dealings involving my former captain."

"And you were assigned to shadow Hurley," Simon concluded.

Patrick nodded. "Hurley was one of the dirtiest captains in the city before his transfer. Turns out Bingham was right to keep an eye on him. Harlem is no Tenderloin, and it took Hurley a while to get the lay of the land, but by the end of the winter he had all of the local pool hall operators on his pay list, making regular protection payments to his collector. He was having trouble, though, getting the pushcart vendors and other small fry to pay the usual premium for their licenses, both because he didn't speak their language, and because they were already paying tribute to various small Black Hand operators in the neighborhood. Then in June, the DA raided the Harlem pool halls, putting almost all of them out of business."

"Thereby cutting off Hurley's main source of revenue," Simon said.

"Exactly. Now, as you may remember, the first Spider letter appeared in late May, about a week before the pool hall raids. The target was an Italian banker, who brought the letter to Captain Hurley and asked for police protection."

I straightened on my seat, listening intently. That must have been the banker Mrs. Fabroni told me about, whom she'd threatened on Felisa's behalf.

"The captain posted an officer in front of the bank, but a few days later, someone managed to plant a timed nitroglycerine bomb in the foyer anyway, which went off an hour after closing time. After that, there were one or two Spider bombings every week."

Billie came over with four cups of coffee on a tray. He smiled at Patrick. "A little bird told me congratulations are in order."

Patrick grimaced. "News travels fast."

Billie lowered the cups onto the table.

"How about putting a little flavor in that?" Patrick asked him.

"It's Sunday," Simon drawled. "The bar's closed."

"I think you'll find the flavor to your liking," Billie told Patrick with a wink.

Patrick took a sip and sighed with contentment. "Now there's a barkeep who knows his business."

I took a tentative sip of my own coffee and nearly choked on the whiskey burn.

"Go on, Pat," Kitty urged, her eyes alight. "Tell them how you figured out Hurley was the bomber."

"Well, like I said, the first Spider bomb

was made of nitroglycerine. But all the other Spider bombs — which, you'll remember, went off *after* Hurley's pool hall revenue dried up — were dynamite. Which got me thinking."

"Wait till you hear this," Kitty said, wriggling in her seat.

He smiled at her, running his fingers lightly up her arm. Turning back to us, he continued, "Back in early June, just after the first Spider bombing, a load of dynamite was left at a construction site on 106th Street in violation of regulations. I was one of the reserves called in to bring it to the station house for safekeeping, until the Bureau of Combustibles could pick it up. On a hunch, I checked the storage room records and compared the number of cases on the original receipt to the number we handed over to the bureau a few days later. I discovered that a case of dynamite and a box of percussion caps had gone missing.

"Now, that was interesting, but it didn't necessarily point to Hurley. It's not all that unusual for things to go missing from storage — a lost coat turned in by some Good Samaritan that no one's claimed, or a stolen teapot held for evidence and never picked up, that sort of thing. I had no way to tell if the dynamite that was missing was the same used in the bombings. Until little Pietro brought the commissioner that unexploded stick."

He took another swig of his coffee, then continued, "The commissioner had already sent the Spinelli dynamite on to Petrosino, so I gave the detective a call to ask if I could take a look at it, to see if it was the same color, size, and make as the explosives we'd been holding in the station house. We couldn't be seen together, of course, so we arranged a handoff."

"That's what was in the bag he gave you!" I blurted out.

He turned to me, cocking an eyebrow.

"I saw you on the street that day, paying the boy to pick up the satchel from the old Italian man. Only now, I know the man was really Petrosino, because he was wearing the same disguise at the café yesterday."

He nodded slowly, his lips pursed. "You must have wondered what we were up to."

I could feel my cheeks heating up. "I'm afraid I did become suspicious."

"I suppose anyone would have, under the circumstances."

"Not Simon. He told me you were the one person on the force whose integrity I needn't question."

"Did he now?" He turned to Simon.

"That's quite a reputation to live up to."

"Just keep doing what you have been," Simon said with a grin, "and you shouldn't have any trouble."

"Anyway," Patrick continued, "the dynamite matched. And Petrosino, it turned out, had made some discoveries of his own. The finger impressions on the later Spider letters all matched each other, but they didn't match the impressions on the first letter to the bank president."

"Which further suggested that Captain Hurley had commandeered the Spider name," Simon said.

Patrick nodded. "We both found it interesting that all the Spider letters used the exact same wording, except for the recipients' names and the amount they demanded. Hurley doesn't speak a word of Italian, so if he was impersonating an Italian extortionist he would have had to copy the original Spider letter word for word. Two days ago, I borrowed a few things from the captain's office and sent them to the lab. His fingerprints matched the ones on the later letters."

A collective sigh escaped us as we pondered the captain's perfidy.

"But . . . wouldn't Hurley's victims guess the death threats weren't really coming from the Spider if his collector was an Irishman?" Kitty asked after a moment.

"Good question," Patrick said, brushing a wayward strand of hair from her cheek. As Kitty responded with an uncharacteristic blush, it occurred to me that her feelings for Patrick went much deeper than she'd let on.

"Hurley got lucky there," he said. "The original threat letter, which Hurley must have gotten someone to translate, instructed the banker to leave his money in a tin behind a statue in the devotional area at Saint Cecilia's Church. The Saint Cecilia congregation is split pretty evenly between Italian and Irish, so Hurley could just keep using the same drop-off location, with Fox slipping into the church to pick up a tin whenever he wanted without attracting notice."

"But what about the explosives?" I asked. "How could he carry sticks of dynamite around without being seen?"

"I didn't figure that out until last night," Patrick admitted, "after Fox was arrested and I was returning his equipment to the supply room. His night baton felt lighter than it should have, so I gave it a closer look. I discovered it had been hollowed out, like a flask baton, only deeper. Deep enough to hold two eight-inch sticks of dynamite. He must have carried the dynamite on his nightly rounds, setting them off in the early morning before his victims were up and about."

"Only Spinelli, being a baker, would get up earlier than most," I mused. "Which Fox must have failed to take into account."

We all sat in silence for another moment, absorbing his extraordinary tale.

"I'd say this calls for another round," Simon said. "Billie! More coffee!"

"Congratulations, Patrick," I said. "That couldn't have been easy, working in secret."

He gave me a half-hearted smile. "I just wish I could have figured out what they were up to before they killed poor Spinelli in front of his son."

I nodded in sympathy, for I knew what it was like to fall short in one's efforts to help.

"And what about Genna?" Kitty asked, turning to me with wide eyes. "Getting those white slavers arrested, and saving all those women!" She shook her head in admiration. "You're a regular heroine!"

"No thanks to me," Patrick grunted. He regarded me somberly. "I'm sorry I let those bastards get you in their clutches. I shouldn't have left you alone out there on the street unprotected. I'll never forgive myself, if it helps any."

He looked so miserable, I tried to cheer him up by saying, "Well, I'm sorry I didn't put your call box key to better use. If I'd gone to summon help earlier, things might have gone differently."

"Oh, I don't know," he said, a glint of humor returning to his eyes. "I heard you nearly blinded one of those thugs with it. Sounds like a pretty good use to me." He grinned at Simon. "We should teach that to the new recruits."

Billie arrived with fresh cups of coffee and set them before us.

Simon lifted his cup. "To Patrick, and a job well done."

We all raised our cups and took a sip.

"And to Genevieve," Kitty said, turning to me.

"To Genevieve!" Patrick and Simon said in unison, raising their cups alongside hers.

As I looked around the table at the hard-drinking cop, his streetwise paramour, and my one-time stable hand, all smiling at me with open goodwill and affection, I suddenly had the feeling that I was exactly where I was supposed to be. I smiled back as they tipped their cups and drank to me. Perhaps, I thought, we weren't so different after all.

EPILOGUE

Teresa stood at the open window at the end of the hallway, watching the crowds on the street below. Garlands of paper lanterns stretched over their heads between the fire escapes, and flags and bunting hung from every window. She could smell the familiar scents of sausage and fried dough drifting up from the vendors' carts beneath the window, and hear the far-off sounds of a brass band mixing with the shouts and laughter of her countrymen.

It was the *festa* of Our Lady of Mount Carmel, which, according to Felisa, was as important here as it was in Italy — perhaps even more so. Italians had been arriving all during the night from far-flung places, many after walking miles on foot, bringing money or jewelry or whatever offerings they could afford for their beloved patron saint. They had stayed with friends and relatives or camped out in the parks, eating and drinking and talking until it was time for one of the hourly early masses, where they would offer thanks for prayers answered during the preceding year and ask for help in the coming one.

The other women from the flat had left hours ago, along with Antonio and his mother. Teresa had stayed behind, having no wish to take part in the festivities — or to see Antonio, whose efforts to see her she had managed to rebuff so far. She suspected that, as an honorable man, he was feeling some sort of obligation to go through with their marriage, however much she must repulse him. She had no intention of marrying him on such terms. But there was no need for them to speak of it. In another two weeks, she'd be gone from the building and from his life. She was biding her time until then.

As the morning progressed, however, something had called her out of the tiny flat where she'd confined herself for the past five days, drawing her to the hallway window. It struck her as nothing short of a miracle that the Madonna had journeyed all the way to New York from Campania, just as she had. The knowledge drove a hot poker into the numbness she'd been working so hard to maintain. Now, as she watched people hurrying toward First Avenue to see the procession go past, she felt an irresistible pull to go with them.

Turning from the window, she crossed to the stairs and descended to the street, merging into the throng. She stayed to the inside of the sidewalk, hugging the wall, overwhelmed by all the noise and color after her days of seclusion. In addition to food, the pushcarts along the street were offering candles and holy cards and charms to ward off evil spirits. As she drew closer to First Avenue, she saw a woman with a cane buy a wax foot from a stand near the corner, which she knew the woman would offer to the Madonna in church after the procession, in the hope that she might be blessed with a cure. Teresa slowed as she drew abreast of the stand, examining the wax limbs and organs displayed there. There was no single body part that could encompass her own sickness, however, and she quickly turned away again.

Nor was there any offering big enough to atone for her sins. She couldn't bring herself to look at the shrine that had been set up at the intersection with the Madonna figurine inside, keeping her eyes straight ahead as she turned right and continued down the avenue. The crowd was so dense here that it was impossible to set her own course. She gave in to the tide, letting it pull her along the sidewalk, only breaking free when she was halfway down the block, where she was able to claim a relatively quiet spot on the curb.

The music from the band was growing closer now. She squinted down the avenue, trying to glimpse the procession through the scores of people constantly crisscrossing the street. The women beside her were becoming more and more agitated, shouting to their children to come near as their husbands tucked in their shirts and combed back their hair with their fingers. The very air seemed to thrum with anticipation.

How many times, she wondered, had she waited just like this at a *festa* in Naples? But thinking of home was a mistake she immediately regretted. Other memories of happier times came tumbling after it, breaking through the wall of forgetfulness she'd tried so hard to erect. Her heart broke as she thought of all she had lost. Before, she had been the daughter of loving parents, a member of a village, the child of a just god. Now, she was nothing but a ghost.

"Here they come!" someone shouted.

The procession appeared at the foot of the block like a shimmering mirage, the white banner with the Madonna's life-size picture seeming to float unsupported above it. It moved closer in fits and starts, coming to a stop each time someone darted off the sidewalk to pin money or jewelry to the banner, swelling and narrowing as congregants joined or left the fray. She spotted the grand marshal in his gorgeous regalia, followed by men of the various Italian societies in their own colorful uniforms. As the banner drew closer, the women around her began dropping to their knees and stretching their arms toward the painted Madonna. One cried out for help with her daughter's difficult pregnancy, while others asked for help with a sickness, or a debt, or a quarrelsome husband.

Once the Italian societies had marched past, the women on the sidewalk rushed out to join the ranks in its wake. The young virgins walked first, dressed all in white and wearing flowers and ribbons in their hair. They were followed by the married women, many of whom carried wax body parts or staggered under the weight of thick, colored candles nearly as tall as they were. Teresa longed to join the throng, but her feet remained planted on the sidewalk. Her sin was too great to bring to the Madonna's ears, she thought, hanging her head in shame.

When she looked up again, the murmuring ranks of penitents, nearly all of them women, were moving past her, bringing up the rear of the procession. They walked barefoot over the blistering pavement or crawled slowly past on their hands and knees, their hair hanging loosely about their shoulders. Some of the crawlers, she noticed, placed pieces of flint beneath their knees to make their penance more complete. Others dragged their tongues along the paving stones. One woman walked past as if in a trance, wailing and beating her chest.

Teresa felt something stir inside her, thinking of what the American woman had said, about God being all-merciful. If the Madonna could intercede on the behalf of all these others, was it possible she could help Teresa as well? Hope bubbled up through the thick sludge of her despair. With shaking fingers, she untied her shoes and pulled them off, laying them neatly on the edge of the sidewalk, then unpinned her hair and laid the pins by her shoes. Fixing her eyes on the receding banner, she stepped off of the curb.

"Blessed Lady of Mount Carmel," she whispered, falling to her knees. "I humbly beseech you, though I do not deserve the name of daughter, to treat me like a mother and intercede on my behalf with your divine son, asking for his forgiveness and the cleansing of my sins." Although she couldn't really believe the Virgin would hear her prayers, just saying the words brought a few seconds of relief. Picking up a piece of flint that someone had dropped on the paving stones, she pulled one knee forward and wedged the flint underneath. "Forgive the unholy acts that I have committed," she murmured as she crawled forward, wincing as the flint ground against bone. She pulled the flint out, preparing to plant it under her other knee, but stopped as a hand landed on her shoulder.

"Teresa, don't."

She looked up to see Antonio standing beside her, his face stricken.

"Go away, Antonio," she said, shrinking from his hand.

He crouched beside her. "Please, Teresa. Talk to me."

"You shouldn't be with me."

He reached out and cupped her cheek with his hand. "Why should I not be with my betrothed?"

She squeezed her eyes shut, burning under his fingers. "We are no longer betrothed. I release you from your bonds."

"And if I don't wish to be released?"

She opened her eyes. "I have been touched by another man," she spat out. "You cannot truly wish to marry me."

"Did he touch your heart, Teresa?" he asked with a frown. "Did your love for me ever falter?"

She stared at him without answering. Of course her love for him had never faltered. But that didn't change the fact that she was ruined.

" 'The sun passes over filth and is not defiled,' " he said, holding her gaze as he quoted the old Italian proverb. "You are my sun, Teresa. You were before, and you always will be."

Hot tears sprang to her eyes. If only it could be true. If only she needn't be forever defiled by what that demon had done. But it wasn't true, and they both knew it. Waving him aside, she dropped to her hands and started crawling again.

To her horror, he dropped onto his hands and knees beside her.

"No!" she gasped, coming to a halt. "Antonio, don't."

"You were entrusted to my care, and I failed you," he said, his eyes bright and his voice ragged. "If you are ashamed, then the burden must be shared by us both." He pulled the flint from her hand and thrust it under his own knee.

"Antonio, no, I beg you. Please, stand up . . ."

"Only if you will stand with me."

She stared at him, her heart pounding. Was it possible? "If you really still love me," she whispered, "why didn't you come to me when they found us?"

His shoulders sagged. "I didn't know how to face you, knowing that I had let you fall into Carulo's hands. I assumed you blamed me for what happened, as I blamed myself. It was only after the American woman talked to me that I understood what you were feeling."

She sat back on her heels, unable to quench the ember of hope his words had sparked. Had the Madonna, perhaps, heard her prayer? "But what would people say," she asked in a daze, "if you were to marry me?"

"Who cares what they say?" His eyes smiled at her behind his tears. "This is America! We'll move somewhere else if we have to, and start over again."

She swallowed. "You would do this for me?"

"I would do this for us." He stood and

held out his hands.

She gazed up into his face, feeling a deep ache in her chest as her withered heart came slowly back to life. She placed her hands in his palms and he pulled her to her feet.

"Shall we continue to the church, *mia cara*?" he asked.

She looked up ahead at the banner with the Madonna's picture, bobbing over the heads a block ahead of them. "Yes, to the church," she said. For today, it seemed, she had much to be thankful for.

READING GROUP GUIDE

1. Sex trafficking is still a major industry today. Why do you think it has managed to persist through the centuries? Do you think Anti-trafficking efforts should be aimed at traffickers, prostitutes, customers, or the illegal status of prostitution itself?

2. Genevieve's textbooks suggest that women are evolutionarily programmed to take a coy or passive role in sexual relations, and that they encourage and are excited by aggressive male ardor. Do you think this is true? If it is, does it create a conflict with contemporary women's desire to be treated as an equal in other spheres of life? How can the two be harmonized?

3. Genevieve feels compelled to help find Teresa, regardless of the risks involved.

Simon argues that she is putting herself in unnecessary danger. What would you have done, if you were in Genevieve's shoes? Do you think she is being unduly influenced by her past? Where would you draw the line between altruism and self-preservation?

4. Although Genevieve is deeply drawn to Simon, she is also well aware of the difficulties a marriage with him might entail. Do you think she is being wise, overly practical, or something else in her desire to take more time before she commits?

5. Do you believe Simon's refusal to engage in physical intimacy with Genevieve is an attempt to protect himself, or merely to manipulate her into marrying him?

6. Pauline tells Genevieve that while many women are tricked into the prostitution trade, the majority enter it voluntarily as a way to escape a life of hard work and near destitution. Can you imagine making such a choice? How do you feel about women who do?

7. Why do you think Genevieve finds Pauline and Angela such good company? Are

there characteristics the three women share?

8. Katie has little sympathy at first for Teresa's plight, seeming to believe that the girl somehow brought her troubles on herself. Psychologists explain victim blaming as a way of making ourselves feel safe, by assigning other people's misfortunes to forces within their control. Can you think of anytime you might have done something similar, without realizing it?

9. Antonio decides to stand by Teresa, despite everything. Do you think many men at that time would do the same? What about today?

10. What role do the members of the Wieran Club play in the story? What aspects of Simon's and Genevieve's personalities are revealed by their interactions with the boys?

11. "The test of civilization is the estimate of woman," according to a quote in the story. Do you agree? How would you say our society measures up today?

A CONVERSATION
WITH THE AUTHOR

Why did you choose to write about the white slave trade?

Because sex trafficking is still a huge problem today, and it horrifies me. Like Genna, I am confounded by the mind-set of people who perpetrate this crime and the customers who keep them in business (to the tune of some $30 billion a year). I wrote about it in part to try to understand it, and also because it touches on the broader question of the balance of power between the sexes, and how that balance, or lack of it, is maintained. In a world where many women are still treated like property or, at best, second-class citizens, I find this a compelling question.

How big of a problem was sex trafficking in Genevieve's time?

It was big. Contemporary writers tend to downplay the white slave panic as a figment of the sexually repressed, nativist, post-Victorian mind. While there is undoubtedly some truth in that view, investigations undertaken by municipal, state, federal, and international bodies during the period documented that thousands of women, both foreign and domestic, were being seduced through deceit or coerced into prostitution. A 1909 report by the U.S. Commissioner-General of Immigration concluded that "an enormous business is constantly being transacted in the importation and distribution of foreign women for the purposes of prostitution, which business includes the seduction and distribution of alien women and girls who have entered the country in a regular manner for legitimate purposes, and to some extent of American women and girls." A Special Immigration Commission report to the Senate that same year pointed out that instead of working in brothels run by women, as in the past, the vast majority of these new prostitutes were controlled by men who "made it their business to plunder them unmercifully." A number of state and federal laws were passed as a result of the various investigations, as well as an international agreement requiring signatories to place lookouts in ports and railway stations, supervise employment agencies, and facilitate repatriation of abduction victims. The plethora of criminal convictions that resulted from these laws attests to the reality of the problem. So do the records of the many private organizations that dedicated themselves to patrolling ports and terminals in search of potential victims, which included the Travelers' Aid Society, the International Catholic Girls' Protection Society, and the National Council of Jewish Women.

Although your stories touch on issues that are still relevant today, they are firmly rooted in another time. How do you keep them true to the period?

I feel a real obligation to try to depict the period accurately. To that end, I immerse myself in newspaper articles, memoirs, photograph collections, and science texts from the time, gleaning not only facts and figures, but also patterns of speech and cultural biases and other nuances that might help make my fiction as true as possible. A great advantage to setting a series in the early 1900s is that there's still a large amount of print material around from that period that's being digitized and made available online. I'm especially cautious when I put words into the mouths of characters who are based on real people, such as

Detective Petrosino. Many of the things the detective says in the book come from actual quotes that were reported in newspapers at the time.

What's your writing process? Are you a pantser or a plotter?

I'm a plotter. Writing a mystery pretty much demands that you figure some things out ahead of time — like who did it and why, where to sprinkle your clues, and what the red herrings will be. But I don't know everything in advance. I use more of a stepping-stone approach, identifying key points along the story path ahead of time and then filling in around them as I go. Often, new twists will occur to me as I'm writing, or a character will demand more space, making the story more complex or taking it in a slightly different direction from what I'd originally envisioned.

What drew you to the mystery genre?

Crimes, especially murders, are usually associated with strong emotions, and strong emotions tend to make for good stories. I view the mystery plot as a device for examining how people behave when they're in extremis, which is where all the interesting stuff happens. I also like the challenge of building a story on two levels, trying to lead the reader astray at the same time I'm laying a foundation that will support the big reveal.

ACKNOWLEDGMENTS

As always, I am deeply grateful to my husband, Larry, for his support. Every writer should have someone like him in their corner.

My sons, Tucker and Chance, inspire me with their own creative ventures. At the end of the day, it really is the journey that counts. I'm glad to be on the road with them.

Being a first reader is a delicate task, and Catherine Clark performed it beautifully. Thank you, dear friend, for your reassurance and suggestions. Jody Scala was also there with answers to my medical questions when I needed them.

Thanks again to my agent, Victoria Cappello, for her efforts on my behalf, and to the wonderful team at Sourcebooks. My editor, Anna Michels, continues to make the publication process a fun and collegial one.

Finally, a big thanks to the readers who have embraced Genevieve and her world and shared their enthusiasm with me. You make it all worthwhile!

ABOUT THE AUTHOR

Cuyler Overholt worked as a litigation attorney and freelance business writer before turning to fiction. She lives in Connecticut with her husband, a psychologist, who is still working on perfecting her. When she isn't reading or writing, she can usually be found on a bike, in the cobra pose, designing her next dream house, or enjoying a good movie. To contact her or to learn more about upcoming books and events, visit her website at cuyleroverholt.com.

The employees of Thorndike Press hope you have enjoyed this Large Print book. All our Thorndike, Wheeler, and Kennebec Large Print titles are designed for easy reading, and all our books are made to last. Other Thorndike Press Large Print books are available at your library, through selected bookstores, or directly from us.

For information about titles, please call:
(800) 223-1244

or visit our website at:
gale.com/thorndike

To share your comments, please write:
Publisher
Thorndike Press
10 Water St., Suite 310
Waterville, ME 04901